PRAISE FOR ELLE MARR

The Family Bones

"With a fresh take on the locked-room mystery, Elle Marr weaves a perilous and pulse-pounding tale of nature versus nurture. *The Family Bones* is a clever, wild, riveting ride that amps up the tension until I couldn't flip the page fast enough. The interconnected threads, subtle clues, and jaw-dropping twists lead to a whopper of an ending."
—Samantha M. Bailey, *USA Today* and #1 national bestselling author of *Woman on the Edge* and *Watch Out for Her*

"'Dysfunctional' doesn't even begin to describe the Eriksen clan during this family reunion from hell. Elle Marr's twisty plot and even more twisted characters make *The Family Bones* a dark, delectable, and fascinating thriller that questions how well we know not only our relatives but also our own minds."
—Megan Collins, author of *The Family Plot*

"Smart, razor sharp, and shocking, *The Family Bones* will keep you up late with all the lights on. A family of psychopaths trapped by bad weather at an isolated retreat—what could possibly go wrong? With dual story lines racing toward a chilling climax, *The Family Bones* is a tense, must-read thriller."
—Kaira Rouda, *USA Today* and Amazon Charts bestselling author

Strangers We Know

"The increasingly tense plot takes turns the reader won't see coming. Marr is a writer to watch."
—*Publishers Weekly*

"Elle Marr is an author to know. Just when you think you understand the motives behind her characters and the way their story lines are being presented—bam!—Elle will hit you with twists you won't see coming. Told from multiple points of view, *Strangers We Know* is about more than Ivy learning of her past and, shockingly, the serial killer within her family; it's also about knowing who to trust and how to discern who's telling the complete story. Because if everyone has secrets, are they truly family or only strangers? Read *Strangers We Know* to find out."

—Georgina Cross, bestselling author of *The Stepdaughter*

"Elle Marr burst onto the suspense scene in 2020 with her bestselling debut, *The Missing Sister*, and followed up a year later with *Lies We Bury*, another trust-no-one murder mystery. With her third novel, *Strangers We Know*, Marr firmly establishes herself as a master of 'did that really just happen?' thrillers. *Strangers We Know* has plot twists so unexpected and characters so creepy you won't want to turn out the lights, and the ending is surprising in multiple ways. Who knew a deranged-serial-killer whodunit could leave you with all the feels?"

—A.H. Kim, author of *A Good Family*

"Dark family secrets, serial murder, and a cult? Yes, please. Twisty and a little twisted, the highly addictive and surprise-packed *Strangers We Know* will have you pulling an all-nighter."

—Heather Chavez, author of *No Bad Deed*

"From the first page I was gripped by *Strangers We Know* and read through the night till the end. The novel is thrilling beyond belief, with suspense and twists ratcheting up on each page. Elle Marr is brilliant at delving into the darkness of a seemingly normal family, and by the time she pulls back the curtains on each character, the terror has built so excruciatingly, you just have to keep going till you find out every single thing—you're afraid to know, but you have to know. This is the year's must read."

—Luanne Rice, bestselling author of *The Shadow Box*

Lies We Bury

"A deep, deep dive into unspeakable memories and their unimaginably shocking legacy."

—*Kirkus Reviews* (starred review)

"The suspenseful plot is matched by the convincing portrayal of the vulnerable Claire, who just wants to lead a normal life. Marr is a writer to watch."

—*Publishers Weekly*

"Marr's #OwnVoices, trust-no-one thriller unravels with horrifying 'THEN' interruptions, producing a jolting creepfest of twisted revenge."

—*Booklist*

"In *Lies We Bury*, Elle Marr (bestselling author of *The Missing Sister*) has brought a cleverly plotted and compelling new mystery with unique characters and truly surprising twists."

—The Nerd Daily

"A deep, thrilling dive into the painful memories that haunt us and the fight between moving on or digging in and seeking revenge."

—*Medium*

"Elle Marr's second novel tucks a mystery inside a mystery . . . The big twist near the end is a doozy."

—*The Oregonian*

"A twisted mash-up of *Room* and a murder mystery, Marr's *Lies We Bury* is a story that creeps into your bones, a sneaky tale about the danger of secrets and the power the past holds to lead us into a deliciously devious present. Say goodbye to sleep and read it like I did, in one breathless sitting."

—Kimberly Belle, international bestselling author of *Dear Wife* and *Stranger in the Lake*

"Dark and compelling, Elle Marr has written another atmospheric and twisted thriller that you don't want to miss. *Lies We Bury* delves into the darkest of pasts and explores the fascinating tension between moving on and revenge. This is a fly-through-the-pages thriller."

—Vanessa Lillie, Amazon bestselling author of *Little Voices* and *For the Best*

"This haunting and emotional thriller will keep you up at night looking for answers."

—Dea Poirier, international bestselling author of *Next Girl to Die*

"A clever, twisty murder mystery packed full of secrets and lies that will keep you turning the pages way past bedtime. *Lies We Bury* hooked me from page one and kept me guessing until its dramatic conclusion."

—Lisa Gray, bestselling author of *Thin Air*

The Missing Sister

"Marr's debut novel follows a San Diego medical student to, around, and ultimately beneath Paris in search of the twin sister she'd been drifting away from. Notable for its exploration of the uncanny bonds twins share and the killer's memorably macabre motive."

—*Kirkus Reviews*

"[A] gritty debut . . . The intriguing premise, along with a few twists, lend this psychological thriller some weight."

—*Publishers Weekly*

"Elle Marr's first novel has an intriguing premise . . . The characters are well drawn and complex, and Marr's prose offers some surprising twists."

—New York Journal of Books

"A promising plotline."

—*Library Journal*

"*The Missing Sister* is a very promising debut—atmospheric, gripping, and set in Paris. In other words, the perfect ingredients for a satisfying result."

—Criminal Element

"Brimming with eerie mystery and hair-raising details . . . A chilling read that shows the unique bond of twins."

—*Woman's World*

"This thrilling debut novel from Elle Marr is a look into the importance of identity and the strength of sisterhood."

—*Brooklyn Digest*

"An electrifying thriller. A must read—Karin Slaughter with a touch of international flair. Just when you think you have it all figured out, Marr throws you for another loop and the roller-coaster ride continues!"

—Matt Farrell, *Washington Post* bestselling author of
What Have You Done

"A riveting, fast-paced thriller. Elle Marr hooks you from the start, taking you on a dark and twisted journey. Layered beneath the mystery of a twin's disappearance is a nuanced, and at times disturbing, exploration of the ties that bind sisters together. With crisp prose, a gripping investigation, and a compelling protagonist, *The Missing Sister* is not to be missed."

—Brianna Labuskes, *Washington Post* bestselling author of
Girls of Glass

"A gripping thriller. *The Missing Sister* delivers twists and turns in an exciting, page-turning read that delves into the unique bond that makes—and breaks—siblings."

—Mike Chen, author of *Here and Now and Then*

THE
FAMILY
BONES

OTHER TITLES BY ELLE MARR

Strangers We Know
Lies We Bury
The Missing Sister

THE FAMILY BONES

ELLE MARR

THOMAS & MERCER

Published by Thomas & Mercer, Seattle

www.apub.com

Amazon, the Amazon logo, and Thomas & Mercer are trademarks of Amazon.com, Inc., or its affiliates.

ISBN-13: 9781542038904 (paperback)
ISBN-13: 9781542038911 (digital)

Cover design by Shasti O'Leary Soudant
Cover image: © plainpicture / Sarah Toure / plainpicture

Printed in the United States of America

For my daughter

The Eriksen Family

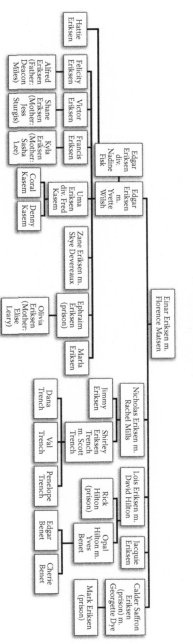

Einar Eriksen m. Florence Matsen

Hattie Eriksen

Felicity Eriksen

Victor Eriksen

Alfred Eriksen (Father: Deacon Miles)

Shane Eriksen (Mother: Jess Sturgis)

Francis Eriksen

Kyla Eriksen (Mother: Sasha Lee)

Edgar Eriksen div. Nadine Fisk

Edgar Eriksen m. Yvette Wilsh

Uma Eriksen div. Fred Kasem

Coral Kasem

Denny Kasem

Zane Eriksen m. Skye Devereaux

Ephraim Eriksen (prison)

Olivia Eriksen (Mother: Elise Leary)

Marla Eriksen

Nicholas Eriksen m. Rachel Mills

Jimmy Eriksen

Shirley Eriksen Trench m. Scott Trench

Dana Trench

Val Trench

Penelope Trench

Edgar Benet

Cherie Benet

Lois Eriksen m. David Hilton

Rick Hilton (prison)

Opal Hilton m. Yves Benet

Jacquie Eriksen

Calder Saffron Eriksen (prison) m. Georgette Dye

Mark Eriksen (prison)

1

News Article

The *Oregonian*
March 22, 2023
By the *Oregonian* Staff

Gunshots rocked the Malheur National Forest in Eastern Oregon yesterday at the Horsefly Falls Resort. *Malheur*, meaning "misfortune" in French, is all too fitting a name, given the six deaths police say occurred during the course of a five-day private retreat. Due to the late-winter cold front that continues to ravage the Pacific Northwest, the resort lost its electrical and battery power sometime during the long weekend. Witnesses say the ensuing panic led to spoiled food, rising tensions, and explosive conflict.

This story will be updated as more information becomes available.

2

OLIVIA

Two Weeks Earlier

The man rages in the packed courtroom, visibly spitting as he denies the allegations of murder. He raps his large fist against the wooden frame of the witness stand where he sits, as he shouts, "I did not kill my father!"

Gathering himself—subtly wiping the whiskers of his chin—the defendant straightens his posture to regard the prosecutor full in the face, to lean forward just slightly over his questioner and flex his considerable presence. "Certainly, a man of my position would not deign to such a primitive act."

"And what position would that be?" the young prosecutor queries, nonplussed by the defendant's show of gentility. "A psychopath?"

Chaos erupts in the courtroom, the sound muffled in this recording from 1945. From the camera's fixed vantage point, the defendant's expression is clear: a sneer curls his upper lip. Then a smile. Voices continue to clamor off camera, and the judge threatens to clear the courtroom, but the defendant slowly turns his gaze to the right. He locks eyes with the camera's lens, terrifying any of the psychology department's graduate students who dare to step back in time with this killer.

I pause the footage on the computer screen. Calder Saffron Eriksen has the dubious distinction, beyond being my great-uncle, of committing patricide—the murder of my great-grandfather. His was the first case I learned of, when I was seven years old and my cousin Alfred confided to me the truth of our family during a camping trip: we were psychopaths. Or rather, our family carries with it a long history of antisocial personality disorder that manifests in myriad ways—psychopathy, sociopathy, borderline personality disorder, and narcissism, among others. At this news, any other little girl might have begun crying or run to her mother. But I only sat quietly, piecing together the clues from my young life. I recalled the way my father seemed incapable of deep emotion; the way my aunt preened, then manipulated her husband into buying her a fancy new car after she crashed her old one; the swift death of my pet rabbit when my aunt Hattie discovered it had pooped inside her favorite shoes.

Calder Saffron Eriksen continues to stare at me through the camera, through the decades to reach into the twenty-first century. A wild sheen coats his eyes. He would later be found guilty due to evidence that proved his motive and opportunity to go after his father; I suspect it was this moment during his trial that began to sway the jury away from his deep blue gaze, his all-American copper-brown hair that curved in the slightest wave.

UC Davis's psychology lab offers only four computers to its graduate students, but access to dozens of films of trials and interviews featuring individuals diagnosed with ASPD. Some—like the one I just watched—are old-timey black-and-white files, grainy even with the best overhead lighting, while others are more recent, displayed in full color with HD. The Freedom of Information Act allows institutions of higher learning access to a long, though not exhaustive, catalog of trial footage. I'll take it any way I can get.

"Olivia, you're still here? It's almost four thirty." Professor Marx stifles a yawn as he enters the small room. His closely cut black hair is nearly covered by a knit beanie. Deep laugh lines crease his temples.

"Right. Yeah, I'm just finishing up." I scan the notes I've made on Calder Saffron's behavior during the trial. I've seen this footage before, many times, and this last moment always strikes me—the instant he stopped acting. When he let the facade of an upstanding young man slip, and he was no longer trying to manipulate the prosecution, the judge, the jury. He simply relaxed and presented his cold, callous self to the world.

Professor Marx nods to the illuminated computer screen, to the twisted smirk of my great-uncle. "Haven't you had enough family time?"

While some grad students complain about visually studying these disturbing individuals, it's the only way to draw primary analysis from subjects long since dead. I don't love it either. It just happens that my dissertation depends on analyzing the footage, and as I near my twenty-third birthday, the age at which psychopathy usually pops up in my family, my mental welfare requires it.

As the head of Psych, Professor Marx has known about my personal interest in ASPD since my third and final year of undergrad, when he prompted me to apply for the accelerated doctoral program. I slide my notebook into the unzipped backpack at my feet. "You're probably right. I've been glued to this cross-examination for an hour now."

He drops a folder crammed with paper onto the table beside me. "Always so dedicated. Go home, Olivia. Enjoy the weekend."

I smile at my mentor, then shut down the computer. Although the end of the semester—the deadline to whip the crap I've written into a convincing dissertation—will be here in less than six weeks, I can feel my eyes morphing into flat-screen monitors.

Outside the brick building, sunshine peeks through a blanket of wispy cirrus clouds. I find my bicycle where I left it—chained to a bike rack, alone. Not an unusual sight, as I don't maintain a lot of friends. Connecting with people, while a skill I have, sometimes feels like an exercise in reassuring others that I'm not like my relatives—an idea I've clung to but haven't allowed myself to fully believe. The terror of what's to come, what could lie latent within me, has always kept me aloof. Growing up, each of my birthdays was eclipsed by dread—terror that this was the year I would snap and reveal I, too, had what my family has come to call "the Eriksen twitch." When I was accepted to UC Davis and moved from Oregon to Northern California, I tried my best to leave that anxiety behind.

As a freshman walking by the psych building, I had an epiphany: instead of allowing that fear to consume me, I could study the disorders that have plagued my family over the generations. I could help people like my relatives—those who desire help, in any case. What better way to support them than by examining the question that lies at the heart of the fear: Nature or nurture? Is it genetic that so many of my family members seem to fall along the spectrum of personality disorders? Or simply circumstantial because we've been swimming in the same toxic fishbowl our entire lives?

"Excuse me? Are you . . . ?"

The voice trails off as I face a wide-eyed girl, a freshman from the looks of her blunt bangs and chin-length bob.

Light blue eyes, like mine, pinch into a smile. "You're Olivia Eriksen. I've seen all your videos, been watching them since I was a kid and just learning about psychology. Can I have your autograph?"

She offers up a pen and the back side of a worksheet. I accept both, then scan the bike rack for a flat surface.

"Oh, let me," she says, turning her shoulder. I scrawl my name, pressing the paper across the canvas of her jacket. The result is jagged and not at all like my usual looping signature.

"Hey, could I get a selfie too? The other neuroscience majors won't believe me without it."

Before I can nod or decline, she slides in close, then holds up her cell phone's camera. I smile, knowing the routine all too well. "I hope you tell your friends about my account. I always appreciate comments from followers."

"Definitely." The student beams, then skips down the paved walkway toward the campus fountain.

When I first started as an undergrad myself, I was surprised by how many people—even faculty members—approached me wanting to discuss the videos I'd created over the years: weekly talks on mental health and my family's experiences with cognitive disorders. At the age of thirteen, sick of scraping by with my mother and receiving zero financial support from my dad, who was in prison, I discovered social media—YouTube at first, then the Instagram and Facebook Live videos that followed. I learned how to monetize it. Viewers seemed to eat up the visual of a prepubescent girl analyzing cognitive conditions. True, I had no place discussing any of it from an academic perspective. Instead, I relied on what I found on the internet and my own personal interactions with family members. Hearsay passed down through generations.

Viewers turned into subscribers, and then subscribers turned into sponsors who asked me to wear their tween-brand clothing label while recounting my uncle Rick's socially deviant fascination with churches and fire. By the time I turned fifteen, I was earning $100,000 annually, and my mother, Elise, was able to stop working night shifts at the convalescent home. None of my high school classmates seemed to care that I was social media famous—they had written me off a long time ago.

Cool air skates across my neck as I launch my bike into the parking lot, whizzing past cars gridlocked in the only exit from this part of campus. My phone trills—"We Are Family," the ringtone I chose for Elise—when I lean right and curve with the road away from the university. A minute later, she calls again. Then again.

Curiosity pulses within me, and I pump my legs faster, eager to get home. The wind twirls my long blonde hair and slices through the wool of my sweater. I shiver as I pedal the final block to my apartment, ready for central heating in the sharp chill of March.

Pausing beside my complex's mailbox, I check my phone. No voice messages. Only Elise's three missed calls.

Inside my mailbox, I find advertisements for "Current Resident," along with a utility bill and a preemptive request from the UC Davis alumni association to donate later this spring.

At the bottom of the pile lies a stiff piece of cardstock. A photograph of a thick forest of trees is framed by a white border and curling accents at each corner. On the back and in large Arial font, a date six days from today is stark and center; beneath it, an announcement:

Eriksen Family Reunion
Extended Weekend Retreat
Come celebrate the Eriksen legacy. RSVP for the exact location.
Confidentiality required.

A fresh gust of wind licks my skin. It's an invitation. To the first reunion in ten years. After the last one, my aunts and uncles decided it was no longer safe to congregate in large numbers with our kin, that we should avoid another chaotic, conflict-riddled retreat.

The sharp notes of "We Are Family" cut through my daze, and I withdraw my phone from my backpack without thinking.

"Mom?" I answer, my voice small, like a child's.

"Olivia," she breathes. "Did you get it?"

All my research into my family's legal history and mental disorders and all the objectivity I exercise as an academic fall away. The internal walls I've built to protect myself from my family's curse—from what might lie in wait for me—falter at the thought of greeting my relatives.

"Olivia?"

"Yes, I'm here," I manage.

"What do you think? About the reunion? Will you go? I just received mine, and I'd love to see you if you'll be close by."

I have zero desire to resume family ties. Imagining myself among people I've successfully avoided for years, even moving a state away to gain a mountain range between us, makes the choice easy. Yet the chance to analyze extended family I've seen featured on the nightly news—no doubt the motivation behind the card's mention of "confidentiality"—is tempting.

My dissertation requires a certain number of primary and secondary sources. Secondary, I have, but primary sources on whether psychopathy is evident from birth are harder to come by. Attending the reunion—with primary sources like my grandfather and my aunts and uncles, all together—could be the perfect way forward.

Then again, the retreat could be the match that ignites the dry kindling of our family pyre—disastrous, just like the last time.

"I don't know, Mom." I curl my nails tight into the flesh of my palm.

My mother clears her throat. "Why hesitate, sweetie? When visiting home again may be exactly what you need."

"Right," I huff. Sharp pain pinwheels along my fist, as Calder Saffron's dead-eyed stare flashes across my vision. "A mountain getaway with the Eriksens. What could possibly go wrong?"

3

BIRDIE

"Quiero un burrito con mucho guacamole, por favor." I wait for the total from the drive-thru clerk of my favorite Adalberto's in El Cajon. High school kids rock the back seat of a beater sedan in front of me to a new pop song that I don't recognize, blaring from their open windows. Oh, to be young. Or, rather, almost twenty years younger.

Back on the 15 freeway, I race home. My baby girl, Brooklyn, will be released from the late-bird kindergarten class in two hours, and I still need to research the dead body that turned up in San Pedro Harbor.

As a stay-at-home mom for the last five years, I admit I felt a bit of empty-nest syndrome when she started school. Then I discovered the dramas of Netflix. The female characters, who were either attacked by romantic partners or issued their own acts of vengeance, held me spellbound tighter than snarled traffic in the Gaslamp Quarter during a Padres game. When I exhausted those stories, a girlfriend of mine turned me on to true crime and the unsolved mysteries that seemed to plague so many women, real ones, who were just like me. A deeper dive through Netflix and other streaming platforms led me to podcasts.

When I open my front door, the entry smells of last night's yakisoba noodles and grilled bok choy. Mental note to self: use less dark soy sauce.

I wolf down my burrito, carne asada and all, then head into my office-slash-closet. At ten feet deep, it has the kind of storage capacity most moms would kill for—some dads too. But my husband, Grayson, enjoys a minimalist approach to his wardrobe. When I first got it in my head to do a podcast on unsolved true crime cases, he moved all the suits he wears for his work as an IT consultant to a freestanding wardrobe with no doors—"The better to see everything at once," he said. When I said I wanted to focus on minorities whose cases are barely given a mention on third-rate online news outlets, he set up the microphone, then the sound insulation between the closet shelves, himself.

I open my laptop. Back in 1977, Pamela Harris was found bloated and floating in the San Pedro Harbor. At barely twenty years old and a newlywed, Pamela never frequented the stretch of bars that led to the docks. The police were dumbfounded as to how a straight A college student from Pasadena wound up all that way south.

"Yeah, I'll bet you were," I grumble. "So dumbfounded as to write off the whole thing as a bad diving accident." I double-click on the photo of the young Filipino woman. Full cheeks and bright teeth dominate her face, and there's kindness to her dark brown eyes. Her husband was cleared after a few months of investigation, before he went on a boys' trip to Cabo San Lucas later that fall and was never seen again.

"Interpol better be tracking this guy." Scribbling notes on a legal pad beside my laptop, I underline the major points.

With only one hour left until I need to pick up Brooklyn, I open the recording program on my desktop. I click the big red button and resume where I paused my latest episode.

"And that's your weekly dose of *Murders You Missed*. Check us out again on Monday for another breakdown. Meanwhile, keep your eyes peeled and your pepper spray flexed."

My phone pings with an email, and I pause the recording. I'll want to edit the episode before publishing it on Monday, but it's at a good spot.

Scanning the details on my phone, I catch the subject line: Li Ming Na. Never heard of her. Recently, my follower count on social media ballooned after I covered the hit-and-run of a Guatemalan hiker in Utah. The episode even got picked up by a megaplayer in pop culture—the website PopBlast—and emailed suggestions for new murders to highlight have flooded in since.

Reading further, I confirm that Li Ming Na is absolutely a candidate to be featured on my podcast. Young and Chinese American, Li Ming Na disappeared in Oregon after leaving her hometown of Oakland, California; she didn't even get a feature on the local news, according to this sender—truecr1m3junk1e@gmail.com. An orphan from the age of nineteen, she had no family pushing the media for answers, and it seems no friends either.

"How awful," I mutter. As a mixed-race woman—of Chinese and white ethnicity—I'm hit in the paunch by the summary of Li Ming Na's death, definitely. For other personal reasons too.

When my older cousin Wendy was found dead by a troop of Boy Scouts, her body discarded on the side of the road, the local news in Bakersfield didn't bat an eye. I was ten when it happened. It was only thanks to my family's persistent (see: pain-in-the-ass) calls to the police that any progress was made on Wendy's case.

I glide through the house, half paying attention to sharp counter edges and chairbacks, grab my keys, then slip out the door. I pocket my phone but continue thinking about Li Ming Na on the drive to Brooklyn's school.

"Mommy!" Brooklyn squeals upon spotting me from the sidewalk. "Mommy, Mommy, I got in trouble and had to go to time-out, and the teacher tried to call you, but you didn't answer your phone!"

"What? What happened?" I say through the open window. I fumble for my cell, waking it from the sleep setting. She's right; I missed two calls from her school on the way here. Damn.

The air is balmy this time of year, and just below El Cajon's seventy-two-degree average. Brooklyn leaps into the car with the usual energy of a five-year-old, her jacket's collar popped to her ears. Black hair that matches my own but with her father's thickness swings gaily in the two braids I wrangled this morning.

Wide eyes stare at me from the back seat. "I kicked a boy."

"Why did you do that? You know we keep hands and feet to ourselves, Brook."

Her brow furrows. "Yeah, but he pinched me first. And he said I should go back to China."

"He did what?"

Brooklyn nods emphatically, as rage twists my face. "Uh-huh. So I kicked him and said he should go back to the dummy store—where—where his mommy bought him."

I can't help smiling. "Well, I'm very sorry that happened. What did the teacher tell you?"

"She said she wouldn't conton—"

"Condone?"

Brooklyn nods again. "Wouldn't let us name call each other. And that I'm not supposed to kick and Paxton isn't supposed to pinch."

I inhale through my nose. "Good. Let's go home. But first we'll stop by for some ice cream to celebrate you standing up for yourself. You were born and raised here, just like Paxton, probably, and no one deserves to be spoken to like that." Twisting to face her, I touch Brooklyn's little knee. "You did good today, you hear me? If Paxton's parents won't teach him the right way to treat people, we have to demand to be treated fairly."

Brooklyn's eyes grow wider. "Mommy . . . you're kind of scaring me."

I release her knee. "Sorry, baby. Mommy gets a little intense sometimes."

On the drive home, Brooklyn requests her favorite cartoon theme song on loop. While she chatters about her day at school—most of it was fun, it turns out—my mind drifts back to Li Ming Na's unsolved murder. To the fact that the police disregarded her death as another accident because it was convenient to conclude the case. And that the media and nightly news barely raised an eyebrow at yet another person of color's tragedy.

"Mommy, can we get Daddy some ice cream too?" Brooklyn asks, scratching at dried food on her leggings.

"Of course, baby. Ice cream for everyone." I smile at her. "And maybe some extra coffee-flavored ice cream for fun. Mommy's got a long night ahead."

4

OLIVIA

"So you're not going to the reunion?" Elise's face pinches in my phone's screen, the way it always does when she's worried. Sun spots dot her temples beside wan brown hair.

I toss my keys on the tile counter of my apartment, then swivel toward my country-style breakfast nook. We switched to a video call, the better for Elise to gauge my reaction to the reunion invite. I prop her against the salt and pepper shakers dead center on the table.

"Why would I? I can go home to Oregon, visit you in Eugene, then arrange for individual hangouts with family members I actually want to see."

"But, Olivia . . . you haven't seen your father's family in years." Her normally singsongy voice turns flat.

"Deliberately."

She sighs. Her light gray eyes shift to the left. "They're not all bad, you know."

"Well, are you planning to attend? You were invited too."

"Who, me? Throw myself back among the wolves when I narrowly escaped the last time?" A short huff pushes from her mouth. "Unlikely. Besides, I've got a new book I'm planning to barrel through that weekend."

"But how can you want me to go hang with the wolves? Your only child, whom you invested everything in, for whom you sacrificed so much."

My sparse living room seems to echo a favorite phrase she often used during my childhood—*Why spend money on stuff when you can heat a house?* A fake potted orchid on the end table beside a fabric couch from IKEA, a cheaply framed photo of Amsterdam's canals hanging above it, and fairy lights that line the ceiling in each corner of the room comprise my lackluster effort at decorating. Though if I were left to my own devices, the walls would be bare except for a hanging calendar; it's good my boyfriend, Howard, intervened.

"You'll be fine. It's different for me," Elise continues. "I've learned that much over the years. Your father and I don't get along, and his family is—"

"Crazy?" My words come out bitter, though I'm not sure why.

"You know I don't like that word. They're not *my* family, and our separation was hard on all of them. They never could forgive me for leaving Ephraim."

"Right," I grumble. "Well, Dad was barely around when I was a kid, and the Eriksens only reached out for those family trips every few years. Must have been so hard to break the silence between themselves and a seven-year-old girl."

"They wasted time that they could have used to get to know you, Olivia. That's their loss. But I think if you went to this reunion, you could learn more now as an adult—more about where you came from— and form stronger bonds with your relatives."

I shake my head, reaching my max with this conversation. She's not listening. "I can do my research from Eugene. Why would I sequester myself with a bunch of strangers, many of whom are incapable of emotional connection?"

Elise leans forward into the camera. "But that's just it. Everyone who's going is on medication, like Cousin Jimmy, and the ones who pose a risk aren't invited. I did a sweep of public records, and Rick is still incarcerated. Your aunt Uma says that Great-Uncle Nicholas and the rest of his family aren't coming."

I pause. Aunt Uma is the one family member my mom keeps in touch with. And I've always trusted Uma to tell me the truth. "Really?"

Elise nods, a smile revealing small teeth. "It's true. Think of the research that you could conduct on-site. You still haven't gotten a hold of your grandfather, right?"

Grandpa Edgar has been slippery ever since I shared that I was researching psychopathy as a birth trait. Months of my phone calls have gone unanswered. "No, I haven't."

"Then it's settled? You can go to the reunion, then spend a few days with me afterward. Besides, many family members haven't been diagnosed with any condition. Isn't your uncle Zane the CEO of a hospital now?" She leans against the headboard of her bed, jostling the phone as she moves. A white Maltese, her baby ever since I moved to California, yips somewhere in the background.

"You know that the lack of a diagnosis doesn't equal a well-adjusted human. Uncle Zane fired half his staff last year after his cat died. You can't tell me that's high functioning."

Elise dips her head. "Okay, sure."

"All right. I'll consider it. For the research opportunity alone, I'll think it over. God knows I could use the help before my dissertation is due." I pause, feeling as though I'm missing something. And I hate that sense of doubt. "Why do you want me to go so badly?"

Elise hesitates. "I just . . . well, I care about you. That's all."

We hang up. I don't know how many relatives will join on such short notice, but I also know that's how the Eriksens like to plan get-togethers—spur of the moment, to avoid unwanted attention.

There's a knock at my door, a rarity for my neighborhood and reclusive neighbors. I check the peephole. Warm brown eyes beneath shaggy black hair fill the view.

I turn the handle, then step back for Howard Ngo to enter. I first met Howard, who's nearly a decade older than me, when I attended orientation for graduate students two years ago. Considering he's the assistant dean of Graduate Affairs, Howard shouldn't be dating me; it's not exactly aboveboard. But I also don't know where I'd be without that charming grin and uncanny ability to know when I'm starved.

"Hey, beautiful," he says, leaning down for a kiss on my cheek. "I missed you." He lifts a white plastic bag of takeout. "Hungry?"

Howard unties the plastic handles, then reveals each clamshell container with a flourish of his hand: beef and broccoli, General Tso's chicken, chow mein, shrimp fried rice, and stuffed eggplant. "Hope it's okay I'm surprising you like this."

Delicious sweet-and-salty smells reach my nose. "More than okay, Howie."

"Good. Because I couldn't stay away," he says with a smile. As he removes our disposable wooden chopsticks from the bag, then rubs mine together to remove any splinters, I lay a hand across his arm.

"You are the best boyfriend. You know that?"

Howard turns a fiery gaze on me, and I can almost feel his desire across my tiny table. Shifting forward over the chow mein, he gently touches the gold chain around my neck. With a dip of his finger, he frees the diamond ring that I keep tucked beneath my shirt collar. "A better question: How did I get lucky enough to call you my fiancée?"

He draws in close for a kiss. Warm and tasting of something minty, his tongue slides across mine. A delicious thrill snakes its way down my belly and between my thighs; I'm tempted to forgo dinner altogether.

When we're on campus, we rarely show any affection, knowing it would put his job at risk. These stolen moments, away from judgmental eyes and in the privacy of my apartment, are all the more seductive.

Not only is Howard the assistant dean and an incredible partner to me during my grad studies, but he's reminded me that I'm more than my family bones—the bizarre smorgasbord of off-center genes that have dominated my line for generations. In his eyes, I'm not some freak show, unworthy of love.

Without prompting, the invitation to the Eriksen weekend retreat returns to mind. Though it's safely tucked away on the counter, beneath a utility bill and my old inhaler, I turn toward it.

"Everything okay, honey?" Howard asks.

I stroke the back of his hand, the way that couples do in movies. "Why wouldn't it be?"

Touching my necklace, feeling the sharp cut of the diamond, I muster a smile. I'm just not remotely sure now is the time to introduce him to my family, to finally announce our engagement.

———

Writing sucks the energy from me during the weekend. Each time I feel like dumping the now-eighty-paged effort into my desktop's waste bin, I remind myself that a doctorate will open doors postgraduation. I can become a tenured teacher or lecturer somewhere and use my family history—my personal knowledge of psychopathy—to my advantage. I can turn it from some gimmick on social media into an accolade.

Saturday and Sunday roll by in a caffeine haze. Howard stays both nights, leaving only once to shower at home. He surprises me with a head-to-toe massage Sunday evening that quickly teases into a three-hour study break. The man has talent. I fall asleep blissfully unconcerned about the competing priorities of the week ahead, once again wondering what I did to deserve such love and nimble fingers.

Come Monday morning, campus is lively. I fall in line behind the other bicyclists of Davis making their way to class. Lectures concluded for me last semester, and the final experiment I was conducting to gauge the mental resiliency of rats has also finished, so I beeline for the film lab.

Two other graduate students I recognize watch a recorded interrogation. They make eye contact when I enter the room but otherwise don't acknowledge me.

I slide into the same seat I occupied Friday, navigate to the folder that contains all the psych department's trial footage, and find the video of my great-uncle, Calder Saffron Eriksen.

"Back at it, Olivia?" Professor Marx stands at the doorframe, a folder of papers under his arm. The two grad students wave to him.

"Yeah, I was just about to pick up where I left off." I smile at him and, not for the first time, notice how attractive he is. Light gray in his hair complements the natural black color, giving him a mature, trustworthy vibe.

"Well, do you have a minute? I could actually use a hand in my 101 class this morning."

I glance back to the video file waiting for my mouse's click to begin. I'll accomplish more here in the film lab, but it never hurts to gain standing in my mentor's eyes. "Sure."

He leads the way downstairs to the massive lecture hall on the ground floor. When we enter the cavernous amphitheater, memories of being an excited eighteen-year-old, anxious to make a good impression and nail my first assignment, return to mind.

Professor Marx strides to the front of the room. Every eye in the four-hundred-person-capacity hall turns toward him, expectant. Although young for his level of success, Marx has been featured in psychology magazines, had his work published in national reviews, testified before the Department of Justice, and worked to overturn wrongful convictions of individuals guilty of mental imbalance, though not necessarily a crime. I follow him, then position myself off to the side.

"Today, we're going to discuss ethics in psychology," he begins. "As in, how do we treat a patient ethically? Well, for starters: complete a PhD; it's important to study and understand the existing research. Next, treat the whole patient, independent of our own prejudices or biases—because we all have those. Ms. Eriksen, can you raise a hand, please?"

Professor Marx motions to me, and I do as I'm told. My cheeks blaze beneath the bright lecture hall lights as all eight hundred eyeballs point my way.

"Ms. Eriksen is a graduate student here at UC Davis. She's done extensive study of psychopathy, a disorder that's often stigmatized and not always treated ethically. Her dissertation will examine whether psychopathy is present at birth. Ms. Eriksen, can you say at this point whether that's possible to know?"

"Psychos? Psycho babies?" a female student whispers in the row beside me.

I smile. "Well, psychopathy is like the crazed killers we see in movies—and it's not. Psychopathy doesn't always equate to violence, right? Most of the time, we see individuals in the news who display hallmarks of antisocial personality disorder."

"Which we covered in last week's lecture, if everyone was taking notes," Professor Marx adds. There's a nervous titter among the students.

"Not all psychopaths break the law," I continue. "Some are really successful. VPs of corporations. Entrepreneurs. Doctors. Some politicians."

More confident laughter this time, and a few names of current senators are shouted out.

"It's true," I continue. "We used to have a pretty antiquated view of psychopathy—like, this perennial image of Michael Myers. But the fact is, many psychopaths are nonviolent, and their profiles differ from men to women."

"I could have told you that." A young woman smirks from the front row.

"Male psychopaths tend to be narcissistic. Self-important and grandiose, while lacking empathy. Female psychopaths desire belonging but still tend to mislabel feelings in others—empathy is hard for them in a different way. Sometimes they display dramatic mood swings."

"I could have told you that!" A male student snickers, and the room erupts in a loud groan.

"Quiet, please." Professor Marx crosses his arms.

"I don't get it," a redhead with dark eyelashes pipes up from the middle of the hall. "If that's all that psychopaths are, they just sound selfish and self-involved. Everyone has moments like that, so what makes these people so bad?"

Murmurs of agreement ripple across the class.

"But that's just it. Moments of caring more for ourselves than others isn't the same thing as the consistent, callous responses that psychopaths display," I reply. "It's the inability of psychopaths to make genuine connections over time or to display empathy in relationships, sometimes to the detriment of those around them, that raises a red flag. Someone with a healthy amount of selfishness prioritizes themselves above others occasionally. Psychopaths, without a compelling reason otherwise, will choose themselves every time."

Memories of my dad startle forward in my mind. Him, staring impassively at my mom; her crying buckets because he had "accidentally" run over her pet Chihuahua that was always peeing in the house.

Professor Marx nods to me. "So, Ms. Eriksen, knowing that as our baseline, can we tell if psychopathy is evident at birth?"

I shake my head. "Psychologically, we are the product of our environments as well as our genetics. It's impossible to know—"

"Exactly. Now, while I look forward to Ms. Eriksen's findings, we can't dismiss the important role of 'nurture' in the nature versus nurture debate—the possibility that the environment might be more persuasive than a patient's genetics or previous diagnosis. It is so dangerous—ethically and empirically—to presume we can predict a person's behavior based on their disorder alone."

Professor Marx pauses, as if for dramatic effect. "So, today we'll discuss modern ethics in psychology, and how certain disorders, like psychopathy, have been misunderstood. Let's take a look at this excerpt from Susan Meier's textbook—"

"Yet," I interrupt.

"Olivia?" Professor Marx raises both eyebrows. The room shifts toward me again.

"I meant, I can't say definitively whether psychopathy is present at birth, yet. But I still have five more weeks before the graduate semester concludes." I offer a shrug to soften my disagreement. Professor Marx only nods.

Soft chuckling follows me as I climb the steps to the main entrance. When I turn back at the top, the students are scribbling in their notebooks, engaged in the assignment Professor Marx just gave. Professor Marx remains in the center of the room, watching me.

Before I can second-guess the impulse, I allow my lips to part in a smile.

Outside the first floor, I spot Howard bounding toward me. Broad shoulders strain the blue cotton button-up that he left open at his collarbone. He's wearing thin-rimmed glasses, and I suddenly have the urge to suggest we role-play bad student–hot teacher later tonight. Part of me genuinely enjoys the taboo of our relationship. But as he drinks me in, brown eyes roving my body, I know there's more between us.

A male student naps beneath a sprawling tree nearby. The concrete walkway that weaves throughout campus feels empty for the moment.

Howard draws me close, then pauses when we're only inches away. "When am I going to be able to tell the world you're my fiancée, Olivia Eriksen? It's only considered taboo to date students. Once the word gets out about our wedding, my boss will probably buy us a blender."

His hand snakes its way into my jacket pocket, pressing against my jeans and rubbing my hip. He lifts his eyebrows. "What's this?"

He withdraws the square cardstock invitation that I grabbed this morning, then scans it. "Eriksen family reunion?"

"Yeah, I just got it in the mail."

A wide grin strikes his cheeks. "Well, we're going, aren't we? I'm dying to meet the rest of the clan. The good ones, anyway."

"Howard, I don't know—"

"I'm only joking. You know that. I'll take the bad ones too." Another smile.

Tears fill my eyes. I'm not sure why, but I feel trapped. Cornered, like an animal, with no escape route to safety. Howard pulls me into a hug, for the first time on campus.

"Hey." His voice is soothing, soft in my ear. "Hey, I shouldn't be making light of this. I'm sorry. You okay?"

I pull back. Meet his reassuring gaze. "Yes. Yeah, I'm fine. I'm just feeling overwhelmed, I guess. Going to this retreat could be challenging. I hadn't made up my mind about it."

"I respect that." Howard steps away, resuming our normal distance in public. "Whatever you want to do."

"Thanks, Howie."

"But—if you did want to go, it would be the perfect place to tell most of your family about the engagement. That could be pretty great, huh? I know you wanted to share the news with your mom in person before we announce to anyone here."

He touches my elbow. "I could be your buffer to the good and the bad ones. You're always saying that truly violent psychopaths are rare and your great-uncle was one of the last. That it's harder and harder to hide those kinds of tendencies these days. I can handle a little manipulation or self-absorbed conversation."

"But can I?" I ask, his good humor starting to catch.

"Olivia, if anyone starts to bother you or annoy you, just squeeze my hand and I'll step in."

I hesitate, taking in his open stance. He makes me feel like I can do anything with him behind me. "You really wouldn't mind going? My mom won't join, but we can see her afterward."

A shy smile crosses his mouth. "I'm wherever you need me to be."

I throw a glance to the psych building. As I take in its slanted green roof and weathered brick facade, I know I've explored all it can offer. Inside its walls lies the available information for my dissertation, and still my writing is coming up short.

I need more. More firsthand experience to analyze, more sources who are living and not simply preserved on black-and-white, static-filled court recordings. Grandpa Edgar has refused to cooperate via phone call. On such short notice, with a little more than five weeks before I turn in my dissertation, a congregation of my relatives is the best worst option I have.

The words I just spoke to a roomful of undergrads return to mind: *many psychopaths are nonviolent.*

I need to return to the mecca of my research. To the Eriksen family reunion and weekend retreat—back to Oregon, where it all started.

5

NEWS ARTICLE

The *Seattle Times*
November 12, 1945
By Chauncey Travers, Reporter

Tragedy struck Sunriver in southern Oregon when neighbors reported a domestic disturbance Friday night. Flashing lights emanated from a house in an erratic pattern until one such neighbor realized Morse code was being used to convey a message: "Help me." Police arrived within the hour to the most gruesome scene Bend sheriff Mark Paulson had ever seen in his twenty years of service: a gentleman lying prostrate on the wooden floor of the home he built by hand, dead of wounds inflicted by an axe; the victim's five-year-old son was found beside the body. Although no one else was present in the home, a search of the ten-acre property found the decedent's oldest son, Calder Saffron Eriksen, alone in the easternmost corner. The local dentist claimed to be admiring the spate of meteor showers this region has recently enjoyed, but his blood-soaked trousers told a different story.

Police are still investigating this shocking homicide as new details continue to emerge. Although authorities took the junior Eriksen into custody Friday night, a more extensive search of the house revealed a basement apartment, previously concealed by a bookshelf. Within the subterranean enclosure? The bones of a young woman, identified only by the scraps of a uniform that belongs to a local hospital. Miss Marie Hendrix has been found after over a decade, mere miles from where she disappeared from the family home in 1933.

Police have not yet issued a formal declaration of guilt against any member of the Eriksen household at this time. Sheriff Paulson only noted that the deed of the house was first recorded in the decedent's name, Einar Eriksen, in the year 1930.

6

BIRDIE

Some murders latch on like pasties and won't let go. And I always check the true crime forums when a new homicide grabs me.

Back when I was first stumbling through these virtual halls, more as a spectator to the forums than a participant, the Eriksen family was like a ten-car pileup. I couldn't look away, couldn't stop reading about them. Einar Eriksen tortured and killed women during the 1930s and '40s, a time when serial killers were way less common than today. His actions all by themselves would be enough content for a docuseries, but then *he* was murdered by his adult son. God only knows what the rest of them have gotten up to in the decades since.

I scroll through the message board subjects, ranging from the classics—the Eriksen family, Richard Ramirez, and Ted Bundy—to the more contemporary—the Golden State Killer and the Cleveland house of horrors. I search for information on Li. The police and media reports that I find online provide the same bare-bones details discussed in the forums: Li disappeared from Eugene, Oregon, where she worked at a bookstore; she was an Oakland, California, resident from the time she was four, but I can't tell when or why she went farther north. Foul play is suspected because she left behind a small child, after she went away for the weekend and friends were unable to reach her.

According to forum sleuths in older posts, Li's former roommate was said to have a motive in that Li owed her a substantial amount of money—somewhere upward of $10,000. Li's boyfriend was cleared of any wrongdoing, despite going away with her. He's quoted as saying that she went for a walk and simply never came back.

"Suspicious. Very suspicious, boyfriend. Why did the police believe him?" I ask an empty coat hanger in my office.

Brooklyn's favorite meal, a dinner of macaroni and Chinese sausage, continues to perfume the kitchen. It snakes its way to me beneath the closet door. She's asleep now, tucked into her bed with a projector of stars rotating overhead for another twenty minutes until the timer turns off the image.

I pause my scrolling and listen to ensure her sound machine hasn't clicked off—the batteries on that thing need to be replaced. Since Brooklyn was born, I've developed what Grayson calls MESP: mom extrasensory perception. I hear everything in this house, as I often remind him with a wink.

The soft whoosh of waves crashing reaches my ears from two doors down the hall. Then I relax.

Multiple other message threads contain mentions of Li Ming Na, but I work my way through the topmost results.

While the boyfriend is usually the prime suspect—for good reason— the police wasted too much time trying to get a sixteen-year-old boy to confess in the murder of my cousin. Wendy and Clayton had been dating for well over six months at the time of her death, and Clayton was known as a star of their high school's wrestling team. It wasn't until later that the cops started suspecting a member of the faculty.

"Who else was in your life, Li? Who is less obvious than your Romeo?" I click on a post dedicated to the roommate who was owed ten grand, Hilarie Dayton. According to a user, SurfsUp56, Li was so far behind on rent and utilities payments that Hilarie tried to kick her out multiple times. But Li always had some new scheme to make back the money, and fast. She worked plenty of steady jobs—as a waitress, at a bookstore, at an herbal medicinary—and still found the time to walk dogs for neighbors, fulfill calligraphy orders for her Etsy shop, and offer Mandarin lessons to local college students.

SurfsUp56 attached a screenshot of an old calligraphy sample that was featured on Li's Etsy page. Black ink sweeps across colorful paper in artistic designs, both in English and in Chinese characters. I open a new browser tab to search for Li's shop, "Beauty in the Eye." Pages of results return, none of them matching the correct name.

"Beatrice Tan. What are you scheming?" My husband, Grayson, leans against the closet doorframe, my sexy tech-nerd edition of Idris Elba. The clip-on lamp I mounted on the former shoe shelf illuminates the kind hazel eyes that first beckoned me across a cruise ship. It was an all-you-can-drink "booze cruise" that San Diego yachts offer on Sundays, but I was punch-drunk in love with Grayson when he caught me eyeing the top-shelf liquor behind the bar; he said the same phrase then: *Lady in red. What are you scheming?*

"Hey. I'm just—"

"Just researching another unsolved case that your ravenous listeners need to know about?" He smiles, then runs a hand across the long top of his hair. "Shoulda known."

"You should have," I tease. "This one seems . . . different, somehow. I don't know. All these cases are sad, especially the ones that never get solved. But this one seems like the puzzle pieces are there and no one bothered to follow up on the threads."

A proud smirk hits his mouth. "So you're going to sniff out the trail? In between making lunches for Brooklyn and planning new arts and crafts activities?"

"Women are excellent multitaskers, babe. It's just wild that there are so many cases, deserving of public support, that get swept away in police archives. Obviously, there's only so much the cops can do, with a workload like what California brings. But still. I think I could help. My podcast listeners seem to think so," I add, recalling the anonymous email that sent me down this rabbit hole.

He bends toward me, then rubs his nose against mine. He kisses me, lingering against my mouth. "Only messing with you. I know what you're capable of. I just ask that you don't forget about us little people in your pursuit of justice."

"Never."

He slides a hand under my cotton shirt, and I reach for the top of his slacks.

———

The glow of my computer wakes me around two in the morning. I must have forgotten to shut it off. I slip from bed, quietly so as not to wake Grayson.

The web page I was reading before is exactly as I left it. I scroll through the other thread titles, scanning for a reason to stay awake. My eyes land on the final thread of the first page: "Police Cover Up Asian Woman's Death."

I sit quietly in the closet. Reread the phrase again.

The original poster, a user named YouNoMe3186, suggests that Li Ming Na's case was solved but the details were never publicly revealed. Instead, the user asserts that her killer would have been in good with the local police or some branch of law enforcement. They must have called in a favor to make her death "go away." The smoking gun, according to YouNoMe3186, four years ago, when they typed their theory? Li Ming Na once shared a photo online of her wearing a man's oversize military uniform.

The replies beneath this message all begin with tongue-in-cheek declarations—"No shit"—"Welcome to reality"—"What victimized

Asian woman? Model minorities live charmed lives duh"—but none of them addresses which branch of the military was captured in that photo, nor on what platform Li Ming Na originally posted it.

When I do a sweep of social media for accounts associated with Li Ming Na, I find they have all been wiped, or the women are entirely too young to be my victim.

Navigating to a direct message, I type out an invite to YouNoMe3186 to chat further. Whether it will come to anything—who knows? But I won't get any shut-eye until I try.

Soft snoring rumbles from our bed—Grayson—and competes with another noise down the hall: talking—Brooklyn mumbles in her sleep.

I'm a woman who has everything in the world I could possibly desire. And I should crawl back beneath the sheets beside my loving husband. Instead, I stare at the inbox of my forum messages, willing my computer to ping with a reply.

7

OLIVIA

March weather is gusty on the drive up. Howard and I split the nine-hour journey into two days to make sure we don't arrive too late on Thursday. Most of the twenty family members who RSVP'd will arrive around noon, according to my uncle who planned the whole thing. Uncle Zane owns the resort where we'll be staying, after falling in love with the property during our last family reunion some ten years ago, then buying it last year. The Horsefly Falls Resort will welcome us with a devoted skeleton crew during the blustery off-season.

The GPS on my phone guides us to Shasta Lake, then east to Modoc National Forest. I drive my car, a red four-door sedan, despite Howard's offer to chauffeur me. The scenery is lush, sprinkled with snow in certain parts, and a contrast to the tiny buds of green barely beginning to form on trees in Davis. A sign we pass reads WELCOME TO OREGON. Memories of sitting by a lake flood my thoughts as I focus on the two-lane road that winds through the mountains.

My father is one of the Eriksen family elite currently in prison—for crimes he absolutely committed. Psychopath though Ephraim Eriksen is, he was never violent. Not with me anyway. Instead, the crime that put him away involved insider trading within the insurance firm he was a partner in; clients gave him information, and he abused his knowledge of the business to share stock tips that earned a handsome profit for them both. Sloppy, with all the federal oversight these days, but I've never visited him to tell him so in the fifteen years he's been locked up.

I recall him sitting me down on the back porch of our home when I was a kid—before my parents separated—with a cone of my favorite ice cream. I couldn't have been more than seven years old, but he told me the story of when his grandfather was murdered by his uncle. Instead of crying like most kids, I sat processing his words, waiting for him to continue; there must have been more—otherwise, why the sweet treat?

He went on to discuss the exploits of other family members: his cousin Jimmy and the early unmedicated battles with schizophrenia; his aunt Lois and her appreciation for starting fires. My dad stole a look at me then, as he asked whether I'd noticed his cousin Ricky, Aunt Lois's boy, and the quirky games he played with their family corgi.

I said I hadn't, and he nodded. "Just as well," he said. "I don't want you to get caught up in our family vices. Mistaking their lives and failures for yours. You're special, Olivia. You're different."

He stroked my hair as he whispered these last words. Then he went indoors.

One month later, he was arrested for insider trading. I never got to question him further about that conversation and what he might have meant by calling me special. My mother called me special often, but not in the same adoring way. In retrospect, knowing what I do about psychopaths, I suppose my father wanted something from me— believed there was something to gain by drawing me close and into his confidence.

A break appears in the trees to my left. A sign stands just off from the road, with words carved into the rotting wood: Horsefly Falls Resort. Beside it, a yellow metal sign warns against wild pigs and elk in the area. Visitors should not approach the animals.

We climb the long gravel road, nearly arrived at our destination.

"Are you excited?" Howard asks, the first words he's spoken in an hour, after I turned on classical music for the drive. He lays a hand on my knee. Squeezes gently.

Not knowing how to reply, I only nod.

As I pull into a parking spot beneath a grand window of a rustic lodge, my aunt steps from wide double doors that open onto a wraparound porch.

"Olivia!" Aunt Uma's voice booms. Her gaze flicks to my passenger seat, to Howard.

I cut the ignition. "Here we go."

Uma, my neurotypical aunt, waves from beside a wooden railing. The thick blue knit sweater she wears complements her short blonde hair, and her narrow frame could grace the cover of a fashion magazine. Aunt Uma, a clear indicator that the Eriksens hail from Norway.

"Do you need help with your stuff?" she asks, all smiles. The last I saw her was five years ago, when Elise threw me a graduation party. Uma insisted on paying for an all locally grown, organic menu.

"We're good," I reply, raising my voice. "Is everyone already here?"

The GPS said we would arrive by noon, the time at which the retreat was supposed to start, but the winding roads up the mountain got the better of me, and we had to stop several times. My cell phone's clock reads a little after three.

"Yup. You're the final straggler. We already had lunch and a passion fruit welcome drink." Aunt Uma gives me a hug by the steps. "And who's your copilot?"

"This is Howard. My boyfriend," I murmur, hauling my suitcase to the steps by the handle.

Howard shoots me a look, then deftly takes my suitcase from me. He shakes my aunt's hand. "Pleased to meet you."

Uma's eyes widen. "Well, we need more than juice to celebrate a new boyfriend. Welcome, Howard."

As Uma leads us through the main entrance and into the reception hall, chattering amiably, I mentally kick myself for forgetting Howard's new status; he popped the question more than a month ago, but we haven't told anyone back in Davis yet.

Overhead, an illuminated crystal chandelier hangs in the center of a vaulted ceiling. Twinkling lights wind along exposed rafter beams, as if part of Christmas decorations someone decided were too difficult to take down. Thick, decorative rugs that muffle our footsteps cover polished floorboards, while a stuffed, taxidermied bear stands upright beside a massive fireplace, stretching sharp claws toward a love seat. Interesting choice.

I touch Howard's elbow, then mouth, "Sorry." He responds by silently wrapping an arm around my shoulders, still towing both my suitcase and his duffel bag behind.

Howard Ngo is a catch; I've known it for some time. Flirtatious women who visit his office hours make that clear, and he takes care of me—is the first person to do so in nearly a decade, really, since I launched my YouTube career. Since before I even hit puberty, I've been ensuring that bills are paid and food is on the table for Elise and me. Now, having someone capable and willing to take charge in my life is a relief I didn't know I needed.

I tip my head back to plant a kiss on Howard's cheek. He turns, brushing his lips to mine, and sends a shiver between my thighs.

"Hello?" Aunt Uma leans on the counter of the check-in desk.

A young woman emerges from an office in the back, carrying a small paper bag with my name written across the front. "Olivia Eriksen? Welcome to Horsefly Falls, and to the Eriksen family retreat," she says.

I take the sack, appreciating its weight. I exchange a look with my aunt. "Wow, Zane is really amped about this weekend."

"Not Zane. His new wife. She's a few years older than you, I think." Thin lips purse together. "Anyway, most everyone is at the yoga center, if you want to say hello after you get settled. I was just heading there myself."

I follow Aunt Uma down the hall to a ground-floor room. "Is Grandpa Edgar there too?"

"He was in the dining hall, last I saw. Talking to someone about the menu for the weekend, and making sure your great-aunt Jacquie doesn't talk to any of the staff. You know how paranoid she gets."

I haven't seen Jacquie, my grandfather's sister, in years, but she was rumored to hear voices as a young girl. As an adult, whenever Jacquie would suggest something off-kilter or display her trademark distrust of the new and unusual, the family would assume "someone else" told her about it.

Uma uses a card key to unlock our door. She opens it wide. Howard waits for me to enter, but I slide my suitcase and the paper welcome bag past the threshold, then return to the hall. "Let's go find him."

Through the back exit, the reception hall opens onto a circular courtyard with a lake a hundred yards off. Lush fields of unmown grass lead to the placid water, and a forest of thick fir trees lies beyond. A carved totem pole occupies the middle of the courtyard.

The three of us walk past the totem pole and the log seating that surrounds it, to a one-story building with a slanted roof. Inside, framed photos of the resort throughout the years line each wall. A few leftover sack lunches are clustered on the nearest table to the door, beside a bouquet of vibrant purple peonies, white tulips, and yellow roses.

"Zane's new wife. Again." Uma eyes the flowers. "I hope those are from a nearby florist. It'd be nice to benefit the local economy if we're all going to trample on nature this weekend."

"I don't see Edgar," I note, scanning the hall for the hunched shoulders of my grandfather among the beige uniforms of the resort staff.

"No, neither do I. Well, I'm sure he'll turn up. We're all together for the next few days, right?" She smiles.

"You say that like it's a good thing," I mutter. Howard's hand slips into mine.

"Olivia?" a voice calls from the kitchen at the far end of the building. "You're late."

Alfred Eriksen, my favorite cousin, grins at me with a bottle of wine in his hand. He wears an orange slicker that could direct air traffic at SMF.

"Already raiding the fridge?" I ask, mirroring his delight.

Alfred was the baby of the family for several years as the first grandchild—the first to make it to adolescence anyway. Although some gray hairs are evident from where Uma, Howard, and I stand near the entrance, Alfred is only nine years older than me. Growing up, he always treated me like we were equals, sharing tidbits of family history the adults didn't want me to know, privately telling me that us neurotypicals had to stick together. His thick brown hair is coiffed to the side, polished and ready for any photos that might memorialize the first day. Naturally. I haven't seen him since the last retreat here. I learned a few years ago that he moved to New York to further his career as a marketing influencer promoting gay culture.

Alfred lifts the bottle of red against a beam of sunlight slanting through a window. "Caught me. There's supposed to be a storm later, and I thought we should start rationing goods."

"Smart. We'll need a block of cheese and a baguette for safekeeping."

He nods, solemn. "You've been forced to a family retreat before." Turning his gaze to Howard, Alfred breaks into a new grin. "And who might this snack be?"

I make the introductions as we move down the aisle between round tables dressed in white linen. Uma clears her throat, still standing at the front entrance. "I'm going to the yoga center, Olivia. Did you and Howard want to join? I know everyone will be very intrigued to meet him."

"Do you mind if we sit for a moment? It'd be nice to relax before throwing Howard in the deep end." I cast an eye at him.

Perpetually calm, even more so away from the suspicious glances of UC Davis faculty and students, Howard shrugs. "I'm wherever you need me to be, honey."

Alfred squeals. *"Honey."*

Howard leans in for a kiss on my cheek. "Why don't I go on ahead and leave you to grab something to eat? I know you said you were hungry. I'll go with your aunt and work on my tree pose."

He winks, then follows Aunt Uma out the door.

Left alone with our appetites, Alfred and I get caught up over a glass of cab and a bag of pretzels. Despite appearances, he says he's excited to go hiking, away from big-city pollution. To reconnect with certain relatives—"You," he clarifies with a laugh. The afternoon passes quickly with the help of an obedient waiter who shows us the alcohol stash for tonight's dinner.

When we ask to taste the resort's finest chardonnay, the server shakes his head. "Sorry. That's in the wine cellar. Off-limits to the likes of me."

"Wine cellar? Can we get a private tour later?" Alfred asks.

"That will put Zane in a good mood—adding our own activity to his retreat agenda." I roll my eyes. "Psychopaths love having control taken away from them."

Alfred smirks. "Good thing we know how to handle those. And what am I here for, if not to ruffle feathers?"

The server smiles, unnerved. "I'll let my manager know you two are interested."

Without a new varietal to sample, we creep to the yoga center. Cloud cover rolls in overhead. I know I shouldn't have abandoned Howard for the last hour, and yet I couldn't help falling under Alfred's spell again; the man can talk, and after several years of living in New York, he's got stories.

We peek inside from the edge of the window frame and find the room nearly empty—except for two people. Uncle Zane and Great-Aunt Jacquie, their voices audible.

"Jacquie, what do you think you're doing riling everyone up?" Zane snaps. Red flushes his pale cheeks. "This weekend is for building bridges. For healing. Not bitching about past wrongs that we can't do anything about."

"I know, Zane. But you can't expect so many Eriksens to get together without some bickering." She crosses her arms over a bony chest.

"I'm in charge here, and I say we leave old conflicts alone. No mention of the last reunion."

"Your mother must be rolling in her grave, to hear you speak to me like that. She would've whipped you—"

"Are you off your meds, Jacquie? Everyone was given enough notice to re-up any necessary prescriptions, and if you didn't take the time—"

Howard walks up from the log seats. He touches my elbow, sweat glistening on his forehead. "Olivia, there you are. Did you get something to eat? Predinner drinks begin in an hour. Your aunt was giving me a tour of the grounds, but I thought we should unpack before then."

We say goodbye to Alfred, who can't take his eyes off my fiancé, then head indoors. Something about having Howard here for support, amid so much tension, makes me feel closer than ever to him.

By the time our hotel door clicks shut, I've already unbuttoned Howard's jeans and pushed them to his ankles.

"Well, look who decided to show." My cousin Coral taps me on the shoulder. I turn from the polished dishware of my place setting, then fumble for Howard's knee. Family members have been more than curious to meet him; Coral's goofy grin indicates that she's no exception.

Blonde hair tumbles in loose, frizzy curls at Coral's rounded shoulders. Autistic and highly intelligent, my cousin has never warmed to me. Not that I didn't try when we were younger. But I admit I wasn't particularly nice the last time we saw each other, at this resort. Alfred and I ignored her and Denny, her younger brother, despite both of them being closer to me in age than Alfred is.

"Coral, meet my boyfriend, Howard."

Zane stands at the front of the dining hall, along a king's table likely specially requested by my uncle. Seated to his right, Grandpa Edgar watches his son, an eyebrow crooked; he looks older than I remember. To Zane's left, a beautiful young woman wearing heavy makeup nudges a fork into place.

"Welcome, everyone, to the Eriksen family retreat!" Zane pauses, lifting his eyebrows expectantly until a smattering of applause replies. "I am so pleased to invite you here, to my and Skye's home away from home, Horsefly Falls Resort. This weekend, we have the finest in luxury outdoor activities available to you and hope that you'll take the time to reconnect, to regroup, and to take new pride in being an Eriksen. There will be a special surprise for the most enthusiastic among you at the very end."

I snort into my empty glass. My uncle Zane is exactly the kind of nonviolent psychopath I mentioned back in Davis in the lecture hall: a doctor, who is self-involved and arrogant enough to believe his weekend would elicit competing levels of cheering from our family.

Alfred catches my eye. "I don't think I can fake excitement for five whole days. You?"

"Depends on how much wine there is in that cellar," I reply. Alfred pours me another round from his bottle.

"As most of you know, we are unplugging this weekend," Zane continues. "All cell phones were turned in to Xavier here, our concierge, upon arrival. Unless you showed up late. Ahem." Zane stares pointedly at Howard and me. A man, tall with dark features and wearing a beige sports jacket, approaches us holding a basket nearly filled with shiny tactile screens.

Howard grimaces, then deposits his smartphone. Not seeing another option, with everyone watching us, I do the same. Although

Zane functions successfully within society, this weekend's opportunity seems to have been too tempting to pass up: full control over our family. He's got the more obvious issues wrangled—violence, disregard for the law and societal norms—but psychopaths, they like totality. Of course Zane would cut us off from the outside world in the name of more effective bonding.

"I don't know that I've ever spent a whole weekend without my phone before," I whisper to Alfred. My cousin mimes hanging himself with a rope.

"Wonderful," Zane says, turning to the concierge. "Now, what can we expect from the staff?"

"Evening, everyone," Xavier says. "If you have any special requests, please don't hesitate to ask myself or any of my twenty staff members. We're here to provide an all-inclusive experience to your whole family, twenty-four hours a day, including spa treatments at our wellness center, group activities such as sunrise yoga, archery, guided hikes, painting classes, arts and crafts, and other opportunities for you to refresh away from city life. If you have any questions, just stop by our welcome desk in the reception hall. Welcome to your Horsefly Falls Resort!"

Zane lifts a glass. Everyone imitates him from their respective tables. Murmurs of "cheers" mingle with clinking drinks.

I count twenty heads across the room and realize I've said hello to only a fraction of my relatives. Could I somehow speak to Grandpa Edgar in private and then leave with Howard, before having to refresh?

Waitstaff emerge from a door leading to the kitchen. Plates of hors d'oeuvres make their way to white-tablecloth destinations.

Dinner and its four courses run smoothly. At one point my great-aunt nearly chokes on a bread roll, but when her husband slaps her between the shoulder blades, she coughs it right up.

Behind me, the main doors leading outside slam against the frame. Alfred and I jump, but no one else seems to notice, not even Howard, who is too engrossed in drink and conversation. Coral leans forward onto the table in a low-cut top, batting big brown eyes at Howard; Howard finds my hand, then clutches it too tightly.

Wind howls along the narrow corridor between the dining hall and the yoga center—a high-pitched scream that seems ripped from a film, or the throat of an animal.

"Was a storm on Zane's retreat agenda?" I ask.

Alfred takes another sip of wine. "It can't be coming, if it wasn't. Not when Dr. Eriksen is planning a party."

I pause, watching my cousin. The years haven't been good to him—he looks older than his thirty-two years. "How's your family? How's your dad?" The non-Eriksen relative.

Alfred pushes out full lips. "Not good. My mom siphoned off the last of his inheritance to fund her dreams of being a writer."

"That costs money?"

"The high-tech writing shed she demanded be built from sustainable materials in the backyard, and the MFA she wanted, did."

"Ah." I take a swig, sloshing the fruity liquid around my mouth. Aunt Felicity has borderline personality disorder. She loves her son in her own way, but it was obvious to me from a young age that she loved him for the way he made her feel. In her mind, her intense fear of abandonment wouldn't come to pass now that she had a child. She took him everywhere, like her own security blanket.

Scanning the room, I spot Felicity's dyed auburn hair by the table closest to her brother Zane's king table at the front.

"We got into it, actually," Alfred continues. He stares past me, to the framed photo of the resort in 1920. "I accused her of stealing from my dad and confronted her about sponging up my college fund all those years ago. That's the reason I went to New York to pursue my marketing career on my own. I didn't have another option, after NYU said they didn't sponsor students pro bono."

"I'm sorry. That must have been really hard," I reply, using the only phrase I can think of. "Hard" being a major understatement. "Did you fight about it here? I wouldn't want to draw attention to bad blood this weekend. You saw the way Zane bit off Great-Aunt Jacquie's head earlier."

Alfred scowls. "It's too late. I yelled at my mother by the totem pole. I know Zane saw me, that Skye, his little wife, did, and most everyone probably, since a lot of people had just crammed into the yoga center. This was before you got here."

Wind whips outside, banging the door again. I get up and try to find a latch to secure it somehow when the door rips from my hand and tugs me forward with it. I stumble out of the hall and into the bright spotlight of the quarter moon.

Howard jumps up from his seat. Together, we shut the door.

Recessed lights flicker overhead. Even Zane appears anxious for a moment. Then, he shouts, "Where's that property manager? Where is Xavier?"

He marches down the aisle, past me and through the door I just struggled to close, toward the main reception lodge. His curse outside—*Goddammit*—is audible over the wind.

The evening concludes early after that. Some relatives, the heavy drinkers, announce they'll be hosting a late-night happy hour with poker in the reception hall, but I shake my head to Howard. I'd rather work on my dissertation. Or gouge my eyeballs with a spoon.

As people don their jackets and brave the weather to reach their rooms, I search for Edgar's hunched shoulders; he's not at the king's table. He must have left after Zane went barreling into the night.

"Shoot," I mutter. "Slippery old guy."

Howard and I say goodbye to Alfred over our empty plates. Stalwart servers pass out small dishes that bear slices of tres leches like parting gifts, and Howard accepts two.

Alfred smirks. "I knew I liked you, Howie. You guys finish dessert; then—since we're not old yet—let's meet in the lobby at midnight. Maybe we can sneak into that wine cellar. There's no way I'll be able to sleep with this tempest brewing."

I lift an eyebrow. "Sounds good, Prospero. We'll see you then."

The lights go out, and voices rise in alarm.

"Everyone, please head back to the main hall and to your rooms," an authoritative male voice commands.

More disembodied voices grumble in response.

A woman's rises above the rest: "'We'll get such a deal on the retreat in the off-season,' he said. 'You're all going to *love* it,' Zane said."

"Keep your hands to yourself!" a different male orders.

"Ow! Is that a fork?" a voice cries. "Who stabbed me?"

Howard and I jog across the open plaza, nearly soaked by rain by the time we reach the lobby. Alfred is nowhere in sight; he must have stayed behind. Someone holds the door open for me, and I accept it without lifting my head. The lobby is pitch black aside from a roaring fire beneath the chimney to my left.

Back in our room, I cross to the window, bumping into the bed, then the desk chair, and pull back the curtains. Moonlight streams through the space. Ornate brass fixtures contrast maroon and green decor. Cabin luxury at its finest.

"Well, that was interesting. Think we'll get our phones back after this?" Howard wipes the rain from his neck. I reach for him, then push his T-shirt and sweater up and over his head. His sharp abs cast shadows down his torso. I drink him in, suddenly insatiable, and slide my hand to the groin of his pants.

After we break in a tufted armchair in the corner, the lights flicker on.

"Thank God," Howard says. "I was wondering whether this place had a backup generator."

We take a bath in the freestanding tub in the center of the room. Being here, immersed among family and all their cognitive conditions, has me on edge. I trace Howard's collarbone and the faint mole above his chest, grateful he agreed to join. I've been intimate in past relationships, definitely. But my emotional and physical connection with Howard goes deeper than anything I've experienced. Feeling his skin beneath my fingertips is akin to foreplay.

"Do me a favor?" I lean forward, into the suds. The necklace with his diamond ring rests between my breasts.

"Anything." He smiles.

"Let's always love each other this much."

Howard slides a hand beneath my hair, then meets me halfway for a kiss. "More, with each day that passes."

Midnight strikes. I return to the cavernous reception hall, before the cushioned settees of the fireplace. Howard opted to stay in our room, and I agreed without asking any questions; it must be a lot for him, too, being here. But instead of finding Alfred waiting for me, I stand alone with the twitching flames. My cousin hasn't yet arrived.

An hour goes by. Alfred still doesn't show.

———

Screaming jolts me awake. Howard hasn't moved beside me. I race into the hallway, through the lobby, clad in the thick cotton of a bathrobe borrowed from the resort, and step onto the back deck without shoes.

Aunt Felicity leans against two individuals I don't recognize. She lifts a shaking arm to point toward the lake. A body floats along the leaf-strewn surface, clad in a bright orange jacket that could stop traffic.

8

JOURNAL ENTRY

October 13
Afternoon
Eugene, OR

Dear Journal—Well, hello, hi, how are you? Thanks to my employee discount at Tilly's Secondhand Reads, I snatched you from the "Fall Deals" table that I set up during last week's shift. Your smooth red leather cover caught my eye from across the room, and I knew I had to have you to record all of my deep (see: medium-depth) thoughts. Bye-bye, spiral-bound notebook from last spring! I have a new confidante.

It must have been my lucky day, because I also met someone. A boy, if you must know. (Cue music!) Or, a man rather, and in the Self-Help section. Anyone looking to improve himself must be a viable dating option, right?

He was tall with dark hair and green eyes that nearly pierced the back of my skull. Boom! Instant-smitten. I offered to help him in any way he needs, and he wondered if Tilly's had a copy of *Self-Help Yourself*—which, of course we did.

One book recommendation led to another, then coffee at the brew spot across the street. Iced coffee for me in the late September heat wave, European-style espresso for him. TDI (Tall, Dark, and Improving) shared that he's a graduate student—finance. He let me borrow a book on meditation he apparently carries with him in the leather satchel slung across his chest (*O, to be a satchel*). We moved on to our favorite movies, best childhood memories, and ended the early-evening meetup by exchanging numbers.

I'm telling you, Journal, I have never felt such instant chemistry with someone. TDI exudes confidence like I've never encountered, and when he pauses to give me—little old college dropout me—his full attention, I don't think I've ever felt so seen. Or so naked before someone I just met. Like he knows exactly what I'm thinking and the precise words to get me to trust him implicitly, with each shard of my broken and needy soul.

Instant-smitten.

We've basically spent every day together since then. Tall, Dark, and Improving took me to see *Armageddon* in theaters on Friday, but tonight was a new level in our . . . relationship? Casual courting? I don't really know what we are so far, except that I'm drawn to him like a magnet, and couldn't stay away if I tried—which, based on tonight, would not be a bad idea.

Over dinner, TDI and I got to talking. I shared that I don't have a relationship with my parents . . . for lack of a better explanation . . . I also admitted that I dropped out of college. It's not something that I'm proud of, even if it was the right choice for me last year, but he made me feel accepted with a half smile and shrug of those strong shoulders.

When I was done laying all my cards on the table, the server arrived with my spaghetti carbonara and his linguine al nero. Something about his plate seemed to unnerve him, and he promptly set down his fork. Looked at me with his forest-green orbs and began his own confession.

"My family has a lot of darkness," he began. "Too much for a lifetime."

That got my attention. "Oh?" I asked, pausing my twirl of pasta.

He nodded. "My father, actually, Edgar. He was the one that found my grandfather . . ." TDI sucked in a breath. "Murdered."

I laid down my fork. "Oh wow."

TDI pursed his lips. "Worse, my uncle did it. He just went nuts, and attacked his own father with the family axe."

I shivered, fear and revulsion careening up my back, I'm not proud to say. I couldn't help it. Hearing an anecdote of this level of horror, for the first time, in a candlelit restaurant, was surreal. I come from suburbia, Journal. Not white picket fences exactly—but some brown, beat-up picket fences that created a much more subdued, if angsty, upbringing.

"Edgar was only a kid," TDI continued. "It really messed him up after that. Messed all of us up, really. Our family is very close, and I think it's because of my father's example. Family must protect each other, at all costs."

He looked down at his untouched pasta plate, like a devastated little boy, and my heart swelled with the desire to hold him.

What are the ripple effects of that kind of trauma? How does a kid carry for the rest of his life the experience of finding his father murdered? How does he pass that trauma down to his kids—to the handsome man sitting before me?

TDI raised his head, then gazed around us. As if only then registering that we were still in a public, romantic setting. "I'm sorry. Was that too much?"

I shook my head, already moving to touch his hand on the red tablecloth to reassure him. "Thank you for sharing. I want to know more about you. Whatever you're willing to tell."

When he made eye contact again, there was a sharp glint, like I'd just said something funny. "Believe me, darling. You may come to regret that."

9

BIRDIE

The freeway is worse than during tourist season, despite it being ten o'clock and well past the morning rush. Fender benders lock in place for miles ahead.

"Move, you idiot!" I honk my horn. If Brooklyn is late one more time, I'm going to be called into the principal's office.

Truthfully, our tardiness is my fault. I was taking notes on the message board posts belonging to SurfsUp56. From Li Ming Na's background as an immigrant born in southern China, to when she was four years old and her family joined cousins who had already established a restaurant in Oakland, California, this user knew details I hadn't seen before. If SurfsUp56 can be believed, Li was naturalized as a fifteen-year-old in Oakland, and then her parents died due to in-home carbon monoxide poisoning when she was nineteen. Shortly afterward, Li dropped out of Chico State and moved to Oregon when she was twenty-one, starting a new life for herself up north.

Note to self: change batteries in our carbon monoxide device thing.

Judging from the way SurfsUp56 seems well versed on all Li Ming Na's details, I wondered whether this user was involved in her case. Maybe they were with the media. When I checked their personal profile and realized they, too, lived in San Diego County, I asked to meet in person. Less than a day later, SurfsUp56 replied with a time and place.

"Mommy, now you have to add to the swear jar," Brooklyn says from the back seat. She doesn't take her eyes from the cartoon episode playing on her tablet.

"Of course, baby. Sorry." I steal a peek at her, then slam on the brakes as a car darts into my lane. Both Brooklyn and I lurch forward. "But is 'idiot' really worthy of a swear-jar contribution? I used to say a lot worse before you were born."

Brook shifts her gaze to mine in the rearview mirror. She arches a thick, dark eyebrow. "You know the rules. One quarter."

"All right, all right. I'll add it when I get home."

"Keep this up and me and Daddy will start asking for a dollar," she says.

When the green Volvo in front of me crawls forward at a sunburn's pace, I can't help my smile. When did my daughter become so smart, assertive, and composed? Who in the hell gave her those genes?

Well, Grayson. Obviously.

The drop-off semicircle is as crowded as ever with parents sending their children out the door.

"Bye, baby. Have fun at school." I pause as she slips from her car seat. "And let me know if Paxton Fairweather pinches you again or says anything rude. I had a nice long . . . uh . . . talk with your teacher about that."

Brooklyn smiles, her pigtails adorably framing her face. "Bye, Mommy."

As she skips to the front door, joining her friends, I watch with a mixture of pride and total retching fear at releasing her into the world day after day.

Once Brooklyn disappears inside, I head in the opposite direction of home. Despite a traffic accident on the 5, I catch all green lights along the oceanfront and reach in record time the restaurant that SurfsUp56 selected. Straddling a busy main road and the concrete path bordering Mission Beach, the beige building displays the usual sun-bleached appearance that's common to SoCal. Salty air makes my mouth water as I walk up to the glass doors.

"Order up!" A cook slaps a silver bell on the counter of the diner's kitchen.

Bacon grease seems to coat my outline the farther I enter Kait's Cakes, one of the cheapest and messiest brunch spots in town. Show tunes blare from garish speakers mounted above framed photos of celebrities who have made their own pancake here, using the self-service griddles attached to the end of each Formica tabletop. Silver-dollar circles of batter line the tables I pass on my way to a booth against the back wall.

The man I approach lifts graying eyebrows. Thinning blond hair dusts the top of his head, but rosy cheeks give him a youthful vibe. He leans forward in the booth, making no move to rise.

"Do_the_Tan_Tan?" he asks.

I nod. "SurfsUp56, I presume." The other user I reached out to, YouNoMe3186, still hasn't replied. When I filtered for that person's posts, I realized they hadn't been active in the last year. A dead end.

"You got it. Also known as Ashley Sherman, former detective for the San Clemente police department."

"Birdie Tan. Novice sleuth." I take a seat opposite Ashley, then note the plate of pancakes in front of him. "Been waiting long?"

Ashley blushes, God bless him. "I admit I arrived early to ensure we got a good griddle. The one down there, halfway along the restaurant, doesn't heat the way it should."

The waiter arrives, and I order a coffee with oat milk and a waffle. Ashley selects the top pancake, then applies butter along the flat surface before rolling it like a fluffy cigar.

"Thanks for agreeing to talk," I begin. "I've been following your posts on the forums, and I think your theories about Li Ming Na are interesting. No one else caught on that she went missing the same weekend that classes resumed at University of Oregon."

Ashley wipes his mouth with a paper napkin. "Yeah, I was always surprised that the police never put more effort into interviewing people connected to the college. Students or faculty. I was still working down here in San Clemente at the time, but later, when I started investigating cold cases on my own, it seemed like a miss."

A different waiter returns with my waffle and mug of light-colored coffee. I drizzle syrup across my waffle until each square is drowning in sugar. Perfect.

Ashley peers at my breakfast. "So, what got you into the forums?"

"I actually have a weekly podcast: *Murders You Missed*."

He smirks. "I must have missed that one."

I smile appreciatively, then wolf down a square. "Very clever. The forums fed a part of me that was looking for answers, you know, when all I was finding were mini-recaps of victims' lives. I wanted more detail, and the forums offered that—in particular, about minority victims."

Ashley nods. He takes a sip of his own black coffee. "There's a lot to dig through there."

"That's my thinking. What else do you know about Li Ming Na's life? I tried looking up her history on my own, but your posts have been the gold mine. How did you know so much about her background, her moving to Oregon, and the odd jobs she held? How did you know about Li owing all that money to Hilarie Dayton, her roommate? Was the San Clemente PD involved in a case that occurred in Oregon?"

Ashley shakes his head, an indulgent smile on his long face. "Definitely not. I've been retired going on ten years now. I continue to obsess over the cases I could never solve, and while I wait for a light bulb moment for each of them, I fixate on the cases that stumped other detectives. Call it a thirst for answers, or professional rivalry. Li Ming Na was an active member of her community who disappeared without notice, and with rock-solid alibis in place for those who knew her. It never made sense to me."

"Right. Lots of questions there."

"And I know so much about this case because I'm not the only retired cop that's sniffing around unsolved murders. There's a kind of . . . symbiosis among us, and I've developed relationships over the years. I have friends up in Eugene."

"Smart friends. In-the-know friends, it seems like. Have you read the Eugene PD's case file on Li?"

Ashley nods.

"Could I see it?"

Ashley pauses. He sips his coffee. Peers around the restaurant. A child squeals somewhere to my left, no doubt tickled by a sugary breakfast.

Ashley leans his elbows on the table to rest his chin in his hands. "I think that would be okay. What about you? I get that you're invested in unsolved cases involving minorities. But we only have twenty-four hours in the day, right? You must have a family"—his gaze shifts to the ring on my left hand—"and other priorities that make devoting time to this stuff hard. What is it about Li's case for you?"

"I lost someone," I answer, matter-of-fact. "My cousin Wendy."

Without warning, my throat closes. Just saying something as simple as her name—when I haven't out loud in years—causes me to blink back tears. Grouping Wendy with all the other tragic deaths that never seem to catch the media's interest churns up memories of my parents long-distance calling everyone in Bakersfield, searching for clues to my cousin's murder.

Then, just as suddenly, in thinking about Wendy like that, remembering my own family's loss and unyielding grief over the years, my sadness shifts to anger. How many families are forced to go on without answers? How many mysterious deaths could be solved if the media and the police spent only a fraction more time and resources on them—diverted some of the energy from the higher-profile cases?

When I don't volunteer further detail, Ashley purses his mouth. "I'm sorry," he says.

I signal to the waiter for another round of coffees. I've got hours before Brooklyn's school day ends, and I'm ready to settle in for the lunch rush. "Tell me about Li's Etsy business."

10

OLIVIA

Friday

The police were contacted immediately. I don't know who called them. Possibly that property manager, Xavier. A man in the resort's uniform said he heard on the radio that our location wasn't the only one affected by the storm. Landslides and flash floods occurred across a ten-mile radius.

The rest of us stood around, dazed, in bathrobes and sneakers— watching Aunt Felicity wail and point toward the lake, over and over again. To be fair, I think most people in her situation would have done the same. Especially when no one wanted to touch the body without the police first viewing the scene.

The body. Alfred. My oldest cousin.

My grandfather Edgar kept off to the side, near the spa and wellness building. No doubt contemplating the degrees of tragedy that have touched the Eriksens over his lifetime.

I know I should feel something. A deep sense of sadness or regret that I didn't show up exactly at midnight, or a few minutes earlier. Maybe if I had, I would have seen Alfred head outdoors instead of making good on his promise to clink a nightcap with me. As it is, I don't feel any of that. I only feel numb.

Alfred's orange slicker bobs against a small wave. I overheard the resort staff speculating whether the fish would have started nibbling on the new addition to their lake. A canoe rocks against the dock that extends from the plaza's totem pole.

———

I peel out of the parking lot of the resort, not bothering to look left for oncoming traffic. Branches litter our path as I drive down the mountain.

"Where are we going?" Howard asks. "All our stuff is still in the hotel room."

We just need to go. Leave this place and these people, whom I thought I could visit for the weekend, then return to my idyllic life unscathed.

"Olivia?"

I swerve to avoid a sapling with roots that occupies my lane. Howard grabs the bar above his passenger window.

The road curves, then descends the hill we climbed only yesterday. I drive over a pile of branches, and my left wheel pops off the ground a quick second. Once we reach the main highway below, the debris is worse. I put the car in park.

"Olivia? Are you okay?" Howard's voice is small, curious, though not insistent. Exactly why I love him—he knows how to get answers from me without pressing. Without making me feel like a freak show for my family history, without him seeming like a rabid fan seeking publishable tidbits to share on his channel.

"Look, based on what you've said," he begins, "I know it must be hard to be back among your relatives. I don't have the greatest relationship with my family either, and the . . . what happened to your cousin is devastating. I get it if you want to flee." Howard stares straight ahead at the log that I'd need a monster truck to traverse. But maybe I can inch around it and still put some distance between us and the resort—us and the orange slicker in the lake.

Why didn't Alfred show last night? I waited for more than an hour before I finally turned in and went to sleep. Was he already floating in the moonlight? My breath hitches, and I fumble for my inhaler in the center console. I haven't used it in ages, but before departing Davis, I decided to toss it in. Just in case.

"Olivia?" Howard waits for me to make eye contact. "I'm here for you. In whatever way you need." A small, reassuring smile curves his lips. "What are you thinking? Feeling, right now?"

"I'm . . . heartbroken. My cousin is gone. We were supposed to meet up last night and—" A sob escapes my throat before I can stifle it, before I can pull myself together. "I think I'm still processing."

Howard doesn't say anything. He only gives my hand a squeeze.

"And I . . . I'm afraid," I continue. The V between Howard's eyebrows deepens. "I mean, it's only been twenty-four hours and already someone has gotten hurt. What if . . . I don't know, what if Alfred's death wasn't an accident?"

"You think one of your relatives was involved?"

"Maybe. Or a member of the resort staff. It's just so weird that Alfred suggested we meet up by the fireplace, then he never showed. I'm sure that sounds paranoid."

Howard grunts. "Not paranoid. Only . . ."

"Callous? Impersonal? Heartless to be wondering if my relatives attacked our family member?" Stress clamps my jaw shut.

"No," Howard replies, his voice soft. "I was going to say 'clinical.' You're only trying to marshal the facts."

A branch with leaves still attached clatters across the asphalt in front of us. "I don't know what to think. And . . . I guess . . . I hope you don't learn something this weekend that scares you away."

"Olivia," he begins. "You're my fiancée. I've been all in since we took that first bike ride along the American River. You remember that?"

Howard traces circles on my hand with his thumb. The day he's referencing was one of the windiest we'd had that spring.

"Of course I do. By the time we finished the route, we both had bloodshot, watering eyes," I answer. "But you said I looked beautiful."

"I did. And you do. I loved that you were down for anything that day, and your willingness to seek out adventure together. I love you."

Something in my chest releases an inch. I squeeze his hand back. "I love you too, Howie."

"And it's all going to be okay," he continues. "I'll understand if someone reacts poorly this weekend. Losing a family member is hard at any point, let alone during a family retreat with . . . well, difficult personalities."

I scoff, fingering the cap of my inhaler. "Putting it lightly."

"No, I mean it. It's completely valid to grieve in all kinds of ways. My grandparents were really the ones to raise me, and when my grandmother passed, I was a wreck. Drinking. Sleeping around. Eating beef jerky for dinner. Not taking care of myself."

I peer at him, hearing him for the first time recall that loss. I knew his grandparents raised him. I've never before heard him describe the aftermath. "I'm sorry."

"It wasn't pretty. But your relatives—they're allowed to freak out in a totally abnormal situation."

I can't help my smile. Few people from neurotypical backgrounds understand the petri dish of my genes. "That's the thing. My relatives—they're not normal. None of us is, when you think about the recessive alleles hibernating inside us."

Howard hesitates. "Yeah. You've said that. But everyone I've met so far appears pretty benign."

"Psychopaths—" I shake my head. "They're not killing machines with some unrelenting need to maim. Not usually. Most are functional, who have adapted to living in society—they've learned there are consequences to socially deviant behavior, so they don't do it. The ones that don't learn end up in jail, where the lesson usually takes hold. They're supposed to appear benign."

I recall my relative's cry last night when they were confronted with a fork during the power outage. "If you watch long enough, that facade starts to slip."

Howard nods, absorbing my Psych 101 lesson. The gentle thrum of the heater fills the car. "So who here is dangerous, do you think? Uma seems warm and welcoming. Even Zane seems arrogant but nice enough."

I pause, considering the answer. "Uma doesn't pose a threat—unless you dislike buying local. As a surgeon and CEO, Zane has too much to risk to behave in totally deviant ways. There are my dad's cousins Rick and Mark, but they're both in prison for murder. It's the rest you want to keep an eye on. No one at the resort has been formally diagnosed with psychopathy, but that doesn't mean the condition isn't lurking."

"Is there some kind of trigger for it?"

Howard's innocent question sends a chill dancing down my back. I haven't told him my concerns about my upcoming twenty-third birthday—the age at which psychopathy is usually apparent in my family. How could I?

Hey, fiancé. You might want to safeguard your checking accounts and sleep with one eye open over the next few weeks. I could start manipulating you for personal gain, via either emotional or physical abuse. Cool?

I take a deep breath. "Generally, no. It's something that's recognized gradually during adolescence. If a condition is triggered due to trauma, that's usually psychosis or dissociation occurring."

Howard lifts both eyebrows. "Yeah, that's . . . that's a lot for anyone to have in their family. I don't think I tell you this enough, but you're pretty amazing. You know that, right?"

My grip on my inhaler softens. Returning his compassionate gaze, I think again how fortunate I am to have him in my life. He makes me feel safe, seen, and accepted in ways I've never been. Flashbacks of middle school, and of being derided as that "axe murderer's relative," return as if to further highlight my luck. "Howie, I don't know what I did to deserve you."

I reach for his hand. Stroke the back of it for a moment, then press it between my legs.

Howard chuckles. "Honey, before we get carried away, maybe we should decide whether we're leaving. Whether we should grab our stuff back at the lodge."

"You're right. Of course. Sorry. Thanks for being so supportive." My cheeks flush against the heat blasting from my car's vent. I pause, considering our options. Allow for the pulsing below my navel to slow.

Shifting into drive, I inch around the branches and log, pulling onto the dirt shoulder of oncoming traffic, wary of any cars that might spin around the corner. But when I reach the edge of the intersection and can fully peer in both directions of the major highway, any hope of leaving sinks in my chest. Compacted dirt from the mountainside and a thick tree trunk taller than me form an impasse I could barely climb, let alone drive my sedan through to reach California, while rocks the size of big rig tires block the narrow two-lane passage heading west toward Eugene. A landslide and blockade, barring any exit from the Eriksen family retreat. Just like the staff member said they heard on the radio.

Beyond the tree trunk, an unlit sign reading GAS in oversize letters is visible.

"I guess that makes it easy," Howard says, as I pull off to the side of the road. Without another word, Howard unbuttons his jeans. He reaches beside him beneath the door handle. The passenger seat reclines as the low hum of the seat's motor fills the car.

11

JOURNAL ENTRY

November 27
Morning after
Still stuffed like a bird

Transformation: complete! I am no longer a single gal, Journal, but a fully coupled-up woman of the world. Last night, I joined TDI for the Eriksen family Thanksgiving—apparently a tradition of sorts during which all members of the family return to the ancestral home, no matter how far the previous year may have flung them. I met TDI's (let's use "Teddy") siblings, cousins, aunts, uncles, and most importantly, his sweet grandmother, Florence.

Although she was kind, it was clear that Florence was no pushover. She had to have been firm to take over as head of the family after her husband was murdered by her own son. (Cringe.) From what Teddy tells me, she ruled with an iron fist to ensure that chores were done, children got an education, and babies were born within the "sanctity of marriage"—per Cousin Mark, a gas station attendant.

Being there among so many lively, happy voices reminded me of the lonely childhood I had growing up. No siblings to bum around with during the summer. But joining the Eriksens last night woke some quiet part of me, previously unaware of what fun could be had in a big family.

Don't get me wrong. I learned a few things I'd rather not have—beyond their earlier tragedies and Teddy's uncle's horrific exploits. For instance, I learned that Teddy's sister Uma doesn't believe in deodorant, Teddy's brother Vic continues to cruise by his ex-girlfriend's house to see what visitors she entertains, and Cousin Jimmy has the temper of a rattlesnake—when Florence announced that dinner would be thirty minutes later than expected, he literally cracked the wineglass he was clutching. But they were all nice in their own way. Teddy was as charming as ever—as if he knew I was a bit overwhelmed in such an environment.

The whipped topping on the pumpkin pie, so to speak? When Teddy's uncle Nicholas called me Teddy's new piece of ass (double cringe), Teddy slammed his hand on the white tablecloth and said, "She's my girlfriend. You should treat her with more respect." I thought that would draw some sharp comments from Aunt Jacquie or any of the other quick-witted and quick-tempered relatives, but they were all silent.

All eyes dropped to full plates except for Cousin Ricky's. He held my stare longer than anyone would call respectful.

12

OLIVIA

Back at the resort, Howard and I don't bother heading to our room. We join the rest of the family and resort employees who are still standing on the back deck. My aunt Felicity lifts a hand, frozen at the lake's edge, as if reaching for the body of her son. Alfred.

I join my uncle Vic along the wooden railing overlooking the plaza. The redness of his eyes and cheeks could be a mark of grief—Alfred was his nephew after all—but the hangover from last night is the more likely culprit.

"Where have you two been?" Vic asks. "I've been out here freezing my you-know-whats off all alone. With no drink."

"There's a landslide down below. Howard and I checked it out," I begin. "Any update on the police?"

Vic shakes his head. "I don't know. It's been an hour. When I used to prank call the police as a kid, they'd always ring me back a few minutes later."

"Excuse me." Xavier, the property manager, emerges from the lobby behind me. Black, closely cut hair seems gelled to the tip. Freckles dot a square forehead. "Has anyone seen Mr. Eriksen?"

"Which one?" Vic returns.

"Dr. Eriksen."

"Zane hasn't come out yet. Why?"

Xavier darts his eyes, scanning the crowd of mesmerized family members still clustered in twos and threes. "There's a problem. Could I speak to you in private?"

"No. Anything you have to say can be shared with all of us," Uma says, appearing from the accessibility ramp by the yoga center. I didn't see her walk up. Her hair is mussed in a ponytail, the sweat suit she wears is rumpled, and dark mascara circles are visible from here.

"All right," Xavier draws out. "I just received a call from police dispatch. The only accessible road to Horsefly Falls has been blocked, and they don't have a free helicopter to fly in. The police won't be coming."

"Not coming?" Uma bellows.

Shouts echo throughout the plaza as each person shifts their attention from the lake to Xavier, then back to the lake and the floating cadaver that the police will not be retrieving after all. Felicity's pallor drops another shade. A new wail teases from her chest.

"What are we supposed to do with the body?" I ask, lowering my voice so that only Howard, Xavier, and Vic can hear me.

Xavier returns my stare with disturbing calm. The lobby door opens behind me as someone else joins us on the wraparound deck. "We have a walk-in fridge. I'm sure we could clear room in there."

A shiver twirls across my neck. The morning air remains brisk, and I wish I'd kept the bathrobe from our room for warmth. Alfred's last words to me were some Shakespearean phrase—how fitting, now in hindsight, to leave on a dramatic note: *There's no way I'll be able to sleep with this tempest brewing.*

"Then the fridge it is," Zane says over my shoulder. "Vic? I'm going to need a hand. Uma, you take Felicity away somewhere."

"What? What are you going to do?" Uma asks. "Where am I supposed to take her?"

"The bar is open. Get her a Bloody Mary."

Zane strides past me. A whiff of alcohol follows—bourbon maybe, and something sweet. Orange juice. I watch my uncles descend the steps toward the lake. If ever there were an acceptable time for a screwdriver before ten, it would be now.

"We'll help you," I call out to Uma, who's already halfway to the totem pole.

"No, I need someone strong." Uncle Zane points a finger at my fiancé's chest. "Howard."

"He's coming with me—"

Howard lifts a hand to stop my protest. "It's okay."

"What? You don't have to do that." I pull him aside. "It's my cousin. My cousin's . . . body."

A glaze rolls down Howard's face. I get the sense that I'm seeing the part of him that enlisted into the army at eighteen, before pursuing undergrad, then graduate school. He never speaks with me about that period of combat. "Really. I'll go. It wouldn't be my first time."

He kisses my cheek. Then he takes the wide steps into the plaza below.

Felicity is ushered inside by Uma, with me at her elbow. She complies without speaking. We three slide past the thick oak door to the lobby's cozy bar located behind the hearth. A floor-to-ceiling window offers a view of the meadow and the forest beyond. I draw a blue linen curtain shut as Vic and Zane climb into the canoe on the lake, followed by Howard.

The bartender, a young woman who served hors d'oeuvres last night, leans over the counter. "What can I get you, ladies?" she asks in a soft voice.

So the entire staff already knows. "A screwdriver for me," I say.

"Bloody Mary. Two of them," Uma adds. Felicity nods without speaking.

When the bartender places our full glasses before us, Felicity reaches for hers with a shaking hand.

"Who would do such a thing?" Felicity asks the polished wood of the bar counter.

"What? What do you mean?" Uma leans away from her older sister. "You think this was foul play?"

Felicity shrugs. "Otherwise, why would Alfie do this to me when he knows my birthday is coming up next month? Why be so reckless and go near the water during a storm?"

I take another sip, then catch Uma's eye.

"Oh, I know it sounds selfish," Felicity offers. "But Alfred and I used to make a big thing about birthdays when he was growing up. When I was too, I guess. I was only seventeen when I had him."

"That's very young to become a mom," I say while my mind races. The thought that someone was involved in Alfred's death had entered my head—why else would he have missed our midnight meeting? Knowing our family, and the latent presence of so many personality disorders, it would be naive to ignore that possibility.

We're locked into the property, given the landslide below. If someone convinced Alfred to step outside to his death, that person may still be among us.

Uma had confirmed to my mom that everyone invited to this retreat was stable, reformed, or heavily medicated. Was she wrong?

"Too young," Felicity continues. "I gave so much of myself to Alfred, and now he's gone." A hiccup turns into a sob. She draws a long sip of her drink, almost draining it to the ice.

When she sets down her glass, Felicity turns to me, her green eyes bright and bloodshot. "You're a psychologist now, right, Olivia? Maybe I should talk to you about some of this. To process everything."

"That's a great idea. You'd love to help, wouldn't you, Olivia?" Uma slides onto a barstool. She waits for the bartender to look up, then points to the celery stick in her Bloody Mary. "Is this organic?"

Professor Marx's disapproving gaze in the lecture hall flashes to mind, when he discussed the ethics of psychology.

"I would, but I'm not licensed," I reply to Felicity. "I have to defend my dissertation in a few weeks in order to finish grad school and then take an exam."

How in the world am I going to corner Edgar this weekend now? Would it be insensitive to ask him my questions, given the death of a family member we both loved?

Felicity places a clammy hand over mine, stilling my thoughts. "No worries, my dear. I don't need some license to know you'll keep things confidential; you're family. And if you told any of these jerks my secrets, it wouldn't matter. They know I'm only too open with my emotions."

"Well, okay. Maybe we can chat later today? After you've had some time."

Felicity clinks her ice cubes together. "How about now?"

Uma returns outside, a fresh drink in hand, sans celery, while Felicity and I head to my room. My card key opens the door with a click, and I push inside. I walk past the queen-size bed tucked against the glass wall that separates the bedroom from the bathroom area, past the freestanding tub in the center of the room and the tableau of a hunting party above it. Two blue tufted accent chairs face an electric fireplace in the corner, and I lead my aunt to the small sitting area.

"Have a seat," I say. I flip a switch, and orange and yellow flames spring to life.

Whether it's the alcohol or grief, I feel . . . nervous. This is exactly what Professor Marx was talking about—the unethical practice of doling out psychological services without professional or legal footing.

My aunt sniffles. "So how do we begin?"

The skin around her eyes is raw—reddened—her normally subdued green eye color sharpened to that of fresh blades of springtime grass. She needs someone to talk to, or at least to keep her away from the lake until Alfred—poor Alfred—is stored away.

Felicity slumps into the chair, gripping the fabric armrests. "Can we talk about . . . about Alfie as a baby? Or maybe we should talk more about my childhood? There's so much about my upbringing, about our family history, that affected how I raised Alfred."

She shakes her head, stifling another sob.

"Whatever you think might be helpful—" I pause. If Felicity is willing to discuss her early years, I could ask her questions relevant to my dissertation. She grew up with Zane, who has all the obvious characteristics of a psychopath according to the Psychopathic Personality Inventory test—a callous unconcern for others, charm, arrogance or vanity. These traits are largely consistent across men and women, except women tend to place more value on vanity and sexual engagement.

Felicity's cousin Mark, Calder Saffron's only child, was convicted of first-degree murder eighteen years ago and has since been diagnosed with psychopathy by prison psychiatrists. I could glean some data for the question that Professor Marx thought was so outlandish and that Grandpa Edgar refuses to even hear: Does psychopathy begin at birth?

Cold air twines down my neck. I hug my elbows, settling into the chair. "How old were you when you first noticed our family was . . . different? How did that difference affect Alfred, do you think?"

She nods, tears sliding down her cheeks. "Oh, I knew early on. I knew it in the way we kids were never allowed to play with my cousin Mark alone. I love our family, but I think that mistrust I was taught caused me to be very protective of little Alfie."

Privately, I wonder if that's Felicity's borderline personality disorder to blame. Her condition would have made her anxious in settings where she didn't feel secure. And that would definitely include her childhood home.

"And," Felicity continues, "I think Alfred started to realize something was off when he was about three years old. His father wasn't around at first, you know, so we spent a lot of time at my parents' house. One day, Alfred pointed at a photo of my uncle Calder and my grandfather, wondering why he had never met them. Even though I told myself I could protect him from the uglier parts of our history, I knew then that he wouldn't have a normal life. None of us does. His innocently pointing finger was a reminder to stay vigilant against the Eriksen compulsions—our little twitch."

Felicity's eyes become glassy. Her shoulders relax. Her gaze shifts to the flames of the electric fireplace and the past.

"Alfred was just a little kid, so I couldn't tell him any of that then. I ended up telling him everything when he was older—probably around ten, which your dad didn't want me to do."

"I'll bet he didn't. He liked being in control of secrets."

Felicity paused. She knows full well Ephraim is in prison for insider trading, and probably knows his antisocial personality better than I do.

"Well, it wasn't just him," she continues. "Your uncle Francis didn't want me to tell Alfie anything either. But I always thought he was being selfish."

Uncle Francis is a narcissist, so that's no surprise. If he's not promoting himself, he's not interested in the conversation. "In what way?"

"You don't know? Francis was suspended from school when he was sixteen. The teacher found graphic drawings depicting the ways he'd murder each of us. My mother, me, my siblings, and Alfred, who just a boy then. Francis didn't want me telling anyone, said he was just doodling. I think he still hopes the memory will die with our immediate family."

"But you told Alfred anyway?"

She nods. "It was his history. He deserved to know all of it."

I lean forward, adrenaline pulsing in my limbs. If my uncle Francis was hiding violent urges and Alfred threatened to expose them, I wonder if Francis would try to stop him—especially if those urges were from decades ago and Francis was embarrassed by them. "Aunt Felicity, when did you last see Alfred?"

Her eyes pinch tight. "He was on his way to his room after dinner, probably around eleven o'clock. When I said good night to him in the hall, I saw Francis disappear into his own room. The one right next to Alfie's."

13

JOURNAL ENTRY

December 8
Afternoon
Writing over a BLT sandwich (excuse the tomato juice)

Hey you—

Work has been nuts; between pulling double shifts at Tilly's bookstore during the holiday season and finding time to see Teddy, I feel like I could fall asleep standing up. My roommate has been bugging me to see *I Still Know What You Did Last Summer* with her, so I agreed to go after work and actually *napped in the theater.* What? Who am I? I love movies and spending time with my friend.

When we emerged and I wiped the drool from my chin, I had eleven missed calls on my cell. All from Teddy. I called him back, thinking something bad must have happened, and apparently nothing did—he only wanted to say hi and see how my night was going. My roommate widened her eyes while I was talking with Teddy; she made a crazy sign by twisting her finger in a circle at ear level, but I ignored her. Yes, he sounded pissed and unnecessarily so, but I also found it . . . I don't know. Sweet. Sweet that he missed me and had become so accustomed to my presence that when I didn't answer or call him back within two hours, he kind of freaked a little.

My mother would have said that's unhealthy, but she's not here to judge.

The next day, Teddy invited me to a birthday party for his brother Zane, the youngest boy of four boys and four girls. His sister Felicity was totally plastered when we showed up at Teddy's parents' house; she kept muttering about how *Perfect Zane gets all the attention*, and I was reminded why I never want kids. Or at least, not more than one—too many sibling nuances to deal with as a parent when there's already pressure enough on the moms to make Halloween costumes, bake homemade birthday cupcakes for class celebrations, and schedule playdates that don't revolve around TV. No, thank you.

The night wasn't completely awkward. We hung out while Teddy's mom and aunts finished making dinner—enough for the army of children they all had, plus me—and shared stories basically roasting Zane. I learned that Zane once set the record for a high school track meet in the 400-meter category and—less impressively—also convinced his chemistry teacher to give him an A in the class by using photos of the teacher and the school principal as blackmail.

Teddy chuckled at that, then asked for tips from his brother.

When Zane criticized the cake that I saw his mother spend painstaking effort on, no one batted an eye—"Par for the course with Zaney," according to Teddy—except for Felicity. She ran out of the house and screamed on the front porch, complaining that no one cared about her recent job promotion at the mall, that she might as well not even exist, until their father, Edgar, went out to comfort her. It struck me as unusual and a little scary, but the rest of the household went right on eating cake.

The whole while, Alfred, Felicity's seven-year-old son, was happy to play with video games alone. But when his mother stormed off, he took his seat at the table and began eating her share of dessert.

Strange family dynamic to witness. I was troubled by so much of what I saw—the lack of emotional understanding all the Eriksens seemed to demonstrate, except for Edgar; the attention-seeking tactics from grown adults; the stories of selfishness that everyone laughed at; and the lack of concern for the child, Alfred, who seemed more stable than his mom.

As we said goodbye to everyone and Teddy took my hand, I wondered what this family did when an outsider wasn't present.

14

News Article

Boise Gazette
July 5, 1993
By Shepherd Greer, Editor

The pyrotechnics of last night's patriotic display weren't the only fireworks that rocked the capital city. During the evening Main Street parade, a man was spotted running naked through the neighborhoods that lead into the commercial district of downtown. Eyewitnesses said they're used to such sights around Independence Day, with one such witness mentioning the clothing-optional cycling event of last year, Boise's inaugural Naked Bike Ride. Not much alarms the urban citizens of Boise's metropolis.

However, the same witness made sure to emphasize that last night's incident was unusual in more ways than one. The streaker, a twenty-year-old man named James "Jimmy" Eriksen, was seen first wearing a track suit and roaming through suburban gardens, appearing to be a local resident. He stopped to speak to several patches of flowers, then apparently became angry with said flowers' response, stomping on the beds in fits of rage. According to the neighborhood watch, this behavior continued for four houses. By the time Eriksen reached the Main Street Fourth of July Parade, he had removed all clothing and was sprinting among the local high school drill team dancers, shouting the lyrics to "Yankee Doodle Dandy."

Police rushed to apprehend Eriksen, which led to a chase in an adjacent alleyway. Eriksen was subsequently arrested and transported to the downtown jailhouse, where he remains today. According to his lawyer, Eriksen has "no comment" about his behavior.

Once thing is for certain: Eriksen exercised his independence yesterday evening, but in a way that was starkly different from other Boise residents.

15

OLIVIA

My first session ends when Aunt Felicity begins to snore, the day drinking overriding her desire to discuss the past. I leave her sleeping in my room and, as the door shuts behind me, wonder whether I should have turned off the fireplace.

In the lobby, the concierge behind the reception desk wears a tight smile. Housecleaning zips down the hall opposite the one I came from, while a woman pushes a cart carrying a tub of ice toward the bar. A pile of bows and arrows, no doubt for the archery that Zane chose for today's agenda, sits by the back door. Uncle Vic, Uncle Francis, and his daughter, Kyla, all squeeze onto the couch of the sitting area beneath the stuffed bear's outstretched claws, opposite Uncle Zane.

"Olivia. Your boyfriend is one stoic dude. Did you know he did two army tours?" Zane asks.

I tuck my hands into the deep pouch pocket of my sweater. I thought he did only one. "Where is Howard, if you're all sitting here?"

"Jacquie got a hold of him. Last I saw, she was talking his ear off over by the dining hall."

"That sounds about right. How was . . . how is Alfred?"

Tears form in my eyes. I lift a hand to my mouth to stifle a sob. "Sorry."

Everyone ducks their head except for Zane. He pushes a breath from his lips. "No, that's okay. Everyone is feeling emotional, Olivia. As for Alfred . . . well, it was not for the faint of heart. Even in my line of work as a surgeon, my knees buckled. He's in the fridge now, wrapped in a blanket. How is Felicity doing?"

He turns pinched brown eyes on me, and I'm reminded that despite displaying a lack of empathy for anyone who isn't himself, Zane is a caregiver professionally. He knows enough about the human condition to imitate understanding and emotional intelligence when the situation calls for it. I wonder if that imitation extends to his private life with Skye. Judging from the giant diamond rings on her left hand, I suspect he shows he cares in other ways.

"Felicity is napping in my room now. This morning took a lot out of her."

"Understatement of the year," Vic mumbles, staring into the fire. He swirls a tumbler of clear liquid, then takes a sip. "Uma said something about you offering up therapy to the family?"

"Sort of." Not really. "Any word from the police?"

Zane shakes his head. "Just that they are trying alternative routes, but none are viable roads for an ambulance or a medical examiner. Part of the beauty of this resort, I always thought."

Vic's sharp eyes dart to Zane, but he doesn't seem to notice. Zane claps his hands together, then gets to his feet. "Well, I know this is all very sad. But it's close to lunchtime, and nothing works up an appetite like grieving. Should we all get lunch, then start on archery?"

My uncle Francis, a portly man with a red beard that extends to his thick collarbone, balks. "Are you seriously suggesting we continue with the retreat programming? Our nephew just turned up dead this morning. And I'm better at basketball."

His daughter, Kyla, my younger cousin, shifts beside him on the sofa. Abandoned by her mom and left to be raised by her dad when she was six years old, Kyla has always been soft spoken. As a pale kid of now sixteen with unruly black hair, she hasn't looked at me yet. Not since I turned the corner and entered the lobby.

Zane straightens his posture to stare down his older brother. "You really think I forgot about Alfred? I closed his eyes with my own hand."

"So? Does that mean you're the grief arbiter? You get to say when it's time to move on?"

"I do during my weekend. This is a safe space for us, where we can be alone and unplug, and yes, where we can distract ourselves from some of life's harder facts. We're here to reacquaint ourselves and to make new and better memories, even if some bad ones get created in the process." Zane raises his voice as if the louder he speaks, the better he can drown out the nay-saying. "Archery is at one p.m., assholes. I'll see you on the field." He stalks down the opposite hall.

When he's well and gone, Vic peers around at the rest of us. "Talk about delusional."

"I think he got in some PR hot water recently," Francis volunteers. "Something happened at the hospital where Zane works last month. All of this 'Family is so important' stuff might be related."

Through the windows of the reception hall, I watch as resort staff cross the meadow toward the lake. One of the two women shouts something across the water, and I notice an individual on the opposite shoreline against the forest. They're not wearing a beige uniform, not like the rest of the staff.

A bartender rounds the corner, carrying a tray of drinks. When she crosses my view, the figure against the forest is gone.

Lunch in the dining hall is a toned-down version of the previous night's dinner. Blue tablecloths instead of white decorate the round tables spread along the perimeter of the building, and a buffet is set up where the king's table stood. I make myself a plate of salmon salad, then eat alone at a table overlooking the water and the archery field farther east.

By the time I've finished eating, no one else has entered the building. I heard dishware clatter in the kitchen behind me, but no other indication of human life. Howard wasn't seated with Jacquie at the plaza.

My eyes land on the corner table closest to the entrance leading outside. Alfred and I sat there last night, continuing our day drinking well into the evening. What happened to him? I didn't know him well enough to comment on whether he was a good swimmer, but the fact that he was found wearing his orange slicker makes a midnight dip even less likely.

Unless. What if the Eriksen smorgasbord of cognitive conditions sneaked up on him recently? My dad's cousin Jimmy has schizophrenia. He was once arrested for streaking through a Fourth of July parade, with zero understanding of where he was. Now, he manages his condition with the right medication cocktail to live a functioning life. Did Alfred have some chemical imbalance he didn't share with me?

Then again, Felicity seemed suspicious of her brother Francis, whose room was right next door to Alfred's. As a gay man, Alfred has experienced his share of aggressors and harassment. If he kept drinking after Howard and I went to our room, would his defenses have been lowered, less sharp than usual? Especially if the aggressor was someone he trusted?

Light glints through the window from the archery field. Someone holds up a bow and arrow in one hand. Their mop of brown hair catches the wind.

"Creepy much?" Coral slides onto the chair opposite mine. "Denny is underage and my brother, your cousin."

"That's Denny?"

The narrow adolescent frame that takes aim at a target a hundred feet away fits my idea of a seventeen-year-old boy's, but Denny is taller than I'd expect. He resembles their mom, my aunt Uma, from here.

"Puberty will change anyone." Coral eyes my empty plate. "You didn't lose your appetite like everyone else."

I ignore the bait and instead note the oversize clock above the entrance doors. "It's nearly one. You coming to archery? Zane is insisting we pretend like nothing happened."

"Isn't that what you're doing?" Coral frowns.

"Sorry, are you—did I do something to you?"

She tucks frizzy hair behind her ear. "Did you? You made plans to see Alfred last night. I heard you. Did you guys meet up?"

"No, obviously. I went to the lobby fireplace, but he never showed."

Coral only stares at me, her expression pinched.

I sigh, my patience running thin. "It seems like you're mad about something."

Coral snaps her fingers. "There's that famous empathy my mother is always saying you have. But why would I be? Just because I'm only two years younger than you and probably should have been invited, too, since I was seated across from you last night? But you've always acted as if I don't exist." Coral folds her arms across her chest. Faking indifference.

She's not wrong. Not exactly. I haven't seen her in a decade, and the last time I did, I was thirteen and she was eleven and still carrying around a doll. The two years that separated us might as well have been twenty. Still, it's interesting Coral is dwelling on a perceived slight, when our cousin turned up dead this morning. Is general self-centeredness to blame? Or some more pronounced disregard for others that I didn't notice before?

Coral waves a hand, clearing the air. "Doesn't matter. I'm glad I won't be anywhere near suspicion once the police show up and learn you had a midnight date with Al."

It takes all my self-control not to snap at her—to vehemently reject the idea that I might have been involved in Alfred's death. I inhale through my nose. "Do you know where Grandpa Edgar is staying? His room number?"

"What?" Coral falters.

"Never mind. We should go." I stand, pushing back my chair. "You coming?"

By the time I reach the front entrance, her footsteps rush to catch up.

Nearly everyone has shown up to the archery field. Denny paused his practice with the bow, and noticeably absent are Felicity and Edgar. The landslide that locks us into the resort for the time being has more than the tragic consequence of hindering an investigation into Alfred's death—it means that Edgar will remain here too. I can't leave without getting the interview and source material that I need. Not after all this.

Howard stands off to the side, against the dining hall. "Hey," he says when I approach.

"Hey." I lean in for a kiss. He tastes of coffee. "Heard you caught my great-aunt Jacquie in one of her talkative moods."

Howard nods. He toes a rock on the ground with his low-top sneaker. "Yes, after she first mistook me for your grandpa's nurse."

"Oh, God. I'm sorry about that." I wince, recognizing the inherent racism—intended or no. "She . . . I don't think . . ." My voice trails off as I realize there's nothing I can say to make my relative's assumption any less frustrating. "I'm sorry that happened."

Howard pulls me in close. "Yeah, it caught me off guard. She apologized as soon as I corrected her. As long as the only time we play nurse is in bed, I've already forgotten about it."

"All right, everyone," Zane shouts. "Thanks for arriving on time. Sandra here will demonstrate how to properly load your arrow onto your bow." He motions to a woman with thick blonde curls dyed blue at the tips. "Sandra, please."

"Thanks, Dr. Eriksen—"

"Are you serious? What the hell is happening with the police?" Jimmy, my dad's cousin, shouts. "Are we just supposed to stay here until Monday with a dead body nearby? Do we have someone guarding it?"

Sandra takes a step backward. Zane flares his nostrils. "No, because no one is going to mess with it. Alfred's death was an accident, of course. Haven't I said to everyone that the police will get here as soon as humanly possible? Let's not jump to unwarranted conclusions."

"Tell that to Felicity. Alfred was your nephew. Why are you acting like this isn't traumatic?" Jimmy adds.

"Oh, because you've always been so sensitive," Zane sneers. "Where was this concern when you traumatized all those kids during that Fourth of July parade?"

"Are you really—? I had a goddamn episode and it was years ago—"

"Why can't they get a helicopter to fly in or something?" A woman with strawberry-blonde hair, my aunt Marla, hugs her elbows. Beside her, my cousin Shane imitates her. At only thirty, Marla is the baby of my dad's siblings; standing beside twenty-nine-year-old Shane, Marla could be Shane's twin instead of his aunt.

Zane spits onto the ground. "Look, this was a horrible accident, and I told the police as much. We have the body stored in a cool place, so they are free to take care of more pressing matters."

Shouts erupt from our group, angry cries competing with swear words.

"Wait—you told the cops *not* to come? Not to prioritize Alfred?" Great-Aunt Lois says above the rest.

"All their birds were deployed to help others at lower altitudes," Zane continues. "The police say the wind has been too unpredictable to fly up here for someone who's confirmed deceased, and their personnel are spread pretty thin across the landslides and flooding in the area. They said to contact them again if the situation escalates."

"You mean, if someone else dies," I add.

My relatives turn to me at the back of the group. Coral takes a step away from me.

Zane scowls. "All right, you idiots. I can see that rational thought isn't going to break you out of this cloud. If you're each so anxious, why doesn't the person that killed Alfred raise their hand? Hm? Scout's honor that we won't judge you, or turn you in to the cops, or tie you up and throw you in with his body in the fridge."

He actually pauses, waiting for a palm to lift.

Pretty awful that he could compare our collective shock and trauma at losing a family member to being under some kind of depressed *cloud*. A quick glance at the group confirms mine isn't the only frown. Although my cousin Shane seems preoccupied with something on his shirt. He picks at a brown stain.

Zane smirks, glowering. "That's what I thought. Now, I'm of the opinion that Alfred, God rest his soul, had too much to drink and fell into the lake during one of the worst storms this area has seen in years. I'm grieving in my own way too."

The collective shock quickly becomes a collective eye roll. A few scoffs round out the disbelief.

"But we took time off from our jobs, traveled large and small distances, and hell, we even got Olivia to come out from her cave in California and to bring her boyfriend. Now, what I'm proposing is that we make the most of the time we have left."

When no one objects further, Zane steps back, ceding the stage to the archery instructor. Sandra demonstrates how to properly use the wooden bow and the fiberglass arrows provided by the resort.

One by one, individuals line up before three different targets, each placed a hundred feet away in a field of tall green grass. Though I'm reluctant, Howard and I slide behind my great-aunt Lois at the farthest target. No one speaks; no one seems to want to be here. I know I can't find a way to convince Zane to abandon the weekend agenda, and the creepy voyeurism that Coral accused me of earlier didn't yield any sightings of my grandfather. It's almost as if Edgar knows I mean to corner him. Especially since all my phone calls to his house went unanswered.

Earlier, I asked Howard if we could wait to announce our engagement to the whole family until I can tell Edgar. Without my dad here, it feels right to tell my grandfather first. Howard agreed, although his eyebrows drew together in that V that tells me he's disappointed.

Lois notches an arrow, then shoots. She manages to reach the target, but the arrow fails to lodge, and it drops to the ground. My turn.

I adjust my feet the way the instructor demonstrated, lock in my arrow on the shelf, then pull the string taut by my ear.

"This is bullshit," Shane says behind me.

"I know, I can't believe we have to do this," Marla replies.

"No, I like the archery. I dislike having to pretend we're all broken up over Alfred's death."

I pause to restring my arrow. I cast an eye at the pair of them and catch Marla's horrified expression.

"Don't say that," she whispers.

"Why not? I barely knew him, and neither did you."

Shane has been working as a model for the last several years, per Aunt Uma. "The perfect job for him," according to her, because he could earn money by keeping his mouth shut. If this void of empathy he's demonstrating is more severe than simply stress-induced, he could be a good substitute interview as a psychopath. That is, if Grandpa Edgar is unwilling to chat about his brother and dad. God knows Zane would rather die than admit he's cognitively divergent.

An arrow shoots from the line closest to the lake. It lodges in the second inner ring of the target. Shouts rise from the victor and the people around them.

Sliding my arrow back onto my shelf, I focus on my bull's-eye. I pull the string taut by my ear. Wait for the wind to die down.

"Shane, lower your voice," Marla says. "People will talk."

"Let them. You're still my alibi for last night, right?"

My elbow jerks, and my arrow flies high at an angle from my bow. Past the target, over the field of grass, and closing in on the edge of the forest, where it lodges into something brown. A head. A human head.

I gasp. My hand flies to my mouth. Someone else makes a scared sound as more eyes seek out my failed shot.

Two steps forward sharpen the image. I should want to look away. But I don't.

"Please do not cross into the field of play," the instructor says. "Miss? Return to the shooting line, please."

I ignore her, and the urge to do exactly what she says, and keep walking.

"Miss Eriksen? Okay, everyone, lower your bows. Lower your bows, now!"

"Olivia, what the hell are you doing? Get back—" Zane's angry voice follows me, then abruptly stops.

Knee-high grass brushes my jeans and the bottom of my vest as I stand beyond the row of targets. Chills lace my back. I try to blink away the scene—try and fail.

From here, it's clear my arrow didn't strike a human head.

It's a severed elk's head. Mounted on a stick.

16

BIRDIE

One waffle quickly turns into two. Then two mugs of coffee turn into a milkshake and a side of fries. I'm making great adult choices today. The diner filled up during the lunch rush, but Ashley and I continued our conversation without a blink.

"Let's circle back to the roommate," I begin. "Li was obviously enterprising and smart. She had sources of income from a few different cookie jars and knew how to make friends, even if she royally screwed her roommate out of ten grand."

"Pretty much," Ashley says. He signals to our waitress for more joe. The waitress returns with a fresh pot, then tops off his mug.

"Do we know that the ten grand was exclusively missed rent payments and utility bills?" I ask. "Would Hilarie Dayton have tacked on interest, or been angling for a portion of Li's Etsy business since Li probably worked out of their apartment?"

Li and Hilarie lived together for two years, according to Ashley. Hilarie claims that she paid an entire year's rent herself, when Li couldn't or wouldn't pony up the cash. If Hilarie saw Li sending out calligraphy orders from their address, I wonder if she thought she was owed a portion of that revenue.

From the kitchen window, an order clatters onto the restaurant's aluminum counter. A bell dings, while Ashley peers at a framed photo of an Elvis impersonator holding a plate of pancakes.

"You're wondering if Hilarie could be behind Li's disappearance?" he asks.

"I am. I mean, I know the boyfriend is always the first suspect—"

"They are, usually. And this one also happens to be the father of her kid."

I pause what I was saying. "Really? I hadn't read that. Was there a custody dispute between them?"

Ashley wipes the corner of his clean-shaven mouth. "Not on record, at least."

"Hmm." I lean back against the cracked red leather of the booth. "Well, that's intriguing. But I still wonder if someone less obvious wanted to hurt Li."

"Like her roommate."

"Or someone," I confirm. During the investigation into my cousin Wendy's death, a major break in the case came after a different student at their high school accused the soccer coach of seducing her. The other members of the faculty were questioned again, then a third time, before the police realized Wendy had been receiving private math lessons from her algebra teacher, unbeknownst to her parents.

My phone buzzes beside me in the booth. Grayson.

"I gotta get this. Sorry." I lift the phone to my ear. "Hey, I'm still at the restaurant. What's up?"

"It's Brooklyn."

"She okay?" I lean forward onto the sticky tabletop.

"Yeah, she's fine. Sort of. She got called into the principal's office, and they need one of us to come in. Like, as soon as possible, I guess."

"Okay, yeah, I'll head over there now."

"Thanks, babe. I'd go myself but I have a meeting in ten. Let me know how it goes. Love you."

We hang up, and I pay for Ashley's and my meals. Ashley understands that I have to go, of course, but I'm only half listening to him as we say goodbye. Instead my mind shifts to my daughter and what could have happened that would warrant an afternoon visit to her school.

Traffic is building up when I enter the freeway, and I navigate brake lights while mulling over Ashley's insights: Li's boyfriend was the father of her child, and she owed a giant sum of cash to someone else who knew her life intimately. What was Hilarie Dayton's alibi for the weekend that Li went missing?

I park in front of the manicured hedge of Brooklyn's elementary school. As I march up the paved walkway, I regret not asking Ashley more about the Eugene case file on Li he mentioned—and failing to grab a shake to go.

"I'm here to see Principal Ramos," I announce to the receptionist. A woman with hard-earned lines across her pale skin, she doesn't acknowledge me but lifts the receiver of a landline.

"You have a visitor. A Miss . . . ?" She makes eye contact with me.

"Tan. I'm Brooklyn James's mother."

The receptionist directs me down the hall to the left. I pass framed photos of individuals, suits and pearls marking them each as belonging to the same club.

I reach the final office and its window of opaque glass, then enter without knocking. Principal Ramos greets me with a closed smile. I've met him twice: the first time during the open house the school held the month before kindergarten began last fall, the second time at the holiday bake sale. The woman seated in the hard-backed chair in front of him turns to glare at me.

"Thank you both for joining me on such short notice. I know you each have busy schedules, so I'll keep this brief: Ardent Elementary does not condone violence of any kind or racism."

Ramos steeples his fingers against his mouth. His thick black hair is spiked like a twenty-year-old's, in contrast to the formal jacket and tie.

"What happened?" I ask.

"Birdie Tan, this is Reina Fairweather. This morning we had another incident between your children, Brooklyn and Paxton."

"Another one?" My nostrils flare. Brooklyn's teacher told me Paxton had learned his lesson. "Why is her son being allowed to attend class with the other well-behaved kids?"

"Excuse me?" Reina Fairweather—God, what a name—swings her golden curls to me. Heavy eyeliner emphasizes narrowed gray eyes. "Your daughter attacked my son."

"And what did he call her? What covert epithet have you been using at home that your kid brought to school?"

"Ms. Tan," Ramos says, "Brooklyn pushed Paxton into a garbage can. He has a sprained wrist."

"She . . . what?"

"She assaulted him," Reina takes up. "And I have half a mind to file a formal complaint against her and your parenting with the school district." A faint smile plays across her lip gloss.

"I . . . I'm so sorry. But Brooklyn is not aggressive. She's kind, thoughtful, and compassionate."

Thinking back on our car ride to school this morning, I reflect that she's more composed as a five-year-old than I've been in my entire thirty-six years.

"The record doesn't show it." Fairweather sniffs.

I lean forward in my chair, directing my energy at Ramos. "But what happened immediately preceding Brooklyn pushing Paxton? What words were exchanged?"

Principal Ramos doesn't flinch. "Ever heard the expression 'sticks and stones may break my bones, but names will never hurt me'? We don't accept taunting as justification for physical injury here."

"Yes, I understand that, and I'm sorry but—"

Ramos lifts a finger to silence me. Anger burns in my cheeks, competing with my motherly shame. "Paxton said the pandemic was all her fault. And that her hair is ugly."

Scratch that. No shame. Only boiling rage. "Because she's part Asian and half-Black."

"He's been watching a lot of cable network reality shows lately," Fairweather says in a low tone.

"He's five. Isn't he?" I seethe.

Shifting narrow shoulders to me, this woman looks up from beneath thick eyelashes. Probably the same stance she adopts when she's getting out of a speeding ticket. "I don't know where he heard those words, honestly. But the pandemic did begin in China."

"Hold on, are you justifying your son's insults? Brooklyn should not have pushed Paxton, but let's not pretend what he said is okay—"

"Ladies, if we could please stay on track." Ramos lifts both hands, palms out. "I'm willing to offer a pass to both students, provided that you as their parents agree to speak to them about their bad behavior. If this happens again, I'll consider suspension and/or a required visit to our school counselor."

Fairweather's plump upper lip curls. "A second-rate public school therapist speak to my son? I don't think so. Look, this was all one big misunderstanding. Kids will be kids, and this was clearly child's play gone wrong." She throws me a glance. "We'll work on it."

Without seeing another way to avoid punishment for Brooklyn, I concede with a huff. "Fine."

I leave the office to the tune of Fairweather thanking Principal Ramos for exercising his authority in such a "judicious manner," then spot Brooklyn seated in the lobby. The little boy next to her, towheaded and the spitting image of his mother, stares at the carpet.

"Mommy?" she asks.

"Let's go, Brook."

When we get in the car, I turn on her favorite song, then pull away from the semicircle driveway.

"Mommy, are you mad at me?" she asks in a small voice. Big brown eyes pinch together.

"No, sweetheart. I'm mad at other people. I love you more than I can string together in words."

And I need to talk to your father about this before I give you an official talk.

As we reach the freeway, the image of Li Ming Na pops into my head. Her shiny, straight black hair, smiling eyes, and pert mouth that could belong to a movie star.

Injustice should be called out whenever and wherever it happens. Especially when the system in place doesn't seem to notice or care. Brooklyn was right to speak up, even though I regret her pushing another kid. People like my cousin Wendy and Li—like Brooklyn, like myself, and like Grayson—deserve notice; we matter, even when it's inconvenient to say so.

Li deserves the truth to be told about her disappearance. And I'm going to find out what happened.

17

NEWS ARTICLE

The *Oregonian*
March 1, 2023
By Arthur Sun, Investigative Reporting

Respected general surgeon Zane Eriksen, MD, is no stranger to controversy in the medical field in the Pacific Northwest. As a resident at Seattle Methodist Hospital, Eriksen performed an unassisted tracheotomy on a patient while in an elevator—an act he claimed was necessary to save the patient's life, despite an attending physician being available on the next floor of the hospital. Later, while completing his first year as an attending general surgeon, Eriksen eschewed the procedure recommended to him by the chief of surgery, Helena Freeman, MD, during a routine surgery to repair a patient's chest cavity after a near-fatal car crash, in favor of a little-known technique that had recently emerged from Norway.

Throughout Eriksen's tumultuous career, he has been considered eccentric but effective—until now.

Last month, during a visit by the hospital's board of directors to Portland Methodist, where Eriksen is currently CEO, Eriksen rejected the entirety of the current roster of resident surgeons, insisting that he alone could perform the day's scheduled surgeries while the hospital was under the increased scrutiny of the board's visit. To his credit, he managed to perform four of the eight general surgeries before losing consciousness in the operating room. A spokesperson for Portland Methodist confirmed Eriksen fainted from overexertion and that he was treated for dehydration immediately thereafter. Meanwhile, the patient on whom Eriksen was operating was abandoned for fourteen minutes, their abdomen cut open and exposed, as Eriksen, prior to passing out, tried to fight off anyone who attempted to "take over" his surgery.

Speaking on condition of anonymity, one nurse in the operating room reflected on Eriksen's behavior as "immature and egotistical," comparing Eriksen to an only child who insisted on getting his way.

Brief research into Eriksen's history confirms he has seven brothers and sisters—far from being an only child. Yet one has to wonder if Eriksen learned the basic tenets of family life with his siblings: sharing, winning and losing gracefully to contemporaries, and how to support the family unit above his own ego.

Although no one plans to undergo a major surgery, this journalist will be taking his vitamins and daily dose of exercise to avoid entering Eriksen's surgical ward, and Portland Methodist, anytime soon. At least until Eriksen has learned how to prioritize the patient's interests and to play nicely with others.

18

OLIVIA

Gasps ripple across the group as, one by one, each person recognizes what I hit. Murmurs follow, and then someone shouts, "What the fuck is that?"

I stride forward through the tall grass, the archery instructor now silent behind me. Blades of dark green reach my hips in an even curtain. Twice, I stumble in what must be shallow gopher holes; then I almost trip on a fallen branch, flung far from any tree trunk. Clumsy footsteps follow my own, and I know without looking that my relatives are approaching; the Eriksens are a curious bunch.

Buzzing becomes audible the closer I am to the elk—flies laying eggs. The stake on which the head sits could be the same type of branch I just walked across. A rancid smell wrinkles my nose—the elk's rotting flesh. The odor is ripe, as if the rain and wind from last night amplified the stench.

I pause ten feet off. My arrow lodged along the elk's crown, forming a clean wound. Its blood must have already drained. From the corner of its mouth, the animal's tongue lolls like some perverse, zany emoji.

Blackness composes the eye sockets. Then the eyes begin moving.

No, not eyes—swarms of ants shifting to burrow deeper into their newfound buffet.

I gag. Heavy breathing reaches my side.

"Mother of God." Vic pauses. Zane is nearly even with us, tramping through the meadow with a reluctant Xavier-the-Property-Manager bringing up the rear. Behind him and farther back, Uma has stopped in the middle of the meadow.

"Are you kidding me?" Zane roars. "How could you allow this to be left over from your last guests?"

"We haven't had any guests for a week. This is the off-season," Xavier says. "There wasn't anything here before Thursday. We did our usual perimeter sweep in case your party wanted to play capture the flag."

"Sure you did. No fucking way. Are you saying this happened overnight? This morning? That one of us did this?"

An uncomfortable silence falls across all of us in earshot.

Zane insists that Alfred drowned accidentally. As I take in the latest cadaver to surprise our group, I'm less certain. If Alfred was the victim of foul play, is this his killer's victory lap?

"I'm not implying anything," Xavier says. "I think we need to wait for the police to arrive, and then we can properly assess what is going on."

"The police aren't coming," Zane hisses.

I turn to leave. Let my relatives make sense of a new disturbing puzzle piece. Howard falls in line beside me, silent as we each try to process what just happened.

Crossing back through the tall grass, I make eye contact with Uma. She seems fixated on the grisly discovery, the dramatics that followed.

"Never in my life have I seen anything as gruesome as this," she says in a small voice. "Well, almost never. Cousin Rick did a number on a church once, setting the rectory on fire. The flames dancing from the pulpit gave me nightmares."

Everyone has stepped forward past the line of targets, as if drawn to the scene, except for Marla. She waits back near a quiver of arrows like a lost child.

"Is that what it looks like?" Marla asks. A window of sunshine has finally broken through the clouds. Her dark brown eyes are a sharp contrast to the pale Nordic coloring we share. Whereas the last time I saw her she was hiding a larger figure beneath baggy clothing, today she wears a tight sweater that shows off a sharp collarbone.

I nod.

"Who did it? Is it a message for . . . for the resort? For us?" She wraps toned arms across her chest.

"It's not clear. There wasn't exactly a note claiming responsibility."

Marla breaks her gaze from the meadow. "Shane didn't do this, Olivia."

Howard widens his stance beside me. I lift both eyebrows. "Who said he did?"

She hunches forward. "I know you heard us. We were right behind you in line to shoot when Shane was running his mouth. Per usual." She scoffs. "But he didn't have anything to do with Alfred's death, or this. Whatever this is."

"Okay, but didn't Shane used to hunt rabbits on your property with Grandpa Edgar, growing up? I remember he was caught skinning one of them."

Marla's eyes narrow. She takes a long pause, and I'm not sure she's going to answer or if instead she'll turn away and walk back to the resort lodge. "Uma said you were offering to talk to the family, since you've got experience in psychology. To deal with Alfred's passing and the trauma of this whole weekend. Is that true? Do you have to hold in confidence whatever I tell you?"

The instinct to say yes, to learn what Marla is holding back to protect her nephew, wrestles with the ethics lessons Professor Marx shared in the lecture hall. Ultimately, I already told Felicity the truth.

"Somewhat. I'm not officially graduated yet. And I'm not licensed. But I am ethically bound to confidentiality."

Marla throws a glance to Howard. She motions for me to follow a few feet away.

"Good," she says, stopping beside the dining hall. "Because, yes, Shane did awful things to those rabbits. More than I'm prepared to ever share with anyone. But he wasn't out late last night, and he didn't go wild elk hunting this morning when everyone was freaked out about Alfred."

"How do you know that?"

Marla shifts her weight to her other foot. She looks off at our relatives, dispersed among the grass. Zane's shouting carries across the meadow to where we stand. "Because he hasn't hunted for years. He swore off of it when I told him I wouldn't cover for him anymore. He's almost thirty, you know? I couldn't keep hiding the crazy shit he was doing out in the woods, with animals or . . . or otherwise."

"What does 'otherwise' mean?"

Marla crosses her arms beneath her chest. "It means . . . Shane has a history of breaking with reality. When he would go hunting, he would come back with this look in his eye sometimes. As if he wasn't fully returned from wherever he came from."

The back of my neck tingles. "He dissociated?"

"No," she snaps. Marla shakes her head. "I don't know. I'm not a doctor. But like I said, he hasn't done that in years. He didn't go hunting this weekend."

Marla and Shane always were close. "And last night?"

She purses her lips to the side. "I know he wasn't out late. Because he passed out in my room after he couldn't find his key."

"You know for a fact he was in there all night? We still don't know when Alfred died. Only that he was last seen around eleven and then discovered at eight this morning."

Marla offers me a stony glare. "There are limits to professional confidentiality and what you're required to report to the authorities. I know that as a lawyer, and I suspect that extends to psychologists as well. I'm telling you he didn't do it."

She turns to leave. Though not knowing what to make of her reply, I touch her puffy jacket. "Did you see Francis last night? After everyone left the dining hall?"

Marla nods. "I saw him seated by the hearth in the lobby. Probably around eleven thirty."

Slowly, Marla spins on her heel. Then she walks toward the main plaza.

If Francis was out of his room past eleven, maybe Felicity is right to suspect her brother. I can't get her accusatory expression out of my head—the anger that was so obvious in her pinched eyebrows, the fear that made her white-knuckle the armrests of my hotel room's chair.

When Howard and I left the dining hall, Francis and Vic were trying to rally the others to grab a fresh cocktail from the bar, to play a game of poker. But while I've fallen victim to my uncle Vic's practical jokes before, and most often when he's been drinking, my uncle Francis is more of a sad drunk. He's generally harmless. If Felicity's suspicions are correct, how heavily was Francis drinking last night? Enough to pass out in his room next to Alfred's before midnight? Or enough to black out while still on his feet, enticing Alfred to leave the safety of the main lobby?

19

Journal Entry

January 1
Morning after
Mildly hungover, McDonald's breakfast doing its greasy thing

Happy New Year, Journal! I write to you from the balcony of a super swanky hotel in Portland at which Zane Eriksen rented a suite for the family to celebrate the arrival of the new year. Teddy and I got a room down the hall. Instead of waking him now, I thought I would catch you up to speed.

The party was rocking, complete with bottle service. I think Zane's career as a doctor might be taking off? Teddy was as sweet as ever, doting on me the whole time. He got kind of pissy at one point when he thought I was flirting with his cousin Ricky. Otherwise, Teddy looked like Freddie Prinze Jr. with his dark suit and iced tips.

One of his nephews, this little kid named Shane, was running around creating chaos. He lifted up ladies' skirts, drank from an old-fashioned that was lying within reach, and even kicked the three-legged dog that someone brought to the party. I asked about his mother at one point, but no one wanted to talk about her. Apparently, she moved to Aspen and disappeared from Shane's life, from Vic's, his dad's, life, last summer with little fanfare. Whenever I mentioned her, because I brought her up twice, the people I spoke with seemed uncomfortable, like she was a topic they'd rather forget. When I pressed Teddy about it later, he said it was a bad breakup for Vic; the family was only trying to protect their own.

Midnight came fast, and Zane went around topping off everyone's glass with champagne (regardless of what liquor was currently being imbibed). Edgar and Yvette, Teddy's parents, mostly chatted with his aunts and uncles all night, but Yvette did make a point of complimenting my dress. I spent most of last month's wages on the shimmery number, and I have no regrets. The tasteful V-neck with its thick straps and skirt that falls perfectly on my hips made me feel like a starlet, and good enough to catch the likes of Zane's wandering eye.

Teddy's parents both seem like nice people. But there's something about Edgar that I haven't warmed to over the last three months. He always seems bothered, like he's upset about something. Like he's scrutinizing everyone, his own relatives. Privately, Teddy has told me I'm not being fair—that I'm judgmental after all I learned about his father and the fallout of Edgar discovering his own father murdered by his brother.

I told Teddy I don't have a judgmental bone in my body. Not after growing up knowing what it is to look put together on the outside, but to really be surviving thanks to the Scotch tape twining your body. Each of us has a silent struggle we carry. Teddy just shook his beautiful, thick hair and said I was getting argumentative again and that always brought down his mood.

After midnight struck and everyone raised a glass, Teddy held out his hand to me. A navy-blue crushed-velvet jewelry box was cupped in his palm. My heart beating wildly, I opened it to reveal the most exquisite pair of sapphire earrings.

He leaned in close, amid the cheering and screams and laughter of the New Year festivities, and whispered, "For my favorite accessory."

I pulled away, searching for the joke in his eyes, but he only kissed me. Softly, and in front of his family and their friends. Emotions warred within me—confusion, hurt, elation, pride—but I let the champagne take over and just kissed him back.

Then the happy cheers turned to an agonized wail. The three-legged dog that someone had brought came jetting out from under a table, Shane behind him waving a shrimp fork like a machete. Shane pursued the dog another ten feet before being reprimanded and separated from his weapon.

Staring at the earrings now, in the sober light of day, I have the distinct urge to return them to Teddy. To put some space between me and all the Eriksens. But, no doubt, a simple conversation with Teddy would turn into a longer face-off about my "lack of empathy." And, after all that I've learned, truly I wouldn't want to be seen as argumentative.

God forbid I speak a word against the precious Family Eriksen.

20

OLIVIA

Archery ended abruptly. More resort staff emerged from a utilities building I didn't know existed behind the wellness center. Howard and I passed a trio of men, one of whom carried a professional-grade camera while the other two lugged a plastic tub filled with ice.

"You sure these people don't want venison? They seem the types to do something totally deranged with that elk," one of the men muttered.

I couldn't fault them there. Almost all my family members eat live delicacies, enjoy free soloing up mountains, or habitually scuba dive in shark-infested waters; the Eriksens don't typically shy away from the frightening or unusual. Today, however, no one seems hungry.

Thankfully, Zane announced on a resort-wide speaker system that the next activity would be postponed for an hour. He didn't give a reason, but he didn't have to; most everyone was at the archery session and saw what was discovered at the edge of the property. I'm sure that word traveled fast among the staff.

When Howard and I return to our room, the bedsheets are freshly rumpled.

"Did Felicity take a nap?" Howard asks.

"I guess so. Although why she couldn't walk down the hall to her own room, I don't know." I catch my reflection in the bathroom mirror, frowning.

Straight blonde hair is tucked up in a high ponytail, the collar of my shirt popped to defend against the strong breeze that continues to surge between buildings and across the plaza. The thick fleece vest I brought on a whim has become my favorite item, and I zip it closed. Sharp blue eyes peer at me. For a moment, I feel dissociated. Like I'm scrutinizing the fashion choices of a complete stranger.

"A nap sounds like a good idea after the morning we've had." Howard climbs right on top, kicking off his shoes as he does.

I sit on the edge of the disturbed bedsheets. The television is mounted in the corner of the room, only accessible by the remote control lying on the nightstand. Tempting. Instead, I open my laptop.

An hour passes as I edit the final thirty pages of my dissertation that I managed to knock out this week. When Howard stretches to a sitting position, I zoom out on the document.

Taking stock of the yellow highlighted gaps throughout, areas where I still need a final primary source to meet the minimum requirements and—oh, nothing major—the addition of actual analysis to finish the paper, I consider my options. Only five weeks remain before the semester ends.

More importantly, my twenty-third birthday is coming up fast—I'll have a new dissertation topic to analyze then: Does psychopathy or some other disorder always appear at a certain age, within a predisposed family? Or just the Eriksens? Do I have less than three weeks before my own condition is triggered? What I told Howard is true: generally, psychopathy is diagnosed during adolescence—but members of my family have also shown initial signs of antisocial personality disorder as delayed as their early twenties. For whatever reason, if a neurodivergent condition is on the horizon for the Eriksens, it appears in both sexes by the time most chemical processes are matured: age twenty-three.

Did Alfred have this kind of anxiety before his own twenty-third birthday, years ago? I haven't known him well in ages, his likes or his dislikes. Although, when we were kids, he enjoyed exploring our grandparents' arts and crafts bin in the garage and would often show me his finds. The giant rubber bucket had all kinds of surprises inside. Duct tape, chains, and plastic tarps stand out in my memory, not all of which made sense for use as artistic supplies. I later learned the bucket was inherited from our great-grandfather Einar—the items within were leftover resources saved from his Eriksen twitch.

At the bottom of the bucket, we discovered a felt cloth protecting paintbrushes. When we asked Grandpa Edgar about them, he gave us a small jar of red acrylic paint and encouraged us to "transpose our dreams."

I save my document on my laptop. Grabbing my vest from the back of the desk chair, I search for my shoes, a pair of dirty athletic shoes thanks to all this rain.

"Going somewhere?" Howard asks, emerging from the bathroom.

"The watercolor happy hour starts soon, and Edgar always liked painting. Maybe he'll show up early. Coming?"

Howard cracks his neck. "Still waking up. I'll meet you over there."

He kisses me on the lips, then sends me out the door.

Though originally planned to take place by the lake, today's art session was moved to the other side of the property, facing some peak called Strawberry Mountain. Past the wellness center and a newer, updated building where I imagine Zane sleeps, I find two rows of easels set up, facing the natural landscape. A white blanket of snow covers the top of the mountain. Burned skeletons of trees surround it, evident from where I pause.

Edgar slouches before an easel in the front row. He's early, as I had hoped. A resort employee I haven't seen before, but who wears the same beige button-up uniform, chats with him using vigorous gestures.

"Grandpa," I say, reaching his side. "How are you?"

Edgar lifts tired blue eyes to me. Deep lines cut around his mouth and into the wide forehead that I inherited and as a teenager used to hide behind blunt bangs.

"Olivia?" His voice is gravelly. Older and more strained than I remember.

"Yes, it's me, Grandpa." Does he not know me? Is Edgar not as sharp as he once was? The painting instructor rearranges brushes in a bucket. I lay a hand on the arm of Edgar's aquamarine sweater. "I've been trying to get a hold of you for months now."

"Oh?" is all he replies.

I purse my lips. I must have left at least a dozen messages on his landline's recording device and spoken to his live-in nurse, who promised to tell him that I called, twice. Maybe Edgar's mind really is going.

"Yes, I'm a psychology graduate student, Grandpa. I've been studying neurodivergent cognitive conditions. I'm writing my dissertation using some examples from our family. Could I ask you a few questions later?"

Not to mention I've been analyzing our family for the world on the internet for the last decade.

"You look so much like her," Edgar says, peering into my face.

Startled, I reply, "Who?"

"Yvette. My sweet Yvette." Something catches his notice behind me. I've seen pictures of my grandmother Yvette, who died when I was four. We shared the same straight yellow hair and narrow eyes that I've had called "mysterious" as well as "critical." But that's where the resemblance stops.

"Grandpa?"

Edgar looks at me again. "Yvette, my dear. We're going to paint with your favorite. Watercolors."

"Olivia, you're early." My uncle Francis stalks between easels toward us. I try to make eye contact with Edgar again, but he's picked up a brush to examine.

The instructor, a man with a braided beard who introduces himself as Dash, offers my uncle a palette of colors. As Francis accepts the plastic tray, his scent confirms what I could have already guessed: he's been drinking—maybe since the discovery of the elk head. Or since last night, when Alfred may have been lured outside.

"Hey, Dad." Francis nods to Edgar, who returns the stoic greeting.

The cloud, or delusion, that Edgar just experienced seems disappeared, but I don't know what to make of him confusing me with my grandmother. Is that why he hasn't returned my messages? Is he slipping in and out of reality? Are there times of the day when he's most lucid?

I take a palette, then follow Francis to a middle row of easels.

"Where did they end up storing the elk and the stake?" I ask, knowing my uncle stayed behind to supervise, or gawk.

Francis sweeps a hand across his white canvas. "They didn't. Felicity came after you left and insisted it not be touched. Said it might relate to Alfred's death, so the police should see it first."

"You mean it's still out there? Like some scarecrow?"

Francis stops adjusting his canvas. He lifts his eyebrows. "Is it a big deal? It's probably some high school kids bored on spring break. Unless you know something I don't and it is related to Alfred."

I peer at my uncle. He searches my face as if for some hidden meaning.

"No. It's disturbing, that's all. Any word from the police?"

"Not a thing. At least the resort has kept the booze flowing—there's that. Did you get to tour the wine cellar?"

I pause examining a paintbrush. "No. Why do you ask?"

Francis shrugs. "I just thought you had. Coral mentioned that you and, uh . . . Alfred . . . had planned to scope it out together. Before, that is."

"We didn't get the chance."

Francis begins experimenting with his color palette while I find my own canvas in the next row behind. When a bar cart is rolled out to our stretch of grass, I'm grateful this was billed as a happy hour event. As more family members arrive, some looking just as bewildered as when I saw them this morning and during the archery session, I accept a delicate stem of white. Chardonnay. Just like Alfred wanted to sample.

While the server offers drinks to the others, I swallow a mouthful, almost painful in its size.

Edgar sits quietly in the front row. A woman in a jean jacket—his nurse, I think—lays a blanket across his lap. He doesn't acknowledge her, but continues staring at his canvas, motionless from behind.

My thesis explores whether psychopathy is apparent from birth. Anyone who spent time with my currently incarcerated relatives, or Calder Saffron, could be good options if Edgar's mental capacities are slipping. They might not be able to speak about my great-grandfather Einar Eriksen, not like Edgar can, but . . . desperate times.

I wonder if my great-aunt Lois would discuss her son Rick and his childhood.

Howard trickles in with the last of my family members. My aunt Marla walks in step with him, whispering something I can't hear, and some instinct within me—jealousy—raises its hackles. I take another sip from my glass.

With a cough, the painting instructor motions for everyone to quiet down. Lifting his red wine, he says, "Let's salute the natural beauty before us, whose ways we'll never fully understand. Let's soak in the magnificence, the way we soak in alcohol content."

A soft chuckle murmurs through the group. Then each of my relatives drinks from their cups.

As stemware is exchanged for paintbrushes, I wonder who among us would prefer to dull the memory of the orange slicker in the lake, of the elk head in the adjacent meadow. And who secretly reveled in the echo of Felicity's wail, while shedding a convincing tear.

21

BIRDIE

Sunshine beats down on San Diego in March, at a cool seventy-two degrees. True to his water-loving forum handle, SurfsUp56, Ashley walks barefoot along the shore's edge. He sidesteps a pile of monstrous seaweed but doesn't break his gaze from the horizon. I call to him, and then he pauses until I catch up.

Scanning the white shells beneath my feet, I think of the last time I came to the beach, more than a month ago. Grayson, Brooklyn, and I spent a whole morning along Pacific Beach, another five miles north. While Brooklyn ran and searched for pink shells among the waves, Grayson took my hand in his, without speaking. It was a small moment. But it reminded me that I have a partner in this messy life.

Grayson and I agreed that Brooklyn was treated unfairly by Paxton Fairweather, and that his parents were probably the ones speaking the nasty phrases that left little Paxton's mouth. We talked to Brook about the importance of standing up for ourselves while also adopting non-violence. I only hope Brooklyn returned to class yesterday feeling more secure in who she is—as much as a kindergartner can.

Who was sticking up for Li when she disappeared, either by her boyfriend's hand or otherwise? The news articles I found on her make it seem like the investigation was riddled with holes, but I don't know if that's my incomplete research to blame; she disappeared ten years ago, and the internet has captured only so much of the past. Although I myself am poking around other options, why did no one seem stuck on the boyfriend? Why was it accepted that she just—poof!—disappeared of her own volition, when she had a child by that man? Acquaintances reported that Li seemed withdrawn the last few years of her life. No one suggested why.

"Hey again." I shoot Ashley a smile, grateful he allowed me to crash his afternoon at Dog Beach. A golden retriever scampers ahead, sniffing other dogs running around off leash.

"Akira! Too far, come back!" he shouts. The dog turns to regard her owner. Then sprints away, kicking up sand in her wake.

Ashley grumbles. "So, what can I do for you? Everything go okay at your kid's school?"

I nod, not ready to hash out those details. "I wanted to talk to you more about Li Ming Na's boyfriend. The father of her kid. What convinced the police that he wasn't behind Li's death?"

The murder weapon in my cousin Wendy's case was a baseball bat that was located a mile away from where her body was discovered. Alcohol was found in her system, but otherwise her body seemed unmolested by anyone or anything else. A small mercy.

After the police learned that the school's algebra teacher was giving Wendy private tutoring after class and that he was a former Division I athlete for his alma mater's baseball team, they brought him in for questioning a fourth time. It was then he confessed to attempting to seduce Wendy, the same as the school's soccer coach did with the other female student. Wendy's death occurred when he tried to initiate a sexual relationship and she fought back.

"Disappearance," Ashley says. "They never found her body."

"Okay, sure." I shrug.

Ashley's mouth tips up in a smile. "Very rarely, a disappearance is just that. Someone is fed up with their life and decides to skip town—yes, even with a kid in the picture."

A black Labrador launches itself into the waves, chasing a bright green ball. The golden retriever that ignored Ashley watches curiously from a distance.

I step over a long stalk of seaweed. "It is possible that Li packed up and left. Is that why the police never declared her boyfriend a person of interest?"

Ashley is thoughtful a moment. I follow his gaze to a trio of seagulls swooping low to the sand about fifty feet ahead. Something seems to jump beneath their frenzied dives. A crab. The Labrador drops the green ball, then sprints into the fray, scattering the birds into the air.

"I don't know, honestly," he says. "Truthfully, I've never been able to find the boyfriend's name. It's not on any of the official records. That always seemed strange to me, like maybe he was a cop himself who called in a few favors."

Just like the message boards suggested. The boyfriend could have been in good with local police. The more I learn about Li, the less I'm interested in any of the other open cases on my dashboard. The calendar hanging above the desk that I pulled into the closet contains my notes projecting the next four weeks of episodes, but all I can focus on is Li. Her history. Her final days.

Ashley shoots me a wary look. "The blue brotherhood protects its own, even if it's not always aboveboard. For better or worse. But that doesn't mean the guy killed her."

I nod. While disappointed that Ashley doesn't have more detail on the boyfriend, I'm also relieved in a way. That means my own checkered research isn't totally at fault. "So, what's your personal opinion? Give me that. Do you think Li simply escaped her mundane life or that her boyfriend was behind her disappearance somehow?"

Ashley stoops to grab a discarded plastic bag. He pockets the trash. "Look, I'm only a retired detective nosing at the scraps of other detectives' failures—because that's what it is, right? An unsolved case upon retirement is a failure. Examining where other cops missed a clue helps me to obsess less over my own mistakes."

Ashley stops walking. He lowers his gaze to mine. "Based on what I've read and dug up over the years, it's not that I think the boyfriend was innocent. It's that I think he was so convincing. Manipulative. Skilled at speaking to law enforcement and have them eating out of his hand by the end of the conversation."

He turns toward the parking lot. "I made a copy of the Eugene PD file on Li's case for you. But don't post it anywhere online. And don't tell anyone you got it from me. There are redacted portions that make a lot of it unreadable."

"Are you sure? I'd love that, but I don't want to cause you any trouble."

Ashley shrugs. Gray stubble punctuates his sharp jaw. "It's a cold case. No one has made any progress on it in a decade. Maybe you will."

A shiver traces my back, the tickle of possibility. "Thanks. I guess I should count myself lucky my boyfriends in my twenties were all pushovers, huh?"

Ashley narrows his eyes. "Birdie, I know you just started in on this game, but people like Li's boyfriend are everywhere. They can look like nice guys in the short term, or anyone else. They're called psychopaths."

22

OLIVIA

Dinner is a somber affair, in contrast to the rah-rah atmosphere of the previous night. Instead of leading anyone in a toast or making a speech, Zane sits quietly at the king's table, bookended by his young wife—Skye—and Grandpa Edgar. Quiet jazz music fills the room, spooling from the speaker system.

Once the entrée plates are cleared away, heads turn expectantly toward the kitchen. Dessert is the last thing on my mind, personally. It was the final dish served before the weather kicked up last night and I separated from Alfred.

"Where's the chocolate? I heard there would be chocolate," Denny mutters.

"It's coming." Seated beside him, Coral clutches a fork she saved from dinner. Howard and I moved to their table, near the front and away from the windows.

Zane pushes back his chair with a scraping noise, then stands at the king's table. "For dessert, there will be s'mores and a fireside chat outside for anyone interested."

"It's too cold!" Jacquie balks.

"And I didn't bring a jacket," Francis adds.

More complaints follow, but Zane flattens his hands, palms down. His upper lip curls. "Portable heaters are being rolled out right now. There will be extra blankets too. I'd encourage each of you to join."

Howard leans toward me. "That doesn't sound optional."

Outside, just downhill of the plaza, red and orange flames grapple with the air in a dugout firepit. I manage to snag a log just beneath one of the five heaters provided for our twenty-person party; the attrition rate of people heading into the lobby is working in my favor. At least, until I spy Edgar being escorted by Felicity back to the fancy lodge behind the wellness center.

She looked like a ghost during dinner. My aunt normally appears in need of a tan, but her skin was blotchy and her eyes empty—hollow, as if all spark of life had been snuffed during the day. I don't blame Felicity for avoiding further festivities while answers regarding Alfred's death are still outstanding. He was her only child, even if her borderline personality disorder, no doubt, added to friction between them.

I shake my head, recalling Elise's enthusiasm for me to attend this family retreat. I doubt the events of last night are what anyone had in mind. And now we're stuck here since not even the police are able to bring in a bulldozer and clear a path.

Seated a few places away on a log, Coral glares at me. She turns back to her brother, Denny. "Who else do you think could have hurt Alfred? We don't know her anymore," she says, well above a whisper. "She was planning to meet him in the wine cellar at midnight."

"Olivia, you want?" Uma hands me a paper plate of graham crackers, cookies, chocolate squares, and two marshmallows. Without waiting for me to accept, she sits beside me.

"Howard? Would you mind grabbing me a hot cocoa from the dining hall?" she asks, sweetly. "I forgot mine on the way out."

Howard and I exchange a look. "Sure thing. You want anything, honey?"

"No, I'm good. Thanks."

Once Howard is on the move, Uma lodges a marshmallow onto each prong of a metal roasting stick. She pops another one in her mouth. "We have to get out of here."

My uncles Vic and Francis and their cousin Jimmy laugh at something one of them said. Great-Aunt Lois is huddled in conversation with her husband, David, and the rest of the group is too far away to eavesdrop on Uma and me. Piano music and the deep notes of violins emanate from the resort's outdoor speakers.

"What? Why?" I ask.

"We need to get out of here before anything else happens." Uma darts her eyes, an aqua green against the flames, around the circle of relatives. "I'm going to tell Coral and Denny to pack up their stuff tonight, that we're leaving tomorrow morning."

"I don't understand."

Her marshmallows catch fire, brilliant blue and orange engulfing the sugary treats. "We can't navigate the roads at night, not if they're still blocked by the landslides. But I'd bet money that the police can't get past the landslide out of some safety policy; I'm sure there's some kind of drivable path, even if it's not pretty."

"It didn't look good when Howard and I went down to the highway this morning." I push out a breath. "But there probably is a way around if you're willing to off road."

Uma blows on her marshmallows, then gives me a hard stare. "You're a psychologist now, right?"

"I'm not licensed."

"It figures you'd go into that field. You were always so empathetic. Observing and acknowledging others' feelings. I remember when you were six, I was upset about splitting from the kids' dad, and you reached a little hand across mine. Just that. No words. You just seemed to sense I needed the comfort."

I let her talk, not knowing where she's going with this thread.

"You were always an intuitive kid, and now you're a psychologist. I'm surprised by you." Uma makes a show of scanning the familiar faces around us. "You'd really be willing to spend another day among this crowd? Think about Alfred. Think about what happened last night, and about that elk head impaled in the darkness out there."

"Do you think someone, one of the family, hurt Alfred?" I lower my voice. Chills penetrate the long-sleeve shirt I paired with my fleece vest. "It's possible that he tripped and drowned. The storm was intense."

I parrot what Zane keeps saying, not sure I believe it myself.

"Yeah. You're right about that. But the storm didn't occur today while you were shooting arrows into the trees, did it? The storm didn't set up that elk carcass." Uma clenches her jaw. "You were born with an old soul, Olivia. But I forget you haven't known these people as long as I have."

She rises to her feet, then squeezes in between her children, Coral and Denny. Someone else comes to sit beside me—Zane's wife, Skye—but I don't bother turning to her.

Uma has always been the stable one amid the rocky waves of the Eriksens. She grew up with psychopaths and watched some of them excel to professional success; she knows better than anyone how well psychopaths can hide their callousness—even Calder Saffron was a respected dentist in town before he attacked his father with an axe.

Alfred was well loved, by our family and others. Still, he ended up in the crosshairs of someone present, if he didn't accidentally drown. No one should have had a grudge against him; the only family member he'd been in contact with for years, from what he shared with me, was his mother, Felicity. But psychopaths operate using a cost-benefit analysis, more so than weighing the morality of offing a relative. So, if Uma is correct, who here would have something to gain from Alfred's death? Who would benefit from it?

A cold blast shoots through the open landscape. Groans rise among the suddenly huddled bodies crowding closer to the firepit and electric heaters. I stand with the older relatives to head indoors as Uncle Vic slaps Uncle Francis on the back.

"We've seen worse than this, haven't we? I ain't going nowhere. Try and make me, Mother Nature!" Vic takes another plug from his whiskey tumbler, clearly more than a few rounds deep at this point.

Francis nods. "Hell, I'd say we saw worse than this only yesterday."

Everyone pauses, the significance of Francis's drunken commentary rippling across those of us remaining.

"You mean, the downpour?" I ask, tucking my elbows in. "Or what happened . . . during the storm to Alfred?"

"What?" Francis wipes his mouth with an open palm. "Are you . . . what are you suggesting, Olivia?"

I shake my head, regretting speaking up. A glance around the log seats, at the shoulders hunched forward to capture my response and faces watching the spectacle I just became a part of, confirms I should have kept quiet.

Francis sways, the alcohol getting the better of his equilibrium, and I wonder again just how much of last night he remembers. Vic's glossy-eyed glare begs the same question.

"All right, everyone, I think we should all head inside. It's too cold for this conversation." Jimmy, their cousin, stands, breaking the tension. Uma rises, then beelines to the lobby.

"Anybody want another game of poker?" Francis asks.

As I reach the deck, I pass two large piles of firewood beneath a gray tarp at the base of the stairs. At least the resort staff checked the weather forecast in advance.

I enter the lobby as Uma's short blonde bob disappears around a corner, toward the gym facilities along the west end of the building. She went away from her room, which is down the hall from mine, in the opposite direction.

"Uma," I call out, letting the door slam shut behind me. I stride to the hallway, but she's already gone, past the fork ahead.

"Can I help you, miss?" Xavier, the property manager, peers at me from behind the broad reception counter opposite the hearth.

"Any word from the police?" I ask. "Are they sending someone to clear the road?"

Xavier sighs. "Honestly, I doubt it. Roads were wrecked across this region, and the debris is backing up traffic on main freeways and heavily used highways. I think we're at the bottom of the priority list, sadly."

I approach the counter. "What about . . ." I lower my voice. "What about the resort's security cameras? Did you see anything unusual on them last night?"

Xavier looks behind me, as if checking whether anyone else is listening. His fingers drum a quiet rhythm on the polished wood. "That's, uh, not exactly clear at the moment."

"What does that mean?"

"Meaning, the bad weather knocked out the power for a few hours. We don't have anything recorded from about ten thirty until four thirty this morning."

"Like, all across the property?"

He purses his mouth. "None of the interior or exterior cameras retained their footage."

A frisson zigzags down my spine. "And now? Are the cameras back up now?"

Xavier darts a look behind me again. "I've shared all this with Dr. Eriksen already—"

"But I'm asking you," I cut him off. Panic, fear, or ego rears its demanding head as I lock eyes with this property manager. "And I think customer service in this situation equates to sharing what you know."

He nods. "Sure. Sure. Well, the cameras do work now. But intermittently, and in line with the additional electrical surges we've experienced since then. There's no telling when or if the footage we do have will be wiped from the mainframe, if another gale hits. But I can assure you and your family, the resort staff will do everything possible—"

I cross to the hearth, trying to process this news, what it means: if there was foul play involved in Alfred's death, the security cameras won't show it. There's no way of knowing whether he was lured away from the fireplace, out to the lake, and then harmed on purpose—whether a family member is to blame, like Uma suggested. Not now, at least, without the police conducting a formal investigation.

A glance through the glass walls of the lobby confirms Howard rejoined the bonfire. Although he's surrounded by my two drunk uncles, he laughs, throwing his head back. Watching my fiancé carry on with the ease and social grace of a party hostess, I'm reminded how he balances me—my blunt approach to conversations, cerebral thinking process, and at times awkward reactions. Howard is so flexible, no matter the situation; he only needs me—a good thing, since we're trapped here.

Did I invite him to a family retreat this weekend? Or the powder keg I worried about when I first learned of this reunion?

Upon arriving at our room, I glance to Uma's door down the hall. A Do Not Disturb card dangles from the handle.

23

JOURNAL ENTRY

July 23
Nighttime

I am screwed. Royally screwed. My manager at Tilly's just announced there will be layoffs to come as a result of a slow summer season and even slower July with school out. There are only fifteen full-time and part-time employees to choose from. So, when I was already working thirty-five hours a week, I need to somehow show I'm even more dedicated and effective an employee to avoid getting fired. My savings has been growing over the last few months, but not enough to make this looming layoff any less stressful.

To make things worse, I got into a fight with Teddy last month about the New Year's Eve party. Yes, it was ages ago, but I've been trying to forget about it all this time and haven't been able to. I brought up his choice of words when he gave me my present—those gorgeous blue sapphire earrings—and how they made me feel.

Telling me that I'm his "favorite accessory" could not have been a bigger disappointment, when I'd already been having doubts about certain of his behaviors: the temper of his that seems to snap whenever anyone frustrates him; the way he excuses the inappropriate actions of his family members; the trivial way he treats me (his favorite accessory) and my feelings when I bring up any of these concerns. I didn't want to voice it out loud before, but since New Year's Eve I've been feeling like his way of thinking is a little . . . narcissistic.

Growing up, I didn't really have a relationship with my father. I don't really know how a man is supposed to talk to a woman, and yet so many things about Teddy's words lately are starting to feel wrong.

Which brings me to my last and arguably most dire point: I'm pregnant.

. . .

. . .

. . .

Sorry, I just had to pause. To let those words sink into the page and watch their ink stain the paper. They're not going anywhere. Just like this baby.

Teddy and I have been dating for nine months. That's it. This is completely unplanned and, I am not afraid to say, unwanted. I am fastidious about my birth control pills. I should be—I have to pay an arm and a leg for them without insurance. So, each morning at eight o'clock, I stop what I'm doing and swallow back the little pill of freedom and autonomy, regardless of whether I'm in a relationship or seeing anyone romantically or not. That daily habit is my confirmation that I'm in charge of my life and my body, that I can predict when my period will hit and when I'll be able to dip into a hot tub without worry.

I know I took my pills last month exactly when I was supposed to.

I also recall that Teddy spent extra long in my apartment's bathroom a few weeks ago.

My pregnancy test came back positive last week. I went to the clinic doctor today. When I returned to my apartment, I went straight for my bathroom medicine cabinet and withdrew the circular compact. The blister pack was exactly as it should be, with three-quarters of the pills gone at this point. I don't know how Teddy did it, but I'd swear to a judge he switched out my real pills for the placebo sugar versions.

I don't have a word for the fury that's coursing through my body, and the despair.

What kind of person would do this? Why do this?

What am I going to do?

This child doesn't deserve to be born into this family.

24

News Article

Spokane Bee
September 22, 2013
By Jameson Winthrop

Local authorities were called late Saturday night to apartment community Silver Springs due to noise complaints. Neighbors reported intermittent screaming, followed by guttural sounds of a sensual nature over the course of several hours. Police arrived to knock on the door at two thirty in the morning, according to radio transcripts, but no one answered. Upon hearing additional screams, officers entered the premises to find the occupants engaged in an act of BDSM.

Twenty-year-old Shane Eriksen was covered in what appeared to be blood. He was standing over a female companion, whom police have not identified to the public. While Eriksen was wearing what Police Sergeant Norm Parrish called "a typical leather harness for the

BDSM community," the woman was naked, bound at her hands and feet by fur-lined handcuffs while wearing a costume deer's head. When police entered the premises, Eriksen charged the two officers, assaulting one with a wooden chair before he was restrained. The woman refused examination by medical personnel, noting that she held the key to the handcuffs herself and had elected to remain bound. The blood found on Eriksen was ultimately determined to be pig's blood.

As of the date of this publication, the woman has declined to press charges against Eriksen and has asked to remain anonymous. Eriksen was arrested on the spot for assaulting an officer and was transported to the local county jail, where he posted bail this morning.

According to Eriksen's attorney, Brent Goode, Esq., Eriksen maintains that any alleged sexual activity, if it occurred, was consensual.

25

Olivia

Saturday

Sobs echo into the hall when I exit my room the next morning. It sounds like they're coming from two doors down, in the room Coral is sharing with Uma. Although I suspect Coral was trying to point the finger at me last night around the campfire, she was right that we don't know each other that well anymore.

Howard and I get off to a slow start. We try to wake up and leave quickly after sleeping in, but I insist on taking a shower together in the glass-walled bathroom. The soap suds dripping down his chest become too distracting, and before I know it, I'm on my knees and tugging him closer, retreat agenda be damned.

Breakfast is offered in a buffet arrangement in the dining hall. I pocket a granola bar since we're already late, and then Howard and I make our way down into the well of the plaza. I overheard a member of the resort staff this morning saying that we should have canceled the hike, but "there's the Eriksens for you."

Past the totem pole, the usual suspects shift their weight in loose-fitting clothing. Most everyone is present—except for Edgar, Great-Aunt

Lois, Felicity, and Coral, Denny, and Uma. Glancing back at the lodge, I expect Coral to open the door and come trotting forward; a burly man in the resort's beige uniform exits instead.

Why haven't Uma and her kids left yet? Why was Coral crying?

Gray skies form overhead. The air is humid. Tall green firs along the mountainous skyline appear like guards looming over us and the valley beneath. High meadow grass sways along the dirt path that slices through the pasture. Someone grumbles their disappointment there weren't to-go mugs of coffee available.

"Olivia, Howard, you guys ready?" Skye asks, a timid smile on her face. Long brown hair with highlights is braided to midway down her back. She's only seven years older than me and married to my forty-two-year-old uncle, but she seems sweet. Nothing like the gold digger so many relatives whispered about after their wedding two years ago.

"Yeah, we're excited for this. It'll be nice to see the forest up close," Howard replies.

"That's what Zane and I are hoping." Skye smiles. "You and I haven't gotten to talk too much, Howard. If you have any questions as a non-Eriksen, I'm an open book." She giggles then, as if Howard couldn't google our family history on such websites as TrueCrimeFamilies.com and ThePowerofGenetics.com.

I scan the group while Howard and Skye chatter away. No sign of my grandfather or his nurse.

I look back to the entrance of the main building again. Uma said she was planning to leave as soon as day broke. Did Coral elect to stay without her mom and brother? Did Uma and Denny already leave, or did Coral convince them to leave tomorrow?

Either way, I was hoping to ask Uma more about our conversation last night. Specifically, what she meant when she implied our relatives couldn't be trusted.

Howard takes my hand, giving me an adoring glance. "I'm just so lucky I found her."

"I feel that way about Zane." Skye darts an eye at her husband.

Uma was the first person to openly question our family's role in Alfred's death, at least to me. Then she disappears. Was she onto something?

Without a better option for whom to interview now, I turn to Skye. "Where did you get your leggings? I love them. That color is not quite blue and not quite purple."

She blushes. "Thanks. Zane gave them to me before this weekend."

"You guys have done an awesome job planning the retreat. Was everyone able to come that you invited? Did anyone say no?"

She hesitates. "Well, we didn't tell Cousin Rick, of course. Too last minute to request a special outing for family time."

I don't bother correcting Skye, but a parole board would not give a family retreat in the Oregon woods, with its many escape routes to Canada, a second thought.

"Okay, what about Edgar's daughter from his first marriage?" I ask. "To Grandma Nadine. Aunt Hattie? She's been in treatment for years. Did she say no?" Although Hattie killed my pet rabbit when I was six, I'm told her psychopathy is being managed with meds and therapy these days.

Skye blanches. Her mouth flutters open, then closed.

"Plus, there's Uncle Ephraim," I continue. My dad's cousin once removed, after whom he was named. "You didn't tell any of them?"

"I didn't know about them," Skye mumbles. "I just wanted . . . I wanted everything to go well this weekend."

She chews her lower lip. Tears well in her dark brown eyes. I feel sorry for her. She probably had big visions of this weekend being her coming-out party of sorts—a time to draw the line in the sand and to be appreciated by her husband's gruff, emotionally and mentally imbalanced kin.

"Well, what about those you did invite? Did anyone seem unusually excited to join?" Someone present could have viewed this retreat as an opportunity for revenge from the start.

Skye steals a look behind her at her husband. Zane stares at a trail map with a resort employee who wears a Crocodile Dundee–style hat, the brim wide enough to catch rainwater.

"Jacquie seemed happy to get together. She called to tell me so. And Vic sent Zane a box of rubber snakes, which I think meant he was excited. Francis was the only one who had a negative reaction. He was upset we were coming back here, after the last time."

I raise my eyebrows. "Any idea why?"

Skye shakes her head. She brings a manicured index finger to her mouth and begins to chew. "I can't believe I forgot to invite so many people."

"Hey, I'm sure you did the best you could," I offer. "If anyone is upset about being excluded, no one here will tell them about the retreat. We haven't been close with Rick, Hattie, or Ephraim in a while."

Skye tilts her head to the side, removes her fingernail from between her teeth. "I thought that was what people said about you."

I stiffen, watching her innocent expression. Is Skye as naive as we all think she is? Maybe she's a better match for Zane than I realized.

Howard squeezes my hand. "Well, we're planning to reacquaint ourselves with the family and to make the most of this weekend. No matter what happens."

"All right, everyone! Listen up." Zane turns to the group with his hands on his hips. Khaki pants and a red plaid long sleeve give him the air of a woodsman, instead of a metropolitan surgeon with a sadistic streak.

Coral and Denny jog from the main lodge to reach us. No sign of Uma.

"Derrick here will begin leading the hike shortly," Zane continues. "He's got a few words of advice and warning, as parts of the trail will be a little messed up due to the recent weather. Derrick. Take it away."

Derrick gives us the lowdown of what to expect: Stay on the path. Don't touch leaves of three. Watch for animals that may have been flushed from their homes. Then we set off, following single file along the dirt. Our group is silent but for the dull crunching of boots on leaves, branches, and other debris that ended up here after the storm. The meadow matches our quiet volume, almost eerie in the middle of the field. Hairs stand on the back of my neck until the path inclines into the woods, where I'm able to blend into the overhanging trees.

"This place is creepy," Coral says three people behind me.

"Like the forest is listening," Denny echoes.

But I couldn't feel more opposite. Within the shadows of the Douglas firs and the pine trees mingling together, levying one unsteady foot in front of the other until the dirt path reaches the trailhead on more even ground, I feel more myself here than I do back on resort property. Even if untold animals are watching.

"Hey, Coral, is Uma coming?" I hang back as Howard passes ahead to a leafy fern.

She slows her pace. Narrowed brown eyes shift to check if anyone else is curious before she answers. "I don't know. She wasn't in our room when I woke up."

"Olivia, how's your mom doing?" Francis waits at the first turn. "I haven't seen Elise in years."

Did Uma take off without her kids? That doesn't seem like her. Uma has always been a textbook neurotypical. Then again, like Professor Marx says, it's difficult to predict anyone's behavior.

"Elise is good. We spoke last week," I add. "She actually convinced me to join the retreat this weekend, funnily enough."

Francis raises both eyebrows. "Why is that funny? She was a part of the family for a few years. She was always nice to me."

I shrug, then accept his hand to step onto a higher shelf of earth. "Well, I don't think anyone would say joining was a good idea now, would they?"

Francis doesn't reply. He helps Coral up behind me.

I let the pair of them pass on, to continue climbing the hillside. Voices filter between the trees where Howard has paused, waiting for me above. Overhead, patches of gray sky perforate the canopy of green so thick that someone could haul a mattress up the branches to live there.

"Everything all right?" Howard asks when I reach him.

"Sure."

"Are you? You've seemed bothered ever since we left our room."

"I'm fine. Really. Just stressed, thinking about my dissertation. You know how pivotal getting my grandfather to talk to me would be."

"And how great it would be to finally announce our big news," Howard replies. "I know you want to tell him first, but do you think we should keep waiting? It's already been two days."

I turn away, not knowing how to reply. My teenage cousin comes bounding up a steep incline like a Saint Bernard. "So, Denny. Is this how you imagined your spring break?"

Denny looks past me. Howard has gone on ahead, no doubt frustrated with me again, and then we're alone at the end of the Eriksen family train. Denny gazes around us, as if he doesn't get out in nature much. No one does these days. Without the rhythmic noise of footsteps, bodies brushing against bushes and low-lying forest growth, the area is calm. Peaceful. Something moves in the ivy beside us. Birds call to one another as tiny paws scramble up a tree trunk nearby. I breathe deep. Inhale the sweet, refreshing scent of conifers, the air still moist after the morning dew.

I open my eyes to find Denny staring at me. "Uh, yeah. Exactly," he says. "Dream come true."

"Any idea where your mom went?"

He grunts, pushing past me. "Not a clue."

We reach the summit of the trail, halfway up the mountain, thirty minutes later. The three-mile hike is more than I've moved in ages; it feels good to have my muscles flex and stretch beneath my skin. The rest of the group is already resting and enjoying a midmorning snack of granola bars, apples, bananas, cured meats, cheeses, and mimosas. Francis and Vic clink what looks like their second glass together when I approach the impressive spread on a picnic table. I lock eyes with Howard, just as Marla steps forward to offer him a plate of food. Funny that she's taken such an interest in him.

"Morning citrus for you, Olivia?" Francis asks. His auburn- and gray-streaked hair reaches below his ears, long and unkempt. A far cry from his marine days.

"Sure." I accept a plastic flute from Derrick, our trail guide.

From the picnic table, the valley beneath is visible in a dip between the trees: the dining hall and a large boxy storage unit beside it, the lake appearing benign from this altitude, and the meadow concealing its dangerous potholes. Beyond the burnt-red tops of the resort buildings, the tree line extends as far as a smaller mountain peak I didn't notice on the drive in. We are surrounded by green and—as a bird sings somewhere above, I'm reminded—by animals. And whoever impaled and decapitated that wild elk.

Alfred loved hiking. He told me so while we held our own happy hour on Thursday afternoon. Did he know Zane had one planned for this weekend?

Meet me at the fireplace. Why would Alfred have gone swimming, if his death really was an accident? Why would he have jumped in while still wearing his jacket?

Uma's skepticism rings in my ears. *You haven't known these people as long as I have.*

No one among our relatives wants to outright say that Alfred was murdered or pushed, or whatever—that would mean someone on the property, someone still roaming free and walking among us, hurt Alfred. I think we were all waiting, during our accidental imprisonment, for the police to arrive and interrogate us before jumping to any conclusions. But they're not coming. I overheard our trail guide telling Zane that another storm is forecast to hit us tomorrow.

When everyone has had their fill of the view and cleaned their plates, we make our way back down the mountain. Mud cakes the edges of the path.

I follow Cousin Jimmy the final steps of the trail to reach the meadow. We continue single file back to the resort lobby when a thought sends me veering toward the dining hall.

"Olivia? Where are you going?" Denny asks from behind. Uncle Vic turns over his shoulder toward me. Howard stops short ahead. A frown draws his face for the first time when he meets my gaze.

"I'm still hungry after the hike. Just want to see if lunch is out early."

"It won't be." Skye pauses from near the front of our caravan, nearly at the plaza. "We asked that it be set out at noon. That's not for another half hour."

I don't answer. Zane, Francis, and Vic took Alfred and placed him in a walk-in fridge in the dining hall without anyone really inspecting the body. What if Alfred is harboring some clue from his killer, or some further indicator that he did innocently go for a drunken swim, or had a psychotic break that caused him to fall into the water?

The dining hall is empty when I peek my head in. Dishes clang in the kitchen. I approach the thick wooden door past the king's table, doing my best impression of a ghost, and pull the door ajar. A man in a white uniform shirt that buttons on the shoulder stands at the stove. He stirs something in a tall pot, humming a tune.

To his right and behind an island, the door of an industrial-size refrigerator is open, revealing large aluminum foil trays on its shelves. Next to it, a steel door occupies the middle of the wall. Taped to the panel in the center, a message on laminated paper warns that nonslip shoes should be worn within.

The cook turns his head away from me. Little white earbuds tucked into his ears are visible as he sings along, nodding his head to the beat. I hold my breath. Then I slide into the kitchen.

I tiptoe along smooth tile to the walk-in fridge, my heart pounding against my ribs. Fearing that the cook will spin on his heel and tackle me, I grasp the handle with a shaking hand. The hermetically sealed door pops open with a hiss. I duck inside.

Foodstuffs line the shelves. Produce, meats, and cheeses fill neat, labeled rolling baskets. An opaque plastic barrel, then three steel kegs, are flush with the opposite wall. A cloud of white air puffs at my mouth.

The fridge's motor vibrates from every corner, resonating within my chest like a jackhammer about to crack my ribs while I process the truth before me: there is no Alfred.

No body. No soaked blanket used to wrap him in.

Despite what my relatives told me, my cousin's cadaver is missing.

26

BIRDIE

Grayson says I'm obsessed. That he hasn't seen me this invested in a victim since I stumbled on the story of a child who disappeared somewhere near Lake Michigan in the nineties and who resembled Brooklyn.

"Mommy? Did you want to take Bunnifred with you?" Brooklyn holds up her favorite stuffie, a rabbit that she's slept with since she was three years old. Faded lipstick marks the white matted fur around Bunnifred's mouth, and she's missing most of her whiskers. Green stains that I never could get out in the wash cover the tip of one of the long ears, from when Bunnifred and Brooklyn experimented with rolling down a grassy hill in our neighborhood. Bunnifred is my daughter's best friend, so when Brooklyn holds her up to place her in my suitcase, my heart crinkles like tissue paper.

"Sweetheart, I couldn't. I need Bunnifred here to keep you company while I'm gone."

"But, Mommy, what if you get lonely? You'll be gone so long."

"It's only for the weekend, baby." I sit on the comforter of Grayson's and my bed, then pull Brooklyn up beside me. "I'll call you every day, okay? You and Daddy are going to have a blast here, finishing your papier-mâché project for Mrs. Washington on Monday."

Brooklyn leans her little head against my shoulder. She smells of the aloe vera–based shampoo I use to wash her curls. "Do you have to go?"

I mull over the answer to her question. Truthfully, I don't. But I need to complete research on Li Ming Na's case for my next episode; I have only one banked podcast episode left, which I'll publish on Monday. I've done all the research I can online and through stalking retired Detective Ashley here in San Diego County.

The case file copy he gave me, from the Eugene Police Department, did hold new answers—new to me, at least. Hilarie Dayton, the roommate, hadn't lived with Li for years by the time she disappeared. Hilarie's alibi that fateful weekend? She was teaching a two-day-long Pilates seminar in Eugene, witnessed by twenty attendees. The details of Li's income were also interesting—she didn't have any. She was no longer working at any of her jobs, or pursuing her side hustles; she was a dedicated stay-at-home mom.

All that I've read in the forums suggested that Li was an ambitious go-getter. Did she willingly quit earning revenue, or did her controlling boyfriend force her to more fully depend on him?

Portions of the case file were redacted, exactly as Ashley mentioned. Thick black Sharpie covered paragraphs of intake sheets and witness interviews. Hilarie Dayton, former coworkers, and resort employees who worked the weekend that Li disappeared all had their own lined sheets, complete with their accounts of Li, her life, and her movements in the week leading up to that fateful trip; the boyfriend is the only person of significance who doesn't have his own page of notes. As the father of Li's kid, it's surprising. So, is information on him missing? Or is it deliberately hidden beneath heavy black ink?

Brooklyn gazes up at me with her chestnut-brown eyes, a feature she gets from me. She deserves my love and attention, always. But Li Ming Na deserves the spotlight that was never offered on her case.

Certain victims of the past barely got a mention in their local newspapers, like Li. If I can promote the details of her case on my podcast, maybe the public will apply more pressure on law enforcement to follow up—maybe some new detail will emerge that will be the key to uncovering Li's fate. I can give up a weekend with my precious Brook if that is the end result.

Drinking in my daughter's trusting face, I tap her nose with my index finger. "I'll be back before you know it."

———

The rental car lobby is packed with travelers at the Oakland International Airport. My flight was a fast hour and a half, but that didn't mean I wasn't anxious the entire time. I hate flying.

"Tan?" A rental company clerk in a starched yellow polo dangles a set of keys from his hand.

"Here." I follow him outdoors to a blue two-door sedan in the parking lot. Across the bay, San Francisco's metallic cityscape shimmers. Did Li grow up here in Oakland and take weekend trips across the bridge? Or did she spend most of her childhood wondering and dreaming about the goings-on of such a famous metropolis from the vantage point of its slightly gruffer sibling? Who was this woman?

I head straight to the motel I booked last night with travel points Grayson and I haven't used since Brooklyn was born. My room is sparse but clean. The neighbors next door debate whether to go into Chinatown now or wait until tomorrow for dim sum. A man goes on and on about his craving for "good siu mai, Goddammit," and I wonder whether they're just loud talkers or if my mommy ESP hearing is in overdrive.

I drop my luggage, then return to my rental. On my phone's directions app, I enter my next stop: the oldest address the internet spit out for Li's background check. Surprisingly, all I needed was her full name, date of birth, place of birth, and a former occupation to accomplish the search. Easy peasy.

Traffic is on par with LA's. Of course. I use the extra half hour to brainstorm just what I plan to do upon arrival: enter Li's place of after-school employment during her senior year of high school, then ask if anyone remembers her.

Brilliant strategy, Birdie. At the least, you're not doing worse than the police did all those years ago.

The ice cream shop is an old-timey staple in Oakland's downtown district. Martin & Sons Malt Shoppe. A pink awning shields the sidewalk and a bench below. Painted blue writing decorates the glass window, advertising green ice cream just in time for St. Patrick's Day. According to online records, Li's parents settled somewhere in the adjacent neighborhood. Ashley says she visited this place frequently as a kid before landing a job here.

"What can I get you?" An acne-riddled college kid beams at me from behind the counter when I step inside. The scents of mint and disinfectant perfume the place, as if an employee just sprayed and wiped the nearest chrome tabletop.

"A milkshake. Peanut butter," I add, scanning the chalkboard menu.

"You got it."

While he spins around to a shelf and gathers supplies, I glance at the cashier: a young woman with thick black hair wrangled into a bun. Too young to know anything about former employees like Li.

"Is there a manager available?" I ask the kid helping me. Both employees freeze. "I had some questions about this place's history."

They relax. The cashier whips out her phone from her apron pocket while my ice cream artist splashes a scoop of peanut butter into a stainless steel tumbler.

"He's not here. But I might be able to help you." He hits a button on a pink machine. "This is my family's shop."

"Oh." I cast an eye around the black-and-white tiled walls. A framed photo of an elderly man hangs in the corner beside a door marked Employees Only. The young man and the grandfather share the same bushy eyebrows and dimpled chin.

"Yeah, I mean—worth a shot. I was just curious if you remembered anyone working here by the name Li Ming Na. She would have been an employee around twenty years ago."

The grandson smiles, warmly. "Before my time, then. Let me call someone." He unlocks his cell. "Sorry, what is this about? Are you family?"

"Yes," I reply, without hesitating. *Not bad, fake-detective Birdie.* "She was my cousin. She always spoke fondly of this place, but she disappeared a while back."

He nods, then slides the milkshake to me across the steel counter with one hand. He turns his attention to the phone. "Hey, Mom. Do you remember anyone named—"

"Li Ming Na," I offer.

"Li Ming Na? She worked at Granddad's shop, I guess back in the early two thousands."

"Or earlier."

The grandson nods again. "Mm-hmm. Hmm. Yeah, there's a woman here, her cousin." He lifts the phone to me. "She wants to talk to you."

"Hello?" I say, bringing it to my ear. Only a college kid whose parents paid for their phone would pass it to a perfect stranger.

"Hi there. Yes, I remember her," his mom says. "She was a big sweetheart. One of my dad's longest employees, actually. I was sorry to hear she disappeared."

The sadness in this woman's voice is heavy. I have to wonder how a part-timer so many years ago left such an impression.

"It sounds like my cousin was a hard worker. Did you get to know her well while she was in high school?"

"Oh, high school, college, and after she dropped out. She worked for the shop for almost six years. I was only three years older than her, so we pulled double shifts all the time together, after she quit school and before she moved—somewhere in Oregon . . . I can't remember where."

The grandson wipes down a glass banana split bowl behind the counter. Sunshine cuts through the front windows to strike the bowl in a searing beam of light. The true crime forums said that Li worked here for only three years.

"Eugene," I say. "She moved to Eugene, Oregon. Did you say she worked here six years? Not three—her last year of high school, then two years of college?"

"Li Ming Na worked for us for as long as she wanted, which happened to be six years. She left when she was twenty-four. If I could have gotten her to stay longer, I would have. I even let her get mail delivered here for a while when she was in between apartments and staying with friends."

"Did you know she had a daughter? A long-term boyfriend when she disappeared?" The gender of the child was written in the case file that Ashley copied for me, but not a name.

"I didn't. That's news to me—even sadder, to leave behind a kid. We lost touch about a year after she moved. Although . . ."

The woman's voice trails off.

"Yes?"

"I think I remember her saying she met someone. Yeah, that was it. She met a guy, then kind of cut off communication after that. She never reached out or answered my calls again."

I thank the woman, then hand the phone back to her son. He hangs up, casting a wary eye toward me.

"Everything okay?" he asks. "Did you need anything else?"

My milkshake drips condensation onto the counter, a slow process that resembles melting. As if the glass bears an altogether different shape beneath the false exterior.

"No. That's it. Thanks for your help. How much do I owe you?"

"Five fifty."

I pay, then take a seat at the window, staring out across the sidewalk to a manicured park. Lifting a slender spoon filled with milkshake, I watch a child twirling in circles beside a sapling. She makes another rotation, then another, before she falls flat on the grass.

Li Ming Na didn't spend three years at this ice cream shop. She spent six, which explains why the address cropped up on her list of significant locations in the background check.

Li moved to Eugene when she was twenty-four years old, not twenty-one, contrary to what the message boards reported.

Li Ming Na may have cut ties with her former life here in the Bay Area—and all the tangible memories of her deceased parents and some of her oldest friends—at the request of a controlling boyfriend, apparently. Unless Li had a type and dated several control freaks, did this same boyfriend invite her to the weekend getaway where she ultimately disappeared?

My jaw clenches shut as a brain freeze takes over. Then all I can do is watch the young girl lying as motionless as a dead body on the park lawn.

27

Journal Entry

Dearest patient Journal—Well, it's been a while. About nine months.

After twenty-seven hours of labor, an epidural, and two stitches, this baby arrived earth side. Everyone was ecstatic—Teddy, his parents in the waiting room, and his brothers and sisters a phone call away—but most of all me! Although, reading my last journal entry back in July (a lot has happened as you can bet), I was pretty furious with Teddy at switching out my birth control pills. But I didn't want to welcome this child alone. I didn't want to be alone while pregnant, even if I couldn't fully trust him anymore.

I've tried to make the best of it at least. Teddy has been incredibly doting this whole while, offering foot massages, back massages, even paying for professional massages, and moving in with me. His older sister Felicity gave me advice on how to prepare for the birth, while Ephraim shared an old family song that I could sing to the baby during labor. Weighing in at a whopping eight pounds twelve ounces, the baby is doing well, but I'm still recovering about a month later. The Eriksens each have been kind in their own way, trying to provide support as me and the baby both get used to our new living arrangement: the baby on the outside of my body, me hovering above.

It's been a year and a half since Teddy and I met. I can't quite believe it.

But I digress. I had to quit the bookshop, an act that felt liberating as well as depressing. It was always my dream to run my own bookstore and offer up reading recommendations to new shoppers and neighborhood patrons. There's nothing better than consuming a good book in record time, then sharing the title with someone who will appreciate it.

So, color me bummed when the time came for me to quit—it was my idea, at least. It was getting too difficult to stand on my feet all day, and Tilly, the shop owner, said she couldn't hold my job for me for the two months I suspected I'd be out of commission, postpartum. Still, it was a heartbreak.

The entire experience of giving birth, while joyful, has been a roller coaster. Blame it on the hormones, but I'm never quite sure if what I'm feeling is actual happiness or some exhausted version of it. For instance, the baby slept five hours in a row—totally unheard of for a four-week-old. So, I thought I would celebrate with a little extra sleep myself, but Teddy lovingly reminded me that I hadn't showered in a week and badly needed it. I gratefully took it (grateful for the hot running water and full water pressure), then couldn't figure out if I was relieved by my fresh Irish Spring scent, or disappointed that I hadn't asked for any of this—either the baby, or the hygiene recommendation from my partner.

Moving on. To celebrate the baby's first month in this world, Edgar and Yvette threw us a party. Their expansive backyard became the perfect place to host some fifty of the family's closest friends—a number I thought was a little much, considering the baby still hasn't received all the recommended shots, but Teddy insisted; he keeps doing that, you see. No matter how sweet and doting he's been over the last almost-year, little things like that continue to remind me how we got here—the degree of betrayal that got me pregnant in the first place.

The barbecue went over well, though. The guests that I didn't know were quick to introduce themselves and to compliment my beautiful baby. Teddy was beaming ear to ear; he was so proud of his little family, as he called us.

Pretty soon the evening started to roll in, but the Eriksens continued to pump the jams and to keep the alcohol flowing. The baby is still nursing—knock on wood, this body keeps doing its magical reproductive thing—so I was the only one sober. A few more friends turned up, along with the volume of Vic's portable speakers that he uses for deejaying. Everyone was laughing, dancing, and eating, and although I was technically a guest of honor, for a moment I felt so damn isolated and alone. Tears filled my eyes as I stood off to the side beneath a birch tree with flaky bark.

Then someone initiated a game. It may have been tag—drunken tag, of course. But suddenly, everyone was running seemingly for their lives, even Teddy. I huddled up against the tree with the baby in the sling across my chest and tried to make myself invisible. Cousin Mark actually tackled an older woman I didn't recognize. Whenever he touched someone, that person became part of his team and then began tagging other people. It was almost like the game was to infect as many people as possible. As if they were all a virus or a horde of zombies.

Pretty soon there were only a few people of the "noninfected" team left, and the zombies were closing in fast. One of them happened to swing their wild line of sight my way and shouted, "There!" Fifteen people rushed toward me and the baby, looking ravenous and ready to devour me, the devil's rage twisting their faces, and I screamed. I thought that might snap them out of their frenzy, but the first person to reach me was Teddy. He clutched onto my arm with a grip like he's never dared use on me before, and I cried out—burst into tears.

That did it. That ended the game. A few people apologized for scaring me, but not everyone. Not Teddy.

Lately, my hormones have been boomeranging so hard, I no longer trust myself to behave normally in social settings. Genuinely, I feared for my life when the horde came rushing toward us. I feared for the baby.

Ironically, not a peep came from the sling across my chest. When I checked to see if the baby had been jostled or was quietly crying too, a pair of wide eyes returned my gaze, completely unbothered.

28

OLIVIA

Vic, Francis, and Zane. When I was a kid, I never knew what my uncles had in store. They were a group that was always laughing, drinking, and casting furtive glances toward the rest of us. Once, when I was seven, Uncle Vic took the apple juice I was drinking, then switched it with beer—his idea of a joke. The bitter taste shocked me and I spit it out, dribbling onto the T-shirt I was wearing that read WILD CHILD.

Another time, when I was ten, the entire extended family had gathered at my grandparents' house. Easter eggs were hidden across their expansive yard, before the area's housing developments sprang up around the rural property. Sasha, my uncle Francis's girlfriend and the mother of then-three-year-old Kyla, discreetly showed me where I could find the best kind of plastic egg, one with money inside; with her help, I found a red egg and its twenty-dollar bill tucked within a spiky patch of weeds behind the house. When I asked for more hints, she shook her head and said that Francis didn't want her giving me an edge. He said it wasn't right, that he never got hints like that as a kid. But I complimented her lavender dress and said how I wished I could be as pretty as her when I grew up. Sasha told me to search behind the oak tree in the corner of the lot. A blue plastic egg was waiting for me up against the exposed tree roots, protecting a fifty-dollar bill this time.

Ecstatic, I ran back to find Sasha among the other adults gathered outside, watching the kids on the hunt for dyed and plastic eggs alike, but she was gone. So was my uncle Francis.

When I asked my father where she was, he only grunted in response. Aunt Uma asked him something then, but a cry interrupted the conversation. It was Sasha, from inside the house in the kitchen.

Uncle Francis came bounding down the rickety porch steps, disappointment plastered across his face. Scared, I dipped behind my dad's legs, but he wasn't having it. He plucked me forward and presented me to his brother.

"The egg. Give it to me, please," Francis said, holding out his hand. By that point everyone had stopped talking. No one breathed.

Slowly, I handed him the blue one with the fifty-dollar bill within. He took it, then replaced it with a different pink egg. As he stalked back up the stairs, I opened it. A piece of trash fell out, paper from a straw wrapper crumpled up.

I fumed over the injustice while the adults returned to their lively banter. Soft cries whimpered through the open kitchen window.

Later that night, when we were leaving, I asked my father where Sasha was. I wanted to say goodbye. My father grunted again. He said she wasn't feeling well and that she'd gone home earlier. Considering Sasha had smiled brightly when I last saw her, I never fully believed him.

———

"Everyone, you'll need a rib, a loop, and a sponge for today's pottery session." The ceramics instructor waves a hand at the wall of materials neatly organized by row. Inside the arts and crafts center, pop music rolls from somewhere out of sight, as if insulating us from the horrific events of the weekend.

Francis and Vic are noticeably absent from the afternoon group. Probably because a pottery wheel doesn't come equipped with a cup holder. Felicity chooses a seat in the front row. I haven't seen her since last night, when she escorted Edgar to his room and never returned to the campfire.

Coral and Denny both grab materials from the wall ahead of me, each in some sort of daze. Uma still hasn't shown up. When Coral passes me on the way to her seat, she sniffles to Denny: "Maybe Mom went for a long walk."

Where is Aunt Uma? Did the stress get to her and she needed to think by herself before leaving altogether?

For my part, I haven't been able to hold a normal conversation since leaving the kitchen walk-in fridge and discovering that Alfred's body is not where everyone said it was. Why move the body, if not to cover up some detail of his death? Which of my uncles did it? Or which of my relatives sneaked in afterward, sometime between Friday morning and now, Saturday afternoon, to displace it?

I asked Howard where exactly they laid Alfred's body, since he was a part of the retrieval team. He said that once they arrived at the kitchen, Zane told him to wait outside.

Instead of joining today's session, Howard said he needed to lie down—that he needed some time alone. I didn't know what to make of that but said I would come back later to check on him.

"First things first," the instructor continues. She tucks a curly strand of black hair into the bandanna she wears, then sits in a cushioned chair at the front of the classroom. "We're going to learn how to turn your wheels in smooth revolutions. No lumpy mugs here. Then we'll begin throwing."

I cast an eye at Coral. She stares down at her wheel without seeing it, tapping the pedal on the ground with her foot.

Felicity does likewise throughout the hour session. When I glance up from my clay, she's moving her wet sponge over her cube with all the engagement of a narcoleptic, spinning the wheel at the bare-minimum speed.

"Well done, Felicity. I love the delicate foot you've made for yours." The instructor tours the room, offering encouragement.

When she gets to the narrow vase I made—because my clay would not behave into a stout mug—she exclaims, "You must be the artist of the family."

Knowing my stick figures are frightening, I don't reply.

Once the session is over, the instructor promises to fire our works of art in the kiln behind the building. While other attendees stand and stretch, to compare their finished products with those of the family members seated closest to them, Aunt Felicity remains transfixed over her wheel, her head dipped.

Relatives approach Felicity to ask how she's doing. She lifts her head, the picture of maternal devotion and mourning, to reply.

"You're so strong," Great-Aunt Jacquie says.

"I'm not strong," she murmurs. "I'm just a woman waking up each day. Putting one foot in front of the other."

"Hang in there," Jacquie says. She lays a hand on her niece's shoulder, and Felicity revives.

No mention of Alfred. Of his last, traumatic moments or the search for the truth of what happened to him.

While the instructor carries our mugs (my vase) over to a table in the corner, most people filter through the door. I follow Felicity outside. A large conifer shadows the doorway, scattering dead orange needles on the ground in a soggy layer.

Alfred confided to me over dinner the first night that he got into a fight with Felicity. Right before I arrived, their shouting match alerted our relatives and several members of the resort's staff that she had spent Alfred's inheritance from his father while he was still underage. Knowing Felicity, a woman with borderline personality disorder, would be furious to be embarrassed in public, and by her only child, I wonder just how upset that made her. Impulsivity is a characteristic of her disorder, along with intense levels of anger. Did she fall into a sharp mood swing that led her to attack her son?

Professor Marx's voice echoes in my head: *It is so dangerous—ethically and empirically—to presume we can predict a person's behavior based on their disorder alone.* Having BPD doesn't preclude Felicity from having healthy relationships, or making choices to keep her loved ones close; plenty of people seek treatment and therapy to do both. To my knowledge, however, Felicity was diagnosed by a psychologist back in the nineties and has been living in denial ever since. Unwilling as she is to manage her emotional extremes head-on, I wonder if she'd rationalize hurting Alfred.

"Aunt Felicity," I say, arriving from behind.

She offers me a weak smile. "Olivia. That was a nice vase you made."

"How are you feeling?" I ask. Dark circles that ring Felicity's eyes are made darker by contrast to her dyed auburn hair. Lines have deepened along her forehead and around her mouth since I left her to sleep in my hotel room. "Do you feel like another therapy session?"

Her expression falls. "I feel like leaving here. But that's not possible."

"No, it's not." I fall in line beside her as she walks toward the lodge.

"Alfred used to love cold days," Felicity says, wistfully. "He would beg to get all bundled up and ask me to build a fire."

"That sounds nice." Alfred said he lit into his mother the first day because she left them penniless, a fact I was unaware of. Was the fire out of necessity? Could Felicity not afford to pay the heating bill during the idyllic memory she describes?

Strange to think you could grow up knowing someone, yet know only the life they chose to share with you.

I clutch my fleece-lined vest higher around my neck. The wind has died down this afternoon, but the temp continues to drop.

Felicity frowns. I follow her line of sight to the dining hall—where everyone thinks Alfred's body is stored.

"I know this must be awful for you, to be so close to him yet without any answers surrounding his death."

She nods. "I wanted to keep Alfred inside the lodge. Somewhere warm that I knew he'd enjoy, but Vic and Francis insisted on the kitchen fridge. What a horrible holding area for my Alfie. My sweet boy. My best friend." Her chin trembles.

"Do you . . ." I hesitate long enough that Felicity pauses her stride. She faces me.

"What is it?" she asks gently.

"Do you believe that he drowned?"

Felicity stares at me, not understanding. Her eyebrows dip together in a tight V. "Do I believe that he died?"

"No, I think that's clear." I try to marshal my words, reflecting on the many hours of psychology sessions, interrogations, and courtroom trial footage that I've consumed over the years. A psychologist must always be impassive, yet empathetic. "But do you think that his cause of death was drowning?"

"Olivia, of course it was. Alfred couldn't swim."

I pause. "He never learned?"

If that's true, it makes even less sense that he would approach the water during a storm, when he suggested we meet by the fireplace at midnight.

Felicity shakes her head. "It was always something I regretted not insisting on when he was a kid." Fresh tears fill her eyes. Her face crumples in anguish. "Damn it! Why didn't I get him lessons?"

I try to put an arm around her, but she slaps me away, shoves me. Shocked, I cry out, "Aunt Felicity—"

"We never should have come here," she mutters. "Alfred and me, we should have stayed away. Or the resort should have had better warning signs of how deep the water is. You know what?" Felicity stalks toward the lodge. "I'm going to find that property manager. That Xavier. Tell him I'm going to sue him for negligence."

149

She pauses, and I almost run into her. "Marla would know about lawsuits," she mumbles. "She's a lawyer. She said she was going to the wellness center after ceramics."

Spinning to the right, my aunt takes off toward the west side of the property.

"Aunt Felicity," I begin, maintaining my distance. "How many other people knew Alfred never took swim lessons?"

"Probably just me." Felicity slows. Then she turns to face me. "Olivia, I don't think you hurt him, if that's what you're getting at. I don't believe what everyone is saying."

"Thank you. I actually went to check on Alfred and he wasn't—wait, what is everyone saying?" I stop short, beneath a pine tree.

"That you were the last person seen with Alfred the night that he died. That it seemed like you two had a heated conversation over dinner."

The emotional discussion she's referencing was about her, actually. Ironic that Alfred's anger in recounting his mother's bad deeds is now being used against me. Instead of sharing with Felicity what I discovered and asking, as I intended, whether she knew Alfred's body was moved, I process this new info. Would someone harm Alfred, then try to pin his death on me? Who is implying to "everyone" that I could have been involved?

"I don't remember any heated discussion." I shrug. "But thanks for telling me. If Alfred drowned, do you think someone pushed him in the water? Led him to the lake somehow and attacked him?"

Felicity purses her lips. She casts a harried glance around us. We're the only two people still straggling back from the arts and crafts building, and we're a good fifty feet away from the luxury hotel wing that Edgar and Zane are staying in.

Felicity clears her throat. "Does patient-doctor confidentiality still hold from our session?"

Professor Marx scowls in my memory, but I ignore him. Alfred is family; he deserves for his killer to be exposed. And I don't deserve to take the fall for it. "Yes, definitely."

Felicity straightens, losing the hunched posture she adopted all day yesterday and today. "I think Francis did it. Francis attacked my son. He's always been jealous of me, since I was the oldest and I married up."

"You're saying your younger brother killed Alfred out of some desire to get to you?"

Felicity huffs. "Stranger things have happened, Olivia. Besides, he's more than some depressed drunk. You don't know what really led to his longtime girlfriend, Sasha, leaving. Do you?"

"Kyla's mother? I thought she went to go model in Europe? After the summer one year." I haven't thought about Sasha in ages. She and Francis separated after eight years together, after the last family retreat when I was thirteen.

"Maybe she did." Felicity withdraws a compact mirror, then fixes the light mascara she's wearing. "Or maybe she was sick of Francis's alcoholism and left him for someone better. He's been alone for a long time. I think he wants other people to be alone and unhappy too."

My aunt resumes walking toward the wellness center while I remain rooted to the ground. Shade from the pine tree overhead seems to suck the warmth from my chest, the longer I mull over Felicity's final implication: Francis's jealousy and depression could drive him to hurt someone he cares about—even a blood relative.

29

OLIVIA

The lobby is empty when I return to the main lodge, save for an employee manning the reception desk and the bartender who said hello from the tucked-away bar. How are they still working, maintaining this false normalcy? Lights flicker overhead whenever a wind tunnel hits the building. The roads still haven't been cleared. Alfred died on the property, his body supposedly placed against a shelf of perishables in the dining hall fridge.

Recalling Zane's promise to unveil some surprise to the most enthusiastic Eriksen on Monday, I can't imagine what he thinks is worth remaining here. Why not call in a private helicopter—or another form of air travel with the money he says he rakes in as a surgeon?

"Excuse me," I say, approaching the woman behind the welcome counter. Delicate braids frame a round face.

"What can I help you with?"

"How are you all—the staff—handling this? Have you guys been trapped together before?"

She stiffens. Then she composes herself with a smile. "No, not since I started working here. But we are finding comfort in routine, I think."

I return her warmth as best I can, without hysterical laughter. *Comfort in routine.* As if none of them has considered there might be a killer locked in with them. Judging from her professional composure, at least she doesn't think I'm Alfred's attacker.

A cold gust of air circles me as a woman enters the lobby. Wearing a white button-up shirt and khakis and carrying a black book—a check presenter—she heads down the hall to the left, to the part of the lodge I haven't explored.

If Alfred hasn't been discovered outside the dining hall fridge yet, it could be that he's still on ice somewhere. A server getting ready for her shift could deposit her personal items in a locker room, or grab a bite to eat in the staff kitchen—likely adjacent to another fridge or freezer.

Then again, he could be flung to the farthest corner of the property by now, or dumped to the bottom of the lake with a concrete block chained to his leg.

I thank the receptionist, then follow the woman along the carpet runner. Later, I should nose around the staff quarters. Pose a few questions to employees about the night that Alfred drowned.

Down the hallway, sandy wood panels appear darker in this part of the lodge. I pass more black-and-white photographs of the property from decades ago. Midway along the wall, a framed poster from a horror movie is the single nonphoto image. Center on the page, a woman with a torn bodice screams as a creature rises from the lake behind her.

The server turns right and disappears from view. I continue close behind, away from a gold placard that indicates guest rooms are to the left. She pushes on a swinging door. As she enters, the light above the doorframe highlights the bronze letters of a different placard that reads EMPLOYEES ONLY.

Footsteps head my way from within, and I swivel toward where I know the indoor fitness center lies. Pausing a few feet off, I busy myself staring at a framed dinner menu from the resort in 1933. Pork loin was paired with rosemary asparagus at the pretty penny of $4.13 a plate.

The flap opens, then closes again, and I double back. Inside the kitchen, leftovers on dirty dishes cover the counter—pasta, meat sauce, and steamed vegetables. Sliding cabinet doors line the area beneath. This must be where the staff eats, or else it caters to room service requests.

Beside a recessed fridge, another door bears a taped laminated square of paper at eye level that reads CAVE.

Laughter rings from the resort hallway, fast approaching, and I rip open the cave door, then fall forward onto the step beneath. A light bulb flickers overhead, illuminating the descending staircase.

A shiver travels my back. The air is cold, though not freezing. Temperature-controlled. Noise from the kitchen is muted.

Fear clutches at my chest, and I strain my hearing for some movement, or a person—Alfred's killer—waiting to attack when I'm too far underground for my screams to be heard.

Zane purchased the resort last year, but our family has been coming here for decades. Did my sadistic great-grandfather have a connection to this place too? Did he get his idea for a basement torture chamber from this property first?

My muscles poise to spin on my heel, back into the kitchen. Then light catches on rows of glass cylinders. Bottles. Wine bottles. I'm in a wine cave. The air-conditioned cellar the server told Alfred and me about the first night. Scanning the rows of dusty bottles stacked floor to ceiling, it's clear to me that this space has been in use for years. Maybe since the pork loin dinner in 1933.

I reach the bottom of the stairs. A corridor of steel walls, keg barrels alternate with wine shelves for fifteen feet in both directions.

Electrical humming sounds from nearby. A motor of some kind—maybe from another fridge. I follow the noise to below the concrete stairwell, to a closed hatch.

With a tug, the door falls open, and I lurch backward. Alfred's mop of coiffed brown hair protrudes from the blanket. Out of some instinct, I lift my hand to rouse him—then stop.

My stomach pitches at the smell. The unmistakable odor of decomposing flesh, and something else. Mold. The blanket that was wrapped around Alfred's body was likely soaked through when it was stored first in the dining hall fridge (if it was ever there), then moved here sometime in the twenty-four hours that followed, before I checked the walk-in myself. His frame fits easily within the storage closet, beside a broom, a Swiffer mop in a bucket, and a generator.

"What happened to you?" I whisper. Revulsion skitters across my neck. I've never seen a dead body before. Not in person, this close. I catch another whiff of decomposition, and my stomach turns in on itself. I choke down a heave.

Why would his killer or killers desire to hide Alfred? Do Francis, Vic, and Zane know that Alfred was moved? Did they move him?

With a shaking finger, I push the blanket open at the head and chest to reveal my cousin. Pale skin has begun to change color, appearing blue and black underneath the wine cellar's dim lighting; his eyes are closed. Black marks ring his neck, where someone strangled him, or attempted to. The orange jacket I last saw bobbing in the lake smells like a septic tank, of rotting algae. Blue veins spiderweb down the open buttons of the light green shirt he wore Thursday night, and bruising is evident across his wrists, like he put up a fight.

A scream builds in my throat. It scratches at my shoulders, pricking my collar. I should be wrestling with some deep-belly grief—the kind worthy of losing a loved one—but I stare at the wool material of the blanket until the urge to fall apart recedes. The precursors of hysteria slink back into the darkness.

I focus my thoughts on the clinical aspects of Alfred's death—the circumstances of his transfer to this concrete coffin—instead. Leaning into the academic part of my brain has always offered me a protective barrier, a means to separate myself from the horrors of my family genes. I take a deep breath.

Why did no one—not Zane, Francis, or Vic—share that someone else was involved? Unless Alfred tried to hang himself before falling into the lake, it's obvious that he sustained some kind of physical trauma. Was it not evident by the time Alfred was fished from the water? Seeing him now, tucked neatly into a storage cupboard beneath the stairs, it's hard to believe this is my cousin—the man who, despite his small stature, would dominate any room, nail any argument, and wield charisma to his ends without fail.

The blanket falls open at his pants leg. A piece of powder-blue paper pokes from the slacks. The same kind as the pad that lies on the nightstand of my hotel room, complimentary of the resort.

I reach for it with forefinger and thumb. It's dry. Crisp in a way that indicates it was never wet. Slanted, disjointed writing occupies three lines: *Apologize to Olivia for angering her. Tell her to remember the last retreat in 2013.*

A cold sheet drags down my frame. I read the message again. I don't understand.

We didn't argue before I went to my room Thursday night. We laughed and said we would meet up in an hour, after Howard and I warmed up from the downpour. The subject of the most recent Eriksen family retreat didn't come up, not once.

Dread washes over me as I recall that Alfred and I wanted to sneak into this very wine cellar the night that he died—that Coral was eavesdropping at dinner Thursday. In light of his death, she's the one who's been spreading that detail far and wide.

Hard puffs of white shoot from my mouth. Panic strikes my lungs, and I can feel them flattening, triggering my asthma. Instead of some clue that pointed to another relative, this note and its location would provide any investigating party with a neon arrow directed at me.

I fold the piece of paper back into a square. Peering around me for cameras, any red dots, or recording devices, I slide it into my vest pocket.

Howard would have told me if he saw anything strange happen, after bringing Alfred into the dining hall. It's possible that Vic or Francis knows more than he's letting on, but anyone could have transferred the body. Someone with the resort, who knows the layout of this property, could be hiding something.

As I pause at the top of the stairs, listening for sounds of movement in the kitchen beyond, I touch the piece of paper once more. The square is still cold, not yet warmed by my flesh.

Whoever moved Alfred bears a grudge against me. And they're setting me up to take the fall.

30

OLIVIA

Once I'm inside my hotel room, I bolt the lock. Howard is somewhere else. I'm alone.

I search for my asthma inhaler within my handbag. Press down on the device, then breathe deep. My lungs expand with soothing muscle memory as I wait for the drugs to kick in.

Those aren't just rumors following me around the property. Not simple, innocent speculation by Coral that "Olivia was the last person to be seen with Alfred." Someone is planting the idea physically, with the poorly faked "note to self" stashed deep in my pocket, that I am responsible for Alfred's death—when of course I'm not.

Unless the many cognitive disorders concentrated within the Eriksen genetics are sneakier than I gave them credit for. I've been so wary of psychopathy jumping out at me these last few years, I could have ignored other signs—of dissociation. Is that possible?

I shake my head. Try to focus my spiraling thoughts.

Psychopathy is most likely diagnosed by the age of twenty-three in my family, or not at all; that age is the proverbial home-free milestone that confirms either its presence or absence. Calder Saffron was diagnosed at age twenty; his son, Mark, at age twenty-two; my aunt Hattie at age twenty-three; my dad, Ephraim, at age twenty-three; and Uncle Francis was vindicated with a diagnosis of narcissism at age twenty-four. Yet dissociation can occur at any time, usually after a significant trauma. What if I didn't merely dissociate but I have what my dad's cousin Jimmy has and manages with medication—schizophrenia? Could I have argued with Alfred before he died?

I lie back on the cream-and-beige bedspread. Stare at the ceiling chandelier. Alfred's death was the first indicator—to me, at least—that this retreat harbored a violent aggressor. The second was during the archery session, when I struck an elk's head mounted on a stick. We still have no clue who might have gone hunting.

The dinner gong rings, long and mournful, pricking my ears. Doors open and shut nearby as people make their way to the dining hall.

Rubbing my still-cold hands together, I try to mentally prepare myself to view another dead body.

Outside, the sun dips well behind the tree line. I cast a furtive glance across the plaza. Shivering in my sweater, I take the ramp of the wrap-around deck, then pass the long shadow of the dining hall, where voices clamor inside. At the edge of the resort's property, the buckets of arrows and archery bows have been hauled away, but the targets themselves remain. I stride between the second and third targets, navigating the thick meadow beside the lake, its blades of grass perpetually lush and damp.

The water is still as I pass. We were supposed to enjoy a polar bear swim this morning according to the original agenda Zane created, but that, at least, was canceled.

I stumble on the uneven ground hidden by the tall grass. For a second, it feels as if I've twisted my ankle. Fear shoots through me as I imagine the rest of the weekend locked in my room, waiting for the police to arrive and arrest me after speaking with my suspicious relatives.

I hobble forward, knowing that's not an option.

Weathered yet intact despite the harsh wind and light rain this morning, the elk's head is as I left it yesterday: buzzing with flies, appearing less pert. Fluids drip from its ears and nostrils. Black blood coats the stake.

I circle behind the idol to where the meadow blends into the woods. Nothing seems out of place on the back of the head. Black hairs sprout from the animal's crown, as if they are all that's left of a once-luxurious coat.

A branch breaks in the trees. I turn, searching for movement, for the wild pigs that are supposed to lurk in the region. Nothing comes forward. I wait another thirty seconds, but the source of the noise waits longer. My skin crawls as if the flies all landed on me in one synchronized act. When I face the head again, a man is stopped in the middle of the field.

"Uncle David?"

The older man twitches his hand by his side but doesn't reply. Great-Uncle David, my great-aunt Lois's husband, has never been particularly talkative—at least not with me. I always assumed he was somewhere on the autism spectrum, maybe Asperger's. He was from that generation that never attributed mental health issues to anything other than "a poor diet" or "melancholy." Honestly, I'm surprised to see him in the field. I haven't given him much thought this weekend, since he's not an Eriksen by blood. He wouldn't be a relative I'd interview.

"Olivia. Am I interrupting?" David leans to the right, like he's confirming with the elk that he's not intruding.

"Not at all. Were you looking for me?"

"I was," he says, glancing around us. "I heard you were providing pro bono therapy sessions for family members, given the—uh—circumstances."

I straighten. Smooth back the light hair that's come loose from my ponytail. Although Felicity's and Marla's sessions were each short lived, I learned important information from speaking to them. Maybe David will have some revelation to share too. "I am. Let's go inside, back to the main lodge. We can find a conference room."

David lifts a hand. "I'd prefer out here, if you don't mind. That way I know no one is listening at the door."

I lift my eyebrows but stay rooted to my patch of grass. "Therapeutic talks can happen anywhere, anytime. What did you want to discuss?"

David inhales a breath that strains the belly of his coat. "It's just that I look at this family and it gives me a lot of anxiety, you know? About where it's going and where it's been. I've been married to Lois for the better part of sixty years, and I saw how broken the Eriksens all were back when I met them a few years after . . . well, after."

"That must have been a shock to enter that environment." What does my great-uncle want? Did he see me exit the staff kitchen?

David nods, pushing out his lower lip. "It was. But Lois was worth it. I mean, she still is. I love our children and our grandbabies."

Rick, the oldest of David's kids, went to prison for murder, and his sister, Opal, has been a recluse from the family for years. "Of course you do. What does that love have to do with your anxiety?"

"Well, I see things. See stuff that the younger generation is doing. It just breaks my heart that Alfred was taken from us, and I think by someone who called him kin."

I tense, worried suddenly that David means to accuse me privately and that's why he followed me. "Oh? And who would that be?"

He drops his gaze to a square of stubborn wildflowers not yet killed off by the freezing night temperatures. "I don't want to go off half-cocked, here. Maybe Alfred and he had some misunderstanding and Alfred's death was an accident, but I think Shane might have snapped."

Relief pulses through me. "Shane? But Marla said she was with him Thursday night."

Shane and Marla seem to me thick as thieves on this trip, being nearly the same age. Though I don't know that I'd trust Marla to tell the truth if her favorite nephew had committed murder.

David shakes his head, glances to the side. "I saw him wandering alone sometime after one a.m. I have a . . . a tic, you see, where I need to confirm a door is locked a few times a night. Lois has learned to sleep through it in hotel rooms; she wears earplugs and an eye mask."

"Okay." So, David has a form of obsessive-compulsive disorder. Maybe in addition to Asperger's.

"And I opened the door, then shut it three times, as I do, and I saw him at the end of the hallway." David pauses, as if to catch his breath. "He and I locked eyes. He'd definitely been upset, and . . ."

"Go on."

David's gaze hardens. "Shane's pants were wet. They were wet up to the knees. And then poor Alfred was found the next morning, drowned. Now what do you make of that? How am I supposed to go on loving and supporting this family with that image burned into my retina?"

A bird—a sandpiper—shoots out from the forest behind us, then glides over the water of the lake. It dips down, grazing the surface with its feet, before landing on the two-person canoe at the shore.

I lick my lips. Try to dispel the nausea that winds its way up my throat. David is the first person to suggest Shane might have been involved, while Felicity seems convinced that Francis killed her son. "Have you said anything to anyone else?"

David's eyes widen. "No, I would never. The last thing I want to do is make more stress for the weekend. And it's not like we're in any imminent danger or anything. If, sadly, Shane was involved, it was probably because he had a grudge against Alfred, not due to some on-switch of bloodlust. You know how young guys can be these days. All testosterone and little else."

"Does Lois share your theory?"

"I didn't tell her. Our son, Rick, just got out of prison on early release. He's still trying to get his life in order on the outside, but she's been walking on cloud nine lately. I didn't want to dampen that joy any more than this weekend already has."

The sandpiper hops along the shore toward the dining hall. I watch for a moment, certain he won't get close to where all the dinnertime noise and conversation comes from, audible from here. Then he discovers a covered garbage bin hidden behind the bushes that hug the building's perimeter. A bottom-feeder.

"Emotional boundaries are key in any relationship," I begin. My words are drawn out as I grapple for footing. "It's important to limit how much energy you dedicate to relationships that drain you, especially in a family like ours. It's all right, and perhaps more healthy, for you to engage in calming exercises that won't exacerbate your OCD."

"Thanks, Olivia. I'll do that."

"Sure thing."

My elderly uncle turns, and then we walk back to the dining hall.

Dinner is livelier than the previous night, as if my relatives are drowning their grief and anxiety in cocktails, while skipping the Chinook salmon and butternut squash drizzled with truffle oil. I find Howard at the same table as before, up front and along the wall, the chair next to him reserved for me with his jacket. A few older relatives I haven't spoken with sit opposite him. They greet me with a smile but continue their conversation.

"Hey," Howard says, barely making eye contact. The gray shirt he wears strains as he hunches over his plate, stabbing a piece of fish.

"Hey, honey. I went back to our room and you weren't there. Did Jacquie corner you again?" I drop my voice to avoid anyone overhearing.

"Just needed to get out." The squash is split in two with Howard's dinner fork.

"Are you mad at me?" I ask, genuinely unsure from Howard's profile. His straight nose and generous eyebrows don't give anything away.

"When are we going to announce the engagement, Liv? Hm? Or do you not want to anymore?"

"Howard." I lean in even closer. Place a hand on his arm that he shrugs off. "Of course I do. I'm just waiting to tell my grandfather first. It's the perfect way to tell my family; we've been over this."

"That, and it gives you an excuse to wait on him to speak to you when he obviously doesn't want to. You're dragging your feet on announcing our engagement, Olivia. And I don't like it."

"Good evening, Eriksen family," Zane begins, rising from his seat.

I know I should excuse myself and walk outside with Howard. I should try and quell his fears by telling him there's nothing more in the world I want than to tell my family he's my fiancé. I should jump from my own chair to interrupt Zane and announce that Howard popped the question.

Instead, I watch Zane make the usual speech, unwilling to do anything yet.

My gaze drifts to my grandfather, seated to Zane's right. Edgar picks at his food but appears fatigued. When the front door opens, his face lights up . . . until a brunette employee walks through carrying more ice in a silver bucket—not the person he was expecting, it seems.

I recall the strange episode that Edgar and I shared during the painting session, in which he called me my deceased grandmother's name. True, I could have told him about the engagement then. But the news may have confused him further—maybe even harmed him. The last thing I need is another relative supposedly hurt by my hand.

Coral and Denny occupy the table closest to the exit, the one that I chose with Alfred on Thursday night. Uma still hasn't turned up. I clean my plate, then down my glass of chardonnay. I bend to whisper in Howard's ear, "I need to talk to my cousin." When he doesn't reply, I stride down the aisle toward Coral.

"Did your mom end up leaving?" I ask. She looks up, while Denny only glances furtively past me before resuming his meal.

"We don't know," Coral says.

"How's that possible? Aren't you sharing a room?"

Coral's usual irritation with me is replaced by concern. "We are, yeah. She said she wanted us to leave early this morning, but when I woke up, all her stuff was still in the room. If she left us, she left her things too. I'm worried about her. I told Uncle Zane she's missing."

I take in Coral's anxious expression and Denny's blank stare ahead. "Did she tell anyone else that she was planning to leave this morning?"

Coral lifts a single eyebrow. "Just you. Funny how people keep talking to you. Then disappearing."

Without a word, I walk away. Push through the wooden doors into the chill night air. I can't stand there while Coral suggests I hurt another family member, not in front of everyone. Not with the image of Alfred's cadaver still fresh in my mind.

The lobby is empty when I reach the warmth of the hearth. I pause beside it, scanning the cushions and throw pillows of the deep love seat, settees, and armchairs. The setting of my midnight meeting with Alfred, had things gone according to plan.

"Well, I'm getting the hell out of here," someone says. Voices travel from down the hall where I found the prep kitchen earlier today, and where Alfred's killer stashed his body. I slide between the coffee table and the love seat, hidden from view.

"How are you going to do that?" a woman asks, coming into the great hall.

"I'm a cross-country runner." The man lowers his voice to a whisper. "I do twenty miles on foot regularly, so I'm just going to walk home."

"Right now, though? In the dark?"

"No, in the morning. I don't want to be here for the next storm that's coming tomorrow afternoon."

"But won't Xavier be pissed? We're all supposed to stay here for the guests while the landslide is being cleared away, and sleep in the long-term residence hall. We got paid extra to be here all weekend and wait on these people hand and foot. I thought . . ." Her voice trails off. "I thought we would have slumber parties all weekend, Jack."

Jack makes a noise. A cross between a sigh and a scoff. "Maisie . . . let's just focus on getting out of here alive. First things first, right?"

A nervous laugh. "Sure. But why the dramatics about staying alive? That guy's drowning was an accident. It has nothing to do with us, or the rest of the staff."

"Have you tried googling the resort's new owner? Dr. Zane Eriksen? The guy is a nutcase with a scalpel. I don't want to be locked in with him if the power goes out later."

"Yeah . . . I guess so."

"Hey, I'm still here tonight. And ready for another sleepover."

There's silence. A sensuous moan comes from the back doors leading to the plaza. I peek over the love seat at the couple embracing, and then I rise from my hiding spot.

It's nearly ten o'clock. Although those employees believe Alfred's death was an accident, we are in agreement about one thing: I don't want to be caught outside my room in the dark with any of my family members—not after taking a closer look at Shane's activities, Francis's checkered past, and the note on Alfred's cadaver.

Using my card key, I enter my room, then flick on the light. Howard's bathrobe hangs from a hook by the shower, but the bathroom is otherwise pristine. I've barely been in here today, thanks to Zane's packed agenda and my own snooping. I scan the space, noting the made bed, the clean bathtub, and my closed laptop on the small writing desk. Despite my learning more about my relatives and their disturbing histories, a poke of regret reminds me that I didn't work on my dissertation today.

What did I hope to accomplish by coming here this weekend? For sure, I wanted to interview my grandfather, to sift through his most traumatic memories—maybe unfairly to him—but that's proving difficult. Between his quick exits and faulty recognition of my face, I don't know how a full conversation would even happen.

The wide bathroom mirror reveals shadows ringing my eyes. I never sleep great. Or, rather, I often feel like I'm sleeping when I'm really awake. A kind of daze takes over when I'm lying in bed, one that never feels restful but always seems to pass the night.

I hit the light switch and illuminate the rest of the bedroom and sitting room with its quaint fireplace. A figure faces away from me, occupying one of the armchairs—the one that Felicity used during her therapy session yesterday.

"Hello?" My voice is strong, covering the jolt of shock I feel. "What are you doing in my room?"

The figure doesn't move. Hair on the back of my neck stands taut, as if a breeze just kissed my skin.

"Hello?" I say again. I step forward. Reach for the umbrella provided by the hotel in a shallow bucket beside the desk.

Gripping my weapon tight, I approach the intruder. From over their shoulder, I notice their hands lie slack in their lap, palms up.

I step wide of the chair and inch forward from the side. A pale face with bright blue eyes stares forward, unblinking and dead for hours. Dark veins career down her cheeks. The black hoodie is zipped to the neck, but she's still wearing the jeans she chose to escape in. Dark red seeps through the fabric at her collarbone. Aunt Uma.

I fall backward against the closet door, clutching my chest, my heartbeat pounding at a sprint. Who did this—how did she get here?

While I can fairly be questioned about Alfred's death since I admit we had plans to meet at midnight, someone wants to ensure there are no doubts about my role in Uma's murder.

Without conscious thought, I stumble to the bed—behind it, to hide from the stark truth of this weekend's latest victim.

31

BIRDIE

The more I know, the less any of this makes sense.

The articles I cobbled together from the internet, police records that Ashley deciphered for me, and links from the forums all stated that Li disappeared at age twenty-nine. But if Li spent six years at the ice cream shop from the age of eighteen, that would put her at twenty-four years old when she moved to Eugene. By all accounts, she was in that college town for eight years, working several jobs and receiving mail at a few different addresses until she disappeared. The math says she would have been thirty-two. Why did no one else catch this? Is this part of that "police cover-up" the true crime forums mentioned?

Ashley has access to the same message boards. Was he up to speed about her true age?

I message him to ask, and he is as surprised as I am.

The rest of Thursday night, I hole up in my Oakland motel room with takeout from a Vietnamese restaurant around the corner, trying to understand what else I may have missed.

Friday, I visit Li's parents' house, the one they died in from carbon monoxide poisoning. Swinging chain-link fences and barking dogs are the soundtrack to my visit, but the park across the street helps me imagine the neighborhood some thirty years earlier: serene, inviting, a haven for recent immigrants trying to survive. I can't find any neighbors who remember Li Ming Na or her family—at least, none willing to discuss them with me.

Driving north across the California-Oregon border gives me plenty of time to mull over how little is actually known about Li's case. She cut off ties to her life in Oakland, maintained superficial friendships in Eugene, quit all her jobs, then took a long weekend to the backwoods of Oregon with a controlling boyfriend. No one was close enough to this woman to know if she was scared of said boyfriend. Not even the former roommate. The more I learn about Li Ming Na, the more it seems she withdrew into herself after her parents died—a form of self-protection that ultimately failed her.

The motel in Eugene that I booked is nondescript. No frills, but it appears safe enough for a woman traveling alone and sticking her nose in other people's business. Much like when I arrived in Oakland, I drop my suitcase in my room, then go out in search of landmarks.

Sidewalks teem with pedestrians this Saturday afternoon. Dark clouds cast a shadow overhead, but I don't spy a single umbrella. I pass an older man in tweed who mentions "that awful flooding" this weekend and whip out my phone to check if I should have brought rain boots.

My screen fills with a photo of Grayson and Brooklyn, laughing into the camera during a trip to LEGOLAND last summer; they're video calling me. I pause outside a bookstore in the heart of Eugene's grid to answer. Our dining room and Grayson's look of surprise replace the photo.

"Oh, hey! I didn't think I'd catch you."

I settle onto a bench beneath the bookstore awning. "Yeah, sorry, I was on the road all morning."

He nods, pushing out his lower lip. "Well, we want you to enjoy yourself and get the answers you need. Brooklyn just wanted to tell you something."

"I lost a tooth!" she squeals, jumping into the camera, sticking her tongue in the void.

"What?" I startle a dog and his owner a few feet away, but I don't care. "My poor baby!"

Brooklyn rolls her eyes. "Not anymore, Mommy. I'm a grown-up."

I can't believe it. At nearly six years old—in one month—my baby's baby teeth are falling out. "Is this soon? Did anything happen? You didn't have any loose when I left."

Grayson slides back into view. He wrinkles his brow as a knot forms in my gut. "She, uh . . . she fell, Bird. She was roller-skating, then fell into the front column of the porch. She's totally okay, but the impact knocked out her bottom tooth."

Brooklyn juts her chin into the frame. A red scrape marks her jaw. I sigh. "All right. I'm glad she's good. You sure she's good?"

Grayson nods, stoic, the way he always is when stressed. "I've been watching her the last hour. Gave her a little Tylenol. She can move her head all the way, right to left, and hasn't had any headaches or anything."

"Okay. Thanks for the full report."

He breaks the tension with a smile. "You got it, boss."

We hang up, with me extracting a promise from Brooklyn to hold off on roller-skating until I fly home Monday. My heart squeezes when she blows me a kiss. For a moment, I have to remind myself why I traveled all the way up to Oregon, a state I've never visited before, only to miss out on a major milestone in my daughter's life.

But I already changed my rental car reservation and flight to leave from Eugene in two days. And I'll be home before anything else major happens. I better be.

Ducking into the bookstore, I breathe deep the scent of leather and paper, and something else. Incense. A young woman wearing a red-and-gold sari top, paired with jeans, greets me from behind a wooden desk. Straight black hair hangs loose across round shoulders. She combs through her tresses with acrylic fingernails painted white.

"Welcome to Tilly's."

"Thanks. Have you worked here long?"

She purses her lips, then grins. "For the last five years. As long as I've been in college."

The name tag she wears at the top of her sari has a piece of masking tape across it. Handwritten in black pen is the name "Van Wilder."

I mirror her tight smile. "Gotcha. I'm looking for someone. She worked here around eighteen years ago, but I don't know how long she stayed. Have you ever heard the name Li Ming Na?"

The young saleswoman shakes her head slowly. Her gaze darts behind me, and I wonder who else overheard my bizarre question. "Sorry. I haven't. Most employees come and go here with the school years. At least as far as I've seen."

"Okay. Well, this person disappeared and I'm trying to figure out what happened to her. Do you carry any books on local crime—or local scandals, that sort of thing?"

"Nothing strictly local, but we do have books that examine national trends. The Eriksens are included in a few of those." She cocks her head to the side.

"Would you know if your manager was working here around 2005, or . . ." Something clicks. Given all my podcasts, my weekly research, and my initial deep dive into Netflix documentaries—I know that name. "Did you say the Eriksens? As in the family of murderers and convicts . . . that live in Oregon . . ."

My voice trails off. Where in Oregon are the Eriksens from? They're still living. Last I checked, one of them is some kind of beauty queen social media influencer—who talks psychology, of all things.

Van Wilder brightens. "Strange, right? They're mostly in southern Oregon, and a few of them used to live nearby. Some went to U of O too. Are you into true crime?"

I nod, too thrown to pitch my podcast.

"The farm where one of the sons killed their father, who was actually murdering women back in the thirties and forties, is about two hours away from here. Super creepy." She makes her eyebrows jump, in a way that suggests she feels the opposite. "One of them used to come in all the time back in the early two thousands. I think he was dating someone who worked here."

I break out of my daze. That timeline could match up. "Do you remember who? Either—which Eriksen or the employee's name?"

She twists her mouth into a corner. White fingernails drum the scratched wooden countertop. "No, I don't. Sorry. Like I said, it was before my time. It's more urban legend."

I thank her, then slide into the nearest aisle. Self-help books dominate the shelf in front of me. The title that seems to pop in bright red lettering among the other spines reads *Kick Your Toxic Relationship to the Curb*.

Li Ming Na moved to Eugene, where lots of people believed she was twenty-one years old instead of twenty-four. She disappeared eight years later, leaving behind a small child and an on-again, off-again boyfriend. So far, I've been unable to track down the boyfriend's name, as the police ruled him out and scribbled all over the case file with Sharpie.

I know that Li worked at this bookstore years ago, thanks to the background check for which I paid a rush-processing fee. Was the Eriksen who was a customer here around the same time her boyfriend? *The* boyfriend?

Questions swirl in my head, clouding my ability to think, so I step onto the sidewalk outside. I slide onto the bench, resuming my seat from before.

Someone has to know more about this Eriksen love interest. The bookstore employees won't be any help, but maybe the local detective who worked the case is still around. Recalling the forum message that suggested the police covered up Li Ming Na's death because of her boyfriend's military service, I wonder if the cops had a relationship with the Eriksens.

I pull up my phone's browser. A quick search using the detective's name—Dakota Peele—returns dozens of results. This guy was active across homicide cases that spanned two decades. When I narrow my search by pairing his name with Li Ming Na's, the hyperlinks end in an article I've already read, written in 2015—two years after she disappeared. In fact, there's nothing more recent than that on Detective Peele.

A different phrase combination—"Detective Dakota Peele goodbye"—confirms my suspicion: he left the state. Peele retired to Minnesota in 2015.

I lock my phone. Turning my face toward the dull sunlight that pierces the clouds, I draw new energy from its rays.

Even if the detective is a dead end, the Eriksens are involved somehow. I can feel it.

32

News Article

Southern Oregon Tribune
May 8, 1995
By Mason Carter, Editor

Ongoing construction at College Town Square will continue yet another month due to new damage. Francis Eriksen, a member of the infamous local family whose dubious history in Bend dates back to the 1930s, was arrested Sunday afternoon at 12:13 p.m. for failing to stop when a police officer signaled for him to do so in downtown Eugene. It was only after Eriksen drove into the new fence perimeter of the square, destroying the last month's progress, that his car came to a halt. When questioned regarding his delay in following the law, Eriksen said he didn't see the officer, or the fence, according to witnesses who overheard the exchange. However, when the arresting officer, Officer Peter Clement, asked Eriksen to step outside the car for a Breathalyzer test, Eriksen became enraged.

Miriam Ben-Ami, owner of local favorite Algerian Eats, says that she had a perfect view of the altercation from her restaurant's front window. According to Ben-Ami, Eriksen stepped from his vehicle, a two-door sedan, then proceeded to physically assault Officer Clement, punching him repeatedly over the head. Eriksen even flung an empty beer bottle at the officer before he was restrained and handcuffed.

Jason Waterford, a student at the University of Oregon who was patronizing the nearby bookstore at the time, says that Eriksen shouted as he was being arrested, "Do you know who my friends are? You don't want to do that." Nonetheless, Eriksen was taken to the Lane County Jail, where he posted bail early today.

Normally, College Town Square sees its share of alcohol-related tomfoolery during finals season. However, rarely are the shenanigans as violent and abrupt as those that Eriksen exhibited yesterday afternoon. Councilman Geoffrey Hutch, who campaigned on promises to make repairs to Eugene's dilapidated city center, maintains that this incident is a minor setback.

According to the Eugene Police Department, Officer Clement is currently recovering from his injuries on paid leave.

33

OLIVIA

Sunday

The hour hand shifts down to reach the three of the clock's face. Apart from the clock's soft glow, my room is pitch black. I tuck my legs beneath me at the edge of the bed.

Aunt Uma is dead. Her daughter, Coral, openly accused me of being involved in Uma's disappearance at dinner. Uma told me Friday night, in view of a dozen others at the campfire, that she was planning to leave the resort Saturday.

Who would stop her from leaving? Then stash her body in my room? How did that person bypass the lock?

After I moved Uma into my closet, I collapsed onto the carpet. Waited for my heartbeat to slow. Debated what to do next. Should I call the police? Add to their list of outstanding deaths to solve at this resort? Allow them to question me openly, as opposed to my relatives, who have done so furtively when my back is turned? But me calling for help in any way, or revealing that Uma was found dead in my room, is exactly what her killer wants. Psychopaths are calculating, and this person will have considered the best way to trap me.

My memories of dinner are clear. Before then, I examined the elk's head on the spike by myself and spoke to Great-Uncle David in the meadow. Each of those moments returns to mind as if in a film. I recognize myself taking the paths to arrive at each location and can name a dozen witnesses who observed me picking at my salmon entrée and side of butternut squash. Sometime during those forty minutes, Uma's killer deposited her body in my room. When would I have had time to sneak back to wherever Uma had been kept since last night—since I saw her disappear down the hall in the opposite direction of her room—then transfer her into my hotel room?

I didn't do this. And yet I have no idea how Uma and her killer managed to access my sitting area when I carried my card key with me the entire evening. Has Howard had his key this whole time?

Her throat was slashed. It was evident through the hoodie, and I didn't bother to check underneath the crusted fabric—although I did stare. I couldn't pry my gaze from the abused area. It felt almost . . . hypnotic. Familiar fear surged, worry that the Eriksen sadism gene will soon activate within me.

Howard hasn't yet returned to our room. He could still be out with one of my uncles.

A new thought grips me: What if something happened to him too?

Panic flattens my lungs, and I turn on the lamp beside the bed. Try to stop spiraling. I tiptoe to my door, then use the peephole. The hall is empty. The handle turns under my palm like a detonated grenade, the sound of the gears shattering the night silence. Light blazes from the hallway, forcing me to squint like a true creature from the darkness. The line between my innocence and complicity is blurring under the fluorescent bulbs. But no one is lurking outside my room. No Howard either.

A lamp along the wall and above a painted tableau of the valley flickers in the tenuous cadence I've come to expect since Thursday night's big storm. Each pulse of the bulb's filaments reminds me of

Morse code, possibly some secret message for anyone watching. I step back inside and let the door click shut.

Located opposite the fireplace and sitting area, the closet is barely large enough for a safe and the ironing board, but a built-in shelf along the wall allows a space just large enough for a suitcase. Or otherwise. I pause before the white folding doors, where I tucked my aunt inside.

I know it was wrong to move her. Uma deserves better than to be dragged and deposited at multiple locations of this haunted property. But I deserve to live my life without going to prison.

Exhaustion from the evening, the stress, and the physical act of dragging my aunt's muscular body across carpet strains my entire frame. My throat clenches like I might burst into tears. Then the emotion passes. Dissipates. Until all I am is fatigue.

I crawl into bed fully clothed. The tang of blood lingers in the room, but I turn on the air-conditioning and try to ignore it. Try to sleep.

Scenes from the meadow drift into my mind. The sun shines bright, full of possibilities, and I know I'm dreaming.

Then there's a scratch from close by. A knock? My eyes snap open and I suck in a breath, waiting for Uma to call my name.

———

The morning comes slowly, although I fall asleep at some point. Dreams come to me in spurts and dark colors and without any real meaning, it seems. When I dress for the daytime activity, I unzip my suitcase as far from the closet as possible.

In the lobby, a fire blazes, warm and comforting in the hearth. As if my evening's revelation and subsequent trauma never happened. A resort employee I don't recognize mans the reception desk when I approach.

"Where are the police? Why haven't they come yet?" My voice is shrill, more so than I intended. The employee, a young man with a fade, nods as if already used to this song and dance. Are there others who have given in to alarm this weekend?

Knowing now for certain that an individual remains close, with the intention of pinning multiple deaths—the deaths of family members I care for—on me, my face twists. "Why hasn't there been an update? Don't they see the situation is getting worse?"

The young man pumps his palms flat on the counter. "Ma'am—"

"Don't 'ma'am' me—I'm twenty-two years old."

He nods quickly, and I know my impression of the hysterical women I've seen in courtroom footage is gaining steam. "Of course, miss. The police have been called every day, and each day they share that they've made no progress. The roads are still uncleared. They want to see how today's weather will pan out."

"This is ridiculous," I snap. Then I take a breath. Try to get my bearings. Reach for a believable lie. "I find myself getting lost in these big hallways. Would you be able to tell me what room Howard Ngo is staying in? He's my fiancé."

I glance around the lobby. None of my family members are out yet, or they've already gone ahead to the meadow. No one I'm related to heard me use the f-word—or reveal that Howard never returned to our room.

Is he hiding from me? Or hidden from view—attacked, then crumpled inside a different closet?

The employee clicks something on his screen. "He's in room 267 over in the Pine Coast Lodge. Looks like he switched rooms last night."

I thank the employee, then trudge outside. Howard's alive, thank God. Alive and angry with me.

The door bangs shut behind me as I resign myself to another of Zane's activities, and possibly the most ironic: survival training.

Part of me knows I should break down, hearing the confirmation that Howard requested a different place to sleep; Howard is my fiancé and my best friend. He must have asked for a separate room once he realized I have no intention of revealing our engagement—not while this shit show is ongoing. Not while, unbeknownst to Howard, I seem to be the chief suspect. I should want to reassure him that our relationship is still on track and the engagement is only months away from becoming a marriage. Instead, relief slides across my skin like a thin poncho; Howard won't learn that Uma is hidden in our room while he's staying in the luxury residence hall, the Pine Coast Lodge. Not tonight at least.

Ahead, congregated in the meadow, my relatives stand among tall grass that reaches knee level in some spots. Great-Aunt Lois is hunched over something on the ground, a few feet away from a resort employee—I'd guess the instructor. The man, probably in his thirties, speaks quietly with Zane off to the side.

The field before us stretches for a quarter mile before it hits forest and mountainside. Located on the west end of the property, behind the luxury lodge and the arts and crafts center, the scene is peaceful, if isolated. I haven't been here yet.

Howard is nowhere in sight.

"Olivia, hi," my great-aunt Lois grunts. She ties a knot on a braid of long reeds. Using deft movements, she twists the braid into a loop, then secures it with a slipknot.

"Did you get an early lesson?" The session was supposed to start five minutes ago, but the instructor, deep in conversation with Zane, seems to be running late.

"A few years ago, I did. During the initial days of the pandemic, while everyone else was working on their sourdough starter, I took an online course in survival skills. Tried to get David to join me, but he wasn't interested. With the apocalypse basically looming over our heads then, it felt like a good time to brush up."

Lois slides the loop around her wrist, then jerks the rope tight. "If one of those elk or wild pigs comes across this baby, they will be in for a quick and painful surprise."

Zane turns and surveys his attendees: Lois, myself, Kyla, and Francis, while Vic, Marla, and Shane now make their way over from the main lodge. Although Zane checks his smart watch, those three seem unhurried. Almost as if they want everyone to see them out and about this morning. Coral, Denny, Howard, and Skye are noticeably absent; the rest of the older crowd has stayed indoors.

I'm still hopeful I can catch Edgar in a lucid moment before I leave tomorrow. If we can leave tomorrow.

I shake my head, horrified by my thoughts. Uma won't be leaving alive, and neither will Alfred. How have my emotions shifted that I'm more concerned about the interview than I am the stress of harboring a cadaver in my room?

Gray clouds roll along the sky, reminding me that there's still much that can happen in a day. Uma knew that better than anyone.

Her voice returns to me: *We have to get out of here.*

"Olivia? Why don't you go first?" Zane stares pointedly at me.

"First for what?"

"Harry here"—Zane nods to the instructor—"just explained the first survival exercise we're doing this morning: finding edible flowers. The field behind us is beginning to bloom, and he showed us which ones to look for and which to avoid."

Harry offers a tight-lipped smile, as if I offended him too. In his palm, he holds up two orange flowers, one with narrow, fleshy petals and the other with short, round petals.

"Zane, I enjoy survival stuff, but should we really be doing this?" Lois steps to her nephew, her voice low. Deep lines frame her mouth in a scowl. "Everyone is emotionally spent, between Alfred's death, power outages, finding that elk, and . . . well, the plain tension of not knowing when help will arrive. You can't keep pushing this retreat forward like nothing is wrong."

"We don't have anything else to do, Lois," Zane barks back. "We're all stuck here, and I'm doing everything I can to keep people from freaking out. What would you suggest we do while we wait for the police? Start fighting with each other? Interrogating suspects to see who has been out hunting? Riot? No. I'm the captain of the weekend, and I'm continuing with the plan."

"And down with the ship," Lois snaps.

Zane wrinkles his nose. "Okay, Olivia. You're up."

"Fine." I scowl, knowing Zane is probably right. Interrogating each other would likely yield fingers pointed at me. "Which ones do I avoid? The inedible flowers."

Zane's disapproval transforms into a smile. "Not only are they inedible, some of them can burn you on touch. You should have been listening to Harry, I guess."

Grinding my teeth, I step forward into the flat, open plain. Behind me, Harry shares his life story, explaining that he was first a Navy SEAL before he became dedicated to preserving and protecting native Oregon flora.

He should have tried harder, because I don't see any live orange flowers in this field. A patch of white flowers grows in a dispersed cluster beside a fallen log. It could be Queen Anne's lace, which I know from living in Davis is edible and a form of wild carrot. I grab three stems, then carry it back to the group.

Harry lifts an eyebrow at my return. "So soon? What did you bring us?"

I present my bundle to him, but he recoils. "Oh no," he says. "What did you do?"

"This is Queen Anne's lace. It's a misconception that it's poisonous."

"I'm sorry, but that's poison hemlock. It's toxic to the skin and the respiratory system, and if you eat a few petals, you can die within twenty minutes."

I drop the white flowers to the ground. My palm itches where it grasped the stems.

Harry eyes my skin. "You might want to wash your hands. Like now."

As I walk back to the main lodge, Harry announces the next lesson will begin shortly: how to avoid getting trampled by one of the animals roaming the area.

Although the itching grows with each step, part of me is pleased to get out of another activity. I pass the dock and the canoe of the lake, arriving almost level with the plaza.

Zane didn't want to discuss the police or Alfred. Is he sticking his head in the sand or genuinely trying to keep everyone calm? The more time goes by since Alfred's death—and now Uma's—the more Zane seems the least affected among those of us left living.

Inside the lobby, the same employee at the reception desk waves me down. "Miss? Are you Olivia Eriksen? You had a gift dropped off."

"A gift?"

The young man reaches beneath the wooden desk, then withdraws a wine bottle covered in dust. A white square of paper is taped to the side, my name scrawled in messy writing on its face.

"Did you want me to uncork it and have it decanted? I can deliver it to your room with wineglasses."

I stare at the dirty bottle. The label shows it's a merlot from twenty-five years ago. "Where did this come from?"

The employee lifts both eyebrows. "Sorry, I actually, uh . . . just went to the restroom down the hall. I didn't see who dropped it off. I found it on the counter when I returned."

"Okay. Thanks."

"But I know it's one of ours. The resort's, I mean. This is one of our vintage bottles from down in the wine cellar. A few of your family members were asking for a tour on Thursday night, I heard. Was that you?"

I stare at his innocent expression. Wait for him to give some indication that he's tightening the noose around my neck on purpose, relishing my discomfort—that he knows more than he's letting on about this smoking gun.

"No. It wasn't." Without a better option, I take the bottle, cringing at my fingerprints on its base. Although I want nothing more than to chuck it in the garbage, as far away as possible from me and from the accusation that I killed Alfred, I can't allow this *gift* to be found by anyone else.

I hold my breath, slinking down the hall to my room. When I shut the door behind me, I drop to my hands and knees. I place the bottle beneath the bed, beside the ironing board that no longer fits inside the closet.

34

Journal Entry

September
(No clue the actual day, so bear with me)
4:08 a.m.

No one really talks about the postpartum experience. Everyone amps you up for the pregnancy, the delivery and labor, and the fact that you need a car seat to drive your baby home from the hospital, but that's it. Nothing about the fourth trimester. Nothing about the trauma inflicted upon your delicate, fragile body while the doctor is trying to save both you and your infant. Zilch regarding the recovery period that follows.

If it weren't four o'clock in the morning, I might have a quip at the end of that terribly ominous sentence. But it is. So I don't.

The first three months were absolutely awful (something else no one warns you about), but Teddy did try to support us in whatever ways he could. Edgar, his dad, keeps popping in to say that it's Teddy's responsibility as a father to ensure we're provided for, and I think that new title is driving Teddy's enthusiasm. Or maybe it's some other motivator—I don't really care. I just need someone to change diapers while I nap for an hour or two, occasionally, and Teddy has done that. Baby still hasn't slept through the night.

Sometimes, like now, I get the feeling the baby is awake purely to watch me. To observe my coos, the songs I sing, and the kisses I plant on little cheeks. It's now been about six months, and although all the books say the baby should be playing and gurgling with me, that never happens when I think it should. For instance, yesterday I made a funny face, some raspberry noises, and only got a stare in return. Then the cat, Whiskers, joined us on the carpet of the living room. The baby reached out with a drool-covered palm and yanked the poor animal's tail like a rope. Whiskers yowled and stopped just short of clawing my perfect child, when the baby released him.

I was horrified. But when I looked at my baby girl, there was just the smallest hint of a smile playing across two chubby cheeks. Part of me was delighted to finally get a smile directed at me. Then she reached out an angelic hand toward Whiskers, who was glowering in the corner with his hackles raised. Almost as if to beckon the cat closer for another go.

35

OLIVIA

Thunder rumbles overhead like an orchestra tuning their instruments before a performance. I join the rest of my relatives at the edge of the field, near where the survival training took place earlier.

I haven't checked the wine cave today, but I'll bet Alfred is where I left him. The note that I found in his pocket, which would point the finger at me, remains carefully hidden in the interior zipped pocket of my suitcase. I would burn it—put any evidence linking me to Alfred's death to bed for good—if not for this growing need for answers. Why me? What did Uma do to deserve being attacked too—then planted in my room, for me to take the blame?

Of all the family members with twisted histories and arrest records present this weekend, the person who seems most invested in maintaining head count is Zane, hands down. If Zane saw Alfred disrupt the family party by fighting with Felicity the first day, then overheard Uma say she planned to leave the retreat, would he have tried to force them to stay? Would he have hurt them? What could then drive him to target me, his niece, as a scapegoat?

There's no way of knowing whether he called the police to notify them of Alfred's death. I didn't see him make any call myself. And I'm not certain that the property manager would disobey Zane if he were ordered against it.

Zane keeps telling us some big surprise is planned for Monday morning. Whatever he's prepared, it had better warrant the emotional hell this weekend has inflicted on each of us.

The air is thick, signaling incoming weather. From beside the trail-head, Shane wolfs down a granola bar he must have saved from the breakfast buffet this morning. Marla fidgets with her jacket's zipper beside him.

I glance toward my uncle and his wife. Zane whispers in her ear as Skye's eyes grow wide.

"What do you mean—" she begins, but Zane shushes her.

He turns away from me, but I catch a few words: "Staff went to check on the final kegs and discovered . . . he's gone."

Skye shakes her head. "We have to stop. What if—"

Zane casts an eye into the forest, breaking off their conversation. As if gauging whether the danger more likely lies therein or among his own flesh and blood. He meets her gaze. "I need this to end well, Skye. We can deal with it afterward."

So, Zane now knows that Alfred is missing. Unless he's the one who moved him and has been taking acting lessons in between surgeries.

Near the tree line where my oldest aunts and uncles cluster together, Coral glares at me.

"All right, Eriksens! It's time for any retreat's penultimate family-friendly game: capture the flag!" The woman I saw behind the reception desk, who wears her hair in delicate braids, claps her hands together—Liz, according to her name tag. "Each team must protect its own flag while hunting down the location of the other team's headquarters to capture their flag. Let's do this!"

We're divided up according to the first letter of our first names. When a drop of water lands on my shoulder, I raise my hand. "Should we be playing now? It seems like that next storm is coming in."

Skye shakes her head, stepping out from behind Zane. "We're going to play as long as we can before it starts really raining."

"Exactly!" Zane stabs the air with a pointed finger. Overdoing it. "And to add some incentive to anyone tempted to skip out of the game, the winning team will get first dibs for the surprise tomorrow."

Skeptical eyebrows rise among our group.

Zane scoffs. "And . . . I'll guarantee the winning team that you'll leave here tomorrow, either via chartered party bus if the roads are clear, or my helicopter."

"Wait—you have a helicopter? And you haven't called it yet?" Jimmy gapes at his cousin. "Call it now."

Zane shakes his head. "Tomorrow. The wind should pick up again tonight, and the sun will set soon."

Jimmy is silent. The rest of us try to process yet another betrayal at Zane's hand. Then murmurs of assent roll through the crowd. Even Edgar appears suddenly energized. We want to go home.

Howard stands off to the side, wearing the gray knit sweater he always looks so sophisticated in. I approach him. Slide my hand into his. "I'm sorry," I whisper so that only he can hear.

"Sorry for what exactly?"

"For keeping our engagement hidden. For prioritizing the drama—trauma—this weekend above us. Above our own family."

He releases a breath. A smile tips up the corner of his mouth. A moment passes, but then his hand squeezes mine. "We have more to discuss, Olivia. I can't keep waiting for you to magically be ready to go public—I thought we were waiting to tell everyone back home in Davis until we told your family first. Now that we have the opportunity, despite the weekend's . . . craziness, I'm ready. Anyway, I appreciate the apology."

"Listen up, people," Zane continues. "Captain for Team A is Coral, Olivia for Team B."

A quick tally of those standing around (not in resort uniform, clutching walkie-talkies) confirms we don't have even numbers for two teams—worse, the disadvantage is to Team B, my own, given that Howard is assigned to Team A.

"Can't Howard stay with me?" I raise my hand.

Zane snorts. "It just so happens, since we're doing this alphabetically, that H ends up on Team A. Besides, we can't have you two lovebirds getting distracted and disappearing into the bushes."

I start to protest, but thunder growls overhead.

"Fine," I say. Howard offers a commiserating glance. At least we're not fighting anymore.

"Two hours to dinnertime." Zane claps his hands, and Skye does the same behind him. "Let's make sure there's a flag captured well before then. You'll each wear a colored flag and belt around your waist to designate your team: blue for Team A, yellow for Team B. You'll take people out by tearing off their personal flags. Once you're eliminated, you must go to the opposite team's headquarters and sit in their jail. All clear? All right, let's get up to our respective bases. Once everyone is in position, Liz will give the signal to start playing."

Edgar and Jacquie huddle together, then round up the troops of Team A. Coral still appears shocked to have been named captain; she joins their circle.

It's disappointing I wasn't randomly assigned to my grandfather's team. He looks sharp this afternoon, maybe even eager to win.

"All right, you guys. Let's crush those idiots on Team A!" Vic nudges my shoulder, then beckons Marla and Shane to come closer. They return his grin with their own, and even eighty-five-year-old Lois seems galvanized, slapping her arms as if warming up her dormant muscles. If there's one thing that excites the Eriksens, it's a competition to beat our own.

"Did we play capture the flag the last time? When we had the family retreat ten years ago?" I ask.

Vic shakes his head; the smell of beer hangs on him like a second skin. "No, it got called off before we could. I had all kinds of pranks planned too."

"Why was it called off?"

"They're moving!" Shane points to Coral's team as they head into the forest to their headquarters. Ours is situated along the northernmost bluff of this hillside, according to Liz, the resort employee. Howard gives my hand another squeeze, then strides toward his group.

"We should go," Vic slurs.

As we set off behind Vic's lumbering frame, I'm grateful that Francis is on Team A; at least Tweedle Drunk and Tweedle Drunker aren't on the same roster.

We find a trail a hundred yards west of where we saw Team A enter the forest. Dewy branches brush my neck and hands as we navigate an overgrown turn; a shiver runs along my spine, the cold amplified beneath the canopy of leaves.

"There!" Lois shouts, pointing above our heads to the next ledge—a flash of yellow between the green. I continue on the reasonable incline of the trail, while Vic navigates the steep hillside adjacent that's covered in some kind of ivy. Poison ivy? I wince, watching the curling plants brush against the bare skin of his ankles and shins.

More thunder claps as I arrive at the clearing, breathing hard; I'm glad I brought my inhaler along. A ladder occupies a small clearing, bearing a voluminous flag on a pole secured to the top step by duct tape.

Vic lurches forward, taking charge. "All right, Lois, Olivia, Zane, Skye, and Marla, you're on offense. Since offense is the best defense, we should only have two people stay here to defend our flag: Shane, and the littlest Eriksen that could, Kyla."

"I'm staying here. No way I'm hiking up and down this mountain in the rain," Marla says.

"Fine, princess. Have it your way. Marla and Shane here. Kyla, you'll join offense."

191

Marla rolls her eyes but doesn't say anything more.

"All right, Team B?" A slender man, a resort employee, emerges from the same trail we just climbed. "They're ready," he says into his two-way radio. He turns and disappears past a thick tree trunk.

An air horn cuts through the woods, echoing from somewhere uphill.

"That's the signal. Game on!" Vic says.

"But how are we supposed to defend the flag?" Shane folds his arms across his puffy jacket. "We don't have weapons, or any rules around how. Should we just . . . attack and take their belts?"

Vic gives a sloppy wave. "You'll figure it out. Besides, with any luck, we'll already have grabbed their flag before they make it halfway here. You two stay put. Everyone else, come with me."

I glance at Zane to see what his take is on all this. He smiles and lays a hand around Skye's shoulders, as if he's pleased to see us all finally participating in one of his activities.

"We should use birdcalls," Kyla says as we walk single file through the forest. It's the first thing I've heard her say in days.

When I took Introductory Psych, I categorized my entire family using the *Diagnostic and Statistical Manual of Mental Disorders*; Kyla struck me as perfectly normal, as far as I could tell. Her hang-ups were typical of having your mother leave you when you were six years old, and of being raised by an alcoholic and unempathetic father.

"Birdcalls?"

Kyla shrugs up to her ears. "Well, yeah. We're in the forest, right? We want to sneak up on the others. Shouting out our plans isn't a great strategy."

"True. But I couldn't whistle to save my life," I reply.

A branch cracks to the right, where the trail disappears and the edge of the hillside steepens. We're only half a football field away from our flag.

Vic lays his hand flat, signaling to us to hold our position. Skye begins to giggle; then Zane grips her shoulder. She stops.

About thirty minutes have elapsed since we all separated in the meadow below. Was that enough time for Team A to mobilize and send a vanguard to attack us?

Kyla puffs up her cheeks beside me. A soothing warble tumbles from her throat.

I lift both eyebrows. One by one, each of us takes note of Kyla's skill, then begins to laugh.

"Where did you learn that?" Lois asks.

"Is that from public school?" Vic smirks.

"Don't tell me—YouTube," I offer.

The tension broken, we continue on. I glance backward before a new copse of trees engulfs the view. Nothing emerges from the hillside.

More than halfway along the mountain, I catch sight of the far end of the resort. The stake with the elk's head is somewhere beneath us, though not visible from here.

"We're almost to the end of the playing field. The game isn't supposed to extend past this point," I say. Although Vic has been acting as the captain, and I have no problem with him taking lead, I don't want to be needlessly wandering in the near darkness. Sunlight has barely made an appearance today. Cloud coverage thickens as night begins to fall.

"Should we climb up?" I add. A makeshift trail, free of potentially poisonous vines, snakes higher at an angle to my left. Our group hasn't seen any flash of a blue flag at this level, either from the other team's headquarters or their personal belts.

Tough luck to be wearing beacon-bright yellow as we are in a forest. I can't help wondering why no one has pounced on us yet.

Another branch cracks. This time overhead.

Vic does some gesture no one understands. When we don't move, he directs part of us above with a wave of his hand; the rest should stay on this same trail. Zane and I take the inclined path, moving as quickly and quietly as we can. Zane's yellow flag wavers in front of my face as he climbs, and I have the sharp urge to snatch it myself.

"Already turning on each other, are we?" Cousin Jimmy, of Team A, stands along a level footpath that continues toward the mountain's summit. He nods to my outstretched hand.

We both pause beneath Jimmy's gaze. I lean into the hillside to maintain my balance. "I was reaching for a tree root."

"Sure you were."

"What does Team A care whether one of us loses a flag? Isn't that better for you?" Zane asks. Zane is ten years younger than Jimmy, but thanks to some hard drugs Jimmy did before he got on his medication for schizophrenia, he looks like he could be Zane's father.

Jimmy stares down below at the rest of our team fanning out and moving quietly. He takes a step backward, as if desiring to keep out of sight. "I don't give a shit about some game. No offense, Zane."

Zane grunts, closest to Jimmy's flag. His calves flex at my eye level. "Whatever. I'm just trying to do right by our family."

"If by that you mean, make up for your public, professional embarrassment—sure."

"Fuck off, Jim—"

"Well, I'm not here for that or any family togetherness. I'm here because I'm broke and we never really all left this place the last time. We left something valuable behind." Jimmy stares off at the resort with a gleam in his eye.

What is he talking about? What would we have left behind? I was at the last retreat as a thirteen-year-old, and I don't remember anything strange about the departure.

"What the hell does that mean?" Zane asks.

Jimmy nods, slowly. "That's too bad. Part of me hoped you knew. I wondered if it would be your surprise tomorrow. Lois, do you know?"

"Jim, you're kind of freaking me out," she says from below. "What did we forget ten years ago?"

Lightning flashes twice, illuminating Jimmy's face in the forest's shadows. "That's what I'm hoping Edgar can explain."

36

OLIVIA

The sky cracks open, and then rain begins slicing through the trees. For a moment I can't see anything, the water is dumping so hard. I lodge my foot into the side of the hill to free my hands and wipe my eyes.

When I open them, Zane has scrambled up to the trail and seems to be chasing after Jimmy. Mud is smeared across my palm. The others have run for shelter somewhere below.

"Jimmy!" Zane calls. "What does my dad have to do with anything?"

Their voices drift away, drowned by the torrent. I huddle deeper inside my vest, cursing my lack of planning yet again for not packing a coat.

"Well. I guess the game is off." I strike my right foot higher into the shallow shelf made by Zane's hiking boots.

Footsteps barrel through the brush beneath me, and I still out of some instinct. Shift my hips to the right to better conceal the yellow flag still attached to my waist.

Shane sprints forward along the trail, coming from our headquarters. Dirty blond hair appears brown, sopping wet in the rain. A leaf sticks to his head as if he crawled beneath the last ten feet of bushes. Did he leave Marla alone to defend our team flag? I open my mouth to ask what happened—whether everyone is heading back to the main lodge and the hearth—and then I see the blood covering his cheek.

He scans the trail behind, then before him. Terror shines in his face, the same kind I watched over and over again on people accused of violent crimes in police interrogation rooms. Rumbling continues, somewhere deep in the gray sky. Shane turns toward where the rest of our team went, and his expression hardens.

New footsteps sprint along the trail from the direction of our headquarters. Shane takes off at a full run.

Marla appears, soaked and muddy up to her knees. "Shane!" she screams. "Shane, where are you?"

A sob cuts off her words. Her face crumples—so many of its features shared with her nephew. "Shane!" she screams again.

The memory of standing with Marla, waiting for our turn to shoot during the archery session, returns along with her concerned admission. *He's almost thirty, you know? I couldn't keep hiding the crazy shit he was doing out in the woods, with animals or . . . or otherwise.*

Great-Uncle David saw Shane standing in the lobby dripping wet on the night that Alfred died. What is Shane capable of, exactly?

Marla whimpers. Then she takes off running.

I shift my weight to the right and find a wider ledge on which to stand, hidden beneath a thick hedge of curling vines. Searching for one strong enough to support me, I wrap my hand around a thick plant, then pull; it holds. If this is poison oak, I'm screwed.

What happened back at headquarters? What was Cousin Jimmy talking about, that we left something behind during the last family retreat? And why would Edgar know anything about it? Considering my grandfather, no doubt, has many secrets locked away, either deliberately or due to shrinking mental faculty, I wonder what Jimmy suspects.

"Olivia?" a voice whispers.

I look up to the next ridgeway. Kyla peers down at me, tension gripping her young frame. "Shane . . . he's kind of . . . he attacked me."

Trembling, she lifts her wrist to me with her other hand. "He came out of nowhere when we were up looking for Team A's flag, right after it started to rain. Pushed me into a tree, and I fell down the hill until I landed on this level. I think I . . . I think my wrist is broken."

Her eyes redden. Her face contorts, and tears spill down her cheeks, mingling with drops of rain. The deluge begins to peter out. Wind whips through the trees to slither at my ankles.

I return to the path forged by Zane. Get to my feet beside Kyla.

"There's more," she sobs. "Something is wrong—with everyone. Great-Aunt Jacquie said I was a mistake. She seemed hysterical, talking about Alfred, and apparently Uma's disappeared. She said I shouldn't have been born, that my mom was too fragile to be part of this family."

"What? Are you serious?"

Kyla nods, jutting her chin out, as if trying to stop crying. She's nearly a foot taller than me at sixteen, but the fullness of her cheeks reminds me she's still a kid—apparently alone in a forest, with a broken wrist.

"Why would she say that?" I ask.

Kyla shrugs. "She's never been super nice to me, you know? It's not a huge surprise. Just really hurtful, I guess. She said she understood why my mom left us, instead of watching me grow up."

Jacquie has never struck me as particularly sensitive, especially given the paranoia she's been prone to over the years. She mistook Howard for a nurse earlier—but this is next level. Even for her. "Well, she's wrong."

Kyla looks at me with raised eyebrows.

"I don't know why Sasha left you and Francis, but it wasn't because she didn't want to see you grow up or she was too fragile. She loved you. I remember that when you were really little." I assume as much, anyway. Sasha struck me as neurotypical and a caring mother. She used to make dumplings from scratch for Kyla.

Kyla stares off at the wall of foliage that hides us from the valley and the resort beneath. "Jacquie just seemed to snap. Then Shane ran up and pushed me off the path. People have lost it."

I glance along the trail that leads to the summit of the mountain. Probably to Team A's flag headquarters too, but the game has got to be called off by now. Between the rain and everyone losing touch with reality, I can't see how anyone could continue. Although I would like to find Jimmy, to find Edgar and learn the family secret to which Jimmy was alluding, staying with Kyla seems like the smarter bet, given everything she just described—and what I witnessed from both Shane and Marla.

"Let's go back down," I say, wiping my face. "I'll bet there's hot chocolate already waiting for us by that giant fireplace. We can get your wrist checked out."

We descend the trail, making sure to avoid the slippery parts made muddy by the flash storm. I remove the yellow flag and pocket it, not wanting it to get caught on any branches. The mile is difficult to navigate, between the wet terrain and slick leaves thrown across the walking path. By the time we reach the bottom and solid ground, my muscles are sore and I'm eager for a hot bath.

The meadow is eerily quiet. The elk's head on its stake remains to the left another hundred feet off, and I try not to look at it—not now, given the chaos. It's a reminder that nature is unpredictable. Anything can pivot, cause you whiplash in an instant.

We cross the tall grass, wary of gopher holes, then climb the steps to the back entrance of the main hall. The lights are out when I open the door. Wind whispers across my neck and through my shirtsleeves. Kyla passes in first, still cradling her wrist.

"Take a seat by the fire."

Kyla does as I tell her, while I peek around the corner to the bar; it's empty. No bartender and no thirsty relatives. The vanity light bulbs that normally adorn the mirror behind the bar are also out. I flick a light switch. Nothing happens.

"Olivia?" Kyla calls. I return to the hearth, where flames cause light to dance across Kyla's young face. "I think the power's out," she says.

"Yeah, seems that way." The chandelier overhead is dark. "Where is everyone? Where are the resort employees?"

"Hello?" Kyla calls, but I rest a hand on her arm. She hushes.

"Something doesn't feel right."

There's a gasp. I turn to the hallway near the prep kitchen, and Liz, our capture the flag instructor, freezes as if I've caught her stealing hotel towels. She inches toward the door.

"What's happened?" I ask her. "Is everything okay?"

Liz continues moving toward the exit at a snail's pace, as if nervous that sudden movements will spook me. "Your family. You people shouldn't be allowed among others."

"What? We were just playing a game. A few of them lost their heads, but we're not dangerous." I purse my lips against the lie, knowing that's what I'm supposed to say.

Her hand touches the wooden bar of the main entrance. "Your family member was killed this weekend—and you're playing games? We found his body in the wine cellar, which you were heard asking about early on."

"What? What are you saying? You think I'm—"

"You must have moved it there. You were also seen carrying a dusty wine bottle that has been in that cellar for decades."

"Hold on, someone left that for me at reception. Where is that employee with the fade top? He knows, he can tell you."

"He told us that it appeared on the counter, and then you magically entered the lodge afterward." Liz doesn't budge from beside the door. "We still can't find our manager."

"Xavier?"

She nods. "You or your family did something to him. And us employees aren't waiting around to be next during this power outage."

"But . . . what about a backup generator? Shouldn't that still work? It kicked on after the last blackout."

She slips out the front door, walking backward, never moving her eyes from me. "Beats me. Xavier has been lobbying for a replacement backup generator for months. The one we have jump-starts, then dies without any warning."

"But where are you going? There's a landslide blocking the roads in both directions."

Liz gives me a hard look. She places another foot outside, as if uncertain whether I might leap at her and drag her back into the lobby. "You can get around it if you climb down the hillside. But it's dangerous. And you need somewhere to go afterward. The staff all live close enough to walk home, or we have relatives coming to get us on ATVs."

She shuts the door, but I spring forward and grab the handle. "Wait."

I look behind me at Kyla, who continues to sit quietly, clutching her wrist. "Could I—take us with you."

A sneer pulls Liz's mouth. "Not a chance. You're on your own."

"Olivia," Kyla says, her voice strained. "Look." She points to the floor-to-ceiling windows overlooking the plaza. Felicity passes the totem pole, supporting Denny as he hobbles up the steps to reach the back doors. Both of them are pale, their clothing wet.

"What happened?" I ask, staring at Denny as he limps indoors. Liz's sprint echoes in the parking lot.

"Twisted ankle, running away from that madman." Felicity grunts, nearly dragging Denny the last few feet to the armchair beside the fire.

"Yeah, both Kyla and I had our own encounters with Shane out there."

Felicity shakes her head. "Not Shane. Though I know he was tearing through the woods running after Jacquie. Jimmy. Jimmy's interrogating everyone about some family secret he heard years ago and not letting anyone leave the summit of the mountain."

Denny groans, lifting his foot onto the coffee table. "They've all freaked out."

Light from the fire casts him in a strange glow. He appears older, more weathered than his seventeen years.

"Well, where is Shane now? Does anyone know?" I ask. When I saw him last, he looked as if he were gripped by some dream state—some post-traumatic stress crisis. "Jimmy at least remains rational for now, even if he's holding everyone captive somewhere in the cold. Shane didn't look well to me. And he attacked Kyla."

Felicity scans her niece, eyes pausing on the wrist she cradles. "I don't know."

"Should someone go find him if he is experiencing some kind of episode?"

No one replies. Each person stares into the flames, the only source of light as the sun disappears behind the trees. Shadows reach for us, stretching from the gallery-style windows. A log cracks, and Denny flinches.

"I've had enough of this place. Enough of this family." Felicity drops her voice to a whisper. "I'm not spending another—"

"Look," Kyla interrupts. She points through the glass. Shane comes lumbering toward us, crossing the meadow along the west side of the lake. His skin is coated in mud, the white T-shirt he was wearing earlier unrecognizable. Blood mixes with earth in smears across his face and neck—one arm hangs limp at his side; I'm not sure whose blood it is. Something glints in the setting sunlight. A knife.

"We should move," I say.

Shane sees us through the glass. Pauses. Then he breaks into a run.

"Go!" I tear down the hall toward my room, fumbling for my key. I slam the stiff plastic against the metal touch pad, but the dead bolt doesn't move. I try again.

"The backup generator," Kyla pants over my shoulder. Denny and Felicity limp toward us. "That employee said it was out. The doors are all stuck in the lock position."

A loud bang resonates from the lobby. Shane has entered the lodge.

I sprint, turning left with the hallway. Upholstered benches lie beneath wide windows, opposite a glass-walled conference room. I try the handle and it turns.

Everyone files in behind me, with Denny bringing up the rear. We dive to the back of the room, where the solid base of the long conference table hides us from the hallway's view. A minute passes. Then another. The sound of our heavy breathing fills the space.

A shadow passes across the wall above our heads, obscuring the dim natural light from outside. Felicity squeaks. Denny and Kyla are motionless on either side of me. My chest squeezes, my lungs flattening. I can't breathe.

My asthma. Where is my inhaler? I search my bag for the small tube of medication I know I brought with me to play capture the flag this afternoon. Where is it?

Shane was carrying a knife. What is he planning to do with it?

Tears prick my eyes. Laying my head between my knees, I suck in a final breath through my nose, try to calm down.

A click booms from the conference room door as the handle turns. Then Shane joins us inside.

37

BIRDIE

Wind whips through the side street where I stand. Frigid air dives down my V-neck sweater and inside the double-lined down jacket I brought with me, making me glad I ignored Grayson's teasing. When he popped into our room while I was packing, he nearly choked on his coffee, eyeing the contents of my suitcase. He asked, "Where do you think you're going? Siberia?"

"I'm a San Diego native," I replied. "Anything below sixty-five degrees gets the winter wonderland treatment." Grayson is from Los Angeles, not too far north of San Diego; he would be begging to borrow my parka in this weather.

I clutch my jacket at my neck. Outside a narrow doorframe of the alley, a wooden sign swings overhead: EUGENE NEW AGE HERBAL MEDICINARY. According to the message boards, after Tilly's bookstore, Li worked at different restaurants for several months at a time before she landed at Iris Stimson's herbal-remedy business—the final address that appeared on the background check, and in front of which I stand now.

Over Thai takeout last night, I tried to locate the detective on Li's case, somewhere in Minnesota. I even called a few phone numbers from my hotel room, with no luck. Hilarie Dayton, Li's former roommate, had maintained a Facebook page dedicated to her local Pilates classes, but it hasn't been updated in seven years. When I tried calling two Hilarie Daytons at phone numbers the internet spit out, one number was no longer in service, while the other was answered by a college student partying at a bar. Too young. And also, too drunk to tell me if she was named after her mother or aunt or older cousin.

I turn the knob of the door, as another gust of wind barrels down the passage. The entry slams open, and I nearly fly off my feet.

"You okay?" A woman with thinning brown hair appears from within. She grips the door with me, and together we close it. Middle-aged, with bright hazel eyes, she gestures to a cushioned bench along the wall. Her gaze roams my parka. "You're welcome to sit if you're just trying to get out of the cold."

I take in this woman's linen tunic and the leggings she wears with slip-on sneakers. Chinese music that my grandmother preferred during the Lunar New Year plays from a speaker nearby. The shop is cramped but cozy, with books on acupuncture and herbal remedies lining shelves, and a small hallway leading somewhere else. Metal turnstiles beside a cash register display dried and fresh plants in plastic baggies.

"No, I'm fine. Thanks. The weather really sneaks up on you here, doesn't it? I checked my app before driving up and there was no mention of a windstorm."

"Ah, not local, huh?" She smiles. Fine lines pleat her temples. "Oregon can have unpredictable weather in March. But nothing's as bad as what's happening in the east side of the state. Our governor just declared a state of emergency to clear landslides from a few days back."

"Wow. Sounds intense."

The woman nods, sympathetically. "Are you shopping, then? We're offering a two-for-one deal on licorice root."

Mint and something else mingle together, perfuming the space. I turn, searching for the source of the smell. "Do you have any Tiger Balm?"

A broad smile pulls her cheeks. "Well, obviously."

She directs me to an apothecary's hutch beneath the window. Waving a hand toward the bottom and middle of the drawers, she pulls a delicate handle to coax one loose. Small yellow circles brim from the tray.

"I'll take two. Thanks."

"Anything else? If you'll be in town for a bit, I'm also offering a discount on a five-session naturopathic treatment series."

A Chinese zodiac calendar hangs above the cash register. Various animals gallop around a circle that conveys the year ahead. As a Tiger, I've always identified with the stubborn part of that beast's personality. Well, obviously.

"Actually, I'm trying to track down an old friend who used to work here," I begin. "Li Ming Na. Does that name sound familiar to you? She would have been in town around ten years ago or more."

The woman—Iris—rings me up on the cash register. "Possibly. Do you mean Ming-Na Li?"

I give a blank stare. "I'm . . . not sure."

Iris plunks my Tiger Balms into a flat paper sack. "Well, if Li is your friend's surname," she says, drawing the words out, "in the American fashion, her name would be Ming-Na Li. Right?"

I don't know if she's asking me because I'm Asian and she assumes I would know, or if she's trying to give me a lesson in Eastern naming practices. "Maybe. But I thought her last name was Na. Li Ming Na."

Nothing in the documents I've read suggests otherwise. Li Ming Na is my victim's legal name, even in the case file that Detective Ashley shared with me.

Iris puckers her mouth. "Right. It could be, of course."

"But you don't think it is?"

"Well, I don't know any Li Ming Na. But I do remember a sweet, spunky young woman in her early twenties named Ming-Na Li who used to help me every weekend for a few years. Ming-Na would translate ingredient lists on new products that I'd receive from brokers in China."

Iris pauses, as if waiting for me to offer translation services too. But I don't speak, read, write, or even recognize Mandarin. My family speaks Toisanese, a totally distinct dialect from Mandarin and Cantonese—and as a fourth-generation American, I'm not even very good at that.

Iris sighs. "Ming-Na was a pretty amazing employee. I was disappointed when she left to become a stay-at-home mom for her little girl. Happy for her, of course—thrilled—but selfishly disappointed."

"I'm sure. It sounds like you knew her pretty well." I speak, not fully grasping what I'm saying. What is the owner telling me? That this trip, literally one thousand miles long, during which my baby hit her first big-girl milestone without me, was a waste of time? That I may have been tracking the wrong name?

"What she shared with me, at least," Iris says. "Only I never called her Ming-Na. I only know that's her full name because, as her employer, I had copies of all her official paperwork. When she worked here, she went by Sasha. Sasha Lee."

I let the name roll around in my head—wait for some light bulb of recognition to begin flashing. Sasha Lee.

It's a new name to me. But not surprising. Plenty of immigrants, across ethnicities, adopt more American-sounding names upon arrival to the States. I have a Chinese name, too, but have little idea how to properly pronounce it myself.

"No kidding. I had no idea she went by Sasha," I begin. "Any chance you have records on her employment still? Her date of birth? An old coworker in California said she was older than I thought she was."

Iris lifts thin eyebrows. Probably, she's beginning to doubt my story of long-lost friendship. "I shredded her personal information a long time ago. But I remember she carried around a fake ID. She accidentally gave it to me to copy when I first hired her, and I noticed the laminate on the edge was coming undone. When I asked her about it being fake, she only smiled and said, 'It's never a bad thing to be considered younger.' Later, she shared that she was just trying to fit in with the college kids in the area. To start fresh with a new crowd."

"Did that discovery change your relationship with her at all? Did you believe her?"

Iris purses her lips. "Honestly, I did my share of odd stuff in my twenties. And she had moved here without any friends or family, from what she told me. I didn't think it my place to judge. How old did you think she was?"

I smile. Try to come off as less suspicious when I speak this time. "Oh, just a few years older than me. Did you ever meet Sasha's roommate, Hilarie Dayton? I was hoping to chat with her, but I can't tell if she's still local."

Iris shakes her head. "No, never. Sasha was a great employee, but she kept her personal life pretty compartmentalized, if I remember right. I knew she lived with another woman her age, but I never met the girl."

"Gotcha. Well, thanks anyway. And thanks for the Tiger Balm."

I turn to leave, and Iris stops me with a hand on my forearm. "If you see Sasha, please give her my best."

Without confirming I will—or can—I exit the shop.

I'll go back to my hotel and do another search on the roommate. Although it's clear the roommate's alibi was solid, Hilarie Dayton might have more to share about Sasha's boyfriend; she could confirm whether he was the Eriksen love interest that the bookstore employee mentioned. And if the city of Eugene won't spill its secrets, I can venture east to the location of Sasha's weekend getaway—that, at least, was clearly written in the case file.

As I make my way to my rental car, snowflakes fall from the sky. Tiny flurries coat the ground in a thin blanket before their unique shapes absorb into the asphalt. Much in the same way that Li Ming Na's—Sasha's—life's details seem swallowed whole.

38

Journal Entry

August 10

The sun is shining and I'm in the great outdoors of Eastern Oregon, so what could possibly bring me down? Dirty diapers in a forest, that's what, Journal. This campground resort offers the higher end of amenities—comfy beds, heating in our respective cabins, maid service, and good food that doesn't come from a box—but it still requires taking my full garbage can of diapers to the locked dumpster on the edge of the property. Housekeeping just doesn't service as regularly as a one-year-old child produces a number two.

The year has flown by. Although it started out a bit rough, with tension between myself and Teddy, I've been grateful to watch him level up—to mature and care for our pudgy little girl—who is now toddling! It's been such a thrill to see those chubby legs taking on the world with the speed and enthusiasm of a baby deer.

It's been hard. But I'm hoping the hardest times are behind us. Which is why I brought my sad, forsaken journal (no offense) to this weekend retreat—to start fresh after so long, and to record my thoughts when I have the time. Don't go expecting great tomes,

Journal. But I will write this weekend at least, while I have consistent childcare from grandparents.

We arrived at Horsefly Falls yesterday, Thursday, and enjoyed a relaxed dinner together outdoors at several picnic tables. There are around thirty of us in all, including Edgar's kid from his first marriage, Teddy's half sister, Hattie. I don't think the first wife was invited, but Hattie looks like she's managing okay.

There's a cook on-site who apparently has big dreams of one day being the property manager and turning this place into a real luxury spot in the woods—Xavier—who said he grew up nearby. When I first started asking questions about the totem pole in the middle of the courtyard, Xavier smirked and called it "a nice form of fiction" that visitors to the campgrounds enjoy. Apparently, the Paiute people, native inhabitants of this chunk of land, never used totem poles.

Today, we've got a hike planned this afternoon and I am so glad I brought my boots. The skies are clear and the sun is out, like I said, but I don't know the forest or what to expect out there. The evergreens are like the ocean for me: once you enter the water, you accept that anything and everything can happen; you're entering territory inhabited by sharks, carnivorous bacteria, undertow, and all kinds of animals beneath the surface of the waves. I'll do my best to be ready, but how well can anyone from the city prepare for coming face-to-face with nature these days, really?

Yvette agreed to watch the toddler while Teddy and I join the group on the trail. She seems thrilled to be a grandmother again. Edgar, less so, but everyone is allowed their own emotions, I guess. I just hope Yvette's around for a long time, for everyone's sake.

Honestly, I was grateful for the reprieve. Teddy is excited to spend time with his family, and for me it's felt more isolating than usual to take care of the baby. We are now both sleeping through the night, but we're still room sharing. I can't bring myself to shut the little human away behind a closed door. Not because the thought of being separated from her chokes me up—it's the opposite. I don't know that I can trust her alone.

The other day I left the baby to nap in my and Teddy's bed. When I went to lie down with her, the way I sometimes do, I felt a stab from underneath the covers. Pulling back the blankets, I found a pushpin—same as the one I stepped on the day before, which had made me jerk and howl from the pain and made her laugh and laugh, watching me. She had placed the pushpin beneath the covers, anticipating that I would join the nap and provide new hilarity. Never mind that I kept bleeding through the bandage and socks that I wore for two days following my injury.

Now, Journal, you might tilt your anthropomorphic head to the side and say that all toddlers display mischievous traits. But you wouldn't be talking about mine. Mine regularly chooses antics like what I described above. So, when Yvette volunteered to watch her, I didn't hesitate for a second to go hiking.

Edgar will probably join the hike, if only to force-mentor Shane. After breakfast this morning (menu: scrambled eggs with spinach grown in the resort's garden, tomatoes, mushrooms, and biscuits), Edgar pulled aside little Shane. The seven-year-old had been playing with his youngest aunt, Marla, all last night and more before we sat down to eat. Apparently, Edgar found that bothersome. I heard him say to Yvette that boys should be running around in the woods, playing with other boys his age or older, swimming in the lake, and catching bugs—not playing with his eight-year-old aunt and her dolls.

I totally respect Edgar wanting his grandson to get out and experience life as maybe Edgar did when he was a child—but Edgar was also traumatized at a young age by finding his father murdered at his brother's hand. Not every childhood is as we expect, you know? Better to not be overly judgy as adults.

About thirty minutes after Edgar reprimanded Shane and tried to pressure him into throwing a football around (picture my eyes rolling), Shane and Marla disappeared. Vic and his girlfriend, Millie, looked for them everywhere and started asking others to help search. Teddy was on toddler duty, somewhere around the lake's edge, so I joined the group, calling for "the twins," as everyone calls them.

While the rest of the adults and older kids went out into the tall grass of the meadow, I saw some movement fluttering the picnic tablecloth from beneath. I lifted the gingham fabric and found Shane and Marla, kissing.

It seemed innocent enough but I admit it shocked me. A seven- and eight-year-old seem a little old to be playing doctor, but it's even more inappropriate when you remember they're related by blood.

I separated them and they turned wide eyes on me, begging me not to tell Shane's dad or anyone else in the family. I asked them how long this had been going on and they both said not long. Marla looked away when she did, so I don't know how much I believe them. In any case, they swore they wouldn't kiss anymore. The rest of the family returned then, and I didn't have the heart to embarrass them, to expose their secret.

While the group went back to their respective cabins to get ready for lunch, Edgar pulled me aside to ask where I found Marla and Shane. I told him the truth: that I found the twins under a picnic table, hiding. Edgar, interestingly enough, asked what they were doing, almost as if he suspected the truth.

For some reason, I felt that revealing the twins' kiss would be devastating to them. So I lied. I said they only seemed to be hiding from Vic, Shane's dad, and his girlfriend—maybe it was time to get them into therapy after Shane's mother moved to Aspen a few years back, and Marla had been having trouble at school. Edgar only nodded, all solemn. He said, "Family comes first." Whatever that's supposed to mean.

When the gong rang, signaling lunch was ready, Edgar brought out a bow and arrow set. Apparently, it was in the resort's recreation cabin, where all the sporting equipment is stored. He presented it to Shane. The sweet kid's face lit up. While the rest of us started walking toward the dining hall, the pair of them went out to the field. Then Shane began practicing how to aim with killer precision.

39

OLIVIA

Monday

The night passes with each of us taking a turn at standing watch. I took the first shift, as everyone else was still rattled by our brush with Shane. Denny took the second watch. Then Felicity, who volunteered to cover Kyla's turn too.

Yesterday, after the conference room door opened, there was a crash that came from outside. I sucked in another trembling breath, trying to stop the feeling of suffocation threatening to reveal my hiding place, when a new click resonated. The door shut. Footsteps led away and toward the main entrance.

I peeked over the dark wooden conference table. Shane was gone. Through the glass wall and the windows beyond, Cousin Jimmy wrestled with something. A wheelbarrow filled with tools of some kind. He managed to lift the wooden handles and move forward another five feet when he dropped it again.

Jimmy's face blanched. And he took off running.

Shane came into view then, a new look of frenzy clenching his expression, as he chased Jimmy into the woods, wielding the knife.

Later, screams outside were audible during the night. But it was too dark to see anything beyond the windows of the hallway. No one among our group of refugees slept.

When day broke, sunshine streamed through the glass opposite the conference room doors. Felicity and I sneaked out to get food from the prep kitchen, but we've otherwise stayed in our hiding spot. We've barely spoken to each other all day, for fear of being overheard and discovered. But now it's four fifteen. A whole day has passed since we were corralled into this room like mice in a psych experiment.

"Anyone know where Zane stashed all of our phones?" I whisper. Throughout the night, images of Shane ambushing Howard somewhere in the forest came to me, as if I'd witnessed the visual directly. As if they were a premonition of some kind. If I believed in that sort of thing.

Felicity grunts. "Knowing Zane, in his luxury hotel room under lock and key."

I bury my head between my knees and suck in a rattling lungful of air. "We should do something. Try something to make this more bearable."

"Like what?" Felicity asks. "The only thing that would improve our situation is Shane being tackled and tied up, and I'm not volunteering. That, or getting rescued."

"The backup generator. If we can get it started, we might be able to call for help. Tell the police about Shane and make them come for us this time."

"But where would we even find the generator?" Felicity asks.

"I think I saw it outside next to the dining hall. The rain seems paused for now, and we can make good use of the break." A lightweight chair that sat beside the firepit tumbles past the window. The rain may have stopped, but the wind continues at full force. The storm isn't over.

"But Denny has a twisted ankle and Kyla an injured wrist. Neither of them is in any condition to go walking or running away from Shane, especially with branches or whatever else flying through the air. What do you think happened to him? Why is he doing this?"

I shake my head, recalling Marla's admission during the archery lesson. "He has a history of breaking with reality. Something must have happened, some kind of trauma to trigger this episode."

"Well, there's safety in numbers. None of the door locks work, so we should stay here together instead of running around outside."

The barricade we made yesterday of wheeled office furniture provides cold comfort.

I shake my head. "Once he comes back, Shane will see the chairs stacked up against the conference room wall. He'll know we're in here; then we'll be trapped. We should get the generator working so we can at least hide in our rooms."

Denny and Kyla watch my conversation with our aunt Felicity like a tennis match. Neither of them speaks up, instead waiting to see who bests the other.

Felicity chews on her lower lip. Stringy auburn hair falls in a curtain around her face. "The police have been called, a few times. They're going to come any minute. They're probably down the road, on their way. We just need to hunker down. It's too risky to be outdoors."

"But what about Coral?" Denny asks, seated on the carpet. "She's stuck out there and doesn't know where I am, or that Shane has gone apeshit."

Kyla remains quiet. I peer at my youngest cousin. She's been through a lot—but she seems stoic within these dry walls. Content to stay out of harm's way, despite knowing her dad, Francis, is still somewhere in the wind. Almost unnervingly calm.

"I'm going," I announce. "Howard is probably looking for me. And I'm not staying put, when Shane can come barreling through here when we're asleep and drooling on ourselves. We have no idea when the cops are coming, and so far, they've given little to convince me they are at all."

I cross to the brass door handle. "I'll be right back. If I get the generator to work, the lights should turn on. You should get to a hotel room as fast as possible. Then you can dead bolt the door."

Stepping into the hall, I listen for movement—either more Eriksens or any remaining intrepid resort staff willing to brave our family but not the elements outside.

Funny to think I came here hoping to get in and out—to leave Saturday with a full interview from my grandfather describing his observations of psychopathy from birth. Maybe even leave with an interview of an aunt or uncle as a bonus.

None of that matters now, though. With my cousin shifting to the animalistic frenzy his aunt witnessed in the past, and my father's cousin Jimmy becoming power hungry during the chaos, it's not clear any of us will get out of here, let alone in time for me to turn in my unfinished dissertation.

In the main hall, I peer at the chandelier overhead. Its glass crystals appear spectral, as if the fixture were a relic from a past life. Long shadows slant through the windows and stretch along the thick area rug. Embers glow in the fireplace, but the flames and their heat have long since died out. The taxidermied bear looks hungrier somehow.

Walking straight, toward the prep kitchen, I glance out the front door. Something white dots the windshields of the employees' abandoned cars. Snow.

I break into a silent jog, my feet landing and lifting with the weight of a ghost. The kitchen door moans open, and I beeline to the fridge. If I do get the generator going, Shane will see the resort's lights flicker on and come inside shortly after—anyone seeking heat would. I won't want to be out of my room when he does.

I pocket a half dozen mini alcohol bottles that could be served on an airplane, then move to the steel shelf of dry goods and fruit. A reusable cloth bag hangs from a hook, and I load it up with a baguette, two blueberry muffins, three apples, prepackaged granola bars I saw at the breakfast buffet, a banana, and a box of raisins. Before I leave, I grab a water bottle that's sitting on the counter.

As I pass through the lobby with my bag of supplies, a wry smile hits my cheek. All the times I thought about the zombie apocalypse and how I might fare when faced with the undead as an enemy, I was kidding myself; it's not the fantasy-based creatures of our imaginations we should be afraid of, but the reality of being locked in with the monsters closest to us.

Outside, new clouds pass across the sickle moon already risen in the sky. Snowflakes dust the banister leading down the deck stairs and into the plaza. The forest line appears black to my tired eyes.

The temperature dropping, I move along the main lodge toward the yoga center. I hug the wood panels until I can dart behind the dining hall, where days ago, I checked for Alfred's refrigerated cadaver.

David saw Shane soaked up to his knees the night that Alfred died. Now Shane is in the grips of some psychotic episode that involves attacking everyone here. Has he been disoriented during the evenings since he arrived? Did he attack Aunt Uma as well?

A ten-foot-tall, rectangular metal box sits elevated on a concrete platform. The backup generator. Instead of a rumbling vibration, like what I've heard from the generator on UC Davis's campus, the box is silent. Dead. With the dim lighting and no flashlight, I squint to read the thick red lettering that outlines how to restart the machine.

According to the square of text, I'll want to verify there's enough fuel in the generator. I scan the side of this panel to find a closed, locked compartment with the word "GAS" prominently displayed. So much for verifying directly.

Next step: *Turn fuel valve on.* The red circular grip is already in the on position, so I turn it off, then back to where I found it.

Turn choke on. Having no clue what that means, I push a red lever back and forth. Then again. Faster. The lever doesn't seem bothered by it, and no friction seems to impede my pushing.

Turn engine on. I press a large black button to the left, leaning forward until it sinks into the metal panel. Gears shift within the generator.

Something catches—*click click click click*—then the engine bellows to life. Rumbling swells in the small space.

I should move. No doubt, the sound is audible from the plaza, in the otherwise desolate quiet—maybe from the forest too.

Turning on my heel, I jog to the corner where the dining hall meets the generator platform. Then the engine cuts out.

Doubling back to the instructions panel, I complete the same ritual—turn the fuel valve off and then on again, turn the choke wildly back and forth, then press the engine start button with all the strength of my upper body—and the motor resumes its blast of noise.

I count to thirty, glancing over my shoulder every few seconds. My frame tenses, ready for an ambush from Shane, when the same gut-punching silence falls over the alley again.

Turning, yanking, pressing through the motions once more, I suck in a breath. The engine clamors anew.

I take off running. Dodge a tarp flying through the air that covered the pile of firewood by the stairs. No longer hugging the brown building facade, I race to the lobby—toward the safety of my room.

No, not my room. Uma is still in my room, and it's now been two days since she was killed. Decomposition is likely well underway, and I won't want to enclose myself with her.

I pull open the back door to the lobby—the generator continuing to hum in the distance—launch myself inside, then take the corner to the hallway like I'm qualifying for a new heat.

Uma's room that she shared with Coral. I'll stay there. Light twinkles from the chandelier overhead like a flashy beacon of safety.

But Felicity stands outside my door, barring the way down the hall.

"I got the generator going," I pant. "We need to get inside!"

Felicity continues to stare at me, her eyes wide and locked on my face. It's then I notice that my door is already ajar, held open by the security latch.

Uma's body is in my closet.

"Aunt Felicity." My voice quakes. "Let's go, we need to get into another room. Get Denny and Kyla out here—I don't know how much longer the generator will keep running—"

Light fixtures flicker overhead. Once. Then they fade to black.

The generator cut out again.

Shadow bathes Felicity's face. Her silence is all the more ominous.

She steps backward, slowly. With a fist, she knocks on the door two rooms away from mine—Uma and Coral's—and it opens. Someone inside is able to turn the handle, despite the electrical outage. Denny and Kyla.

"You killed her, Olivia. Uma. All this time, I've been wondering where my younger sister is; you killed Uma. From what Kyla shared with me, and the staff shared with her—you killed Alfred, too, and moved him to the wine cellar."

"Wait a minute. No. The staff got it wrong. I didn't touch Alfred or Uma."

"Your room was my safe space," she continues. "It's where I felt most comfortable and supported after Alfred died, so I came here first. Uma's stench was reeking up the whole place. And you didn't touch her?"

"No—well, yes, I placed her in the closet because—" I grapple for the right words as panic clenches my throat. Fresh sweat breaks across my neck. This isn't happening. I'm not being accused of two murders— of killing the family members I was closest to.

"You placed her in the closet?"

"Well, I didn't know what else to do. I couldn't—"

"Couldn't tell anyone else or call the police?" Disgust tightens her small features.

"No, I . . . It felt like the best plan at the time," I finish weakly. Tears fill my eyes, although I don't know if my aunt cares. My voice is thick as I muster a reply: "This . . . this isn't what it looks like."

"Goodbye, Olivia." Felicity sneers. "You're the worst our family has to offer. I'll be sure to tell the police that when they get here."

I blink, and then Felicity is gone, having slid into the room and shut the door behind her. Another moment passes, and then the security latch clips in the darkness.

———

I stood outside my hotel door for another five minutes in a daze. Trembling racked my body. I leaned against the silk wallpaper for balance as I processed my new reality: my relatives weren't coming back out; they would not have a change of heart. I was alone, with a proverbial branded letter *K* across my chest. A killer, in my aunt's and cousins' eyes.

Kyla told Felicity what Liz, the resort employee, said. Why did she do that? Does she really think I hurt Alfred? Or did she simply want to turn Felicity against me?

All the times I wrote off Kyla's quiet demeanor this weekend, and when she was a kid, I never once considered what might be going on in that head of hers. I had assumed, in my own arrogance, that she was neurotypical. But what if Kyla has other motives in shutting me out right now? The same blood runs in her limbs as ran in Calder Saffron's.

Kyla's wrist has taken on some bruising in the last twenty-four hours, but it's clearly not broken. Was Kyla attacked by Shane at all, and insulted by Great-Aunt Jacquie? Or was it all a ploy to get me to trust and pity her?

As Uma's odor reached my nose like a curling vine, I remembered I should find new shelter. Shane would be along any second. Waiting like a human sacrifice on the patterned hallway carpet would do me no favors.

Damp pine needles mute my steps as I approach a tiny house outside. From this angle in the shadows, the arts and crafts building reminds me of a converted cabin—similar to the yoga center, the wellness center, and the sports hut. Heavy charcoal clouds rolled in while I was indoors, and enshroud the resort like it's midnight.

I slink to the front of the arts and crafts building. Pressing down on the handle confirms the door is locked. Whether by a physical key or an electronic one stunted by the broken backup generator, I don't know. Creeping along the back of the building, I approach the first window, then try to push the glass up. It won't budge. I continue forward, well aware that the slight overhang provided by the roof barely conceals me from view. Anyone standing in the vast field leading into the forest and mountain range in the distance, where I demonstrated my lack of edible-flower knowledge, would have a clear view of my skittering path.

The next window is already ajar. I duck down. Rising slowly, I pause when the arts and crafts room is in full view. Two people are already inside. A man and a woman, naked.

The woman straddles the man on the cushioned chair that the pottery instructor occupied during our session. He buries his face in her chest, gripping her backside as she moves in a carnal rhythm.

Thunder cracks as lightning slices through the nebulous sky. The room flashes, illuminated for a moment. Shane pulls Marla's hair, and she arches backward in a silent moan.

Horror roots me in place—no, not exactly. Fascination. Epiphany.

Marla vouched for Shane the night of Alfred's murder. She said they were together that night because Shane lost the key to his own room. They were together then.

Unable to tear my eyes from the scene before me, I can only assume Shane and Marla have been together every night since we arrived. If that's the case, nothing Marla has said to me this entire trip can be trusted.

I sink to the ground beneath the window, my mind racing. Marla is Shane's aunt.

Nausea roils my stomach. Sweat lines my temples. Then the cold earth is a shock to my fingertips that jolts me to crawl forward. To keep moving and find someplace safe to hide.

40

NEWS ARTICLE

The *Eugene Horizon*
August 25, 2013
By Anne-Marie Gu

Authorities investigating the disappearance of Natasha "Sasha" Lee continue to be baffled by the young mother's abrupt departure from a campground resort in the Malheur Forest reserve. Two weeks ago, Lee attended a family gathering at the Horsefly Falls Resort, about six hours from Eugene. Witnesses described her as participating in the planned activities Thursday and Friday, then disappearing on Saturday. When family members checked her cabin, she was gone.

A known suburbanite who enjoyed taking her six-year-old daughter for walks in Eugene's downtown district, Lee previously worked a part-time job in an herbal medicinary, and she volunteered with her local animal shelter on weekends. She is described as a devoted mother, which is why her disappearance is all the more confusing to investigators; no one believes she would willingly leave her child. Moreover, according to the police, it was not Francis Eriksen, her longtime partner and the father of her daughter, who reported Lee missing, but the animal shelter at which she volunteers when she failed to show up for her shift last week.

Although previously convicted of two misdemeanors, Eriksen, who has a record of military service in the Marine Corps, is not suspected of involvement in Lee's disappearance at this time. Eriksen maintains that Lee left him and their daughter without so much as a note, let alone an indicator that she was in trouble. Lead Ranger Tomlinson for the Malheur Forest, who is conducting the search for Lee, confirms that Eriksen has been cooperative with all branches of law enforcement thus far. Former Lieutenant Governor Evan Peterson also contacted police investigators to urge them to resolve the case quickly, his first public address in a year. Last year, Peterson made headlines of his own after scandalous photos of him and local exotic dancer Kyss Kyss Bang Bang were leaked to the *Eugene Horizon*. The photos' sender has yet to be identified, although a handwritten note that accompanied the photos confirmed there are "plenty more where these came from."

A friend of Lee's suggests that there are more sinister motivations involved in her disappearance. Grace Huang, a former classmate from Northern California, says that in the past Lee had made comments suggesting that she feared for her life when she found herself alone with Eriksen for extended periods of time. Six years ago, before her daughter was born, Lee confided to Huang in a text message that Huang shared with the *Eugene Horizon* that Eriksen was jealous of anyone who held personal interactions with Lee. In fact, on two occasions that Huang was aware of, Eriksen insisted that Lee quit her part-time jobs to devote herself fully to their relationship. Once their daughter arrived, Lee cut off communication with Huang.

Now, Huang and others who knew Lee to be an independent, free spirit are raising questions to local authorities. Namely, What role did Eriksen play in Lee's disappearance?

41

BIRDIE

Sunday night, I called Grayson. I told him I wasn't coming home on my flight and that I didn't know when I'd be back. He, naturally, freaked out. After I apologized for the dramatics, I explained everything: I've been searching for Li Ming Na this whole time, without realizing that Li was her surname. I'd assumed that Na was her last name, that she had legally chosen the American way of leading with her given name on formal documentation—"Li Ming Na."

Recalling that the ice cream shop knew her as Li Ming Na too, I wondered when she adopted "Sasha" as her American name. Was it when she moved to Eugene and desired to blend in? Was she trying to leave behind the grief that she associated with Ming-Na Li, the nineteen-year-old girl whose parents died? Sasha Lee certainly sounded confident. She could be American, Russian, or from the Deep South with that spelling, an offshoot of a *Mayflower* family tree.

Asians are not a monolith. They come from diverse backgrounds across continents and islands. Many of us try to be allies to each other, while remaining wildly ignorant of other Asian cultures that are different from our own—I knew all that. Yet I couldn't help feeling a gut punch of disappointment and responsibility. I should have realized her last name was "Li" and not "Na," or I should have considered it at least. Was I so American that the option didn't once enter my head?

After I processed my mistake overnight, I woke up and set my laptop on the writing desk of my motel room. An internet search for the roommate, Hilarie Dayton, finally yielded helpful results on the tenth page back. I confirmed she had moved up to Tacoma and would be too far to reach in person on this trip. Another dead end.

Several more articles from 2013, the year Sasha disappeared, popped up in my search results, using "Sasha Lee" as my keywords. Lunch came and went, thanks to a Korean BBQ truck parked on the corner, and then I migrated to the motel lobby's on-site business center. I printed out an article that mentioned Grace Huang, an old friend of Sasha's. A dozen Grace Huangs were still alive in the Bay Area, as far as I could tell, but I couldn't determine which one was interviewed by the *Eugene Horizon* all those years ago.

Frustrated, I added the printed page to the binder I had brought with me and slipped it into one of the clear plastic sheet protectors. The rest of the articles and reports and certain forum message threads were all those that I found compelling before I left San Diego.

In the same article, Francis Eriksen was identified as Lee's longtime boyfriend and the father of her child. Their relationship must have been the basis for the rumor that the Tilly's bookstore employee shared with me: a former coworker dated one of the Eriksens. Francis, as the bookstore Romeo, seems like the obvious Eriksen in Sasha's disappearance. Just to be sure, I did a Google sweep of those male family members with arrest records—histories of violence.

Francis was not unique, it turns out. Adult males in the Eriksen clan with arrest records, who would have been between the ages of twenty and forty-two during the year 2013, were Ephraim, Francis, and Zane—all siblings; Jimmy, another cousin; and a nephew, Shane. The other eligible man in that age range—a Cousin Rick—is currently in prison; with only online records at my disposal, it was impossible to confirm when his stint began. Once I finished, my binder on the Eriksens and Li Ming Na could barely close.

How was it covered up that one of the Eriksens—a family notorious in southern Oregon—dated a woman who then mysteriously disappeared? Wouldn't the local media go nuts, amplifying that angle of the story? *Another casualty of the Eriksen orbit?* But the article I found was the only one to link "Sasha Lee" with "Francis Eriksen."

I recalled the true crime forum posts that suggested Li Ming Na's boyfriend was ex-military, then Ashley's assertion that psychopaths are skilled manipulators. Was Francis Eriksen in good with law enforcement, despite his two misdemeanors? Someone could have been muzzling the rest of the media against including his name in their reports and pressuring police to omit him from the official case file. Those redacted portions were extensive. After finding the article, it seemed like Francis's name and Li's alias, "Sasha Lee," could be part of the blacked-out paragraphs.

The lieutenant governor of Oregon urged police to resolve Sasha's case quickly. How much did "resolve" equate to "ignore and archive without examining the Eriksens further"? Noting the scandal that this former state leader experienced the year prior, it was possible he was being manipulated—but by whom?

Ashley's voice popped into my brain then, from our conversation on the beach: *People like Li's boyfriend are everywhere . . . They're called psychopaths.*

Snowflakes continued to fall during my frenzied research, visible through the ground-floor window of the business center. When I emerged at dinnertime, the white dusting had all but evaporated.

———

Logging trucks barrel through the mountains, blaring their horns at my two-door sedan rental. I swerve to the slow lane, gripping the steering wheel tight. At only two hours into my six-hour drive through the woods, a headache shoots through my temples, driven by stress and shitty coffee from a gas station at the edge of Eugene. Tuesday-morning traffic heading east through black ice, pummeling wind corridors, and cloud coverage so thick it feels like nighttime challenges my previous admiration for Oregon's natural beauty. I could really use an Uber SUV right now.

According to the case file that I spent all yesterday studying instead of flying home, Li told friends at the animal shelter that she would be taking a weekend getaway with her boyfriend's family; she last used a credit card at a gas station out in the wilderness of Eastern Oregon, and booked a stay at the Horsefly Falls Resort. With nothing left to go on and an already-disappointed five-year-old at home in San Diego, I set off this morning to visit the scene of the crime.

Brake lights flash along the decline ahead, and I slow my speed. The road drops as a blind curve leers in front of me. Bright yellow signs warn to decelerate to thirty-five miles per hour, and my car begins to shake the more pressure I apply to the brakes of this cheap rental. I switch to the fast lane, praying no big rig appears in my rearview, then take the sharp turn as slowly as I can manage at fifty miles an hour. The smell of rubber shoots through my air vent, but I hug the mountain and manage to gain the straightaway without killing anyone.

My six-hour drive turns into seven due to icy road conditions and my own fear of slipping off into one of the many canyons that I pass. Twice I pull over just to catch my breath. The farther east I drive, the more inconsistent cell phone reception is—until I have zero bars of service. The Wi-Fi radio playing from my phone's Bluetooth cuts out. The only source of comfort to me now is my GPS, guiding me through the twisting forest landscape.

At last, I'm directed to exit. Tree branches litter the ground of the off-ramp, but none so large that I can't drive over or around them. I turn left, beneath the highway, and follow a two-lane road for seven miles.

A restaurant that I pass appears abandoned, with no cars parked out front or lights on within—strange, because a marquee along the side of the road advertises a Friday-night special, the date from three days ago visible in smaller block text. Someone would have changed the date recently. The owner was expecting customers.

Neon lights cut through the darkness setting in. Although it's not even five o'clock, night—or the illusion of it, thanks to thick fog creeping in from the valley beneath—has begun to fall.

A blinking sign flashes the words No Road Access Ahead. I keep driving another hundred feet. Then a gas station appears.

I pull over to park in front of the single-door entryway. Inside, a man stares at me from behind a display of cigarettes perched on the counter.

Bells jingle as I cross the threshold. "Hi. I'm heading to Horsefly Falls Resort. Is this the only gas station nearby?"

Sasha Lee's last credit card transactions were at a gas station and at the resort itself. If this was where she filled up her tank, someone here—the owner, if the property hasn't changed hands since then—might remember the investigation.

Brown liquid dribbles from the man's mouth. Tobacco chew. He wipes it with the back of his hand. Stains mark the collar of the white T-shirt he wears beneath a zippered sweater.

"This is it," he says. "We have a monopoly on all fill-ups this side of Route Twenty, normally."

"Why 'normally'? Has something happened to disrupt that?"

The man lifts both sandy-colored eyebrows. He chuckles, his cheeks ruddy despite the warmth of the store heat. "You tell me."

I follow his gaze past my shoulder. The fog remains thick, and even more opaque from inside a brightly lit convenience store. Then the fog lessens. Shifts. Shapes become clearer.

A landslide the height of an RV blocks the road entirely. Tree debris, earth, rocks, sticks, and mud all cake the road to form a barrier that no rental sedan or even a school bus could move on its own.

I turn back to the store clerk, speechless.

"Pretty bad for folks out here, trying to get from point A to point B, right? Well, from what I understand, there's a family retreat going on up the mountain at the resort. They're all stuck there, with the resort employees who haven't jumped ship and walked the two miles down."

The clerk lifts a white metal mug from the counter, then spits into it. "Going on five days now, they've been trapped."

A family retreat, ten years after the last weekend getaway that Sasha Lee attended with Francis Eriksen? There's no telling who's up there now, but I've come too far to turn back without seeing this resort for myself. The family might even be happy to see a new face.

I scan the wall behind the clerk until I find the items I need. "I'll take a can of bear spray. And two water bottles. And a fill on pump number one."

Both eyebrows disappear beneath his baseball cap. "Coming right up."

42

OLIVIA

From the window of the sports hut, whose old front door luckily wasn't locked by either electronic or physical key, I note the layer of frost hugging the pine needles littering the ground outside. Repeating to myself the events of yesterday and the weekend does little to reassure me—they all happened, no matter how horrific: two of my family members were killed; each death was staged to make me look responsible.

Bringing Howard all the way out here was a mistake—wherever he is. It was too cold, too dark, and felt too dangerous to go traipsing around looking for him last night after capture the flag. Does that make me a terrible fiancée? What does that say about me, if he spent his night searching for me while I huddled inside a conference room? I can only wonder if he went peering into dirty windows and spied the same scene I did.

After I saw Shane and Marla together, I tried to digest what I had just witnessed: Shane and Marla are lovers.

Moments I've observed between them surged forward. Marla coaching Shane at the archery session, their whispered conversation, them eating together during most meals, both Marla and Shane agreeing to stay behind to guard Team B's flag alone. How long has this been going on? Depending on when their relationship began, this could have affected Shane in dozens of different emotional and mental outcomes— not the least of which is dissociation.

I run a hand down my face, safe and warm behind a barricade of sporting equipment that I shoved against the cabin's door. Considering Marla is only a year older and Shane probably has twenty pounds of muscle on her, I shouldn't assume she initiated it. But they're twenty-nine and thirty years old now. Do they have the right to be with whomever they choose?

The more I observe of Shane's behavior, the more he fits the bill of a psychopath: self-absorbed, unconcerned with social conventions, deferential only to consequences that might hamper his plans. Typically, psychopaths view relationships in terms of utility—what they offer to the psychopathic person. It makes sense that Shane would engage with Marla, since she's a successful lawyer who has probably given him free legal advice over the years. I don't know what would motivate Marla to jeopardize her career for him.

My stomach churns beneath my rib cage. Anxiety and hunger melding into one. I inhale through my nostrils, anxious to stop another asthma attack before it begins. I found my inhaler at the bottom of my handbag, trapped between the lining and the exterior shell, but I know I should conserve the medicine. The night ahead may be long. The smell of dirt and grass lodged in various athletic accessories reminds me I'm alone and removed from my relatives. The scents ground me, pulling me back to reality.

Today is still Monday. Depending on how bad the next storm is, maybe the police, the fire department, the mountain rangers can come tomorrow and rescue those of us left—the ones who have escaped Shane's murderous rampage.

Why would he kill Alfred? My great-uncle David said that Shane was soaked up to the knee the night that Alfred drowned in the lake. Why else would Shane be wading into a pool of water except if he were involved somehow in our cousin's death? Marla insisted she was with Shane all night, swearing he wasn't part of any attack on Alfred—but she's been lying about more than I ever realized. Is David telling the truth, then?

I can't just stay here, waiting. Shane is not Alfred's obvious killer—I am, if the first note I found tucked into his pocket is to be believed. I need to keep searching for answers.

Another less paranoid part of me recalls the mystery Jimmy was referencing on the trail yesterday. What did our family leave behind during the last retreat?

The metal bars of the soccer net scrape against the wooden floor of the sports hut as I push it aside, straining the jeans I chose for traipsing around the mountainside yesterday. Metal framing and mesh shelves remain from the days when this resort was merely a campground and this building was a cabin. Six beds would fit comfortably in this layout. Was the sports hut in operation ten years ago, when I was last here as a thirteen-year-old? Or was this place a cabin then? My memories of that weekend are sunny and carefree until cousin Rick's crime directly after.

I step outside. Moonlight washes the meadow in a white glow. A rush of cold air snakes beneath my vest and through the buttons of my black plaid shirt. I sling my handbag and my bag of supplies higher across my chest, then walk toward the forest. One of the trailheads ends somewhere on this side of the property.

Heavy gray clouds line the sky. More rain is on the way. With an eye toward the ground for uneven surfaces or gopher holes that might cause me a twisted ankle like poor Denny, I march as quietly as I can manage with two bags bouncing at my hip.

I take the first distinct path that leads up the mountain and pass a patch of white flowers. Frost covers the pointed leaves—either poison hemlock or Queen Anne's lace. Why didn't I pay more attention to that lesson? Where is that retired Navy SEAL instructor now?

A branch cracks to my left, up the hillside, and I freeze in place. Shane?

I count my breaths—*one, two, three, four*—working to maintain a decent rhythm. Then I continue forward, taking care to set each foot where it won't make a sound.

In my bag of supplies, the plastic packaging of the granola bars rubs together like steel wool, heightening my nerves. My muscles ache after another ten feet of the climb. A thick pine tree blocks the view of the valley down below, and after another look around, I slip the reusable bag over my head and into a pocket of upturned tree roots. Once I get the lay of the land and understand how things have evolved (devolved, more likely) during the last twenty-four hours, I'll grab it on my way back to the sports hut.

Up the path, a tight switchback careens along a steep incline of the mountain's face. I scan the ground for muddy patches in the moonlight, fearful of losing my balance.

A shadow lies motionless on the trail ahead. I pause. Take a tentative step forward. It doesn't move. As I creep closer, the shape of an animal becomes clear—a raccoon, dead and surrounded by a black pool of liquid. Blood.

"Olivia." My great-aunt Lois crouches behind a bush along the next turn. She rises to her feet. Dirt covers her pale cheeks, her ash-blonde hair wild with leaves and bark entangled within. She wields a steak knife.

"Don't move," she says.

My face blanches. She heard the rumors and believes them. "Lois, put the knife down. I didn't hurt Alfred or Uma, I swear."

I raise both hands palms forward. For a quick second, I falter and step an inch down the hill.

"Olivia!" Lois whisper shouts. "I mean it, don't move."

"But I'm trying not to . . . I just—"

Lois surges forward with a speed and agility I wouldn't have thought possible. She pauses not three feet from me. "Shit," she breathes.

"What?" My heart racing, I search her face for aggression—some sign she's going to use the knife to stab me through the chest before I can muster a better defense than "I didn't do it."

Lois turns strained green eyes on me. "I don't remember where I put it."

"Put what?" I whisper.

"The snare." She darts her gaze at our feet. Her face crumples. "It was just here."

When I first arrived at the edible-plants session, Lois was working some braided reeds, tying them with an elaborate slipknot. I search the ground for something similar beneath the encroaching vines and black earth. If the snare is nearby, thin tree roots are the perfect camouflage.

A sob bursts from Lois's mouth. "Where have you been?" she asks me, pointedly. "Last night was hell on earth, and you turn up now looking clean and showered."

"Come closer and you'll learn I'm definitely not showered."

"Jacquie is dead." Her voice breaks. "Your great-aunt Jacquie didn't make it through the night. She thought that someone was watching us from the woods—not Shane—so she went down the mountainside alone. Nearly got into it with Jimmy, who's been insisting our camp is the safest place right now. She never came back. Francis has disappeared, and so have Zane and Skye."

"How do you know Jacquie's dead? Did Shane do it?" I throw a wary eye at the knife Lois still holds, then the raccoon behind her. "Did Shane do that, or did . . . ?"

"Shane has been attacking anything that breathes, leaving surprises up and down the trail." Lois glares. "But Jacquie, we think it was hypothermia. We found her body. Jimmy is to blame for her death. If he hadn't held us up at the summit, raving about some family treasure left behind here, we would have gotten indoors before the power outage.

We could have been holed up in our rooms, with blankets and barricades against Shane. But then the snow started and it made more sense to stay where we were without knowing where he was. I haven't seen Shane since yesterday, when he snapped."

"So your snare was meant for Shane?"

Lois's jaw hardens. She throws me a new appraising look. "It's meant for anyone trying to harm me. I've already lived a life full of murder and betrayal from our family. I'm not subjecting either myself or my husband to that again."

"Okay. Have you seen Howard?"

Lois squints. "He's not with you?"

"I . . . No, he's not."

"He said he forgot something in his room and went back right before capture the flag started. What were you talking about—Alfred and Uma?"

"Me? I didn't. I was asking about Howard."

She peers at me, unwavering. "No, when you first walked up here. You said you didn't hurt Alfred or Uma. What happened to Uma?"

The ground seems uneven beneath my feet. "She's . . . she was found dead."

"What?" Lois's face crumples. "What happened to her? Who thinks you killed them?" Emotion twists her mouth as she stares into a copse of tall shrubs. "Coral thinks you had something to do with Alfred's death. Now her mother is dead."

"I didn't hurt either of them, I swear."

She reaches for me and I smack her hand away, sending her off-balance. Lois jerks backward, her feet swept out from under her, and she lands hard on the ground. Deep-belly grunts burst from her throat, like an animal clawing her chest. The woven snare she made bites the skin at her ankle.

"Are you okay? I didn't mean to—" I try to help Lois up, but she recoils.

"You . . . you did this. You . . . wanted me to get hurt too. Coral was right. What they're all saying about you is true, Olivia." She whispers, struggling to speak, but her meaning is clear. My relatives have turned against me. Have they done something to Howard—are they using him as bait somewhere to lure me closer? Waiting for me to come searching for him so they can ensnare me too?

Voices clamor from above. "Lois! You okay?"

"I'm over here!" Lois shouts, finding her voice. "She's here! Olivia's here!"

I take off running. Leaves and branches slash at my arms and legs as I sprint down the trail, narrowly missing tree roots meant to twist my ankle.

More shouting follows, but I don't pause to listen for footsteps. I don't pause for anything—not searching for Howard. Not my bag of food. Or the sound of the real killer hurtling down the mountain after me.

———

The door to the sports hut is as I left it, and I slide inside with a yank of the handle. Whirling, I grab the goal net, the bin of sports equipment, and the chest of baseballs, then stack them to bar the entrance. My barricade restored, I cross to beneath the window beside a rusted bed frame built into the wall.

Moonlight pierces the cloud cover outside as the gray masses shift overhead. Long shadows stretch from fir trees across the meadow. The forest's ghosts seem to reach toward me, as if cursing how I escaped their grasp.

I sink to the floor. The wood groans beneath my weight as my heartbeat slows, as I process how badly public opinion has turned against me.

Now that I've spent hours inside the sports hut, I do remember these stout converted buildings from the last retreat. But they were cabins for sleeping then, weren't they? And before? Were these structures present back when the pork loin dinner was being served during the 1930s?

I find a comfortable position, leaning against the wall. The floor protests again. No, a single squeaky board.

Leaning to the left, then right, I find the one that first cried out. It's been plied, manipulated. It's warped and curling upward at an edge. Crossing the hut, I grab a hockey stick from the corner, beside a plastic crate of golf balls. Jamming the stick into the negative space between the board and the wall takes a few tries. Then the board groans, giving way by a centimeter.

There's something underneath. A dull red color.

The back of my neck tingles. I cast an eye around the room and confirm I'm surrounded by old athletic equipment. My obstacle course that blocks the door appears sturdy.

I reach into the dark space between the floor and the foundation of the old building. I fumble around in the thick dust and dirt, unsure of what I'm even looking for. Then I touch paper. Nudging the object around allows me to grasp it with forefinger and thumb until I can bring it forward. It's a book.

A journal.

The first entry is upbeat. Then the writing—and intimate confessions—become sporadic, its author not appearing to hold themselves to a consistent routine. She's a woman, at least. I skim a few pages. She doesn't come off as happy, but maybe that's the postpartum depression speaking—she had a baby toward the end.

"Aunt Sasha?" I mumble out loud. Kyla's mother, Sasha Lee, was always thought to have run away from her daughter and my uncle Francis for some modeling career. How long has this journal been here? Pressing my fingers to the lined pages, I know I need to read each entry to find out.

I reach back beneath the floorboards and touch something else. Delicate fabric. Lace. Or straw. I give a light tug, and the material releases into my palm. I pull my hand out and up to the slanted light of the window—it looks like dark, coarse string. I peer down into the floor space at a different angle. A bulbous, smooth white skull returns my gaze farther within, remnants of black human hair covering the surface in patches. A skeleton.

I jump to my feet. Human hair tangles with my fingertips, and I slap and wipe it on my jeans, on the old office chair, on a basket of Wiffle balls. My chest constricts, my muscles tense, poised for a fight with the dead, and I trip over a baseball bat propped against another box as I scramble to the door.

When I reach the soccer goal net that I used as the foundation for my barricade, I pause. Jimmy was ranting about something valuable being left behind after the last Eriksen family retreat. Was it this journal? Or this body?

"Who buried you here?" I whisper to the corpse beneath me. With everything going on in the forest and the resort, I wonder if I am first to locate it now.

I take a slow step back to the mesh wire bed frame. Cast an eye at the red leather book lying closed now. Its author must be Sasha. She didn't escape to Europe, far from Francis's controlling grasp—she was killed.

Cold air rises from the foundation of the sports hut to twine my neck. Whoever killed Sasha had no intention of her or her words ever being discovered.

And now I've positioned myself beside yet another dead relative, doing the killer's work for them.

43

Olivia

Tuesday

I don't sleep the whole night. Despite desiring as much space as possible between myself and this cadaver, I was riveted by Sasha's journal. The mystery of who placed her here, who killed her, must be found in its pages. I read as much as I could before complete darkness took hold in the sports hut.

Early on, Sasha was excited in her journal entries. When she begins spending more time with her Tall, Dark, and Improving boyfriend and his family, that's when things take a turn. The way Teddy dismisses her concerns in favor of his family's comfort seems to dim the energy this woman had. Seeing my relatives' names in this journal, the identity of the boyfriend seems obvious: my uncle Francis.

I recognize certain facts that have been shared with me over the years, such as that they met in Eugene. But I always thought their meet-cute was when Uma insisted Francis visit a new herbal-remedy clinic in town that specialized in relieving back pain after an old injury was acting up from when he was in the marines. Sasha was an employee there at the time—not any bookstore, I don't think.

I stare past the grimy windowpane of the sports hut. Faint sunrays, visible earlier in the center of the sky, have long since disappeared. A crow flies overhead, weaving above and below a gray blanket of clouds.

If the person buried beneath me is Sasha Lee, my uncle Francis's girlfriend, then the callous baby mentioned in the journal must be Kyla, my younger cousin. Does she know that her mother never left the resort and didn't abandon her? Has Kyla been manipulating everyone into thinking she's some helpless pity case ever since?

There's a scratch at the door. A knock. "Olivia? Are you in there?" a woman's voice whispers through the thick wooden panel.

I don't move from where I'm seated on the office chair. No one followed me when I ducked back inside yesterday. The voice doesn't belong to Skye, and I can't imagine Coral would desire to partner with me to get out of this hellhole. The woman doesn't have the smoky voice of Felicity, who should still be hunkered down in Uma's room, too fearful of me to approach now. That leaves Marla.

"Olivia, I need to talk to you. I've looked for you everywhere, and Shane thinks you're in here."

Shit. If they know I'm here—if Shane is still in some fugue state—the last place I want to be is this converted cabin. God knows I'd prefer to be miles away from *another* dead body.

"Olivia." The voice pauses. The handle slides down, but the door isn't forced inward. "Shane isn't well. I need to get him help. The others are talking about tracking him down and tying him up—even his dad, Vic. Will you help me? If they get Shane, they'll come for you next."

I stare at the crack beneath the doorway, the sliver of light that keeps this place from being considered warm. "Come to the side," I say. I stash the journal in my handbag, then ensure the loose floorboard is tucked back in place.

"What? Olivia?"

"Come to the window on the side of the building." I rise from the chair as her footsteps crunch along pine needles leading away from the door. Her face appears in the square frame seconds later. She lifts a hand to shield her eyes, the better to see inside. When she spots me, her hopeful expression shifts to a frown.

"I should have known," she says. "While everyone else is fighting for warmth and food, you're nice and dry indoors."

I step closer to the smudged windowpane. Marla looks to me just as well rested as she's accusing me of being—and I know why she might seem more relaxed. "Why are you fighting for food? Just go into the dining hall. That should be unlocked like the main lodge, right? And Shane is probably allowing you to do whatever you want."

Marla makes another face. "The food is spoiling, genius. There hasn't been electricity for close to forty-eight hours, even if Shane were letting me come and go as I please—but why do you think that?"

"Why do you think the others will come for me after they catch him? Why should I step out and trust you?"

She pauses a moment. Peers past my shoulder to the two baseball bats I've taken to calling Pedro and Babe. "They think you killed Alfred and Uma. Edgar, Lois, David, Jimmy, Vic. Once Shane tells them where you are, they'll come for you."

"Do you think I killed anyone?"

Marla purses her lips. "No. But the police are still MIA, and now I'm starting to think the property manager never even contacted them. I think the family is interested in finding Jimmy's lost trinket or whatever, but they'll settle for tracking you down as the killer."

My stomach grumbles. I don't trust Marla. But I also left my bag of supplies out in the forest. I've nearly finished my water, and the apple and remaining granola bars that I kept in the hut are dwindling fast. "Why are you warning me? What do you want?"

Marla hesitates. "There's been more violence than anyone could have guessed this weekend. I don't want a new casualty that could have been avoided."

Casting another eye at my youngest aunt, at the sincere worry she wears, I'm tempted to believe her. And what she's saying does have some sense to it: if the group catches Shane, suddenly I'll become the biggest threat on the property. "Fine. I'm going to get some food."

She stands back as I work the window open. She watches me climb forward but doesn't offer a hand. "Didn't you hear me? The food's gone bad."

I exit the cabin wearing my handbag across my chest, with a baseball bat in hand. If I'm going to step outside my barricade, to willingly join Marla, Pedro is coming with me. I scan the meadow before me. No sight of anyone. No Shane. No sign that the area's nocturnal animals are beginning to stir.

We cross the property to the dining hall, with me watching the fields for movement. Marla appears so at ease she could be on a Sunday stroll.

Inside the industrial kitchen, stainless steel surfaces appear dull beneath the sole window. A burlap bag lies overturned on the gray tile floor, wilting celery poking its leafy head from within. Half-empty, open jugs of spoiled milk, coffee creamer, and quarts of yogurt cover the island counter in front of the recessed refrigerator—all rotten, from the smell of things. An open metal shelf that I last saw stacked with grains—loaves of bread, muffins, bagels, dinner rolls—and fruits is picked clean. Not a trace of sesame seed left behind.

"Didn't believe me, did you?" Marla gloats from over my shoulder.

I reach for the walk-in fridge handle, determined to find something salvageable to eat.

"No, don't do that—"

Stale air rushes my nostrils—amplified by the stench of death. The shelves are far from barren, instead holding more containers of rotten, fully perished food. On the floor of the walk-in fridge, a body is wrapped in a hotel coverlet normally found on the foot of a bed.

My stomach turns. I creep closer, allowing the light from the open door to guide me. Someone else died, and I don't think this body is

Jacquie's. Was this the work of the storm, Shane, or that person who is so bent on targeting me?

The body wears black nonslip sneakers. Using Pedro the baseball bat, I lift the bottom of the blanket to reveal tailored khakis. I lower myself to the ground, conscious of being close to yet another corpse—closer than I ever imagined while back in the safety of the psychology building. My breath hitches. I spare a second to worry that an asthma attack might strike.

With shaking fingertips, I reach for the top of the blanket, then pull down. A constellation of freckles dots a square forehead. Xavier the property manager.

Unwrapping the blanket reveals open black eyes, the pupils fully dilated, and a mouth slack-jawed. Shivers twirl up my spine staring into the face of a dead man; I'm unable to look away. Grim fascination pulls me forward another inch. A whiff of the sharp cologne he wore stings my nose.

I sit back on my heels, breathless. Why did I just do that? Why didn't I do that with Alfred or Uma—or did I? Maybe this twisted magnetism that I feel when I'm so close to death is the result of my warped mindset this weekend; I simply didn't recognize it until now.

Who did Xavier offend? Someone attacked two of my family members, then attacked a resort employee who has probably never met anyone here before, except for Zane. Zane has been clear in his hope that we would embody a functioning family this weekend—something entirely foreign to the Eriksens. I don't see how a nonrelative could have affected that goal.

If Xavier was killed before Uma, when I know she was alive sometime late Friday night, his attacker could have taken his keys, cards, and identification—even the master key that Xavier no doubt wields as the property manager, which allows its user to access any door on the resort. His attacker must have used the master key to place Uma in my room.

I step back into the kitchen, shutting the door behind me.

Marla lifts an eyebrow, standing at the entrance. "Did you find what you were looking for?"

I swallow back bile. "Have you seen anyone? Did anyone follow us?"

"No. But I haven't checked."

"Because you think I'm the killer? That I attacked Alfred, Uma, and the property manager? Or you're just looking for some way to clear Shane's name?"

Marla crosses her arms. "Why would I want that?"

I take in Marla's suspicion, the scowl baiting me to reveal that I know their secret. Her lover-slash-nephew is struggling with his grip on reality and was last seen waving a butcher knife like it was a canoe oar. The last thing I need is for Marla to sic Shane on me.

"No clue," I reply. "I'm only reeling. Trying to digest what I just saw."

Marla softens. "This is crazy. This whole thing is otherworldly right now."

"Don't you have some police connection you can call to get us out of here? As a lawyer, don't you have some law enforcement contacts on speed dial?"

She shakes her head. "I am a litigator. But I handle mergers and acquisitions, Olivia, not criminal law. And the landlines are still down."

Part of me hoped Marla somehow had kept her cell phone hidden from Zane—the tiny part of me that still hopes Howard is alive. "Well, where are the others? I heard that Jacquie died in the night," I add, speaking softly.

Marla nods, tossing the strawberry-blonde curls that frame her face. "They're scattered in the woods."

"How, though? We learned next to nothing during the survival session—" Shouts come from outside. Marla and I barrel out of the kitchen, then rush to the window. David dances in the meadow beneath the twilight, far more spry than I've seen him this whole weekend. He twitches his body, jumping first left, then right, then sprinting another ten feet before dropping to the ground, where he disappears in the tall grass.

"What is he doing?" she asks over my shoulder. "It just finished raining again, and the grass is still slippery."

David pops his head up, scanning side to side. Then he breaks into a sprint, far faster than he should be capable of going at his age.

Suddenly, an object flies from the forest's wall of green, and he jumps as if the grass reached up to grab him. He continues pounding his feet forward, then stumbles—a gopher hole. His limbs flail as he struggles to stand again; then another object surges from the trees.

"Is that . . . a bird?"

Marla grunts. "I've never seen one move that fast."

David lunges to the left like a running back giving it his all on the field, narrowly avoiding another object. He high-steps another ten feet.

The movement of the object is almost like a slow-going bullet. I recognize the quick way the object slices through the air, faster than a ball, and has David spinning like a marionette. An arrow.

Another arrow pierces the meadow's perimeter, striking David in the chest. I gasp. The impact counters his forward momentum, and he stills, upright, before collapsing to the earth.

Marla bites back a sob. "He saw me and Shane together the first night, making love on the dock by the lake. Shane thinks that David has to go, just like Jacquie did after she spotted us kissing in the woods. Being caught with me is what triggered Shane."

I whirl to face my youngest aunt. She's admitting it—that she and her nephew are lovers, and that she's conspiring with Shane to kill our relatives. I tense all over, no longer sure what she wants from me. Not to help me, despite what she said by the sports hut.

When David suggested Shane might have attacked Alfred, he must have wanted to direct attention to Shane—though not directly reveal Marla and Shane's affair.

"That's Shane out there?" I ask. "With the bow and arrow from our archery session?"

"Sharpened arrows, yes. I told him not to—I tried—"

"But I thought Jacquie died from hypothermia," I add, backing away from Marla, moving toward the kitchen. A knife was sitting on a pile of dirty plates. I don't know if I have it in me to attack a relative, but I don't want to be harmed by one. Marla is admitting everything. By telling me this, she's marking me next on Shane's list. I jerk the baseball bat in front of me, between me and Marla.

She only nods, matching my steps backward with her own forward. "Jacquie did die from hypothermia. Because Shane wouldn't let her keep the jacket she had. Shane pushed her into the lake to make sure she wouldn't warm up while still outdoors. He's got a gun, Olivia. Took it from Jacquie, who's always thinking someone might attack her and so brought it along."

The dining hall is empty save for tables and chairs aligned with the walls, offering a clear escape route to the only exit. But I know I wouldn't make it in time, not with Marla on my heels. And once in the fresh air, who's to say Shane won't come charging into the meadow with his mercenary's arrows—with his gun?

I continue my retreat until my hand touches the wooden panel of the kitchen door. "So you killed the two people who knew your secret. I never saw anything."

Marla grabs the bat from me, yanking it free. Her face crumples. "Didn't you? Or were you too focused on the ceramics wheel to watch us in the arts and crafts building last night?"

"Give me the bat."

"No, Olivia."

I yank open the wooden door, then reach inside and grasp the knife where I last saw it. Sharp pain pierces my flesh as I grab the blade first. I find the handle, then stab it toward Marla.

She hasn't moved. "I don't want to hurt you, Olivia. Shane has lost it. He's . . . he's scaring me. I'm an attorney, and my career could be ruined if our relationship comes out, and all he's doing is shining a spotlight on us. You have to believe me. You're the only one out here who understands psychology, who can help him, and he says he doesn't remember attacking anyone, or that he feels like he was watching someone else do those things, and I . . . I don't know what else to do."

Her eyes dart to my shaking hand. Blood drips onto the floor beneath me, adrenaline pulsing in my arms. I edge around her, farther into the dining hall.

"Shane is dissociated," I say. "I think that's obvious. But why are you protecting him? Why are you . . . involved with him?"

Dissociation does not necessarily lead to violence. Usually, if someone breaks with reality, like what Marla is describing, they're in some kind of fugue state or depersonalization that leads to more confusion once the episode ends—not bloodshed. Shane seems to shift between awareness and total ignorance of his actions, but I wonder how much of this he's actually enjoying. Given his history of hunting, how much of the weekend's events should be linked to a dissociative episode?

Marla fixes me with glossy eyes. "Why do you think, Olivia? I love him. I've always loved him. Even when he's asked me to do things I'd rather not—BDSM, role-playing with animal costumes, you name it. I can't say no to him."

Disgust should be my first response to such a confession. Pity. Incest of any form is incredibly damaging psychologically. Instead, I take in Marla's earnest expression, the mixture of shame and defiance that stills her face, and I let my shoulders fall. Marla, at least, isn't going to attack me. "Okay. Yes, I saw you together. And I'm not going to tell anyone about you."

I continue backing toward the exit. "Not yet anyway. But if you come for me before the police arrive or try to pin any more murders on me, then you can bet your stellar legal career that I will spread the word faster than you can say 'viral.' Now, get in the kitchen."

"What do you mean, 'pin murders on you'?"

There's no time to argue, not with Shane lurking outdoors. My only priority now is to clear my own name—and I doubt I can do that with Marla following me. Despite what she thinks, I can't help Shane. "Get in. Now!"

I direct her with the knife until she stands, hesitating, before the door. With another poke as motivation, she retreats along the white tile into the kitchen with my baseball bat.

The king's table is set and ready to host another dysfunctional family dinner, left over from Saturday night. Shoving it forward, I drag it across the kitchen doorway, blocking Marla inside.

My palm throbs where I gripped the knife's blade. As I march up the aisle toward the exit, I snatch a cloth napkin from a place setting and press it to my flesh.

The air is humid outside. As if a new round of rainfall is about to descend on this miserable property. I scan the meadow where David remains, dead or close to it at this point, and likely still under close watch by Shane from the woods.

Marla seemed sincere in her love of Shane and fear of the impending doom on her career. But while she may not have hurt me herself, I'm sure Shane would tie up my loose end in a hurry.

Dark clouds unfurl across the evening sky, shielding me from the moon's intrusive spotlight. Although I won't be crossing the meadow to reach the forest anytime soon, Marla shared an important piece of information in between confessions: everyone was accounted for as of this morning.

Edgar may still be alive. He's had a front seat to the deranged minds of our family since his own childhood and might know more about Sasha's death at this resort than he cares to admit. Recalling Jimmy's desire to speak with Edgar—back when capture the flag was the only cat and mouse game we were playing—I know I'm not the only person to suspect it.

44

OLIVIA

I avoid the sports hut, despite the hunger pangs churning my stomach for the final apple that I hid at the bottom of a bin. Shane is up to speed about my location, and I don't want to be trapped in there with a busted hand—not for a second.

The luxury hotel wing is a dead end. It's locked from the outside.

Red has soaked four inches of the cloth napkin that I tied tight across my palm. But the knot I made holds.

Darting to the ancient conifer that shields the sports hut, I survey the open field. Thick fog in the distance hides the mountain range.

I clutch my handbag along my body. The grass is tall here, slick with rain. A branch snaps from behind the wall of green somewhere to my right, but I continue forward, sprinting fast and lifting my knees high. Marla might be loose from the kitchen by now. She'll tell Shane that I know of their relationship as soon as she's able to find him.

I follow the trail up the initial steep incline and beneath a canopy of trees. A bird whistles a song, low and sweet. The sound is quickly imitated by another, then another. It feels like years ago that Kyla first suggested our team communicate by birdsong, instead of two days ago.

A half mile later, I reach the flag headquarters for my team. The clearing is empty but for the flag still waving high at the top of the ladder. Alfred, Uma, Jacquie, and now David are all dead, along with the property manager, Xavier. Where would the rest of us be hiding?

A chill lingers at this elevation, though the frost has melted away. I reach into my handbag, searching for my nearly empty water bottle, when I hear it: the sound of running water. A creek bed or pool of rainwater nearby. If I were a survivor of two nights fearing for my life against Shane and the elements, I'd need something to drink.

I follow a dirt path I didn't see during the five minutes I spent in this clearing on Sunday, deep into a shallow tunnel of branches. The route seems to end in a pile of leaves knocked free from adjacent trees and swirled around with each successive windstorm. I crunch forward, saying goodbye to any advantage of surprise. The air is thick within this foliage cave.

My feet catch on a rock, and I lurch forward, grabbing a tree trunk with my sliced palm. Pain sears my skin as peeling bark stabs my wound.

I stumble forward. Branches lift higher above my head, giving way to a small riverbank. Clear water gurgles along a narrow channel. The water is ice cold when I lean down to fill my bottle.

"Look who's come to visit." Grandpa Edgar peers at me from the opposite side of the creek. His deep frown emphasizes the loose skin around his jaw. The gray winter sweater I last saw him in is torn at the elbows, and mud cakes the knees and shins of his khakis.

"Grandpa," I say, getting to my feet. "Where are the others?"

"I don't think they want you to know."

I stare at my grandfather, absorbing the most clearheaded response he's offered since I arrived to the resort. At least he doesn't think I'm his long-dead wife. "You recognize me?"

Edgar is stoic. "How could I forget that face? That voice that's been calling me for months now."

Chills crawl along my skin like a platoon of ants. "So you listened to my messages."

"Not all of them."

"Okay, you're . . . mad at me?"

"Not mad, Olivia. Wary. I didn't want to believe it, of course. But the others say that you've been behind the violence this weekend, and you haven't exactly been around to disprove them. I've lived close to that kind of personality for too much of my life."

"Who is saying that about me? Is it Coral? Lois? Were you avoiding me then, when I wanted to interview you?" Disbelief wars with anger inside me, recalling how earnest I'd tried to sound on those calls.

"Jimmy, Lois, Francis, Coral. Especially Coral. We've been talking, in between staying warm and keeping watch for Shane, and we all agree you seem to have been close to each victim. You were one of the last of us to speak to Alfred, and apparently Uma was found dead in your hotel room closet. Coral managed to speak to Denny through the window of the resort, where he's staying now." Edgar turns his head, as if listening to another conversation. Someone whispering.

A bird whistles a high two-note song. My relatives are communicating, just like Kyla wanted.

Realization dawns on me in a cold wave. "You were faking it earlier. When you called me Grandma Yvette by the watercolors session. You've been completely in charge of your faculties this whole time."

Edgar furrows his heavy brow. "My dear, how do you think I've managed to survive this long when surrounded by family such as ours?"

Something moves in the brush behind me, but I don't turn around. Edgar maintains eye contact.

"So all this time," I begin. "You simply didn't want to discuss your memories. Your firsthand recollections."

My grandfather nods as a beam of moonlight shifts to his cheeks. "It doesn't do to dwell on evil, Olivia. There's darkness to our family line, and the ones who enjoy it get what's coming to them. The rest of us must cut them off. Keep those relatives as far away as possible once we learn who they really are."

"You mean your older brother, Calder Saffron, and your father."

"Not only them, Olivia. Other family members have been just as bad but are much better at hiding their . . . proclivities."

"Like who?"

Edgar purses thin lips. He rubs dirt from his whiskered cheeks. "There are the obvious ones, you know. The ones the news outlets would gladly do an hour-long special on, but whom we've done our best to keep off the public radar."

"We?"

"The family, Olivia. With genes as dubious as ours, we have to protect our own—at least, the kin who don't indulge in the Eriksen twitch."

He turns and climbs to the ledge behind him, up where I heard whispering.

"Aren't you going to invite me to come with you?" I ask. "Doesn't Jimmy want to interrogate me about the lost treasure left behind last time?"

I haven't breathed a word of my discovery in the sports hut. Whoever buried the body there would not want me disclosing their secret, and I'm not ready yet to reveal my leverage. Still, now I wonder whether Jimmy is merely baiting the rest of us—whether he's the assailant who put poor Sasha beneath the floorboards, or if it was someone else. My uncle Francis.

Edgar looks at me from over his shoulder. The memory of sitting on his knee and of him tickling me, my young laughter filling the room, returns to me with a sharp pang. Of regret? Disappointment?

He draws his eyebrows together. "There is no treasure, Olivia. The only thing we left behind was a broken poker table and trashed cabins that caused the previous owners to ban us from the property. It's only because Zane bought the place that we can come back. But I'll let Jimmy know you're around the mountain today."

"Have you seen Howard?"

Edgar doesn't reply.

"We're engaged, you know. Howard is my fiancé." Speaking aloud the words that I've been avoiding the entire weekend should feel liberating. Instead, they sound hollow in the forest, without the person I'm supposed to be marrying by my side.

At my confession, Edgar pauses. "Are you proud of yourself, then? You fooled someone new."

He withdraws farther into the foliage.

"Any word from the police?" I shout to his back. Edgar lifts a hand without turning; then branches cover his path.

Bubbling fresh water fills the space, cacophonous.

Any hope of writing a compelling dissertation, one that might be published after I graduate, is long gone. My goal of uncovering who killed Alfred and Uma—and who was trying to make it look like I attacked them both—and now Xavier, is laughable in the shadowy coverage of Malheur Forest. All signs continue to point to me for those initial deaths, even as Shane seems to vie for second place in the race toward prison.

Edgar's casual words boomerang in my ears. *There are the obvious ones, you know. The ones the news outlets would gladly do an hour-long special on, but whom we've done our best to keep off the public radar.*

Zane, of course. The megalomaniac surgeon with a god complex whose psychopathic tendencies could be featured in undergrad courses. Who else would be so "obvious"?

Shane. Although, prior to this weekend retreat, I had never heard of him having more than brief and ultimately harmless run-ins with the law. Aside from Marla's admission during the archery session, Shane's unhealthy interest in shooting and animals was a blip on the conversation radar when I was at family functions. I had my own suspicions of Shane, definitely. But they weren't truly piqued until Great-Uncle David approached me in the meadow for an impromptu therapy session. What did he say? *Shane's pants were wet. They were wet up to the knees. And then poor Alfred was found the next morning, drowned.*

If Marla is telling the truth, that Shane didn't kill Alfred, why would David lie about seeing him soaked? Especially if what he had actually witnessed was Shane and Marla together on the dock.

He said something else: *Our son, Rick, just got out of prison on early release.* My dad's cousin. I have vague memories of a lanky thirtysomething who kept to himself before he was convicted of a robbery turned murder. David had shared with me the good news about Rick's release, and that Lois was on cloud nine about it.

There are the obvious ones, you know. Skye said that she hadn't invited Rick here because he was still in prison.

Birdsong twirls through the air, three notes creating a cyclical melody. I always wished I could whistle. Ten years ago, at the last retreat, Rick tried to teach me and failed. I realized then I didn't have that talent. I followed Rick everywhere, reveling in his ability. I thought it hypnotizing, and I was jealous that I would never have such a skill.

Turning toward the consistent notes, I begin to follow the creek bed. Up it climbs, past the trail I walked on early Sunday evening, and above the secondary trail that I spied from my position on the hillside, clinging to the vines. The footpath continues before disappearing over a summit to slope downward.

Tendrils of smoke rise from an abandoned campfire, tucked inside the off-the-path enclosure, the gray plumes trapped by thick branches above. Below, a break in the trees affords a view of the open meadow east of the dining hall, but otherwise I can't see the yoga center or the main lodge. Someone has been camping at the very edge of the resort's property.

I stare at the pair of trees forming an X. The urge to crawl beneath them, to swing from their leaning trunks, swells in my chest. I've been here before. I listened to Rick whistling here.

Someone whistles still.

A voice rings out overhead: "There you are, Olivia."

From the ridge, a man peers down at me, triumph written across his lined face. Hair that I remember as blond appears brown beneath the dark clouds. My father's cousin glares at me with black eyes.

"Rick. Why are you out here?" I ask, fearing the answer.

A sneer lifts his mouth, revealing a chipped tooth. "Why, waiting for you, of course."

45

NEWS ARTICLE

The *Bend Herald*
August 12, 2013
By Willard Everett

DEVELOPING STORY—Local authorities have confirmed a shooting took place this afternoon in the Malheur National Forest. A man opened fire at a Gas N' Go service station off Route 20 a little after three o'clock, killing the store attendant after witnesses say he demanded cash from the register in "tens and twenties."

The suspect, identified as thirty-nine-year-old Richard "Rick" Wilton, is the nephew of Calder Saffron Eriksen, who was himself infamous for committing patricide in 1945, and the grandson of Einar Eriksen, whom authorities found to have tortured and murdered women in his home's basement.

Prior to being fired upon, the store attendant was able to alert local police to the situation by pressing a panic button. Witnesses say that Wilton appeared relaxed while robbing the gas station, using a 9mm handgun and wearing only a baseball cap and sunglasses to mask his identity.

Maritza Smythe, who had stopped in for gas on a road trip to Idaho, said the suspect seemed surprised when the gun discharged while the attendant was still gathering the store's cash. Smythe recounted that she was seated on the floor with her hands zip-tied in her lap, but she observed the suspect jump at the gunshot's loud noise. She said that when Wilton turned to face her and the other three hostages on the linoleum, he had a crazed look in his eye, as if he then meant to kill the rest of them too. "Instead of appearing panicked, this guy suddenly seemed bloodthirsty," Smythe recalled. "Like killing that guy triggered something in him."

Luckily, local rangers and a nearby police officer on extended patrol from Bend both arrived within seconds, answering the initial distress call that the attendant had the wherewithal to place.

After a brief standoff, Wilton was arrested. An attorney for the suspect has not yet been announced. Wilton may be remembered for setting fire to a local church ten years ago in Sun Valley.

This is a developing story. This page will be updated with more detail as it becomes available.

46

OLIVIA

A gust of wind whips through the branches at this height, sending a shiver down my backside beneath my vest. It was Rick. He's been stalking us this entire weekend—or maybe before? Why else would he have hidden himself away?

My thoughts reel as I try to process the facts. Rick is here, released from prison early just as David said. And now David is dead, shot through with an arrow.

"How long have you been waiting?" I ask.

"Since you've been down there with the comfort of central heating." He takes note of my widened stance, then smiles a yellow grin. "You don't have any food, do you? I haven't eaten since yesterday, and everything's gone rotten down below."

The years have thrown Rick into a blender, then poured him into the shape of what must have been a man. Whereas some ex-cons emerge from prison as sculpted frames of muscle, Rick gained a paunch around his midsection and a shaved head. A flock of birds is tattooed on his left temple in flattened letter v's, like distant cartoons. His shoulders strain the thin T-shirt he wears in what must be forty-degree weather, while sweat drips from his forehead. I haven't seen my dad's cousin since the last fateful retreat at this resort. Rick was arrested shortly thereafter for committing murder. I always wondered whether he regretted it. Judging from the frenzied look in his eye, the way he licks his chops like an animal, and how he's concealed his presence the whole weekend, I no longer have my doubts.

I shake my head. "You attacked Alfred. And Uma, didn't you? Are you and Shane trying to take out family members together?"

Rick shakes his head, bemused. "I gotta tell you, Olivia, I've thought about this moment for so long. You found me—at our spot. We played here last time, remember?"

"What are you talking about?" A memory flickers. Before it burns out just as quickly as it appears.

"Shane wouldn't know which hand to masturbate with if Marla didn't lay it all out for him," Rick adds. "Been that way since he was a kid, so there's no way he'd be able to pull off something as complex as this."

"As what?" I ask, growing impatient. Rain splashes the wide, flat leaves of the branch beside me.

"A revenge bid. Think about it. No one else other than me on this retreat roster could have gotten in and out after each kill undetected. Except for maybe you."

Rick tips an imaginary hat to me, and I sputter, "I'm—what do you mean?"

His face drops. "Have you managed to rationalize everything, then?"

"If you mean the games we played last time, that was all within the rules."

"Was it? Was tripping Sasha in the canoe and watching her knock her head on the dock considered sportsmanlike conduct?"

My chest constricts. Images of myself standing along the shoreline and staring at a bobbing object in the water return with blurred clarity. "That wasn't a body. That wasn't Sasha."

Rick narrows dark eyebrows. "It was."

"You're lying. You came here for revenge on Alfred, Uma, and myself for some reason. That's why you've been planting signs that point to me as the killer with each death. Only I don't know why you've been targeting me. And it's not because you and Sasha were so close and I supposedly killed her."

In saying the words, the feeling of déjà vu washes over me. Rain begins to pick up, dotting my vest in thick drops that roll down the polyester. *I didn't kill anyone.*

Rick sneers, his shirt now soaked through. Water runs down his cheeks, but he doesn't wipe his face. "It's because of you I went to prison. You manipulated me into acting as your accomplice, helping you to hide the body in her cabin. If I hadn't done that, I would have left this shithole instead of staying the night. I wouldn't have lost all my money to Francis in a nightlong poker game, and I wouldn't have had to rob a liquor store on the way home and accidentally killed that cashier. I've thought a long time, in a tiny cell, about where I went wrong. The people that led me to that moment. You're at the top of that list."

"I don't remember that," I reply, still trying to make sense of what he's saying. Recalling the disturbing anecdotes from the first half of the journal, I add, "Francis must have killed her. I'm not responsible for Sasha's death."

The feeling of the desiccated hair in my palm from the other night returns as if to disagree.

"You are. Francis held a twenty-four-hour poker game that was witnessed by nearly everyone on the property and which gave him the perfect iron-clad alibi. And I got taken in by a thirteen-year-old, who got off scot-free in the years that followed." Dark eyebrows pinch above dead eyes. "When you realized what you'd done, you peered at me with these big blues, tears streaming down your face. 'Uncle Rick,' you cried. 'Help me.' When burial was over and done with, you laughed and clapped your hands and asked me to teach you to whistle. Followed me around for the rest of the day to make sure I didn't reveal your secret to anyone."

My lips part. But no defense comes to mind. I remember that—sticking to him like his shadow in these woods.

"Your actions put me on this path," he continues. "Sent me to prison and made every sneeze that I made before and after my sentencing seem like some grand clue to my violent impulses. When in fact, I was never a psychopath. I knew what that looked like, having grown up in this family, and I didn't show any of those traits."

"But you set fire to a church. Uma told me."

"Of course she did." He scoffs. "Uma was in Sunday school when I was helping to prep for mass. She witnessed a lit candle fall to a velvet drape, but not me knocking it over. The rectory went up in flames after that, but it wasn't because of me."

I rack my brain, searching for the fact that disproves what Rick is saying—that shows I didn't commit murder as a child. "But you killed the gas station attendant."

He shakes his head, his scalp glistening in the rain. "It was an accident. It was only meant to be a robbery since I lost all my money to Francis the night before. When I entered the store, I kept my hand in my pocket, then pointed it to make it look like a gun. The guy at the register refused to hand over the cash, then whipped out his own semiautomatic. We wrestled and the gun went off, killing the guy. But the newspapers never reported that it was his weapon, and the police didn't believe me that it was an accident. Once they learned I was part of this family, I was as good as gone."

Rick pauses. He stares over my shoulder into the trees behind me. "Ironic, when you think about it. After the last ten years, I'm now seen as this dirty prisoner—but you're the true monster, Olivia."

I step backward. Away from his words, and the trapped feeling that tightens my chest. "No. You killed Alfred. And Uma. And the property manager. You're the monster."

"When I overheard you and Alfred talking Thursday night about the wine cellar, about how angry he was with Felicity, the opportunity to frame you was too good. Alfred went looking for more wine in the dining hall after everyone left, and I came in from where I was crouched beneath the windows. I knew my chance had come. Then, your favorite aunt Uma—well, she's always been the worst. Telling everyone who will listen how I was some bloodthirsty madman since forever. The world is better off with less of our DNA in it."

"And the property manager?"

"Xavier was collateral damage. I needed the master key to the rooms, and he saw me one day in the forest, saw my face, after two women told him I was out here."

White-hot fear grips my shoulders. Rick, my relative, has done a far better job at setting me up than I realized. "You couldn't have Xavier identify you as the killer, when you've been planning for me to go to prison for the murders."

"For two of them at least. People should see you for who you really are, Olivia. All this while that I've been in prison, watching your videos online—some of them about me—you've been exploiting this family without owning up to your deeds."

I shake my head. "I don't understand. You served your time—you could have just moved on with your life. Why hurt so many of our relatives to get to me?"

"Move on? You think ex-cons can just exit prison and rent an apartment—find a job that pays above minimum wage? You are the reason I'll never have a normal life again." Rick smiles another yellow grin. "Now if I'm branded as the embodiment of the cursed Eriksen genes, it's only fair that some of that dirt rubs off on you finally."

I scan this man's face. Flushed cheeks peppered with gray stubble, sharp black eyes that seem content to devour me from above, Rick is unrecognizable to my childish recollection. His hatred for me is clear. For a moment, I feel transported to watching the old videotapes of psychopaths accused of murder, them dearly wishing they were free of handcuffs so they could throttle their captors.

But Rick isn't a psychopath, not according to him—he's just a ruthless murderer intent on getting revenge. Psychopathy can appear to be many other disorders—sociopathy, for one. The ability to deny, to justify, and to rationalize horrible actions is part of its powerful skill set.

Rick descends the ridge, taking a steep path to the right, stepping on flat rocks for stability. "Don't try to run," he says.

I falter backward. Behind me is the clearing where I saw Edgar about a half mile back. Too far for me to escape.

"Okay, I admit—you did make it look like I killed Alfred and Uma. But no one but us knows about Sasha's body. Why haven't you told anyone about her?"

Rick jumps the last few feet, landing on the muddied path with a thud. He withdraws a folding knife from the side pocket of his cargo pants. "Wrong again. I sent Jimmy an anonymous note last week and planted the idea that your grandma Yvette's diamond-encrusted ruby ring was buried on the property, with Sasha; he'll find her body and discover you killed her because of the added insurance I tucked beside her."

Realization stabs my chest. "The journal. But what does the journal prove?"

Rick only smirks. "You're screwed, Olivia. After I saw Shane and Marla together, I encouraged Shane to protect their secret however he thought best. I know a guy from prison who can make them new identities if they decide to start over somewhere. Shane has been a better distraction than I could have asked for while I knocked out my plan. The storm this weekend was a happy surprise."

My stomach roils. The branches overhead provide faulty shelter against the rain that's now pouring in sheets. Water trickles down my back.

"But your dad. David. Shane attacked him, shot him with an arrow."

Rick turns his head to spit. "Regrettable. But David never came to visit me in prison. Not once."

"The elk head. What was the point of attacking a random animal if this whole weekend was about revenge?"

Rick grins. Scratches his head with the knife's handle. "You gotta hand it to Shane. He's got a real flair for theatrics. The guy has a few too many screws loose, but he's so damn good looking, no one seems to care. After he and Marla were caught by David, doing it on the dock Thursday night, Shane got bored and went hunting. When he ran into me in the forest, I told him a trophy like that should be put on display."

I stare at my relative, someone I've known my whole life. While I've been so concerned with nature and being born with some psychopathic gene, Rick is the poster child for the nurture side of the argument that Professor Marx would support: he wasn't destined to be a psychopath; he was molded and presumed to be one by the world until he cracked— and gave them his own brand of ammunition.

"Rick, listen to me. I don't remember what you're describing—"

He lunges forward, knife in hand, and I dance back. He smiles.

"What was that, Olivia? This rain is so loud out in the open. If someone screamed, I doubt anyone could hear."

He stabs at the air again, slashing my vest. A puff of white fleece pokes from the blue polyester of my midsection.

"Wait! Wait, look! None of this is my fault. Or yours either. If I did kill Sasha by accident, I was a child. I wasn't responsible for whatever happened, and someone should have been watching me."

Rick narrows his eyes on me. "I was watching you. You laughed and doubled over when she fell and hit her head."

Memories of watching a woman fall on the dock snap forward. Rick's description of my laughter unlocks some part of my brain, and I can see Sasha's black hair whipping behind her as she crashed against the wood. The canoe we occupied together dipped dangerously in the water from the shift in our weight, but I wasn't concerned. I laughed, reveling in how clever I was to trip Sasha by extending my leg. When Sasha didn't rouse after her skull connected with the reinforced deck, I was surprised. Tripping her was nothing more than a joke—a prank— like the kind Uncle Vic was always playing on me, and not malicious. But the amusement I drew from the whole situation was worth the momentary doubt. My laughter, young and sweet, rings across the years to return to me now.

With new horror, I lick my lips. Rick is beaming. We both know I've recalled the truth. Despite that fact, admitting I'm responsible will only lead me to disaster. Nothing has changed for me, not really. A bead of rain slides down my cheek like a false tear.

"We're the product of our family, Rick," I begin, searching for my footing. Some way to convince him to drop this vendetta. "We didn't choose this life. We were born into it. If our actions led to pain for other people, it's because of the fishbowl we were swimming in as young, impressionable people."

Rick was a fully grown man when he accidentally killed someone, but I leave out our respective ages. Everything I know and have been studying about psychopaths confirms that most of them make excuses for their behaviors—it's their defense mechanism, and one they'll repeat until they march death row. Although he doesn't self-identify as a psychopath, he's walking a thin line.

But I'm doing the same thing. Making excuses for myself, my actions—when they led to a woman's death. What is wrong with me?

"Oh, I'm well aware of that, Olivia. Believe it or not, you're just another cog in the wheel of Eriksen dysfunction. Edgar is the last of the old guard to blame."

Twigs crunch on the path behind us. "What makes you say that?" a voice calls.

I turn to catch Edgar emerge from the foliage, then plant his feet wide. He scans us both with narrowed eyes. "Keep going, Ricky. I'd like to hear more about this theory of yours."

47

BIRDIE

The two-mile uphill trek is brutal. After scaling the landslide that was visible from the gas station, using tree branches and rocks for footholds, I slipped on the other side, then fell ten feet to the ground. My jeans ripped at the knees, and the back of my jacket was slick with mud. Landing the way that I did, my ankle felt twisted for a moment. But I gritted my teeth. Walked it off. *I've come too far,* I thought to myself, along with enough swear words to buy my family a nice steak dinner.

I limped along the first thirty minutes of the road. Although I tried calling Ashley, reception was completely shot, maybe due to the recent storm. When a fourth attempt didn't connect, I dropped a pin to him in a text and hoped it went through. Just in case. I also left the car at the gas station off the highway. If anything happens to me, the rental will serve as my smoke signal that I got into trouble somewhere on the mountain.

Dirt, leaves, rivulets of water, and mud made the path even more of an *American Ninja Warrior* episode—especially in high-top sneakers that I thought I'd be exclusively driving in. My feet hurt and my under-arms are chafed from sweating so much, but at least I have my parka that Grayson teased me about. The wind howls as I reach a battered one-story lodge. Shutters, partly unhinged, slap against the building's face. It's now past eight o'clock and pitch black. Branches and trash lay strewn across the steps of the main entrance, like a dumpster lid got blown off nearby. The place looks deserted. Li Ming Na's last known location.

Inside the lobby, I choke back a scream. Beneath faint moonlight streaming through tall windows, a giant taxidermied bear stands guard by the fireplace and nearly causes me to soil myself. Who chose that decorating theme? *Why?*

I try a few light switches with no luck. None of the lamps even flicker above the fireplace, at the welcome desk, or on the end tables beside deep armchairs. Thick silence feels like a ghost hovering at my side. Drinks half-full of water—melted ice cubes and liquor, from the smell—are arranged on a tray on the empty reception desk, as if someone meant to take them elsewhere. The cold air of outdoors is cut in half, but I close my parka tighter at my neck. The heat hasn't been on here, maybe in days. What did that gas station attendant say? *There's a family retreat going on up the mountain at the resort . . . Going on five days now, they've been trapped.*

Something crashes to the ground around the corner, down a hallway to the right. I freeze, searching for a place to hide.

But no one comes. No other sound emanates from either direction leading away from the main lobby rotunda. Shouldn't there be someone working? Or did every member of staff leave on foot?

Not quite ready to rejoin winter in Oregon, I wander down the hall in the opposite direction of the noise. Away from the guard bear. Padded carpet cushions my steps. I creep along the baseboards anyway, wary of squeaky floorboards.

I pause in front of a framed movie poster—the only one of its kind. Framed photos line the rest of the walls, black-and-white images that become color as the years roll on. An image of a lake—maybe somewhere on this property?—captures children jumping off a dock, the resort in the background. I lift my cell phone to read the bronze plaque beneath: 75TH ANNIVERSARY OF HORSEFLY FALLS RESORT, 2016.

Hanging beside it, there's a photo of a young woman laughing with a girl in front of a cabin. A large brass "8" is visible above the door. To the side, a looming pine tree casts shadows on the ground.

I angle my phone for a better look. The woman could be Asian, but she could be any number of ethnicities, the way that her face is partially turned. The plaque beneath reads only "2013." The year that Li Ming Na disappeared.

My lock screen lights up the hallway, and I turn it around to savor the image of Grayson and Brooklyn laughing as she discovered a pink shell on the beach.

I came a thousand miles to learn something tangible about Li Ming Na's disappearance and likely death. Sasha Lee deserves closure. She deserves someone to fight for her, like my cousin did, and countless other unnamed faces who might not have beauty-pageant looks or the right last name. I'm so close to answers, I can practically hear my own voice describing my findings on next week's podcast.

Popping my hood over my hair so that my head, torso, and upper thighs are doused in black, I return to the lobby. I reach the back entrance, two heavy glass doors with thick horizontal wooden handles, then slip outside.

Freezing air whooshes down my neck, as I move quickly from a ramp to a lower plaza. Walking in the dark, hidden in my makeshift invisibility cloak, I scan the courtyard on high alert. The bear spray I bought is tucked in my jacket's deep pocket, but I hope to get in and get out before anyone notices the resort's new party crasher.

Several cabins that I peek into along this part of the property look as if they've been converted recently. From sleeping quarters to centers of other activity, remnants of the cabins they once were are still evident: drapes cover the windows, bunk bed frames are used as shelves, and the faded outlines of removed numbers above doorways are clear.

On the edge of the property, before an open meadow and moonlit mountains in the distance, I see it at the last cabin: the shape of an eight, a lucky number in Chinese culture. The cabin that the woman in the photo was standing in front of.

Holding my breath, I twist the doorknob to enter. It turns, but the door doesn't budge. Peering around the corner, I spy a crate beneath one of the building's windows. A push against the window's dirty pane drives the sheet of glass upward with a moan.

"This is crazy," I whisper to myself. "What are you even looking for, Birdie?"

I cast an eye behind me. Certain that no one has seen me yet, I crawl into the former cabin.

Sporting equipment fills the bunk beds turned shelves. Basketballs, baseballs, kickballs, and soccer balls overflow from plastic barrels. Lacrosse sticks occupy a corner, upright, and as I move through the cabin, the scent of leather hits my nose—a pile of baseball mitts in an open storage container. Food wrappers—from granola bars—litter a yoga mat beside a disturbed floorboard; someone was here recently. And left in a hurry. The wood rises an inch above the rest, obviously displaced in the starlight streaming through the window, as if hastily laid down.

My heart thumps against my ribs. I steal a glance past the window-pane, searching for signs of movement outside. Listen to see if anyone else has climbed the rickety step to reach the door. A coyote howls somewhere close.

Sweat gathers beneath my arms as I stoop low. Using my cell phone as a flashlight, I lift it close to the disturbed wooden board.

Everything I've lived, everything I've done, has brought me to this moment. Regardless of what I find underneath, I'll never stop trying to give a voice to those who have been silenced. I won't be able to. Not now. Call it the Aquarius in me. I'm finally seeing the water I've been swimming in—seeing it for what it is—instead of meandering along as just another complacent goldfish.

With a shaking hand, I lift the board, then push it aside. It clatters to the floor. Underneath, darkness peers back at me. I twist my phone to the side until something white appears. Motionless. Steady. Pale.

I duck down. Chalky white returns my gaze. A skull. A human skull picked clean by something years ago, shiny beneath the orb of my cell phone's beam. Strands of black hair hug the crown of the head. Empty eye sockets look straight up, and then a beetle crawls forth from a round void.

I turn my head, then drop to all fours. Vomit splatters onto the yoga mat. Liquid connects with a plastic box beyond, and then I heave again.

The door handle is jimmied. Someone is trying to get in.

The tentative effort pauses. Then something slams against the door. Again. Again. Terrified but weak from fear, I sit watching, until the handle breaks. A barrier of sporting equipment inches backward as the door creaks open. Horror douses my chest as I register a body standing in the doorway, backlit by the night.

"Who are you?" a deep voice calls.

Stunned, I can't reply.

"Never mind. It's less fun that way."

Chills trace my jaw as this person steps forward. The impact of their feet resonates across the cabin, approaching me, vibrating beneath me, as I back into a corner.

48

OLIVIA

"What are you doing here, Ricky?" Edgar asks, his tone wary.

"Nice to see you again, Rick. It's been ages, Ricky, my boy." Rick pauses, clearly enjoying this surprise. "Exactly what you think, old Ed. I'm joining the family retreat. Despite not being formally invited, of course."

"But I thought you were in prison. When did you get out?"

Rick scratches his head again with the knife's polished wood handle. "That's the thing about mothers, right? Mine has been sitting beside you for days while all of this"—he waves his hand around us—"has been going on, and she didn't even mention that I was released early on good behavior. Did she?"

Rick rests his foot on a rock. He drops his head while maintaining eye contact with Edgar. "The thing is, I was saving up all my bad behavior for when I met you lot again."

Edgar glares at me. "You've been working with him this weekend?"

I shake my head. "No, I only just discovered—"

"You've been planning this for ages. Haven't you, Olivia?" Rick interrupts. "You just couldn't help yourself, who you really are, and went after both Alfred and Uma. The icing on the cake was killing the property manager for fun. Isn't that so?"

Edgar darts his gaze between the pair of us. Soft grunts are audible from the path overhead. "What is going on?"

"But it's better that you found us; it is," Rick continues. "Tell me, Uncle. Did you suspect I was out here, or were you following your gut and tracking down Olivia? Trying to make sure she didn't harm anyone else?"

Edgar is silent. I shrink backward, recognizing the latter is true. He doesn't trust me.

Rick's stomach rumbles within earshot. "God, I'm starved," he says. "You have any food in that bag of yours?"

He grabs my purse, and I'm forced to slip it over my head or be yanked forward with it. A quick look, him pawing at my inhaler, then chucking it into the bushes, confirms I wasn't holding out. He finds a breath mint, then pushes the bag back into my arms. I trip and fall to the ground.

The vines of the forest floor are tough on my palms. Bringing my hands forward causes fresh blood from my bandaged gash to ooze through the cloth.

My thoughts return to the film wing of the psych building. Images of killers, predators, serial rapists—Calder Saffron on trial—all pass across my mind's eye as if I'm flipping through a jukebox panel of songs. Their expressions, their true reactions, and the faked emotions that they believe will earn them leniency. Which is Rick presenting now? Does he actually want to hurt Edgar, his uncle and my grandfather? Or is this all meant to distract me—to manipulate me, as he swears I did him?

Professor Marx said back in the lecture hall, *It is so dangerous— ethically and empirically—to presume we can predict a person's behavior based on their disorder alone.* What has Rick demonstrated in his actions since I found his campsite? He's willing to harm family members for his vendetta against us; he's confident that he's in control; he believes down to his muddy sneakers that I'm responsible for his pain. He doesn't trust me either.

"I would eat bark if I knew it was safe to eat," Rick adds, grimacing. Another grunt from the trees this time. It's getting closer.

"You could have just come down the mountainside, Ricky," Edgar says. "You didn't have to wait up here . . . plotting."

Beside me, a patch of orange flowers peeks from under a rock—flowers that I know someone said were edible during the survival lesson. If they have narrow petals.

I scan our surroundings, slightly protected from the ongoing rainstorm beneath a thick canopy of leaves. A green bush to my right nearly covers a spherical plant with white blossoms.

Queen Anne's lace. Or hemlock. I pocket a fistful when Rick isn't looking. More grunting sounds as if it's only feet away.

"Me, plotting?" Rick stabs his own chest with a finger. "No, you must be mistaken. Olivia here has been masterminding all the fun and games."

"Best weekend I've had in ages," a voice calls out. From down the path, in the same direction Edgar and I came, Shane emerges, dirt smeared across his face like a mask, pushing someone forward—a woman I don't recognize.

Shane gestures with a butcher knife. "Found the girl digging around one of the cabins. She's not resort staff."

Wearing all black, she could be Howard's shorter cousin—they both share dark hair and brown eyes, but she's smaller in stature. She should never have come here, whoever she is. Cowering beneath our stares, she makes eye contact with me, a silent plea to the only other woman present. Another mistake.

I can't help her fight against whatever Shane has planned—not against both Shane and Rick.

"Why did you bring her up here, Shane? Who are you?" Rick asks the woman.

"I'm . . . I'm a podcaster. I'm Birdie," she says.

Rick pauses, as if he didn't quite hear her. "What the fuck is a podcaster?"

"She's a narc. A mole. She's trying to dig up more dirt on our family." Shane steps back to take her in. "Which one of us are you doing an episode on, hmm? C'mon, don't be quiet now. Or do you need a microphone in front of you?"

He steps suggestively toward her, grabbing his groin.

"Knock it off, Shane," I say.

"Why should I?" He whirls on me, more in control than I've seen him in days. "Why should any of us? We're the fucking Eriksens, for crying out loud. We take what we want, right? Isn't that the way? Great-Grandpa Einar did."

Fear is stark across the woman's face, while Edgar looks like he might be sick.

"Shane, this isn't the plan," Rick adds. "No outsiders involved."

"But she came to us, Uncle Rick. To *us*. Like that elk that just showed up, all ready and willing for the slaughter."

Rick shrugs. As if that logic is airtight.

"Shane," I begin, searching for calm. Grasping for the psych training I've been choking down the last five years. "I know you're experiencing some kind of episode right now—"

Shane grabs the woman by the jacket, threatening her with the giant knife. Shocked, she cries out, locking eyes on me again. He throws a glance back to me. "This isn't an episode, Olivia. This is bloodlust. So I'm going to need either blood or lust, and if you're not volunteering for either one, someone has to step up!"

Swirling black clouds rumble overhead. New rain breaks, falling on my shoulders as a meager sound cuts through the noise. The woman.

"You're . . . Olivia Eriksen? The social media star? You're all Eriksens?"

Edgar, Rick, and Shane direct their gazes to her. Then to me. "Yes," I say.

She peers at me, as if we're the only idiots in this forest. Her breathing is short and stunted, like an animal making its last play for life. "I've seen your platform. My followers are always asking me to do an episode on you and your family."

I pause. "How many followers do you have?"

"One point two million. I cover true crime." Birdie scans our group. "If you're Olivia Eriksen, then you must be Shane Eriksen. Rick Wilton. And Edgar Eriksen."

Rick raises both eyebrows. "A quick study."

"But where is Francis Eriksen? Where is Li Ming Na's boyfriend? The father of her kid?" Birdie asks. "Her killer?"

"Who the fuck is Li Ming Na?" Rick shouts. "Why is this person still talking? I've waited ten years and did jail time to wrap this up. Let her go, Shane. She's not supposed to be here."

Shane whips out a gun—the one he took from Jacquie. "What's it going to be, Olivia? You decide: Should I kill her? You're team captain."

Edgar swings his attention to me. "So, you *were* directing everything this weekend?"

"No! That's not—I wasn't. Put the gun down, Shane," I say.

"Choose, Olivia! If she lives, we have to find something else to play with, though. You volunteering?"

"You're not thinking straight—"

"Count of three, Cousin. One. Two." Shane glares at me, his mouth curled in a sneer. Tension stacks between us like the landslide on the main road below.

I shift my body forward, knowing there's only one answer. "You can't have her."

Something tears through the bushes, grunting and snarling as it hurtles toward us. An animal crashes our circle—a wild pig with tusks ready to disembowel—scattering us to the sides. I dodge behind a tree, mud splashing my face. Shane drops the knife, then whips his gun from Birdie to the animal as it leaps toward him, its gullet wide for the kill.

Shane's face goes slack, as if he's dissociated again. The pig squeals, gives a war cry, and redirects its tusks toward my cousin's belly; then Shane shoots it in the head. The animal's mass crashes to the ground, rolling to the edge of the mountainside.

Birdie whips out her own gun and showers Shane's face in a pepper cloud—not a gun, bear spray. I duck my head and cover my mouth, while Shane screams. He clutches his eyes, then aims wildly with his gun as Birdie scrambles from his path. Shane shoots once, twice, wildly into the air—and Rick jerks forward, grabbing the gun from Shane's fist.

With a click, Rick pulls the trigger. The gunshot erupts, echoing in the cavernous acoustics of the fir trees. Smoke lingers at Shane's chest. Dark liquid oozes from his white T-shirt, glinting in the moonlight, as he lifts a hand toward me. His face contorts in pain before his eyes roll back into his head.

"Marla," he moans.

Then his body collapses to the earth.

49

BIRDIE

Shane Eriksen slumps into the mud. I can't speak. Can't move. Can't breathe. Rain continues to pitter on my head like dull waterboarding. Panic clamps my throat shut, but my feet stay planted to the earth. I should run—sprint away from these wackos and back down the road to my car, to safety and to my baby girl and Grayson.

These people—this fucked-up family—remain motionless. I don't trust it, but they seem in just as much shock as I am. Animals among the trees are silent, the gunshot still reverberating between branches, vibrating in the skin of every living thing on this mountain.

Grayson. My first true love and the best person I've ever known. I should have kissed him again before I left, a third, then a fourth time. The scent of his special toothpaste that he mixes himself, baking soda and mint extract, floods my nose in some taunting fit of memory. God, I would give anything to smell him right now. To be protected in his arms.

Am I going to die here? What will he tell Brooklyn?

Fresh tears wet my eyes. My sweet girl. The last time I held her was five days ago, when she offered me her stuffed bunny for company. Had

I known how the weekend would transpire, I'd have taken Bunnifred with me. Or hell, I wouldn't have ventured past San Clemente.

We should have given Brook a sibling so she wouldn't feel so alone when she learns I've been killed. Regardless of what happens now, these people won't let me leave. I've seen and heard too much. I'm a loose thread.

My fingers ache, clutching the giant can of bear spray I purchased from the gas station. At least I know it works—although I probably emptied the entire canister into Shane's face.

Everyone is frozen. Shane Eriksen lies flat on his back, staring up at the trees like he's lost in thought. Then he rolls down the hillside, crashing into bushes and branches as his body connects with each.

Olivia Eriksen, social media influencer, tried to reason with him, as if that were possible. But she wasn't with him on the hike up here. She didn't see the way he sneered at me when I crawled away from him on the cabin floor down below—how excited he seemed by my show of weakness and fear.

The old man, Edgar Eriksen, can't stop looking at the spot where Shane rolled out of sight, between the dirt path and the tangle of vines on the hillside. Tears, or rain, dot the loose skin of the man's cheeks as he watches on. I wonder what tragic scene from his life is replaying across his vision right now.

Seeing something like what Edgar would have as a kid, the discovery of his father axed to death, has got to mess you up. Maybe to the point of continuing the family legacy—of committing horrible crimes against strangers, who were minding their own business, seeking out answers to unsolved murders on a weekend away from arts and crafts projects.

Morbidly enough, part of me would jump at the chance to interview all the members of this poisonous family tree. But the rest of me knows that will never happen.

Not from the way Olivia Eriksen is peering at me now—like she doesn't see me—or the way that Rick Wilton is side-eyeing me. Like I'm collateral damage to the weekend. Even if Olivia appeared to be logical, normal, when she asked me about my social media following, the fact is she was distracted by it.

Shivers course down my spine. I think again of my husband. A surge of compassion punts the fear from my chest as I think about my family, the grief they'll feel at my loss, what they'll do with the hundreds of dollars saved up in the swear jar, thanks to me.

Rick Wilton lowers the gun to his side. "He was never going to make it out of here alive anyway. Shane was a loose cannon."

"Was that it?" Olivia asks in a quiet voice. "Or did he know too much? Did you always intend for this?"

The sky cracks overhead. Lightning flashes, illuminating our circle of soggy bodies. My cheeks flush with heat as tears cascade to my jaw.

Neither Olivia nor Rick displays any emotion. No grief at watching their relative get shot in the torso, then disappear over a hillside. No terror. No regret.

I am going to die here. All for a true crime obsession that led nowhere—to new dead ends that will confound the police for years. In an ironic twist, I'll become what I've been consuming: the latest person of color whose death gets a pitiful mention during the nightly news. And there's not a single damn thing I can do about it.

50

OLIVIA

I wait for a surge of hysteria to fill me. Panic. Loss. Rage.

A break in the storm occurs, and Birdie's sobs reach my ears. My vest is soaked. I close my eyes.

Devastation or fury should be consuming me, that after all I've lived—my dad's imprisonment, my struggle with Elise to make a life for ourselves, my turning to social media and selling the Eriksen trauma, then busting my ass at grad school to be taken seriously as an academic—Rick is going to pin each murder this weekend on me. Alfred's, Uma's, the property manager's, and now Shane's.

Rick will kill Edgar, then likely off the podcaster, Birdie, too, to ensure there are no witnesses to his presence this weekend. From the way Marla was speaking earlier, I doubt she knows Rick was responsible for the retreat's chaos. Only Shane was up to speed, and now he's gone. A tidy ending to his messy contribution.

No sharp emotion comes. I feel numb.

Rick lifts the gun toward Edgar, and my grandfather flinches.

"Ricky, my God. Isn't this enough for you?" Edgar pans to the forest and gestures to the valley beyond. "This weekend's carnage?"

Rick scoffs. He moves toward Edgar, prowling. But I need Edgar. I need Birdie and Edgar now.

"Wait," I say. In a daze, I dig into my pocket where I tucked the flowers away. White petals, round and innocent, spring forward.

Since I found him, Rick has demonstrated that he doesn't trust me. Most psychopaths think of others in terms of utility, versus trust. But he's also confident that he's in control. Even when Shane took him by surprise and brought Birdie to the mountaintop, Rick simply bided his time until the gun was within reach.

Professor Marx smiles in my memory, alongside the countless psychopaths whose interviews I've consumed over the years and whose behaviors can change on a dime depending on what suits them in the moment. *The environment might be more persuasive than a patient's genetics or previous diagnosis.*

Rick hasn't eaten since yesterday.

"Wait," I repeat. "You said you were hungry earlier."

Rick squints at my outstretched hand. He hesitates, searching my face for something. Then he takes the flowers and bites the heads off whole, leaving butchered green stems. He chews and swallows, then holds out his palm. "Any more?"

I shake my head. My heartbeat thumps in my wounded palm, tension coiling my stomach. "None."

"Too bad." Turning back to Edgar, Rick smiles. "All the years I was imagining Olivia's demise, I didn't fail to think about you, Uncle Ed. She started me down this black path, but the entire family turned me into a monster, taking their cue from you."

"Me?" Edgar lifts his head.

"Your unnerving shame, the deep fear you showed whenever someone unlike yourself came to family dinner on Sundays," Rick says, raising his voice. "Your prejudice is what set the tone for this family, everyone coddling you after you discovered Einar's body, and no one trying to protect the rest of us who were just left of center. Your PTSD or whatever you call it is the reason I am who I am. Who Shane was."

Edgar narrows his eyes. "I didn't force you to kill anyone at that gas station, Ricky. To kill Shane now. Did I shame you into homicide?"

"The gas station was an accident. And Shane didn't leave me a choice. He was dangerous, waving that gun around," Rick seethes. "But you don't care about intentions. You never have. All you've ever done is judge deviance before you tried to understand it. You labeled me a psychopath and a murderer without a second—"

Rick stops speaking. He coughs. His hand rises to his throat as if to scratch, and then he turns to me. "What did you give me?"

He slashes at me with the knife, but I stumble backward. My palm burns. "Flowers."

His skin turns red; then purple climbs his neck to reach his jawline. "Not . . . edible."

Rick dives to the ground, searching for something. He thrashes about, trying to return to his feet, but tumbles back to the dirt. He inches his way through the bushes, horrible noises rising from his chest, agonizing cries that cause me to cringe. He vomits twice but continues to moan. Squeals of pain could be from another wild pig roaming nearby, rather than my relative as his insides liquefy before us.

I glance back to Edgar, but he is riveted, frozen where he stands. The voice of the Navy SEAL who led our survival training snaps forward in my mind: *If you eat a few petals, you can die within twenty minutes.*

Rick ate several whole flowers, and the quantity shows. He convulses in a bed of greenery, nearly hidden but for dirt-covered, trembling sneakers.

When the retching stops, all becomes silent in the forest. Edgar meets my gaze, horror stretching his face. "What did you give him?"

"Poison hemlock. He was going to kill you, then make me take the fall for it. I . . . I couldn't allow that to happen."

Edgar pauses, unnerved by my candor. "Why, though? Why not let him attack me, then give him the flowers?"

Birdie is frozen on the edge of the circle.

"Because, Grandpa," I begin, "as you're always saying, family comes first. You're the head of this one."

Edgar pauses. His eyes dart toward where Rick collapsed. "I used to say that. But I haven't thought that since the first family retreat here. Your grandmother Yvette tried to tell me I was overreacting."

Yvette died when I was five. She wasn't at the first one. Is Edgar actually confused? "You mean the retreat ten years ago."

He shakes his head, then peers at me from beneath a heavy brow. Someone comes tramping up the path, footsteps crushing branches while a woman hums a tune. Lois. A shriek rips from her throat at discovering her son's lifeless body.

"No. The first one," Edgar says. "Twenty-two years ago."

51

Journal Entry

Day three of the Eriksen family retreat

Today was one for the books. I don't know that I've ever felt this anxious, and after the last year of my relationship with Teddy, that is saying something.

I confess that I'm no longer sure I should be recording my thoughts like this.

Last night I returned from a walk with Yvette and the toddler, and found Teddy sitting on my bed instead of his own; we each have twin beds here. I think he found you, Journal. That he read my private thoughts about him and his family and the child we share. Now, poring over the words I chose months ago, but which accurately reflected my feelings then, I am filled with dread. We are likely at a turning point, me and Teddy. I don't know how much longer I can or should stay with him.

You're probably concerned that I've had too much to drink or am on the rag again. But that's not the case. I'm definitely not boozing the way that I normally would all the way out here in the woods, because I'm still breastfeeding the toddler. After a year, it gave me a sense of mommy pride to provide the nutrients to supplement solid food, but even that seems like it might be at an end. Hear me out.

A good mother would never write these things where her child might find them years later, or anyone else that might judge. But I suppose what Teddy says must be true: I'm not a good mother. I'm a nice accessory. I never believed it until now, when the idea seems to have wriggled into my brain, burrowing like a parasite that begs for more gray matter to munch.

You see—the toddler appears to feel the same way as Teddy.

Today, before bedtime, it was time to nurse. Everything was going normally, and I had paused from stroking soft baby skin to peer out the window. Yvette was scolding Shane for disappearing into the woods again. Edgar, Teddy's father, was swinging a racket with someone out of sight.

Then sharp pain pierced my breast. My baby girl had bitten me. When I cried out, she only seemed encouraged, and she bit me again, using the sharp new front and bottom teeth that only recently came in to draw blood. Red spots dotted her beautiful lower lip.

Tears filled my eyes, I was so overwhelmed by the moment and what just happened.

When the toddler looked up at me again and seemed to understand I was hurting, she laughed. She tried to bite me again, but I lurched backward to protect my skin and held her at arm's length. More giggles that each felt akin to slashes from a blade. For some reason, I glanced through the window then to find Edgar staring at me, mirroring my expression down to my dropped jaw and wet cheeks. He knew, as I did then—she's an Eriksen, and more Teddy than she is me.

I have no doubt that Teddy will seek out my journal again this weekend. I'll tuck it away somewhere safe in this cabin until we leave, beneath my bed, but things already feel different. As if we've crossed into foreign territory together, and not necessarily for the better.

Part of me did love Teddy once. But now it all feels utterly useless to pretend that Ephraim Eriksen could ever have been someone Tall, Dark, and Improving—someone worthy of the nickname TDI, because he's not. Looking back over the pages I've written, the truth is stark: Ephraim Eriksen is not on some path of improvement, if he ever was. He was always himself with me. I just wasn't interested in seeing who he was.

And now we have a daughter together. Olivia is sleeping in the twin bed that we share while I write this at the edge of the cot. There's no part of me that loves her less, and I'll raise her the best I can to recognize emotions in others and to imitate them if she's unable to feel them herself. But where before this trip there was unconditional maternal understanding, now there's concern mingled with . . . fear.

52

OLIVIA

Red and blue lights shift across the windows of the main lodge. Police officers in uniform navigate the property like ants, swarming the formerly empty plaza in single-file, orderly lines, along the shore, the meadow, and the adjacent buildings that comprise the resort.

I bring my inhaler to my lips to breathe deep a new lungful of medication—then stop short.

After Edgar confirmed the first family retreat took place the year of my first birthday, and that my mother was in attendance, I withdrew the journal that I'd found in the sports hut from my bag and read to the end. It wasn't Sasha's journal but my mother's. Elise didn't speak much about the first few years, often explaining it was too painful to recall those early days—before she split from my dad and decided to raise me herself with his intermittent involvement. I knew she worked at a bookstore in Eugene and the local library before she had me, after leaving college. But I had never heard mention of a previous family retreat, neither from Elise nor anyone else in the family.

For my tenth birthday, she gifted me a journal that I ultimately never used. With it, she offered the warning to always keep it in a safe location, that if I were to record my thoughts and feelings in it, to ensure I knew exactly where it was. She shared what seemed like a mundane detail at the time: the last journal she had, she'd tucked between the floorboards of the place where she was staying, then accidentally left it behind when the weekend was over.

Rick must have thought it a good idea to bury Sasha in her cabin, the farthest one on the property. When he pried up the loose floorboards, he would have found the journal from twelve years prior—read it or maybe skimmed the last page, as I should have earlier. It was his own form of insurance, like he said, that points to me as the imbalanced baby—Sasha's unfeeling attacker. The journal, plus his word against mine, would have caused the authorities to investigate me.

The aluminum canister of medication in my palm, with its fragile plastic cover, shines beneath the police spotlight overhead. I've been asthmatic from the time I turned thirteen. Looking back, that was also the age that I began remarking the differences between myself and other teenagers: I was much less emotional, much more calculated, and seemed to lack a basic penchant for the usual age-appropriate drama. With my inhaler, I was suddenly a participant in shocking conversations or aerobic activities during PE or on a sports team, not merely a bystander observing the mood swings of neurotypical teenagers. Asthma was psychosomatic for me.

I allow the plastic to drop to the waste bin of the plaza. Packaging from marshmallows, chocolate bars, and graham crackers cushions the inhaler's fall, the artifacts from an anxious Friday night. The totem pole above seems to tower against the gray skies, an imposing judge, witness to the executions that followed.

"Olivia."

I lift my head. Howard peers at me from a few steps above.

"Howard," I breathe. "Where have you been? I've been looking all over for you."

Despite everything, Howard glares at me. "No, you haven't. If you had, you'd know I've been hiding in the luxury lodge since Sunday, waiting and hoping you'd come find me. But you were too busy playing Hunger Games out here."

"That's not true," I reply, weakly. "I tried the Pine Coast Lodge. It was locked."

"But why, though? Not out of some concern for me. I don't know how I didn't see it before, but when push came to shove, you didn't care." He huffs. "About us. Our engagement. You never did. You only used me for as long as it was convenient, back in Davis. Out there"— Howard raises a hand to the mountain—"it wasn't."

My fiancé, the man who has been my constant for the last year and helped me in so many ways, looks at me with disgust. And, I think, sadness. I should mirror him, shouldn't I? A natural emotion here would be loss or regret, compassion for this person I've emotionally wounded. Instead, I feel detached. Empty of genuine remorse. I could fake it, of course, I know how, and in hindsight it's what I've done all my life. Yet leaning into the clinical part of my brain offers more satisfaction—more clarity. None of the ambiguity that clouded my efforts to connect with people in the past.

"I'm sorry," I finally reply.

He shakes his head. "I don't think you are. No, don't—"

I pause sliding a finger beneath the collar of my shirt, to retrieve his ring. I lift both eyebrows.

"I don't want it. Whoever you are, you're not the woman I proposed to. Not the woman who made me fall in love with her. I don't want the reminder of how easily I was fooled."

He turns, then climbs up the flat, wide steps of the plaza. He's leaving me. I think in movies, this is the dramatic moment that the remaining partner cries out for their lover to stop—to return and hear them out. To accept a tearful apology, a declaration of loyalty and wrenching fear at losing their person forever.

Howard walks past two police officers to disappear inside the main lodge.

A minute goes by. Howard doesn't reemerge, and maybe more importantly, I don't go after him. I don't speak a word. Internally, I note that I'm content to remain exactly where I am.

On the way down the mountainside with Edgar and Birdie the podcaster, the rain paused while I searched the path for some sign of Marla. Although Rick and Shane were behind most of the death of the weekend, Marla may have been complicit; I didn't want to be surprised by her, if she knew that Shane was killed. She was an accomplice to him, however unwilling, determined to keep their relationship hidden at the cost of certain relatives' lives. I believed her when she said she was scared of Shane. But I also knew, according to the movies, that love—real love—makes people irrational.

Edgar was wary of me as we descended together, rightfully. He didn't say it, but once I read the final journal entry on the summit and connected the confidential dots of my mother's experience, I realized why he'd been avoiding my requests to interview him, even going so far this weekend as to pretend to confuse me with his late wife: he was afraid of me. I was the sadistic baby who took pleasure in her mother's pain, and Edgar saw that moment from the window. In hindsight, the memory of him tickling me while I sat on his lap as a six-year-old was rationalized in my mind, just like Sasha's death. He wasn't being playful; Edgar wanted me to get down, and his repeated attempts to dislodge my arms from around his trunk made me giggle. He knew who I was, what I was, from the moment I drew blood while nursing.

When we reached the meadow, the police sirens were audible. The road had finally been cleared, five days after the initial storm created the blockade. According to the first sergeant I spoke with, the cops thought they could leave us longer than other situations deemed more pressing around the region. They thought we'd enjoy the family time.

Another cop shared that some retired detective in San Diego had phoned them. Told them to come up here. Apparently, he wouldn't stop calling the station until a team of officers agreed to find a way to drive to the resort. When pressed for a solid reason why they should, the detective said "symbiosis." Whatever that means.

After interviewing Edgar, paramedics came bounding down the hillside with a body on a stretcher—an unsurprising fact, given the casualties above. What throttled me was seeing Shane carried past. He was alive. Barely, according to a paramedic who barked an order to a different man in scrubs to start a blood transfusion. Shane would confirm Rick's vendetta and clear my name, I hoped, since I still wasn't sure of Edgar's interpretation of what went down. I breathed a sigh of relief.

Zane and Skye emerged from the luxury residence hall as soon as the police stepped from their cars. I overheard them explaining to an officer that after the storm deluged our capture-the-flag game, they locked themselves on the topmost floor and refused to answer anyone's cry for help. As the owner, Zane had another master key that worked just fine, despite the power outage. The big surprise for our family that he dangled like a carrot all weekend? A photo shoot with him and a reporter, which he planned to distribute to local media outlets. He believed that a PR blitz would ease fears that he was a self-serving wild card at the hospital.

When I heard him explain to Francis, who came out from hiding in the indoor fitness center, that the photographer bailed days ago, I shot Skye a glare. She knew the "surprise" the whole time and used the promise of it to ensure everyone followed the weekend agenda, when it was only a canceled PR gimmick. Skye is a better partner to Zane than I gave her credit for.

Francis was self-serving to the end, hiding in the same building as his daughter, Kyla, without searching for her once. Although, it turns out, his alcoholism didn't drive Sasha away.

Birdie the podcaster was questioned for twenty minutes by a series of police officers, who all seemed genuinely confused about why she was here. A short while after she was released, a team of uniforms went to the sports hut where Sasha is buried. One of the officers emerged, then waved over a more senior official wearing a suit and trench coat.

So Birdie knows too.

She has lingered beneath a lamp along the back deck's railing. For a while, she was on the phone with someone, reassuring them that she was okay. I thought when she hung up, she would leave, return to her world, and thank her stars she can walk away from the Eriksens in one piece. Instead, she's been watching me since then, as if trying to memorize my face.

"Olivia?" she calls out. "Can I talk to you?"

I meet her halfway at the top of the plaza stairs. Police officers who were swarming the grounds earlier have largely disappeared indoors.

"I wanted to thank you," she begins. "For standing up for me."

I nod, because I still don't know what she wants from me. And, in hindsight, reading people has never come easily to me anyway. But I know what I need from her.

"Sure thing. Are you still wanting me on your podcast? My chances of finishing grad school are shot now—for this year anyway. My social media channels are going to need the promotional push."

She startles, as if taken aback. "Yeah. Definitely."

"Good."

"I'd also like to . . . that is, if you're willing . . . talk about Sasha Lee on my podcast."

I regard this woman full in the face. A police spotlight that some crew set up behind me, when they were searching the grounds for survivors, illuminates every muscle spasm, each fine wrinkle, mole, and freckle of her skin. She makes no sign that she knows the truth: that I'm Sasha's killer, by prepubescent design.

Birdie hesitates. "Rick said that he waited ten years to finish what he started. What was that, exactly?"

I weigh her words. "I think it's obvious, isn't it? He killed Sasha. Or Li Ming Na. Is that what you called her?"

"Sasha's legal name." Birdie nods, slowly. "So it wasn't Francis, her boyfriend, who did it. Even though he has a history of violence. Rick buried her."

"Yes. He admitted to it, before you arrived. He must have originally planned to kill us all at the last retreat," I lie. "It's a shame Sasha had to wait a decade in order to be discovered—by you, is that right?"

She tilts her head to the side. "Yeah. Only, I was wondering if someone else got there first."

"Did someone?" I ask, my heartbeat ticking up.

"I probably shouldn't talk about it." She rocks back on her heels. "I haven't told anyone where I found her, except for the police. They said not to while they're still questioning people. Honestly, I had never heard of her before I received an anonymous email. I was hoping to ask Francis, to see whether it was him that wanted her story told, but he's refused to speak to me."

"Francis, care what happened to his longtime girlfriend? I doubt it." I scoff. "He hosted a nonstop, twenty-four-hour poker game the final night of the last retreat. Now that I think about it"—*now that Cousin Rick jogged my memory*—"I don't think Francis even mentioned Sasha was missing until the next morning."

Understanding now how deeply Rick blamed me for his imprisonment, I'll bet he sent Birdie that email; he had more than enough time in prison and access to the internet to learn Sasha's legal name, Li Ming Na. He wanted Birdie to track down the truth—to expose my role in Sasha's death—and didn't want the effort to be traced back to him. His clueless act on the mountaintop was all for show, knowing he is less than credible as a convicted murderer. He needed Birdie to find the body and the journal—to piece the facts together herself—although I doubt he predicted she would visit the resort the same weekend as us. Birdie was a final form of insurance, in case his plan went poorly. What had he said about Shane—*There's no way he'd be able to pull off something as complex as this?*

Birdie nods. "That explains it. I've been wondering why the police never called Francis a suspect—or even a person of interest—in Sasha's disappearance. I guess the poker game, with its witnesses, and a push from the lieutenant governor made them give him a pass."

"That, or blackmail," I add. "I've heard stories of Francis going off the rails when he was younger. And he wouldn't hesitate to use information against people if it works to his advantage. Most narcissists wouldn't."

Birdie pauses. "This is going to sound weird. But does your uncle know someone named Kyss Kyss Bang Bang?"

"Excuse me, miss? Were you a guest this weekend?" A man approaches me from the staircase of the main lodge. He wears a suit and tie beneath a black slicker, his close-cut hair still bearing raindrops from the last sprinkling an hour ago.

I've been interviewed by the police and other related law enforcement personnel several times now, and I don't recognize this new addition. Turning back to Birdie, I add, "Let's chat about dates for my episode later."

The man follows me as I return to a seat along one of the log benches. "I'm Tom Morales, reporter with KALL-10 News. I'd like to ask you a few questions, if you're willing. The police said they'd finished with you."

Lost in my thoughts, I nod.

"This was a family retreat gone terribly wrong. Did you see disaster coming?" the reporter asks. He lifts his cell phone toward me, already recording. "How do you feel?"

I start to reply the way I know I should, the way I've studied in other people my whole life, then made an academic career on, but I stop myself. I take stock of the question and the actual answer: I feel nothing. Rather, I feel blunted, with none of the heightened emotions I should after being abandoned with murderous relatives in the backwoods of Oregon, losing a fiancé, knowing now I won't achieve my graduate degree.

Memories of ignoring calls and texts from suitors my own age return, along with the excitement I felt when Howard, the assistant dean of Graduate Affairs, showed an interest. Even the voracious sexual appetite I've always had seems like a neon blinking light, as female psychopaths are known for it. I haven't truly cared about anyone who didn't affect my life directly. Maybe Elise knew that all along. That must be why she insisted I spend more time with the Eriksens this weekend: to better understand my condition—psychopathy—in ways that she could never educate me in as a neurotypical.

In hindsight, even my dissertation, which explored whether psychopathy was evident from birth, was self-serving. Despite being anxious about turning twenty-three, the age at which the condition becomes undeniably apparent in my family, I've been ignoring reality: since I was old enough for Elise to teach me to smile when someone called me pretty and to cry when a movie depicted the demise of a beloved family pet, I've been imitating the empathy that my more socially successful peers demonstrate without effort. I wonder if I subconsciously hounded Edgar for his interview these last several months not only for my grad paper but to confirm what I already guessed: while existing published studies all suggest psychopathy can't be discerned until a child is older, Edgar and me, we knew the truth.

Tom the reporter raises a thick eyebrow. "Miss? Could you state your name, please, then tell me what happened in your own words? How do you feel?"

"I'm Olivia Eriksen. And I feel . . . fine."

The reporter asks me a few more questions, typing notes into his phone. I answer in short sentences, not really listening. As Edgar steps from the lobby onto the deck, then shuffles to where I'm seated, the reporter huffs.

"Well, thanks for your time." He approaches a group of police officers standing closer to the lake, leaving me alone with my grandfather.

Edgar retains his frown. He nods to the red journal I hold in my lap. "Did you finish reading?"

"I did. It's Elise's. She wrote in it during the first family retreat you mentioned."

He doesn't recoil. "I thought I recognized it."

I glance at the deck, where police officers consult each other. My remaining living relatives were interviewed in the lobby earlier, after the grounds were searched, but I haven't seen anyone outside in some time. Marla insisted she accompany Shane to the hospital and left with him in the ambulance earlier.

"Where is everyone?" I ask. "Or are they avoiding me? I think some of the family still believe I killed Alfred and Uma."

Edgar shakes his head, thin white hairs catching the air. "Jimmy took off. Once he was cleared by the police to leave and he confirmed that Sasha wasn't buried with any valuable jewelry, he left in a hurry. Coral knows now that Rick was behind everything."

"And Kyla? Does she know about her mother? About Sasha." The last I saw Kyla, Denny, and Felicity, all three of them were sipping mugs of coffee brought by the paramedics. Funny to think I had convinced myself only a day ago that Kyla was a psychopath.

"She does."

Birdie the podcaster leans against the railing by the steps, looking off toward the dark meadow, though I doubt she can see anything beyond the police spotlight.

"And what about you?" I ask. "Why are you talking to me now?"

Edgar focuses on the wooden bench for a long moment. "Why did Rick say that you set him off on a black path?"

I speak the lie without hesitation. "I don't know."

Edgar grunts. "Did you argue with Rick the day that Sasha was killed?"

"No."

"Strange he would single you out, then." Edgar looks at me from the corner of his eye. "But maybe Rick was right. I've been biased. Fearful of . . . what do you call them? Certain *neurodivergent* conditions. Maybe I wasn't fair to him. To you."

Edgar clears his throat. Dumbfounded by the semi-apology—which I don't deserve—I only nod.

"In hindsight, you weren't the one we all should have been concerned with this weekend. And seeing how easily Rick justified his behavior—blamed it on me—I wouldn't be surprised if he killed Sasha after some misunderstanding. A perceived insult. He probably buried her in the first place he thought of to get rid of his guilt. Maybe his own cabin."

"The sports hut. Rick buried her in the sports cabin." I snap my gaze up to see whether any cops have returned and may have overheard my knee-jerk admission. I haven't divulged how I discovered Sasha's body first, or any detail that might swing suspicion back to me. Rick is dead; I'm the only one who knows what really happened.

Edgar gets to his feet. "Either way."

"Grandpa?"

He pauses. Turns over his shoulder to hear me before he goes, much in the same way he did back on the mountaintop, before he disappeared beyond the gurgling creek.

"If I call you tomorrow for an interview, will you answer?"

I know now that Edgar has avoided me all this time, out of some concern—some fear of me. But he also had no obligation to join me on the log seats, to hear me out or confirm that he believes me when I say that Rick was the true vengeful relative this weekend.

After another moment, Edgar dips his head. "Yes."

Happiness—real joy—snakes its way down my stomach. I might be able to turn in a completed dissertation on time after all.

As Edgar leaves me to sit alone in the plaza, Birdie locks eyes with me from across the deck. She narrows her gaze, as if she heard our whole exchange—my accidental confession that I know the location of Sasha's burial. As if she has some kind of superhuman ability to eavesdrop.

A cold breeze twists my hair across my neck. Does Birdie know the truth now too—that I'm responsible for Sasha's death?

I am a psychopath. I see that finally. But I'm nonviolent at least, like Zane, like my father. That should count for something.

No longer exercising the intense self-control that I have for years, my arsenal of socially acceptable reactions, I feel free—maybe for the first time ever.

And then I can't help myself.

While holding Birdie's eye contact, I allow my mouth to twist up into a smile.

Acknowledgments

Writing a book, then having it published for the world to read never gets old. I am indebted to the Thomas & Mercer team and everyone at Amazon Publishing for being the very best in publishers. In particular, my editor Megha Parekh was so supportive when I first came to her with this idea. She is an amazing champion of my books, better than I could have hoped for. To Gracie Doyle, Brittany Russell, Sarah Shaw, and Lindsey Bragg: thank you for being part of another novel of mine.

To my developmental editor, Charlotte Herscher: thank you for your support and insight as we rode the roller coaster of edits together. This story is more compelling (I like to think) thanks to your keen eye. It was a pleasure working with you. Likewise, thanks must be paid to the copyediting teams (Haley Swan, Rachael Herbert, Kellie Osborne, and others!) and proofreaders who make the final text of this book sing.

To my agent, Jill Marr of the Sandra Dijkstra Literary Agency: thank you for answering my emails as if I were your only author (I am far from it) and allowing me to bounce ideas off you always.

To the talented cover designer, Shasti O'Leary Soudant: thank you for applying your creativity to yet another of my books. I love this one, much as I was thrilled by your cover designs for *The Missing Sister*, *Lies We Bury*, and *Strangers We Know*.

Many ideas, events, and personal experiences influenced my writing this time around. True crime podcasts have exploded in availability, but there are several that I must call out and thank: *My Favorite Murder*, *That Chapter* YouTube series, and *Tenfold More Wicked*, you have each held my attention rapt in every setting of my life—not the least of which is right before bed, thereby forcing me to dream of the incredible true stories that you highlight. Thank you for providing interesting and compassionate content. My character Birdie would approve.

Michelle Lema, My Bean, one of my oldest friends. You are supportive to the hilt, and I am so lucky to know you! Your creativity and work ethic have always inspired me.

To my husband and my family: I remain in awe of your endless patience and passion for my writing. Your enthusiasm for plot holes and plot twists mirrors my own, and I'm grateful you're willing to discuss them over sushi. In particular, thanks must go to my daughter, who was literally with me every step of the way as I wrote this novel.

Lastly, if you've read this far, thank you, readers, for following me on this journey. I hope to continue writing suspenseful, thrilling stories for you that feature a diverse cast of characters. Thank you for connecting with me on social media and telling your book clubs, friends, and family about my books. I am grateful to you every day.